DOORS OF DARKNESS

EDITED BY
CALEB J. PECUE

INTRODUCTION BY
CAMERON CHANEY

TERRORCORE
PUBLISHING

DOORS OF DARKNESS

A Terrorcore Publishing book / published by arrangement with
Caleb J. Pecue

PRINTING HISTORY
Terrorcore edition published 2023

ISBN: 979-8-9889138-0-1

Terrorcore Books are published by Terrorcore Publishing

Contents

Fern Street

If tradition holds that a red door signifies welcome, then the tattered cover of a horror novel must be like a door slathered in blood. "Come on in," it says. "Nothing here can hurt you." Deep down, you know it must be true—what lies within is a harmless spooky tale and nothing more. But as you reach for the doorknob with curious wonder, you may suddenly draw back and ask yourself whether it's really such a good idea.

I got my first taste of this predicament at a yard sale as a child. Like always, I leaned into my book-detecting senses and sniffed out the nearest box of musty old paperbacks. I was on the prowl for R. L. Stine's *Goosebumps* and maybe some Christopher Pike or *Point Horror* novels—same as any other young tyke in the '90s. What I found instead was far from the kid- and teen-friendly horrors I was seeking.

From the bottom of the box, I unearthed a paperback published by Pocket Books in 1990. The cover art, created by the legendary and prolific Lisa Falkenstern, depicted a woman resting peacefully on a massage table . . . helplessly oblivious to the monstrous hands emerging from the shadows behind her, poised as if to strangle her. A splash of light revealed in her stalker's eyes the purest gleam of evil.

The novel was *Thrill Kill* by B.L. Wilson, its title displayed in a jagged, blood-red font.

Out there in the blistering sunlight, surrounded by bargain-hunters, I was completely transfixed, morbidly fascinated by what I saw on the cover. When I asked my dad if he'd buy it for me, he shrugged and said yes without giving the ratty thing a second glance. I was delighted. It wasn't until I was all alone in my bedroom that night, staring at this disturbing piece of art, that I began to feel uneasy. Maybe innocent little me wasn't ready for a big scary book like this after all. Did it really belong on my bookcase, a few tiers away from my collection of Little Golden Books?

I held on to *Thrill Kill* for a while, but it eventually left my shelf for a charity donation box. Intrigued as I was by Falkenstern's artwork, I was also petrified by it. I decided I didn't want that book in my room even a moment longer, and I certainly never wanted to read it . . . or did I? No sooner than I had given it away, I was consumed with the utmost regret.

Why was that? What made this book so inviting and disconcerting at the same time? I suspect it had something to do with the "red door" effect. Though I was scared, the cover enticed me with its dark and forbidden fruit, tempting me to wander the mysterious corridors of the story inside despite my fear.

To this day, I've never stopped hunting for another copy of *Thrill Kill* for my personal library, where it could now sit alongside the hundreds of other vintage horror paperbacks I've amassed over the years. While the state of modern publishing has ensured that most horror book covers share the same minimal graphic design as their counterparts outside the genre, it's those wild vintage horror books from decades past that cry out to me from thrift store donation bins. To say they don't make them like they used to would be an understatement: embossed neon fonts, murderous dolls brandishing blades dripping with blood, diabolical banjo-strumming skeletons, full-cover holograms, die-cut covers accompanied by eerie step-back art . . . When was the last time you saw any of these things at your local Barnes & Noble? I'd wager a guess that it's been a very long time indeed.

This is why I've "rescued" so many vintage horror books from used book purgatory in recent years and exposed them to a fresh audience on my YouTube show *Library Macabre*. In my pursuit of forgotten gems to feature on my show, my home has transformed into a kind of museum (or shrine, you might even say) in tribute of vintage horror, with each bookcase bowing — and sometimes buckling — beneath the burden. While publishers push further and further away from the horror norm of the past, those old horror paperbacks are still out there, moldering in the darkest reaches of used bookstore basements. They deserve a home. And more than anything, they deserve to be in the hands of eager readers.

Thanks to the renewed interest in these musty little books, brought on by channels like mine and the nonfiction masterpiece *Paperbacks from Hell* by Grady Hendrix, we now have books like this one: *Doors of Darkness* — a brand-new collection of horror fiction curated in the spirit of groundbreaking author Charles L. Grant, a master of "quiet horror," whose anthologies have stood the test of time as the best of the genre.

Like Grant's Oxrun Station and Greystone Bay books, *Doors of Darkness* features a host of terrifying tales that share a frightful setting. Fern Street is an eerie, atmospheric locale like none other. Each residence is home to the grisliest of happenings: murders, unexplained deaths, disappearances, hauntings — a great place to raise the kids.

What skeletons will you uncover in the walls of Fern Street's decrepit structures? You'll have to open each door to find out. After all, if a horror novel is a haunted house, then a horror anthology is an entire haunted neighborhood.

Cameron Chaney
September 4th, 2023

To those brave enough to venture beyond closed doors,
may your screams echo in the halls of eternity.

TIME IN MY WAKE
E. P. Clement

786,
787,
788,
789,
790,
791,
792,
793,
and—

Droplets continued to leak down the faucet into the mildew-laden drain. I hadn't stopped counting since she left for her morning run, like clockwork, every Saturday. The kitchen table rocked back and forth with its reliable wobble while I tapped my elbow and counted. The stupid sink leaked for ages, wreaking havoc ever since I moved in.

With summer in full swing, the whole house sweltered like an oven, the spiteful rays of sun conspiring with the outdated A/C unit. I could feel my blood boiling, oozing through my pores. In this heatwave, all that remained was the hollow outer shell of anger holding my body together. If I'd been counting correctly, I think we were at 817 drips.

Mittens slinked into the room, the light pitter-patter of his paws almost indistinguishable from the dripping until he hopped up onto the counter. His white paws stood out against the sleek black fur of his body; the cat reached a curious paw into the sink and shook out a few tiny droplets from between his claws. This heatwave baked more than just me in this godforsaken house.

"You're gonna wanna get down from there, Mitz."

With a hop down and an attitude, Mittens bolted toward the creak of the front door, ignoring my grimace completely. Typical. The old brass knob still rattled, loose in its jamb from wear and tear, and with her entrance back into the house, I propped both forearms over the rickety table. There she was, right on time at 839 drips.

Her reddened cheeks and shiny forehead greeted me first as she limped through the threshold of the door, her sneakers squeaking with the quick pivot into the kitchen. Her uneven breathing already exhausted me of my patience. Without even a hint from me, her gaze drifted to the irritating waterdrop torture coming from the sink.

"You'll never guess what's wrong," I mused, folding my hands over my mouth and running my fingers over the dry crust of my bottom lip. Everything felt tender.

"This stupid fucking sink." She lashed out, making her way over the speckled linoleum tiles to the bane of this relic house. She leaned over the pale green countertop — *Original 50s mint skylark,* the red-lipped, smooth talking realtor had gushed during the walk-through — in order to leverage a tight grip on the handles. Her forearms tensed with the effort, twisting and turning, but to no avail.

I picked at the scab on my lip. "You know that's not gonna work, come on."

She groaned in defeat and tugged at the roots of her hair, slick from the sweat of her morning run. The steady drip *plinked* into the basin like a sick joke, her feeble effort an undeniable failure. Her attention turned to our pantry as she yanked off her t-shirt, crumpled it into a sweaty ball, and tossed the stewing remains onto the floor of the living room.

Eye rolls aside, I stretched back into my chair. Nothing ever changed. In only her sports bra, she snagged the bright yellow box of Pops from the cabinet, the almost expired milk from the fridge shelf, and her favorite polka-dot bowl. She kicked out the chair across from me and plopped into its worn seat with a soft grunt.

"You ever get tired of the same cereal every day? Maybe you need protein. You know eggs, bacon, ham?"

She hummed to herself, shoveling a heaping spoonful into her mouth and chewing in loud defiance. Her magazine, left out from yesterday, lay wide open next to her placemat. She flicked her eyes over to where I sat and then swallowed with an audible gulp.

"Sorry, I'll just shut up — I know you hate it when I judge you."

Mittens meowed behind me, hoping for a taste of the cold milk from her cereal bowl. Another spoonful pushed its way past her lips. She fingered the next page of *Runner's World,* following the article neatly titled, "Stay Loose: An Exercise Program to Follow Your Running." I didn't need to look over her shoulder anymore, the pictures demonstrated various yoga poses for an improved cool down program after long distance training. Her eyes carefully studied the models trapped in the boxes of the page, tracing their limbs in the reflection of her gaze.

In her shoes, I would be less concerned about pretzel-shaped contortions and more worried about plain old strength and agility. But I kept my comments to myself this time. They fell on deaf ears.

The rest of the morning drifted through the haze of suffocating heat, like an unwanted sauna of space-time. When her sweat overflowed the crook under her lip, she finally jumped in the shower with half the day already wasted. Mittens had stayed away from the sunny windows, creeping low to the ground for the cooler air, and laid down on the beat-up hardwood floor in a pitiful sprawl.

The heat only added fuel to the fire in my belly as

pain twitched with a raging vengeance. But I'd grown accustomed to this routine with time, these aches and pains now a familiar friend that greeted me with a rancid smile. I allowed the pain to sweep through me, no longer tensing or protecting myself from the worst of it. It wandered in the halls of my body aimlessly, while I tried to busy myself with the house.

I lumbered down the hall, avoiding Mittens and his chosen spot, only to hear the rush of the shower from beyond the closed door. I imagined the cold relief across her skin—the icy shock to her system, a pleasant break from this hell of a day. A pang of jealousy made me freeze outside the bathroom door before I shook my head and pushed on. The battered brown door ahead guarded my bedroom. A medium-sized space decorated as sparsely as possible, only the basic double bed and dresser in matching dark maple and a thick round rug in the center of the room. I never wanted much of my own.

Instead, I turned left into the smaller guest room, its door propped open by a thin wedge. With the A/C busted, the solitary window along the back wall stayed open halfway, a bird's nest in the nearby hedge chirping with animated excitement through the breezy gap. The sound of happy cheeps kept me company.

I paced for a while in there, burning nothing but time in my wake. I stomped my feet over the thrifted purple shag, noiseless in their impact. A dusty mirror hung over the closet door, speckled with dirty smudges along the edges. Its reflection appeared hollow, dreadfully lonely in a room meant for hosting friends, family, anybody wanting to visit. I scoffed at its pointlessness; why this room was ever filled with furniture, only to remain unused, was beyond my comprehension.

The screech of a Cooper's hawk shrieked outside, sounding far up above the roof, and signaled now was the time to return to the kitchen. I wasted no more time dawdling in the guest room and strolled down the hallway with a certain tension in my chest. The pain in my gut lingered and my crimson shirt felt damp to the touch.

When I turned the corner, she already stood at the counter, a bright yellow towel wrapped and tucked over her slim figure, with a piece of celery hanging out her mouth as she chopped an array of vegetables into chunks. The stockpot on the stove rolled to a gentle boil stuffed with enough chicken thighs for a small army.

"Only you would cook on the hottest day of the year — *soup,* of all things."

She lowered the heat of the front burner, pausing her chopping to stir the thighs from sticking to the side of the pot. Grandmother's recipe meant the simmer had to be low and slow, drawing out all the nutrients and careful not to mix too much of the fat into the broth. She chewed more of the celery in a satisfying crunch.

I sat back down at the table to monitor. She appeared unbothered by my unwarranted supervision. More vegetables became victim to her knife, cut to messy bits and pieces and soon to be tossed into scalding waters. An empty bowl sat readied next to her cutting board, meant for the thighs' ice bath in order to shred the meat from the bone. No artistry in her carving or her chopping, a poor imitation of better idols. Before she could finish the last of the onion and carrots, the shrill ring of the house phone interrupted her work.

I leaned back in my chair, crossing my arms as she skipped across the linoleum to answer after the fourth ring.

"Hello?" Her voice sounded chipper, despite the oppressive heat. Her wrist flicked the knife in the air, half-aware she'd forgotten to leave it on the cutting board.

Murmurs of sound filled her ear as she pinched the phone into her shoulder in order to unravel the twisted cord with her free hand.

"Hey, Mom. Little busy."

I seethed. "Always too busy for your mother."

Her eyes washed over Mittens, who was making his last appearance of the day due to the enticing aroma of chicken. She refocused on the stockpot and the remaining vegetables at the counter.

"I'm cooking with Nana's recipe." She sucked in her bottom lip, not really listening to the yammering on the other end. "Yeah, yeah—yes! I know it's a heatwave, Mom. But I felt like I needed it. Who am I to question divine cravings?"

She rolled her eyes, stretching out the cord to test its limits. Confident the phone could reach, she took steps toward the stove to check the chicken, letting the curls of the phone cord extend to a tight, straight line.

"I know. I should call more." The metal spoon clanked as she stirred, steam rising over the pot. "I'm still training for that half, though. Most of the time, I'm running when I miss your calls. And that's why I'm making her soup; my muscles need it."

This conversation was a dead end on a road going nowhere. All I wanted to do was slam the phone into the cradle for her. End this misery for all of us. But I sat in festering silence instead. This household was a torture chamber with front row tickets.

"Mom, it's just Fern Street. I promise I'm safe when I run. There's really no need to worry about me," she whined, spooning out some of the fat that floated on the surface of the simmering broth. There was more exasperated noise from the phone outside of my earshot.

"No, it's thirteen miles, not thirty. That'd be more than a full marathon!" She laughed and switched ears to hold the phone in place.

And I hated her for it, that ugly laugh. She really had no idea what she was in for.

The conversation came to a quick close with the realization her thighs would soon be overcooked. She hung up the phone with a sudden goodbye, no I love yous or talk to you laters. The phone cradled in its resting place with an angry cord. With the chicken placed in the ice bath, she returned to chopping the vegetables. I never wanted her knife more, but I waited.

When the soup was done and the egg noodles strained, she prepared a huge bowl for herself and crashed on the couch in the living room. Television blasted the same sitcom with rerun after rerun. The afternoon dimmed to evening with her feet up on the couch, eyes dreary from hours of television, and her toweled body spread across the lumpy, mustard sofa. Daylight drained into nighttime with minimal effort.

When sleep flirted with her mind, she slapped the power button off on the T.V. set and walked past the kitchen. She retreated to my bedroom and closed the door behind her to turn in for the night. Uninvited from my room, I wandered back around to the kitchen. The worst crime of the night was her carelessness as she forgot the rest of the soup on the stove, the leftovers soon to be rendered inedible by morning. The beautiful knife, cutting board, bowl of chicken bones with melted ice, and food scraps abandoned to the elements. The chef's knife whispered to me, gleaming in the early starlight. Its steel possessed a magnetism drawing me in and dazzling me in its affection. The way its edge could slice and filet, a tool she abused and abandoned without due care.

My fixation broke with the chiming of the clock, striking eleven times with determination, and I fled to the guest room before I missed the pay-off. In the cover of darkness, I wedged myself in the corner by the closet for the best view of the back wall. A sudden hush fell over the chorus of crickets outside, and I refused to blink in anticipation.

On cue, the cracked window of the guest room opened all the way, the screen outside already removed and a soft glow of a flashlight clicked off with the entrance of the intruder. His clothes were plain, dark, and nondescript as his right leg and arm perched through the opening, like the night birthed him straight through the aching womb of 101 Fern St.

I pressed against the closet door, a quiet onlooker, as he carefully steadied his feet on the shaggy rug. I hadn't even thought about how carpet absorbed sound, not once when I purchased it; I had liked the purple tones that complimented the cream walls. But I guess all things in life have unintended consequences.

In the dark of the room, I could only see the faint outline of his stocky figure standing still, listening intently for any movement. He'd done his homework on the layout with his eyes fixed on the open door. I waited for the show like a peasant at the gallows, anticipating the delight of a gruesome punishment. The glow of moonlight revealed the knife he clutched near his waist and a sliver of teeth showing through his sharp leer. His feet caressed the ground with calculated, soundless steps. With exactly thirteen steps out of the room and into the hall, he staggered his body in a strong stance outside my bedroom.

From the hall, I watched on as he cracked open the time-beaten brown door with a quiet creak. He moved quickly into the room for her, a tight grip on the knife at his side. I never liked following him into the bedroom; it always felt a little too personal and crowded. Maybe next time, I'd work up the nerve.

A scream. Her scream. The scream curdled blood and stirred spiders from their corner web hideaways. They scurried away, smarter for the retreat. Just like Mittens, who oddly did not show his visage for this part of the night.

The hall light flicked on as he dragged her by the hair into view, a deep crimson spewed over the walls of the corridor. Her eyes bulged with the hand crushing her neck, her nails dug deep into flesh. His flesh — exposed at the wrist and nicked in small etchings by her sharpened nails.

"Just like Mom taught you." My tone stayed flat.

The wild curls of her hair splayed through his fist, his arm swinging back and forth to throw off her balance. The wood floor seeped red into the crevices between the old planks like a fresh lacquered stain. He released her throat, a momentary reprieve, to fix a better grip on his blade, already wet and ruined.

Then, again, another scream erupted from her lips. Her eyes, black and brimmed with desperation, seeing through him and through me. They were vacant as he stabbed through the side of her nightshirt.

"Help!" she choked. "Help me!"

His gravelly voice grunted in unison with mine, "Shut up, bitch."

Feet flailed along the floor as he yanked her into the living room, nearly hitting her target but missing his knees by mere inches. But her struggle didn't last long. One solid wallop to her head sent her into a daze; her limbs lost any semblance of coordination as she tried to resist. His knife pistoned a flurry of attacks along her torso. Falling to her knees, she whimpered. And I hated her for it.

The assailant kept his eyes on his prey, relishing in the sound of her hitched breaths from the wound that punctured her lung. Blood poured out of each stab with steady streams to the floor. Her pajama shirt was torn and a deep crimson soaked through to replace the powder blue color. Invigorated, the man shanked hard into her belly, tearing through her abdominals and piercing a few good organs.

Minutes were left. The clock ticked toward 11:15 already and I moved closer for the finisher.

His gruff panting echoed around the room as he watched her claw at the ground, trying to make her way to the front door. In this pitiful state, she looked like a worm groveling to an unforgiving sun, squirming to its death on the sidewalk. Her body slid next to the wall where she tossed her sweaty t-shirt from this morning.

She seized up when he stepped on her back and made a funny choking sound when he drove his boot into her chest to flip her over. Her face, battered and tear-ridden, held desperation in the blues of her eyes. Her sight loosely set to the mess of the kitchen, the spark of a knife glinting in the twilight.

"Why do you even bother?"

In a blink, her hand snatched the used shirt crumpled along the baseboard and threw it in his face, distracting him for maybe a full second. She utilized that momentum to launch a strike right in the groin —one last stand—and it could have worked if she'd had a little more oxygen and blood left pumping through her. Instead, her strength fell short, and the blow faltered. The man caught her and pulled her close to him.

In this intimate proximity, his knife stuck into her like a coroner's scalpel as he drew the blade down to slice open the rest of her abdomen. Her shirt, like her skin beneath, flapped freely and mattered less and less to the confines of her dignity.

She fell to the ground with a heavy thump, face first, before his boots. The tide of red rushed around them, unable to withdraw back to its source. I kneeled next to her, under his gaze, as shallow breaths spasmed in her ribs and her eyes glazed over. She coughed into a weak sob.

I laid down on the floor in the pool of blood, unbothered by the tidal wave of death. I'd swim in it if necessary. On my side, I brushed her hair back to look into those sad eyes. The reflection of my own. It was a mirror, dusty and smudged like the one in the guestroom, but functional nonetheless. The same fear, memory, and darkness were encapsulated in the prison of those eyes. With only five breaths left, I wondered why I ever talked aloud when the end result was always the same.

She tried to pick her head up, but her cheek seemed glued to the mess below her.

"Stay down. Trust me."

He crouched down, lifting up her chin in tense examination.

"Why?" Her last exhale framed the existential question.

"Million dollar question, isn't it?"

Blood sputtered out of her mouth, pooling at her lips. Proud of his work, the man stood over us, beaming at the last spasm of her rib cage and the gory scene he'd painted so prettily around the floor. He waited until her body fell limp to move her, stepping past me and gripping her wrists to flip her over. He hoisted the lifeless form and repositioned her onto the couch.

The rest of the scene unfolded in all its ritualistic majesty. The single rose on her lap, the book of poems opened on the coffee table to Robert Frost, the dainty crossing of her legs. Like a true sculptor, the man carved out the hidden beauty from the woman of this antiquated house, styling the room to his liking and adding one more piece of death to his collection.

By now, I almost admired his attempt to make this corner of the world his own. I sat back at the kitchen table to watch the rest of the modeling, the quiet gentleness as he adjusted her hair over the bruising that bloomed on her cheek and patted the split of her lip dry. It was a bittersweet contradiction of his treatment before and after death, the violent cruelty to endearing worship of flesh.

And yet, this was my doom. To be stuck in the same loop of waking up and ending my life every single day in this shithole without deviation. After an infinite number of reruns, my reality shifted. This person I watched every day felt less and less like me. I started to hate her the more I observed. I hated how weak and stupid and pitiful she looked when she died. To waste her last day running alone, reading a brainless magazine, watching endless television. She deserved to die for leaving the goddamn window unlocked and open, rushing her own mother off the phone trying to warn her. She was careless up to the point of her very last hours.

With the latest iterations of death, I'd started to study him, my killer, much more. A reverence grew with the little details I'd missed in the beginning, too disturbed by my own end to notice the care and precision in his final strokes of punishment for a life wasted. In death, my body was repurposed to be one of his art pieces, a collector's item with sacred purpose.

I waited for midnight, uneasy. I hadn't learned anything new from this iteration. I wondered if tomorrow I'd learn something new about him and if that would finally break me of this eternal curse of repeating my death over and over.

If not, at least I got to see her punishment again in all its gore and glory at 101 Fern St.

102

THE RABBIT'S FOOT INN
Laura E. Mangi

Room 5

"Guys, be quiet. My parents are going to hear us."

"Oh, come on, this house is huge and they're way on the other side."

Three of the four teenage girls giggled as they turned out the lights in the old-fashioned room of the Inn. They lit candles they found in their room and turned on flashlights they got from the library of the old Victorian house.

"I—I don't think we should do this," the fourth girl whispered as she sank onto the floor, clutching one of the floral, ruffled pillows from her bed.

"Don't be such a baby," the Ringleader of the group said harshly.

The girls sat in a circle on the floor, setting a board on the dusty green carpet and a planchette on top of the board.

"Yeah, like, isn't this what you're supposed to do at sleepovers?" the girl nearest to the board said, chomping loudly on her bubblegum.

"I swear you guys, if my parents hear us, I'm so dead."

The last girl sat down with two lit candles and placed them on either side of the board. The candlelight illuminated the letters and numbers on the board and the four girls surrounding it. The Ringleader placed her fingertips on the planchette, encouraging the other girls to do the same.

"No, I'm not doing it," the Scared Girl said. "It probably won't even work." She tried to make the words sound like a challenge, but inwardly meant them as a reassurance to herself.

"Suit yourself, you baby."

The other three girls placed their fingers on the planchette as the Ringleader said in her most ethereal voice, "Spirits of this old, dusty house, come to us. Make yourself known."

Everyone held their breath, waiting for the planchette to move.

"Spirits, we want to communicate with you. Come to us. Let us know you're here."

An audible creaking came from near the window.

"What was that?" the girl asked, nervously smacking the gum in her mouth faster.

"I didn't hear anything," the Ringleader insisted. She cleared her voice, but somehow her face looked paler in the warm glow of the candles. "Is there someone here with us?"

All four of the girls gasped loudly as the planchette moved over the word, YES.

"Oh, hell no! You're moving this, aren't you?" the Gum-Chewing Girl said loudly.

"Shhhh!" both the Ringleader and the other girl hushed her. The Scared Girl shoved her face into the scratchy pillow that smelled of mothballs.

"Who is with us? Tell us your name!" the Ringleader continued, despite objections from the other girls.

The Scared Girl could hear the scratching of the planchette against the wood, despite digging her face deeper into the thin pillow. They just had to be doing this as a joke, she kept telling herself.

"You guys, I swear we're not moving it!"

"What's it spelling?"

The Ringleader was about to say the first letters when all of a sudden, the candles blew out in a gust of wind, and the flashlights grew dimmer and dimmer until they went out. The room became heavy and thick with darkness. All the girls screamed and scrambled over the bed to the window, the only source of faint light from the moon.

"Okay, I am seriously freaking out! Stop doing this!" one of the girls yelled.

A low, guttural, inhuman laugh slowly emanated from the other side of the room, closest to the door, ringing loudly in the girls' ears.

The three girls were too terrified to scream.

The Scared Girl rose slowly from the floor, the moonlight from the window casting light across her face that was stretched into an impossibly large grin. Her head was cocked at an odd angle and her eyes seemed to reflect the light as a cat's would in the dark. The slow, deep, animalistic laugh reverberated throughout the room again, coming from the girl.

"Stop it! Stop it!" the Ringleader screamed as the other girls sobbed.

"Don't be afraid," the Scared Girl said in a deep, growling voice that didn't belong to her. Her smile grew even larger, exposing her teeth that glinted in the moonlight.

Moving suddenly like an animal, she clambered over the bed to where the girls were huddled together and massacred them all with her bare hands.

❋ ❋ ❋

Rain pummeled my windshield and wind caused my old, beat-up car to shake. I looked out the window searching for a street sign or anything, really, so I could get my bearings. My crumpled map covered up most of the windshield that was getting foggy at this point. The flimsy wipers furiously swiped back and forth at top speed, but barely cleared anything. It was summer and had been warm when I first left for the hour-long drive from my former home, but the sudden rain made the temperature here almost freezing, so I cranked up the heat. Lightning flashed, and I got a glimpse of the street sign: FERN ST. I was where I was supposed to be.

Slowly, I pulled up and parked in front of 102 Fern St. On the corner, sat a huge Victorian-era style home that had been converted into an Inn back in the 1900s. Maybe once it was beautiful, but now it was run down. Ivy was strangling every post around the front porch that wrapped around the entirety of the house. The grass was overgrown, covering the sidewalk, and it looked like a front window had been broken and never repaired. The old wooden sign stuck in the front yard was faded, but you could still barely make out the words: "The Rabbit's Foot Inn: Vacancy"

Lucky me. It was my job to renovate it. I hadn't even seen the inside yet and I knew this was going to be a difficult task. I groaned as I was taking stock of what I could see through the rain. There was one feeble porch light that periodically flashed on and off, making it even more difficult to see.

I honestly don't know what I was thinking. I used all of my savings to buy this property, convinced this was my calling after my divorce. I had made the final decision to end my marriage and every other day I regretted it.

Today was one of those days.

I grabbed as many bags out of the backseat of my car as possible and braced myself for the cold downpour I was about to run through. I managed to make it through the tall grass growing around the sidewalk and up the stairs to the front door without tripping or dropping anything. The front door had been painted a pale, sage green and was chipped enough to see a beautiful dark wood underneath. Green seemed like a strange choice against the burgundy siding that was wrapped around the whole house. The porch and trim were all white, and at a glance looked like it was in semi-decent condition.

My heart was suddenly pounding as I grabbed the ornate brass doorknob to go inside. Sure, I was nervous, but my heart was pounding like I was terrified. Taking a deep breath, I twisted the knob and stepped inside.

As terrified as I had felt before, the instant I was inside, the feeling was gone and replaced by a sense of familiarity. Probably because the inside had the decor and smell of my grandmother's house.

"Hello?" I called out as I dragged my bags across the threshold. It was a strange setup. There was a small foyer that opened up to a long, wide hallway. Almost immediately to the left was a vacant front desk where I could see what was presumably a little office attached to it.

The inside of the Inn had floral, dusty pink wallpaper that stretched from the tall ceilings to the wainscoting where it switched to dusty pink and gold vertical stripes. *Yikes*. The carpet was a dark hunter green that had an ivy pattern on it. Ornate brass candelabras with unlit candles lined the hallway along with generic paintings of unknown children playing outside.

"Can I help you?" I jumped when I heard the old woman. She had the husky voice of a longtime smoker.

"Hi, yes, sorry," I responded. "I'm Holly Hudson and I'm the new owner!"

She looked me up and down, then immediately turned around and walked back into the little office she came from.

I looked around nervously for a split second, thinking I was in the wrong place again.

She reappeared suddenly and slapped a stack of papers on the desk in front of me.

"Sign these, then I'll show you around," the woman said. She was very short, the top of her shoulders barely clearing the top of the counter. Her gray, feathery hair was so thin that it seemed to move independently around her face when she walked.

I pulled my pen and paperwork from my realtor out of my bag to make sure I didn't forget about it, and got to signing their paperwork. There were more papers than I expected, and they all looked like they were typed on an old typewriter. I realized that I probably should have read the fine print, but I was too nervous. I had made a huge, impulsive decision to buy this place and now it was officially my property.

What had I gotten myself into?

❄ ❄ ❄

Room 3

The large wooden door stuck as she wrenched it open and slammed it behind her when she got inside. Panic filled her chest instead of air, and she couldn't catch her breath from all the running.

"Please, can I get a room for tonight?", she said breathlessly to the attendant at the front desk. The old woman eyed her suspiciously. It was unusual for a woman to come to the Inn alone.

"Just tonight?" the old woman asked curtly.

"And tomorrow night. Please, I can pay for both right now," she caught a glimpse of herself in the mirror behind the desk. Her blonde hair was falling out of the pins in her hat, her clothes were disheveled, and the bump of her belly made her skirt sit in an unflattering position.

"Down the hall. Room 3," the old woman said as she forcefully set the key down.

"*Um*, is there a room on the second available?" she asked nervously, constantly looking towards the door.

"No. We're all booked. Room 3 if you want it," the old woman turned and took the money that was sitting on the counter.

"Fine. Thank you," she snapped her coin purse shut, grabbed her suitcase and hurried down the hall to Room 3.

Finally, she thought as she locked the door behind her and leaned against it. She placed her hand on her bump and sighed out of relief. *It's okay, he won't find us here.*

For the first time since he had found out about the baby, she didn't feel panic. All she had to do was stay here until the train left on Thursday, then she'd be free to go back to her mother's house. She couldn't stay with him. He had gotten mad before but not like that, and he had everything wrong, but he just wouldn't listen to her. She had done some bad things in life, but adultery wasn't one of them.

She could barely hear the other guests in the dining room down the hall, but she was still too nervous to join them. At least the room had a radio to add some distracting background noise. She unpacked the dresses she had thrown haphazardly in the suitcase and hung them up in the closet. Thankfully, the bedroom had a joined bathroom where she put her toiletries and thanked God for the large clawfoot bathtub.

Time was passing at an impossibly slow pace, so she lit a cigarette and went into the bathroom to draw a bath. The warm water on her body felt amazing. The soreness of the running and sheer terror over the last few days seemed to evaporate. She put out her cigarette and closed her eyes, finally letting herself fully relax.

Suddenly, the door to her room opened, then slammed, and the lock slowly turned. She sat up quickly in the bathtub, sloshing water over the sides of the tub and saw him. His once kind, green eyes were filled with malice as he looked at her. His clothes were pressed and expensive, but his dark hair was messy. He wasn't particularly tall, but he seemed to tower in the doorway of the bathroom, her only way out.

"Please listen to me," she cried, hoping and praying he would have mercy on their baby.

A strong smell of musk hit her nose as he slowly walked closer and closer to the tub, making her stomach turn.

"You have to listen to me, I didn't do—"

"Whore," he interrupted her as he wrapped both hands around her neck and pushed her beneath the water's surface until she stopped fighting back.

***

I finished the paperwork and looked around, waiting for the short, gray-haired lady to come back. There was a thin layer of dust covering the paintings of a little girl in a big fluffy dress doing various activities. I walked down the hall away from the front desk, unable to look away from the paintings. Her face looked strangely adult-like on a child's body, as her face had a gaunt, sunken look to it. She had straight blonde hair, wide brown eyes, and full lips that never smiled in any of the paintings. No matter if she was playing ring-around-the-rosie with other faceless children or in a tree swinging, her too thin face always looked sad or afraid even.

I don't know why I was so drawn to them. They creeped me out a little, but I couldn't figure out why that little girl felt so familiar to me. I was deeply fixated on the last painting in the hallway before Room 3. The girl was hiding behind what I assumed was her mother's dress, so only half her face was visible. I felt my heart begin to race in a sudden surge of fear as I looked into the painted eye that felt as though it were staring back at me.

"You ready?" the croaking voice of the short woman said behind me. I jumped and felt silly at how scared the paintings made me.

"*Oh!* Yes, I'm ready!' I responded, trying to catch my breath. She looked at me skeptically, then nodded her head in the opposite direction towards the staircase.

"So, who is the little girl in the paintings?" I asked.

"No one knows. They assume it was the daughter of the family that originally owned this house," the woman shortly responded.

"Oh. Do you know a lot about the history of the place? I mean, my realtor hinted at a kinda crazy past, but she didn't go into much detail." We walked back in the direction of the front desk, where the stairs were opposite of it. I grabbed all of my bags, and she didn't even offer to help. *Great, she hates me already.*

"I have been here for a long time," was all she offered.

"Here's where you'll stay."

She stopped in front of a door with a large, ornate placard that simply said PRIVATE and handed me the key.

I unlocked the door and stepped into my new home. The ceiling in the bedroom was tall since that was where the turret of the house was, giving the room a castle-like feel to it. The same floral-patterned wallpaper was now blue instead of the green that claimed the second floor. There was a small kitchen and an uncomfortable-looking couch in front of the oldest looking TV I had ever seen. Good thing this place needed a lot of work, so I wouldn't have much time for TV.

My room was beautiful, though. There were large windows that faced towards the back of the house, where I could see the garden and the rest of Fern Street. The bed was on an ornate, old-fashioned bed frame with carvings on the wooden posts. Off my bedroom was the bathroom, and all that mattered to me at the moment was the large clawfoot tub.

I walked back out to my living area, and the woman was still there.

"Do you want me to show you around the rest of the house?" she asked.

"Yes! I'm sorry though, I failed to ask you your name," I said, feeling ashamed of myself for being rude.

"Marcia," she said, then promptly turned and walked out of my room.

Okay then, I whispered to myself. *Let's go on a tour of the Rabbit's Foot Inn.*

❈ ❈ ❈

The Cellar

The three maids all gathered in the back of the kitchen, waiting for the chef to make breakfast. The attendants of the Inn were all supposed to check out at 9AM, promptly, then the maids would do their daily rounds to clean the six rooms of the Inn.

A tall, dark-haired man walked into the kitchen, and the chatter between the maids and the clammer of the kitchen stopped.

"As you were, Chef," he said to the head cook and the two assistants. The man made his way through the kitchen towards the maids.

"Good morning, ladies," he briefly locked eyes with a light-haired maid, then quickly looked away before anyone could notice. "I've just received a letter that we are having an important guest staying at the Inn tonight, so we will need all of your assistance in the dining room and if they require services tonight, you will need to attend to them then as well."

The maids all nodded in agreement at his request, and he gave one lingering last look to the light-haired woman and left.

"Mr. Hudson is so handsome," a dark-haired maid stated after the man left.

"You shouldn't say that," the older, third maid said in a hushed voice. "He's a married man *and* our boss."

"Oh, I don't think he'll stay married for long," the dark-haired woman continued. "Some of us don't have an issue with that." She looked pointedly at the light-haired maid, who stared back and tried not to blush and give herself away.

The truth was that they were in love. She never expected that this would happen. She had shown up at the Inn, fleeing an abusive father and mentally absent mother. It was raining when she came through the door and the kind woman at the front desk gave her a towel and showed her to the room of the owner, Harris Hudson. He generously took her in and gave her a job. The physical part of their relationship started later, when they began talking more, when it was her turn on the late shift. They thought they had kept it a secret, but clearly people were beginning to notice.

"You and your magic tricks are a sin!" the older maid whispered as she quickly stood up and hissed at the dark-haired maid, "They used to burn people like you!"

She quickly hurried off, leaving the two other women alone.

"I suppose you'll be the one working the night shift tonight," the dark-haired woman smirked, and her eyes became hard and cold. "See you later," she said and walked out of the kitchen, leaving the last woman alone and shaken from the conversation.

The evening came and went. The servants and maids put on a big production for the important guest of the evening without any issues. The light-haired maid had received a handwritten note from Harris during the dinner and felt the cold stare of her dark-haired coworker on her back for the rest of the evening.

When she finally got a moment alone, she read the note in the all too familiar handwriting of her lover:

Meet me at midnight in the cellar, my sweet.

At five to midnight, she carefully and quietly crept outside to the side of the huge house, where the cellar doors were open and waiting for her. She hadn't taken a light with her since the full moon was bright and lit her way. She carefully made her way down the creaky stairs.

"Harris? Are you here?"

She heard a muffled sound come from the corner of the cellar and suddenly the cellar doors slammed behind her, shrouding her in darkness. There was a blow to the back of her head and then nothingness.

She wasn't sure how long she had been out, but when she woke, she was tied by the hands to the ceiling with a gag in her mouth. The dusty, small cellar was lit with candles and she groggily looked across the room from her. Harris was tied up in the same way she was, with the dark-haired maid drawing a strange sigil on the dirt floor between them.

"Tonight is the last night you two will ever be together, I'm afraid," the dark-haired woman took the pins out of her hair, letting her long curls tumble around her.

"I just need a little of him, and a little of me, and then we'll be together forever." She pulled out a knife, cut her palm and three drops of her blood into a vial. Walking over to Harris, she did the same to him, a muffled cry sounding throughout the cellar when she cut him.

"Unfortunately, love requires a sacrifice," she said, walking over to the light-haired maid, brandishing the bloody knife. "I'm so sorry, dear," her voice was remorseless as the dark-haired woman made a motion and instantly the light-haired woman felt dizzy and weak, slumping over with her weight being held by the bind on her hands.

Muffled screaming emanated throughout the cellar as Harris screamed and tried to get to her. She focused on his eyes, the last thing she saw before eternal darkness.

❅ ❅ ❅

Marcia led the way, moving quicker than I had expected. She led me into Room 6, which was pretty standard looking. As we walked down the hall and around the corner to Room 5, I couldn't help but notice a sense of foreboding creep over me. The hallway was covered in old paintings and mirrors that made me feel like I was constantly being watched.

"Did your realtor tell you about this room?" Marcia asked after several moments of silence.

"No, Miss Davenport just told me that in general this place has a history of, *um*, bad things happening," as I said the words, I began regretting my purchase deeply.

"Well, back in the 60s there was a situation with some young girls and what we think was an intruder. Poor things were almost unrecognizable. Three of them were 14, and the youngest was 12. None of them made it and they have no idea who killed them." Marcia said all of this matter-of-factly, as if she wasn't telling me an absolutely horrific story.

"That happened in here?" I asked, horrified, looking at the flower-covered double beds and little TV that sat on the drawers. The room was unassuming, no sign that anyone had been brutally murdered in it.

"Yep. We replaced the carpet, of course, but everything else was fine to keep using." Marcia shrugged and left me in the room, walking out to the hallway.

I took one last look and ran out to meet her. The foreboding feeling had turned to a heavy panic. When my realtor said bad things happened here, I wasn't expecting murder.

I barely remember Room 4, since my thoughts were preoccupied with the poor girls that died here. I made my decision that every room was going to need a major renovation, and I would take out as many loans as I needed to make it happen.

We made our way back downstairs, past the front desk and paintings of the little girl, to Room 3.

"This is one of our larger rooms," Marcia stated, opening the door. "The woman who had my job as manager before me told me a story about some woman who drowned in the tub back in the 40s. Story is that she drowned herself because she was pregnant with a child that was not her husband's. This is our most updated room. The bathtub kept flooding."

I didn't know how many more horrifying stories I could take, but luckily, that seemed to be the last one. Marcia took me into Rooms 1 and 2, the last rooms on our tour. The downstairs rooms were bigger and more up-to-date than upstairs, which made me and my pocketbook feel better.

She showed me the large kitchen and connected dining room. Apparently, the Inn had a nice restaurant, maids, chefs, and groundskeepers back in its heyday. Marcia finished off the tour in the library, where allegedly one of the original owners had hung himself.

Marcia sat herself back at the front desk as I moved my stuff into my room. I was so relieved I didn't have to pass Room 5 and desperately tried to keep all the stories out of my mind for the night.

My car was finally emptied, and I got as much as I could unpacked with no help from Marcia, of course. I was exhausted, but my mind was buzzing with thoughts.

Why did this place creep me out but comfort me at the same time? Why hadn't I run screaming when Marcia told me about the murders and suicides that happened here? Why was I so determined to fix this place up? Why did I want to live here again?

*** *

Weeks passed, and it felt like I had barely scratched the surface of what needed to get done. First thing I did was rearrange and paint Room 5 and got rid of the musty old comforters and replaced them and the dresser I repainted from the thrift store. Bright, sunny yellow. That would get rid of the dark, ominous feeling I had every time I passed that room. *Right?*

The front porch was my next project. I replaced the broken planks and gave it a fresh coat of paint. I added flower pots and hung ferns around the entire wrap-around porch. I tackled as many weeds around the outside as I could every day. The backyard had a little, worn down garden that no matter how hard I tried, I couldn't seem to get rid of all the dead foliage. One day, I got up the courage to wrench open the cellar doors, which was a lot of work and ultimately disappointing, since I discovered the whole thing had caved in at some point and was never fixed.

Every day at the Inn, it felt like I discovered a new secret that was hidden away somewhere. In the attic, I dug through old photos, all the articles from the newspapers the Inn was mentioned in dating back to the 20s, and more old paintings of the strange little girl. The newspaper articles and photos shed light on the Inn's history. I discovered that at one point in the time, high-powered people would pass through the town and stay at the Rabbit's Foot Inn. It was consistently regarded as one of the best places in the area to stay until a maid that worked here was arrested for attacking the owner at the time. Then the news was nothing but bad. On top of the murders and suicides already told to me by Marcia, there had been a kitchen fire and almost every owner since the early 70s had died in the Inn in some way or another which did not put my mind at ease about being the owner now.

As fascinating as I found the history of the home, I also found it changed the way I felt in my new home. No longer did I feel comforted by its strange familiarity. I constantly felt like I was being watched, like there was someone waiting for me around every corner. Every now and again, I felt like I was in immediate danger. I tried my hardest to get as much done as I could so

I could be doing something instead of sitting around feeling afraid.

The work distracted me from the world. I barely interacted with my neighbors. I saw many of them give me looks of pity as they drove or walked by. Even they must have known I faced a hopeless challenge. I hadn't heard from my family since I moved here, and I definitely hadn't heard from my ex-husband. Although I wouldn't anticipate hearing from him since he was off with his new girlfriend. Marcia wasn't great company, but at least she was there. We hadn't had a single guest since I bought the Inn. Hopefully that would change quickly because I was running out of money.

One rainy day that turned into a rainy night, I took a bath and settled into bed with a book. Marcia had left by then. Those were the worst parts of the night. I hated knowing I was alone in this house that was most likely haunted. I tried to focus on my book, but it was no use.

I got out of bed and walked to my door, hesitating at grabbing the doorknob. Usually, I was good at pushing the feelings of dread and being haunted away and could function normally, but this time felt different. The rain was pounding on the windows as I took a step into the hall. Running through my mind was every bit of information I discovered about the Inn. The murder of the girls; the suicide of the pregnant woman in the bathroom; the death of four of its previous owners, all of their faces from newspaper clippings flashed through my mind on endless repeat.

I froze at the top of the stairs. A young girl with an adult looking face and big brown eyes stood at the bottom of the stairs, staring back at me.

❋ ❋ ❋

Private Room 7

She stood alone in the bedroom, rain pounding furiously against the windows as lightning flashed around her, lighting up the room. Sobbing, she sank to the floor. There was no way she could deal with this. There was nowhere else she could go, no family she could depend on, no money.

She couldn't stay here, though. Not with them here. The way they had surrounded her, closed in on her so she could barely escape, screaming her name at her over and over again made her paralyzed. They were going to torment her for the rest of her life if she didn't get out now.

Get out. That thought made her stop crying and start thinking about a way to get out of the house. Wiping her eyes, she looked out the windows. The house was huge. There would be no way to jump out of it without getting seriously hurt or worse. Grabbing what she could, she ran to her door and hesitated.

She stopped breathing and listened as hard as she could for any sign that they were still out there. It was hard to hear with the rain and intermittent thunder, but she was satisfied that they weren't thereafter listening for a solid five minutes.

She made it all the way to the stairs when they appeared all around her. Little girls, a pregnant woman, a maid, and many other faceless people appeared at the bottom of the stairs, in the hallway behind her, everywhere.

"Why are you doing this to me?" she screamed. All at once, the figures began screaming her name. Over, and over, and over, screaming only her name. She closed her eyes and covered her ears, sinking to the ground. It wouldn't stop, they wouldn't stop. She needed to escape. She had to get out. Pushed by adrenaline, she stood up and ran back towards her room, since that was the last place she was where they weren't drowning her in screaming.

Bursting through the door, she raced to the phone that was mounted on the wall, but there was silence. Panicking and sobbing, there was only one way out, only one way to escape them. While she stared out the window of her bedroom once more, she heard them. They came in this time. Their faces appeared in her doorway, one after the other, distorted and screaming.

She made eye contact one last time with the brown-eyed little girl in the front of the group. The girl wasn't screaming; she was smiling.

No other thoughts entered her mind as she took a deep breath and jumped out the window.

❈ ❈ ❈

I couldn't move a muscle as I stared at her. The girl from the paintings. My mind couldn't make sense of what I was seeing. This wasn't real.

Thunder crashed, and lightning flashed outside, illuminating the girl's face. If I could move, I would have run for the light switch, but I couldn't.

"You need to know," her high-pitched voice rang out clearly over the rain.

"Know what?" I somehow managed to whisper back. *This isn't real, this isn't real,* I kept saying over and over again in my head.

"Holly," she said, as she took a step up the stairs.

"What?" the word barely escaped my throat. I was suffocating. Air felt trapped in my throat.

"Holly," she said again, and took another step.

I could feel tears in my eyes. *This isn't real.*

A pregnant woman who looked like she was from the 40s appeared on the stairs next to the little girl. The sudden sight of her shot adrenaline into my system and I was able to take a couple of steps back. I knew this woman. The picture of her from the newspaper article about her tragic suicide.

"Holly," she said, in the same kind of loud, clear voice as the little girl. "It wasn't a suicide, ya know? It was his baby, after all. He just didn't want us."

"What is happening?" I'm not sure if I actually said those words out loud or not.

"But you should know this, Holly," she looked at me knowingly.

"What are you talking about?" I kept backing up until I was against the wall in the hallway. A maid and a twelve-year-old girl in pajamas appeared.

"Holly," they said in unison.

"Why do you keep saying my name?" I was finally able to scream.

"Because we know you, Holly," the little girl said. "And you know us."

"Holly, Holly, Holly," they all started screaming my name, and I ran.

I ran to my room and locked myself in. I was hyperventilating and somehow made my way into my bedroom.

What was happening to me? I had to be going crazy, right? I only knew them because I read the newspapers about them.

He just didn't want us. That's what the pregnant woman said. *But why?*

Suddenly, in a flash, it came to me. I knocked something off of my bedside table as I sat down, trying to keep myself together.

I know what they were telling me. My name. Our name. In my mind's eye, I could see a dark-haired woman slitting my throat as I hung by my hands, staring into the eyes of the man I had stared deeply into so many nights before. I could see a man I once loved hold me underwater, while I fought to tell him that he was killing his own baby. I could feel the darkness that overtook me and how good it felt to rip those other girls' throats and faces to shreds with my bare hands. I felt the glass shatter on my face and my bones break as I hit the ground. I remember the swing, the children I played ring-around-the-rosie with, and the skirt I hid behind when I was frightened, and how hot the fire in the kitchen was as it engulfed me.

How would I die this time?

ON THE DOTTED LINE
Caleb J. Pecue

She caked the candy-apple red lipstick across her pale lips, licking the slit between and moistening them thoroughly before moving on to the rouge that she applied with an equally heavy hand. When she was done, all the signs of her true age disappeared, transforming her into a twenty-year younger version of herself. So long as she kept her head held back and her nose slightly tilted upward, just as she had been so elegantly taught in etiquette school, Delilah Davenport resembled each of the professional photos plastered on the "For Sale" signs in the neighborhood, down to the tight-fitted red suit jacket with the purple heart brooch and voluminous blond wig, which looked as natural as real hair.

She stepped out into the sunny afternoon, greeting the man on the steps, and after a few moments, she flipped the sign on 103 Fern St. to display the "sold" side and in her mind that would have equaled dollar signs, typically. However, this one was different, as she couldn't get the vision of the man out of her head. The black tie and coat, the diamond-encrusted wristwatch, the Rolls-Royce. It all overshadowed what would have been her commission. She envisioned a multi-millionaire and was pleased to see such a figure buying a more humble abode.

Astor Wainwright.

Even his name had an air of luxury, so much so that she felt goosebumps flitter down her spine upon hearing it pronounced so cleanly in his not-quite British accent that she'd have labeled as exotic.

"Don't you want to go over the fine print?" she asked, handing him the deed she had drafted a few hours before, after receiving an email request to do so. Standing in the front yard, he assured her that the pictures online were reason enough to swiftly act.

"These things go quick nowadays!" he stated, and they both chuckled.

"You're not wrong," Delilah replied, masking her fear that he would have pulled out suddenly with awkward laughter that made her feel like a teenager.

She had only sold houses on Fern Street a few times before. In fact, she was rightfully upset when her boss asked her to show it. She attempted to persuade him with her seniority, but she wasn't about to resort to their level. She didn't even need to ask what the younger realtors did to get out of it.

She knew.

It wasn't that she hated Fern Street, per se; but rather, it took forever to sell a house. And yet, 103 had only been on the market for a day; the mulch around the sign still had its fresh scent of being just placed. Earlier that morning, she was cursing the very fact that she'd been tasked with selling it, and now she was standing with a briefcase entirely filled with large bills. It was rather uncouth and something, up until then, that Delilah had only seen in movies.

Who pays in cash? she wondered, but let the notion fall out of her mind as quickly as it had entered.

As she chewed on the peppermint bubble gum which she had tucked at the back of her mouth, a clap of thunder rolled far off in the distance, the storm clouds not yet impeding the sun overhead.

"Sounds like rain," the elderly man said, stating the

obvious. It had been forecast for nearly a week to be the "Storm of the Century," but Delilah had a penchant for ignoring the media hype wherein everything was "urgent" or "alarming" or "unprecedented." Delilah tried to get on with her life at that moment, as she believed spontaneity was the key to a long, youthful life. That, and the money, which Astor had promised. No storm would have stopped her.

"Shall we crack it open?" Astor asked, nodding toward the bottle of champagne that Delilah had almost forgotten she was holding, and with a nod herself, the two of them walked back up the steps and into the house, closing the creaky door behind them.

Delilah let out a yelp as another clap of thunder coincided with Astor's firm shutting of the solid old door. Inside, mahogany and a smokiness filled one's senses in a display of vintage decor.

"All original," Delilah started her sales pitch as if he could've still pulled out. "You just need to air it out a little, and—"

"Darling, you don't need to convince me. Where's the damn pen and I'll sign the bloody thing already? I mean, you do have my money already." He laughed again, looking down at the briefcase still firmly clasped in her hands.

She struggled for a moment, digging deep into her pocket with her free hand, and finally pulled out a fountain pen, used for only the most special moments. The pen had been used several hundred times over the course of her forty-year career and with it, many lives had been essentially started.

And some, ended.

The divorce paperwork, twenty years ago, struck a sour note with her, but her trusty pen signed off and freed her from the hell that she had lived in for eleven years. She'd have rather not relived that part of her life, yet failed a second marriage not five years later. Delilah pushed the memory from her mind.

The cork on the champagne made a loud pop as Astor

pulled it with his perfectly kept, white teeth —*Money can buy you anything* — and some of the liquid spilled on the stained butcher's block. Delilah reached for a napkin next to a charcuterie board, but Astor immediately grabbed her hand.

"No bother. It adds to the flavor," he stated, explaining to her that "a butcher's block stores valuable microbes that could enhance flavor if left to germinate." She had no idea if he was joking, but she laughed anyway, pulled her hand from his, and she drank from her glass as he sipped directly from the bottle.

"Would you like some cheese?"

Astor picked up a slice, placed it on a cracker, and instead of eating it himself, he leaned in and brought it up to Delilah's lips. With a laugh, she coyly took it in her mouth, thinking of her second husband, who at first showered her with gifts and later showered her in bruises. Her first husband gave her the alliterative last name; her second gave her another type of double d's. Neither of which she hated, much to the chagrin of the former Mr. Delilahs.

But she had sworn off men, now.

"Oh, I'm sorry," Astor started, "Wouldn't Mr. Davenport be upset?"

She'd have been lying if she didn't say she felt the goosebumps rising up her back again; the little hairs on her neck standing on their ends.

"Mr. Davenport is dead," she stated, which wasn't exactly the truth. This was her ruse; an out that most took to change the subject.

"I'm terribly sorry," he stammered, and for a moment, Delilah saw him faltering, his persona interrupted. He wasn't the perfect character he projected. This humanized him, made him seem more real and less of a fantasy.

"No worries, that was a long time ago," she said, taking the cheese this time and feeding it to him. He accepted it with a smile.

After a few more minutes of feeding each other, Astor asked, "Where do I sign?"

"Here," Delilah pointed to the paper, "and here. And one more... here, where the little x is."

"Is that it?" Astor asked.

Delilah shook her head. "I guess that about wraps it up. Congratulations, Mr. Wainwright."

"Mr. Wainwright? Woah. I haven't been called that in a long time. Astor is fine, please. Mr. Wainwright was my father and his father before that. I come from a long line of Wainwrights that I would rather leave behind."

"That makes two," Delilah started, but after awkward eye contact and confusion, she clarified. "Well, pasts left behind, I mean. But, honestly, it can't be all that bad if you drive that fancy car and carry a briefcase of money, right?"

"I suppose you're right," he said, sitting down on the barstool. "Money isn't everything."

Money buys anything, she thought again.

"But it wasn't my father's or his. My money came from the lottery. Happenstance, you see?"

Money buys happiness. Money could have made the divorce easier.

"My father spent his lion's share of it. Hell, even to this day... I put him in a home back in Denver. Cut him off, except for the essentials. He's in his nineties anyhow. What could he need?"

Money could have made my life easier.

"Denver? I wouldn't have placed you there," Delilah said.

"A transplant, originally from Boston, if you could imagine."

She couldn't. The accent didn't fit.

"So, you don't have any family?" Delilah asked.

He shook his head, took another drink from the bottle, emptying it.

"Whoops," he said with a chuckle as he tipped the bottle upside down, presumably to illustrate its emptiness.

"No Mrs. Astor?"

"Gosh, no. I'm intolerable, insufferable." Delilah

shook her head. "I'm a waste of space on this overpopulated planet. Thus, the downsizing."

Downsizing?

Delilah moved to the other side of the counter, plucked a strawberry from the board and pressed it to her lips, sucking it, staining them a deeper, brighter shade of red. She slipped off her suit jacket, bearing her white button-down underneath.

"Can I be honest with you?" Astor asked.

Delilah shook her head, rolled up her sleeves, and unbuttoned the top two buttons of her shirt, exposing her second husband's gift, never mind if she continued, she'd have exposed her scars. *Don't think about it, Delilah.*

"I think you're one of the most beautiful women I have ever seen. The moment I laid eyes on the ad posting attached to your image, I knew I needed to meet you."

Astor stood up.

"If I'm completely honest, I knew you weren't married. And that your two husbands are dead. Money can really buy whatever information you want, as long as you pay the price."

Delilah picked up a knife on the counter, sliced one of the larger strawberries in half, took the other half in her mouth, seducing it. Over-animated, she slurped the juices from it like a babe from its mother.

"I'm sorry for doing that, but I cannot trust everyone. Winning the lottery has taught me to be more cautious. That's why I picked this neighborhood. A place where no one knows me. A fresh start. I'm selling the Royce. This watch," he said, and unfastened it, "means nothing." He tossed it into the garbage.

Money buys stability.

He stood up, moved around the island opposite to her.

"Money means nothing," he said, catching up to her as they danced around the center of the room.

Nothing?

He pulled her close to himself.

"Hell, I'll give it away. Yes, give it away."

"The money?" Delilah asked, not quite understanding

where Astor was going.

"The car, silly. I don't need it here. Money—there still is a use for it, but I feel nothing for it."

He tugged her collar with his forefinger, caressing the seams with the tip. He pulled her close to himself and whispered in her ear.

"I think I love you."

This struck Delilah as absurd. *Love me? How can he love me? He doesn't know me. It's one damn picture.* Yet, for a moment, she pictured herself with him, as crazy as it sounded. A life where he got her anything she wanted. She had already been married twice before. Why not a third? Hollywood celebrities eclipse that number. Why couldn't she be happy? Didn't she deserve happiness, too?

Then the moment was erased. As he drew closer and closer, the scent of his cologne hit her. A Ralph Lauren or something—a musky, manly scent. A memory of her life before.

The bruises.

He brought his lips to hers, sucked the residual strawberry from them, exposing herself as the fake woman she was, and bit down slightly. Most women liked that, he thought.

With a cacophony of memories floating around, she tried once more to envision herself with him. Each time, floating back to all the failures before. She swore off men; she reminded herself.

He kissed her again.

"Delilah, I love—"

His profession was cut short by the blade. Silenced like the dead husbands before.

It pissed her off. The move wouldn't be so bad this time, at least, she thought, and picked up the suitcase of money as Astor slumped over the butcher block.

Delilah Davenport turned the sign at 103 back around, got into her Pinto, and drove down Fern Street, and exited the neighborhood.

Delilah Davenport.

Double D.
Deeds & Death.
Mrs. Astor just didn't have the same ring to it.

104

WHAT LIES BEHIND THE FENCE
A. L. Davidson

How peculiar the yard behind the crooked white house was. Hidden behind a tall privacy fence, slats overrun with ivy and worn down paint, the triangular lot held many secrets. It sat at an odd angle on Fern Street, slightly caddy-corner to the rest, as if it were a hideous hag attempting to hide its face from the onlookers. The house number had long since fallen off, though the sun damage left a prominent 104 burned into the exterior, and its odd placement in the neighborhood left many wondering how long the horrific place had been standing. Even among the other unsightly places along the street—like the overrun and neglected, empty lot where 115 should have been—it stood out as ominous.

The facade of the home was tinged with a mossy-green hue, a layer of ivy crawled along its eastern wall and half-obscured a dirty window that hardly let in any sunlight. An art piece made of driftwood swayed on the porch, twisting in the unsteady breeze that signified a storm on the horizon. The lawn was always overrun; the mailbox was always overflowing. The mortgage, however, was always paid, so no one dared try to intervene.

It was an eyesore. One that caused whispers among the locals, with enough fervor that it stretched out as far as the neighboring community, and was a common gossip topic among the youth. They would often ride by on their bikes and try to peer over those tall fence slats, wondering what secrets were hiding behind the tightly clustered panels of wood. Hoping to sneak a peek at the reclusive owner, who was said to stalk the halls of the home.

"Are we doing this?" Jamie asked in a hushed voice.

The sun started to set on the horizon, draping the neighborhood in an orange-soaked palette. The adventurous duo's shadows were cast across the cracked pavement, long and ominous. As Alexander leaned on the handles of his bike, he rocked back and forth with anticipation. Jamie looked on nervously behind his coke-bottle glasses, biting at his thumbnail with his eyes locked onto the slanted home.

"We've been planning this for weeks, it's now or never!" Alexander said with a chipper tone and a gap-toothed smile.

"I dunno, it sounds illegal," Jamie reminded.

"Don'tcha want to know what's back there?"

"Well…" Jamie groaned, "Yeah, I do. But my mom'll kill me if she finds out."

Alexander laughed and parked his bike just out of view in the safety of some unruly bushes, beneath a flickering streetlamp that was plastered with missing posters featuring a chubby-faced boy. The amount of missing posters around these parts was concerning. A lot of kids never made it home after dares were enacted, a lot more were snatched up by a man they should have been able to trust. Even the pews didn't feel safe anymore.

Jamie followed Alexander's lead and quickly darted after his friend, who began making his way toward the tall fence.

As they approached, they crouched down in the shadows and snuck along the property line. Struggling to stifle giggles, the boys turned their eyes up toward the fence. They knew it would be futile to climb, they'd done enough stakeouts and gathered enough intel to know that it held no gates, that the ivy that crept across the panels was too loose and light to hold them upright, so they'd have to use other means to take a peek at the mysteries within.

Alexander hushed Jamie as he approached the fence. He looked up into the dust covered window that lingered on the edge of the entryway that butted up to the patio. Cobwebs hung in the corners and the thick layer of grime turned the panes a grey-green that looked sickly. Alexander could see the overhead light in the entryway flicker, a few moths bounced against the old bulb's surface. A rocking chair could barely be seen inside and he swore it moved slightly.

"See anybody?" Jamie asked.

"Nope! Let's keep moving," Alexander said with a giddy glee.

They surveyed the home carefully over the summer months, trying to find a way into the unknown without causing alarm or breaking the law. The fence was too slick to climb, too rigid and tall, and the awkward dips in the ground around the perimeter made it hard to prop something against it to assist in their efforts to scale it. Having seen one too many movies, they worried that their fingerprints would be found and the FBI would swarm their houses, so they opted not to touch anything that could leave evidence.

The roof seemed unstable, with plenty of slipping slats and tiles, and the siding was a bit loose, so getting up that high without falling or making noise seemed risky. So, after much consideration and conversations held around the flicker of the television and handfuls of popcorn, the boys finally found their route and the perfect night to execute their plan. One darkened by a storm on the horizon and the increasing earliness of sunsets in autumn.

The porch was their way in. They noticed a small section of it caused a strange cutout to be made in the fence, like a tunnel burrowing into a mountain to allow travelers to pass through. It sat flush against the porch, with nary a sliver of a gap to look through. There must have been a section that continued on into the unknown, and a small boy-sized hole was made in the rotten wood just on the other side of the stairs. They would crawl through the soil and peer into the curiosities that sat hidden behind the fence and flee victoriously under the cover of darkness. It was a flawless plan.

Alexander waved Jamie over and the two of them slowly moved around the slanted staircase that led up to the porch. They laid prone atop the warm, dry grass and began making their way into the house's underbelly. Earthworms shifted around their hands as they clawed their way through the small opening, pebbles moved from the force of their palms. As Alexander's body entered the open space, a small gasp escaped his lips.

"What?" Jamie questioned as he tried to avoid Alexander's foot.

"It goes under the whole house," Alexander whispered excitedly. He shifted out of the way and let Jamie crawl up beside him.

The boys took in the expansive underside of the home, studied the storage bins and mismatched bits of furniture and home decor that littered the area. A few gaping holes in the flooring could be seen on the far end, peering upward into the home, and a musty, fungal smell wafted through the openings.

Mason jars sat half-buried beneath the dirt and the warped slats of the busted would-be flooring made it look like the ground was eating up the house. It was hard to determine what the objects inside of the cracked, dirty containers were from this distance. A soft glow came from one of the holes poking through the slats of the flooring, and harsh shadows flickered by as the home's occupant moved about.

"It's a crawlspace," Alexander noted.

"It's spooky," Jamie added with worry. "Maybe we should leave?"

"No way!" Alexander said with quiet disbelief.

"But—"

"We've planned this for—"

Jamie slapped his dirt-covered hand over Alexander's mouth. With the dulling of his voice, Alexander honed in on the strange sound above him. The wood was creaking, making a horrid groaning noise as a hefty weight was placed upon its surface. Dust fell down with each thunderous step, trailing across the middle of the crawlspace. The thuds were uneven, the specks of dust that fell on the right-hand side seemed heftier.

They heard a mumbling.

"We should go," Jamie whispered, hardly loud enough to be audible.

It was too late. Alexander was already on the move, overwhelmed by curiosity.

Jamie reluctantly followed. They bypassed a broken milk crate, its letters faded with time and warped from the excessive moisture. Inside sat the curled up skeleton of some rodent, alongside several herbs and dried lavender sprigs. One of the previously obscured mason jars held a coiled snake in a vinegary substance, and the ground was overrun with mushrooms.

They crawled through the cramped space, careful to not disturb the clustered objects and draw more attention to themselves. Alexander stopped just out of sight of one of the openings. He peered up into the room and found himself looking into a kitchen. The floorboards were in need of dusting, the cabinets were slightly off-centered and a pot on the stove was boiling over with greenish-colored bubbles. He saw the overhead light was hardly hanging on by its wires. He could smell a familiar scent, it was burned into his brain after the many BBQs his father held over the summer. Someone was cooking meat.

He crawled a few more paces forward to try to get a better look inside of the disgusting space and the shadow that was moving across the wall. No longer intrigued by just the mystery of the hidden backyard, he wanted to know everything about this home and its strange owner with the heavy footfalls that seemed to shake the Earth.

"Alex," Jamie whispered nervously.

Alexander tilted his head to the side to gaze up into the hole. A cloud of dust shot down from a heavy footstep above. He quickly wiped his eyes and tried to rid them of the irritants.

Blinking rapidly, he blearily attempted to focus on the world around him.

Something stared back.

A hand, gnarled and claw-like, shot down through the hole. Attached to an arm of unnatural length, the sharpened fingernails snatched up his hair and yanked him forward. Jamie slapped his hands over his mouth and watched in horror as his friend was lifted up into the home with a bloodcurdling scream.

The terrified younger man quickly tried to back up, tried to find his way back to the entrance with tears in his eyes and dust accumulating on his glasses. As he finally locked onto the entrance they came in through, he saw a disfigured, grotesque face staring at him with a wicked grin full of yellowed teeth.

A heavy metal barrel was dragged to the opening and pushed up against it with such force the wooden slats bent, locking him inside of the crawlspace and, as the dawning realization of his doom hit him, his screams joined his friend's in a chorus of frenzied panic.

Alexander flailed and kicked as his eyes locked onto the discolored, wild stare of the monster that snatched him up. Unnaturally tall with heavy, massive feet, the mountainous woman stomped happily with a guttural giggle escaping her lips. Her tongue hung loose between gaps of missing teeth, saliva dripped down her chin onto her bare, sagging breasts. She held onto the screaming young boy's head with a death grip and began trudging through the kitchen toward the back door that swung loosely in the wind.

He saw the horrors of the home as she carried him through the hallway. Saw the mismatched limbs and torsos of boys his own age hanging from hooks with bundles of florals and herbs dangling from amputated fingers and poking through severed necks. Mushrooms grew freely on the walls, flickering candlelight caught the curved edges of large glass jars holding eyeballs and organs. All Alexander could do was scream until the wiry-haired woman shoved a large clump of dirt into his mouth.

The old crone stepped out into the yard and continued to giggle, surveying the chaotic landscape as she went. Tears welled in Alexander's eyes, his jeans grew wet as his bladder emptied in a panic as he finally gazed upon the secrets he yearned to see for so long. That boy-sized hole in the porch was not made naturally. Oh no, it was made with a purpose. One that openly invited curious and bored teenagers into danger.

Lying in shallow graves, half-covered by dirt and sod, were the bodies of several emaciated boys around his age. Missing boys. Classmates. Teammates. Boys on missing posters that hung above his discarded bike. Their heads and hands sat above ground, moving slowly with desperation as heavy fungi grew from their pores. Hamster water bottles, hung from chicken wire, kept them barely hydrated, kept them barely alive.

"New fertilizer! New fertilizer!" the gnarly, wicked old woman said with a laugh as she dragged her recent prey to the backyard.

With a harsh motion, she tossed Alexander into a freshly dug grave. He hit the ground with force, knocking the wind clean out of his lungs as he inhaled the dirt. He gasped in agony and tried to orient himself, only to come face-to-face with the sunken eyes of his classmate, Jimmy, who had been missing since Memorial Day. Jimmy opened his mouth to speak but could only make a guttural sound as the budding plant life that overwhelmed his gums and tongue restricted his ability to converse.

The owner of the decaying house with the tall privacy fence stood above her new bag of organic plant food with a bloody, dirt-caked shovel in hand. The necklace of human teeth that hung around her wrinkled, greenish-hued neck swayed in the wind and her possessed eyes glistened with sickening glee. As Alexander tried to crawl away, she pressed the pointed end of the tool into his chest.

"Bad boy, stay put," the woman croaked as she slapped his chest with the shovel.

Immobilized, all Alexander could do was feebly wriggle as heavy clods of dirt and dried sod were tossed over his body, weighing him down with the force of a hungry Mother Earth who was delighted to have a new meal to satiate her. The owner of the white house gleefully stomped and whistled a tune as the thunderstorm and the cover of darkness finally came in, drowning out the young boy's cries for help, lost behind the tall slats of the mysterious fence on Fern Street.

PEOPLE TO DEAL WITH SUCH THINGS
Jackson Robinson

By the time Father Sam Green stumbled onto Fern Street, the sky had already begun its transition from the cheery blue afternoon to the pink and yellow of early evening. A chill had come into the air and the streetlights were coming to life one by one with a loud *clanking* sound, followed by the hum of fluorescent bulbs warming up. Sam was drunk and hadn't intended to come to this side of town. He'd simply left the cottage and started walking. His feet had found their way down here all on their own.

He knew that this wasn't really the best part of town, but he didn't really care. There were bigger things on his mind that fine summer evening than what might be said about him if he were seen walking through the "bad part of town." There was Father Gregson, for instance. Sam still couldn't quite believe everything that'd happened with him. Not all that long ago, he'd wanted to be just like Gregson. So sure and steady in his faith that he could stand before the altar, before God himself really, and confess that he'd lived a righteous life. Now, whenever Sam thought of him, all his mind could conjure up was the image of Gregson hanging from the ceiling fan in the cottage they shared. His face had been badly bruised, and Sam didn't know if it was from an off-the-books interaction with police before he got sent home or if that was just the way blood pooled in your face when you hung yourself. The reason for it didn't really matter. What mattered was that every time he closed his eyes, he saw that swollen and bloated face hanging there in the cottage living room and it made him want to scream.

He'd gone and drunk half the church's wine cellar to try to tamp that urge to scream down, but all he'd really managed to do was make himself drunk. A lot more drunk than he'd been in a long time. And while the thought of going outside so a good old-fashioned burst of fresh air could shock him back into sobriety had felt like a good idea at the time, he was starting to think he might be better off just finding a nice quiet place to lie down.

"Hey Sammy," someone hissed at him.

He turned toward the sound.

It was coming from a thin man with a shaved head standing on the deck of the house closest to Sam. He was leaning against one of the support beams like a greaser in an old movie.

"Whatcha doing down here?" He asked.

He was smiling like he knew something Sam didn't, and it made Sam's skin crawl. He looked first up the street then back the way he'd come, unsure of if the man was talking to him. The street was empty save for a teenager lying atop the porch roof across the street. Sam turned back to the man.

"I'm sorry, do I know you?" He asked. His drunkenness only slightly noticeable on the word "sorry." As a practiced drinker, Sam knew how to keep from slurring his words. It was a must, considering that some mornings, he really did need a little extra something in his coffee to get him going.

The man either didn't care or didn't notice. He just went on talking.

"You know, it's fucked up, isn't it? What Gregson did

to that kid. Kinda makes you wonder how there could even be a god in heaven in a world where someone like him could hear the calling, doesn't it?"

Sam's heart dropped into his stomach. He'd known sooner or later word about Gregson would get out. It was a small town, after all. But he hadn't really expected people to want to talk to him about it. How was he supposed to explain what Gregson had done? And furthermore, how the hell had this idiot found out about it so quick? As far as he knew, the police hadn't made any statements yet and he sure as hell hadn't told anybody.

"Heard about it on the phone," he said and gestured back towards the house with his thumb. "That's what you're wondering about, isn't it? How I knew about all of them and Gregson and everything. That's what it said you'd be thinking about when you came by. Said you might not be thinking the nicest thoughts about me too, but I'll let that slide for now. On account of you not knowing who I am and where you are. Come on in, I'll show it to ya. We hear all sorts of crazy shit on that thing. You're gonna love it."

Sam didn't move.

The man straightened up as much as he could and looked down at him.

"You don't believe me? That I got a little secret line to God? Well, a god."

Sam smiled his best *it looks like we may have a problem here* smile and said, "Of course not. There are no secret lines to God. He speaks with all who call upon him."

"Well, that's where you and I disagree. And I have to say, you're certainly not being very *faithful* right now, Sammy? But then again, for a priest, you've always been sorta lacking in that department, haven't ya?" the man replied, grinning.

Sam scoffed. His smile disappeared, and he stepped back, throwing his hands up in the air in a drunken *who has the time for this shit* gesture. He cast his eyes down at the ground and shook his head. "I don't know what you're talking about," he said, trying to ignore the flutter of embarrassment he felt in his chest.

"No?" the man asked, arching his eyebrows. "Because the phone said you might be struggling to understand just how your god could let such a thing like Kathrine Teague even happen. I believe its exact words were that you'd "lost the faith", Sammy. Now, does that sound like you?"

The photographs of Kathrine Teague the detectives had shown Sam flashed in his mind. She was only six years old when she went missing. Thinking about it made his chest hurt, and he had to push the memory away before returning his attention to the man on the porch.

Sam didn't know how the man knew about Gregson or Kathrine Teague, but Sam knew why he was hackling him and accusing him of lacking in faith. People did this all the time. Not to him, but he'd heard about it. Nonbelievers took a certain amount of joy in trying to get the teachers to question their doctrine. They believed that if they could just convince a few of the people called to teach The Word that there was no God, then they would be safe. He supposed it wasn't much different from when the church quizzed scientists about the soul or the creation of the Earth. The satisfaction of such an act stemmed from their own fears of God and, as much as Sam didn't want to admit it, his own fears that science was starting to have a pretty good case.

But, of course, this man wasn't going to rattle Sam. Even on a night like tonight, when it felt as if his entire world had just been flipped on its head. Sam's faith would persevere. Sure, it'd wavered in the past, but that was a long time ago. Today he was solid. No matter what. Sam just also felt the need to tell this man that.

"I think you have me mistaken for someone else," he replied.

The man just kept on smiling.

"Oh, not a lot of priests come wandering down this street, Sammy. I think I got the right one. This is where all the whores and lepers hang around, you know. Hell,

Rottingwood is just over yonder. You might tarnish your reputation just being here. Especially if it got out how drunk you were."

Sam hoped his cheeks didn't look as flushed as they felt.

"Didn't think I knew about the wine, did ya?"

Not wanting to admit defeat, Sam looked up at the man and said, "I have a glass of wine every now and then with dinner. My doctor says it's good for my heart. That's no business of yours."

"It's probably not. But I know that you had quite a bit more than a glass at dinner. Hell, I can smell you from here. But hey," the man held up his hands, "I'm not here to judge. God knows I've had my share of drunken nights. I just want to share the faith with you, brother. One holy man to another. Come on in and take a listen. Believe me, you don't want to be out there once it gets dark. It's dangerous."

Sam looked around once more. Their conversation had, so far, gone unnoticed. But some deep part of himself wouldn't let him. Maybe it was the wine, or maybe it was just the day he was having, but he wanted to shut this man up. How dare he accuse Sam of lacking in faith. He was going to march right into that house and tell him just how wrong he was and why.

He started up the path. He didn't notice the lights in the second-story windows flick on and he certainly didn't put together that they looked like eyes watching him. And the porch was like an open mouth with a long, concrete tongue lolling out across the yard for him to wander up.

❊ ❊ ❊

The inside of the house reminded Sam of the house he'd grown up in. It opened into a near empty hallway with scuffed and scratched wood floors and a couple picture frames hanging from its walls. It stunk of cigarettes, but there was another smell too. One that wasn't as easy to articulate. It was a kind of ozone smell that reminded Sam of thunderstorms. It made his arms break out in goosebumps and he felt the hairs on the back of his neck lift up.

"The phone's up on the second floor, but if you want, I can grab you a beer before we head up. Just between you and me, of course," the man said and winked.

Sam sighed. It was impossible for him to hide when he was frustrated and judging by the way the man smiled and said, "We'll just head upstairs instead," it was clear that this had been his goal all along. Maybe it would've been better if he'd just gone home to sleep off his drunk in peace, but Sam was never one to back down from an argument.

He followed the man upstairs.

He led Sam down a hallway that ran along the staircase to a small, messy bedroom with a red telephone sitting on the floor in the middle of it. The phone wasn't really anything special. It reminded Sam of something you might see in an old movie. The only impressive thing about it being how red it was.

"This is it," the man said and gestured toward the phone.

Sam guffawed. He hadn't known what to expect when he followed the man into his house, but this surely wasn't it.

"That's great," Sam said. He couldn't help but smile. All the anger and aggression he'd been feeling towards the poor old guy was slipping away from him. He wasn't being vindictive or judgmental. He was just crazy. How he knew about Father Gregson was a mystery, but maybe that didn't matter. The man was just sick.

Still, he didn't miss a beat.

"You don't believe me," he said. "I get it. You have to…*experience* it to really understand it. After all, seeing is believing. Isn't that what you used to tell your parishioners every time you read about some miracle recovery in the news? *If you could only see this, you should be able to believe in God.* Of course, you never seemed to bring up the ninety-nine out of a hundred who didn't make it, did ya?"

Sam stopped smiling. Perhaps the anger and frustration weren't completely gone, yet.

"Just try it."

"Try it?" Sam asked and looked down at the phone. "You must be joking. It's not even hooked up to anything."

"Some people just don't wanna open their eyes, Sammy," the man said. "Gregson used to say that, didn't he? That if people would just open their eyes, they'd see your god everywhere. Well, Sammy, I don't know about yours, but mine talks back. And pretty regularly at that. Just go have a listen."

Sam didn't move. For a second there, the man had almost sounded like Gregson. He told himself that was just because the man was using Gregson's favorite expression — an expression that was probably about as common as God works in mysterious ways — but there'd been something more to it than that. The man's voice had taken on a tremble, and it'd gone up as he'd said it just like Gregson's voice had after his stroke.

"Go on," the man said again. In his own voice this time. "Take a listen. Prove me wrong."

Sam crossed the room like a death row inmate crosses the room to his final chair. He was nervous but couldn't quite say why. When he got to the phone, he bent down and lifted it from its cradle. He wasn't sure if he should speak into it or just press it against his ear.

Just do it, Sam. It's nothing, he thought. But despite how much he told himself it didn't matter and to just get it over with already, something deep inside him was telling him to chuck that phone across the room and get the hell out of there.

But such advice is rarely listened to, and Sam pressed the receiver to his ear.

There was a sensation a bit like one of those old hand buzzers. The kind they used to sell in drugstores that would send a mild jolt up your arm when you shook hands with someone. Only this was no two-dollar trinket. Sam's teeth snapped shut and every muscle in his body was suddenly trying to contract at the same time. He felt his bladder let go and he could smell his hair and skin burning from where the phone was pressed against him. Somewhere in the distance, the man was laughing. The lights in the room dimmed and flashes of blue and white light began to arc across the walls and ceiling.

He had time enough to form the thought, *this isn't how it's supposed to feel when God speaks to us* before the humming started. It radiated up through him like a low-grade fever. Starting somewhere deep inside his chest and rattling out into his head through his fillings. Within it, he could hear a voice coming through. It said, "I am of the new gods. And I say unto thee, though art Samuel, and thou shalt care for my church."

Sam tried to scream, but his jaw wouldn't loosen.

As the voice spoke to him, Sam watched bolts of electricity descend from the ceiling towards him. Like pale blue hands coming down from the night sky to lift him up to whatever heavens they promised. They touched his cheeks, caressing him the way lovers caress each other after a long year apart, and Sam's world went black.

❋ ❋ ❋

Sam couldn't remember hanging up the phone. Or stumbling across the room to try and open the window, but he must've, because that was where he woke up.

Across from him, the man lay on the floor. In all the excitement, the old bastard's heart must've given out. He lay on his back with his hands clutching at his belly. His head at one point had rolled onto its side so that he was looking at Sam. He'd died grinning. Which would've been bad enough on its own, but both his eyes had rolled up into his skull, leaving just the whites to stare across the room at Sam.

Serves you right, you dirty, old bastard. Sam thought.

He wanted to spit it across the room at the corpse, but he was worried he might be on camera. He told himself that what'd just happened was not the result of some new deity rising from the ether to destroy life as he knew it, because there were no such things in the bible. No, this whole thing stank of one of those horrid undercover prank shows gone terribly wrong. He saw them all the time on the church's Facebook page. He, of course, didn't have a social media account. Vanity was a sin after all, but he maintained the church's account and that required him to be familiar with what was out there. The videos were all the same. Some fool with a camera would go up and harass someone until they snapped and then said fool would upload their reaction to YouTube for a laugh. The whole thing was sickening. The plan here had clearly been to lure him in off the street — why him, he didn't know, but that didn't really matter — and then bring him up here where they had a dummy phone with a couple of hand buzzers loaded into the receiver set up so they could scare the living Christ out of him. Whoever he'd talked to on the phone was probably just some out of work actor reading a script in the other room.

Probably, he thought to himself.

The only problem was that they hadn't counted on the old guy having a bad heart. He'd croaked during the climax of the whole thing, and Sam was pretty certain that he'd almost died himself. A malfunction in the hand buzzers most likely, but that didn't matter. He was going to sue them all until their fucking heads spun. The church had lawyers, and this was a dream case, he just knew it. That was probably why they were waiting so long to come in and check on him. If Sam just died, there'd be no one to call the cops, and they'd be off scot-free. Or maybe they were already hightailing it to Mexico. Well, if that were so, there were people to deal with such things and just as soon as he could stand on his own, he was going to get a hold of them.

It took him another twenty minutes of lying there, trying not to let his mind obsess too much on what'd just happened, before Sam's legs stopped twitching enough for him to stand up on his own.

He hobbled across the room, giving the phone a wide berth, and stepped over the old man's corpse into the hallway.

It didn't cross Sam's mind that as a priest; he had a certain obligation to try to perform some sort of Final Rite for the body of the man. But if it had, he probably wouldn't have done it. He was too angry to be performing any sacraments today. He was going home where he could lock the doors, pretend everything in this cruel world simply did not exist, and go to sleep.

Sam made his way down the stairs as fast as he could, which wasn't very fast considering he had to lean against the banister for support. He crossed the main hallway to the front door in as close to a run as his body could manage. He spun the deadbolt, unbolted the chain, and twisted the door lock, but when he pulled on the door, nothing happened. The handle twisted, and he heard the latch disengage, but it was like the frame had shrunk two sizes and the door had stayed the same. It wouldn't come free.

Sam stood there dumbfounded. He ran through the cycle of twisting all the locks in the opposite directions and tried the door again, but to no avail. He tried just slapping the door with the palm of his hand as hard as he could in hopes that the vibrations would loosen it from the frame, but it was useless.

The door was stuck.

When it was clear that the door wasn't going to open, Sam went looking for a window. In the living room, he found a large portrait window that looked out onto Fern Street. It was divided into three sections that all slid open individually. He went to the center section, flipped the latches on top, and tried to push it open, but it wouldn't budge. He might as well have been trying to move the mountains. He didn't understand it. Sure, his arms felt a little weaker than they normally did, but he should've been able to open a sliding window and yet, as much as he tried, the window refused to open.

He tried the other two, and both refused to budge.

Desperate and frustrated, Sam wandered to the back of the house to try the door there. They couldn't all be stuck, right? But as much as he yanked and pulled, the backdoor also refused to give. He tried a handful of other windows in the kitchen, bathroom, and back bedroom, all with no luck before deciding on breaking out of the house.

In the kitchen, he found a barstool that looked heavy enough to smash through a window, but light enough that he'd be able to lift it in his weakened state. He took it back to the living room and stood in front of the portrait window.

He got as close to it as possible, not caring if he got glass on him or not. Just wanting to be out and away from this godforsaken house forever. He gripped the stool by its base and swung.

It bounced off the window with a hollow *bonk.*

He raised the stool up and swung it again. It bounced off the window and this time, as it came back, Sam almost lost his balance. As if the window had actually pushed the stool back. He swung again and again, anger giving way to desperation, but the window would not break.

* * *

A few hours later, Sam was sitting in the living room with his head in his hands. He'd been praying. Not that it'd done him any good. Though he would never admit it, it rarely did these days. Even on that day, he'd found the skull of Kathrine Teague in the garden, it hadn't done him much good. How long had he spent praying that day? Hours upon hours full of contemplation. His knees still ached from all the time he'd spent on the kneelers. There was only one person who would've put the skull there, and Sam knew just who it was. He just didn't want to believe it. And he thought that if he just prayed hard enough, some sort of relief would come. But there'd been no relief or answer, or cosmic shift within him. In the end he'd gone to the police, because he hadn't known what else to do.

And now, even after what felt like a lifetime of praying, he didn't understand what the hell was going on. He'd tried all the doors again. He'd tried smashing different windows. He'd even spent a good twenty minutes just banging on the portrait window with his hands, but the only attention he managed to attract was that of an old black cat with graying fur around its nose and white feet. The doors wouldn't open, the windows wouldn't break, and no one would come to help. He had a cell phone, but it wouldn't turn on. A side effect of whatever'd happened with that damn phone upstairs, no doubt. And as far as he knew, there wasn't another landline in the house.

As if to punctuate this thought, the phone upstairs started to ring. Sam shut his eyes and let out a long and frustrated sigh. This couldn't be happening. Things like this weren't supposed to happen. Not to good people at least, and he was a good person. He volunteered, helped out around his community when he could, and even donated a small amount of the pittance that the church paid him to local charities. Not to mention he'd committed his life to the church. And was he perfect?

No.

Sometimes he drank too much. Sometimes he was a little loose with what people told him in confessions. But was he as bad as Gregson? Certainly not. He was the one who should be stuck in this house, not Sam.

The phone continued to ring.

"Just go answer it," he told the empty room. There were tears in his voice, but he tried not to notice. "Maybe that's what they're waiting for."

He got to his feet, careful not to anger his already sore muscles any more than he already had, and walked into the hallway. He looked up the staircase. As much as he wanted out of this house, he certainly didn't want to answer that damn phone again.

But what other choice did he have?

***

Sam froze at the top of the stairs. All the spit in his

mouth had dried up and there was a clicking sound in his throat when he tried to swallow. His heart was thumping double-time in his chest and he felt like he might pass out if he didn't get his breathing under control soon.

The old man's body had moved. It should've been sprawled across the doorway to the back bedroom. Half of it lying unseen in the bedroom and the other half stretched out into the hallway. But instead, it sat propped up against the doorframe with its hands in its lap. Its head was cocked to the side as if Sam had just asked it to answer a complex equation.

It was impossible. The man had been dead. He had to have been. Your eyes didn't roll back into your head like that unless you were. And if he wasn't, then why hadn't he tried to come downstairs when Sam was trying to smash the windows out? Why hadn't he made some sort of noise to try to tell Sam that he was up here? No, he had to have been dead and if he wasn't, then he certainly was now.

Which meant what, exactly?

Sam didn't know, but he felt guilty all the same. He kneeled down and pressed two fingers under the man's jaw and waited. The phone was still ringing, but Sam figured if the call hadn't been dropped by now, it probably wouldn't be. He didn't feel a pulse and the skin there was cold.

Like touching a corpse, he thought, and his stomach rolled. He pulled his hand back quickly.

He crossed the room and looked down at the phone. He didn't want to pick it up again. He didn't know if he would survive picking it up again. There was a pretty pronounced flutter in his chest that hadn't been there before he passed out and his muscles kept twitching. Still, when he ran through his options, he didn't know what else to do. It wasn't like he could just leave.

He kneeled and picked up the phone. He didn't press it to his face this time. He held it in front of him and angled the receiver up towards his mouth when he spoke.

"Hello? Who is this?"

The voice on the phone made all the blood in Sam's body run cold.

"It's me, Sammy," the man's voice came through. "I'm a part of the house now. I live in the walls and when the house requires it, I will give myself unto thee to be consumed. It's our purpose, Sammy. It's our calling as holy men. I have seen the new gods and they are magnificent. It is an honor to serve."

Sam turned around and looked at the body.

It's a prop. That's all. The real guy is probably off in some sound studio watching all this unfold on a little TV screen, he thought, but he didn't really believe it. The body hadn't felt like latex, no matter how much he wanted to believe it had. It'd felt like the dry and papery skin of a corpse.

It's just a show, he told himself. *Don't let it get the better of you.*

He glanced around for cameras. He didn't see any, but that didn't mean there weren't any.

"What the hell is wrong with you people? Let me out of this house or I'm going to call the police!" Sam said.

"The house will let you leave just as soon as you accept it. Abandon your god, Sammy. Abandon your life. Abandon your hope ye who enter here." The old man started to laugh.

Sam slammed the phone down in its cradle, then kicked it across the room. It smashed into the wall and made a *clanging* sound and started to ring again. Louder than it should've been able to. As if Sam wasn't exactly hearing it, but it was appearing in his head like an intrusive thought.

He plugged his ears against it and walked out of the room, delivering a swift kick to the corpse in the doorway as he did so. This dislodged a hollow burp from the corpse's throat that made Sam shout.

He didn't have time to think about the implications that came along with that, because as he made his way down the hallway, the house started to shake. He turned onto the staircase and gripped the banister as he made his way down. It was chaos at the bottom of the stairs. Picture frames fell down and crashed all around him, and Sam struggled to stay on his feet as he crossed the hallway to the door.

"The doors won't open, Sammy. Not until you accept your new post." The man's voice came from behind him, but Sam didn't want to look. He knew that if he turned around and saw the man standing there, his face would be swollen and bloated from death and his eyes would be rolled into the back of his head. Not much different from the way Gregson had looked, and it dawned on Sam that he'd been seeing a lot of dead folks lately and he almost laughed. "Abandon your god," the man called. "Abandon your life. Care for their house or else the new gods will rise and consume the earth."

"Shut up!" Sam screamed and slapped the door again. "Let me out of this fucking house or I'm going to burn it down!"

"Turn around, Sammy. Face me," the man said.

"No," Sam moaned, but he started to anyway. Shutting his eyes tightly in hopes that the door would simply open, and he would be pulled away from whatever this hell was.

"Open your eyes." The voice was no longer that of the man, but that of the thing he'd heard on the phone. That hum.

Sam couldn't help himself. His eyes did open and what he saw made him forget every bible lesson he'd ever had. He started to scream and collapsed onto his hands and knees.

The man who'd brought him into this nightmare stood at the bottom of the staircase, his arms held out to his sides like Jesus waiting to be embraced. His face was bruised from where the blood had settled, and purple veins stood out like spiderwebs beneath bits of his pasty white skin.

"Accept me," he said and as he did, he lifted off the ground and rose slowly toward the ceiling.

"Fine, just please let me out of here!" Sam screamed

and turned back to the door. He spun the handle once more and this time, there was a little gasp of air as the seal broke and the door swung open.

The house was suddenly quiet. As quiet as a church, as the saying goes. He looked over his shoulder. The walls had stopped shaking, and the pictures had stopped falling. The man's body lay in a crumpled heap at the bottom of the stairs. As if it'd been dropped from a great height.

Sam crawled through the doorway onto the porch where, just a few hours ago, the man had called to him.

He was still crying, but he was getting himself under control. Mainly by repeating over and over to himself that what he had seen wasn't real. It would become a mantra that he would maintain for the rest of his short life.

Sam didn't want to look back, but he did just the same, telling himself that it was just a funhouse. Something you would see at a carnival. It was a funhouse designed to scare someone very specifically, but that was all it was. The voice he'd heard in his head, the ringing, all of it a product of carefully hidden speakers and cameras. The shock and the body, bad props. Even the levitation could be explained away to nothing more than a couple of carefully hidden wires.

That was all.

And the doors had simply been set up to open whenever whoever was in charge figured they'd screwed with him enough and flipped the switch.

That was all it was. A prank. And still, he couldn't shake the fear he felt. And when he went home that night, his sleep was light and troubled.

He dreamt of an enormous bright coin hanging in the middle of a blood red sky. It was the sun. And something impossibly large and human shaped was rising up in front of it, blotting it out. He tried to hide from it, but it called his name. It asked why he'd abandoned his post.

When he woke up, he was screaming, but to the changing world outside, it sounded like he was laughing.

106

GIVING UP THE GHOST
Tobin Elliott

The room's warmth is sucked away, leaving an icy coldness. All light retreats, leaving a deep, pervasive darkness.

And now, instead of two of us, there's three.

Mom is still on the bed, prone, sleeping. But Mom is also sitting up on the hospital bed, her hips occupying the same space as the prone figure.

I stare at this other Mom, and she smiles back at me. "Hey, Lee," she says.

※ ※ ※

I sit in my mother's living room — the kitchen chair hastily dragged in, turning increasingly more uncomfortable as the hours wear on — and stare at the old woman on the hospital bed. Her hair is in disarray, but thankfully, the nightgown they'd put on her that has an annoying habit of working its way up to her waist is covered with several layers of blankets. She's always cold now, her tissue-thin skin not able to retain heat anymore. Her mouth hangs open as she sleeps, her eyes rolling under onion-skin eyelids.

The hospital bed feels overwhelming and formal in my mother's informal living room. We'd done the hospital visits way too many times, and when the hospital decreed that she could no longer stay there, I knew better than to bring her to my home.

She'd ruined my life enough in the past three decades. I'd rather pay to have her stay in her own too-big home on Fern Street, with a rotating stable of support workers coming in to tend to her needs.

Her needs. I flick my eyes toward her again.

Katherine Blanche Clarke. Mother of one, grandmother of two. Ninety-three, with a history of high blood pressure, strokes, and a reliance on an almost Elvis-level cocktail of painkillers and medications.

Katherine Blanche Clarke. Known forever as Mary for some forgotten reason.

Mary.

My mother.

And the thought comes to me, as it does for every one of these interminable visits to her home…

Wonder if this is the time she gives up the ghost?

And then I feel a little guilty, because I don't feel guilty about thinking it.

* * *

My mother was, at one time, my world. After she separated from Dad, I was just five years old, so it was the Mary and Leo show for quite a while there. And she was a great mom.

I wish she could have stayed that way.

* * *

When I was getting ready to visit my mother for the weekend, I didn't bring much. I'd already left some old clothes and toiletries in the bathroom upstairs. She'd never use that bathroom again, so I figured it was safe to claim. To get ready this time, I just grabbed an old paperback that I remember liking in my younger years. *Nightmare Seasons*. Knowing how long the day would be, short stories were going to be better for my lack of concentration.

Yeah, this isn't my first rodeo.

Hell, this isn't even my first rodeo this year. It's just late February, and we'd been to Emergency twice. Now this. Hospitalized at home.

Getting old ain't for pussies.

My mother had been mostly healthy until the first stroke hit her, about five years ago. Then, with lessened, weakened mobility on her right side, along came the falls, the bone breaks, and the occasional additional stroke, sometimes mild, sometimes not so much.

It had taken a reasonably healthy woman in her late-eighties, still driving, still cooking up a storm, always baking and out visiting, and beat her into submission, leaving her a housebound, frail and fragile shadow of her former self.

She probably should have given up her two-story house at 106 Fern St. for a tiny senior's apartment, but she flat out refused to consider "an old folk's home where everyone's just waiting to die."

Instead, she's still at her Fern Street home, sandwiched between a lot that should be condemned, and a house with a crazy lady. Instead, my mother just withers away in a rented hospital bed, condemned and crazy herself, waiting to die.

We'd gone through a lot together, her and I, and somehow survived it all.

Mary and Leo.

Mom and me.

Together against the world.

But, eventually, I grew up and, as one does, I went through a few girlfriends until I met Lea.

Yeah, I know. Leo and Lea? Way too cute. Pathetically so.

But she was the one. And my mother seemed to like her a lot. At least, until we got married. It was like a switch flipped in her head. Mom got mean. Mom got nasty.

She was no longer the mother I'd known.

Sure, yeah, I'd heard of the dreaded mother-in-law thing, but I never expected my wife to have to deal with that shit.

God, was I wrong.

The living room is a small oasis of non-activity, so not like when we're in the hospital. Aside from a nurse stopping by to check the saline drip that's keeping her hydrated, we're in that endless purgatory of waiting for whatever comes next.

Five hours in, it's barely noon. I keep picking up the paperback, and putting it back down again. The thoughts and the memories don't want to stop.

I look out the window. Fern Street's quiet now, no jogger, no more old music from the house next door. Not since that day I startled that kid when I tried to cut mom's lawn. There was a hell of a commotion there the next day. But, none of my business, I have enough of my own shit to deal with.

One more time, I try to read one of the stories, but my eyes slide over the paragraphs, retaining nothing.

I give up and close the book and set it on the table beside me. Maybe it's the motion, maybe it's the whisper of the book on the surface, but my mother's eyes flutter open.

She looks around in confusion, then squints. With her age and the advancement of cataracts, I know she's likely seeing blobs of shape and color at best. I stand and approach the bed, getting myself into her field of focus.

Her eyes quit roaming and settle on me. "Bill?" she says, but tentatively, with a hint of…what? Fear? Trepidation? God knows that's pretty much how she approached all communication with her long ago ex-husband.

"Leo," I offer.

She squints again, and I can almost see the roil of confusion. Bill has been dead almost forty years. He drowned himself in cheap whisky in a shitty basement apartment, one bottle at a time. Mom had pulled us out of that shitshow almost fifteen years prior to that.

"Bill?" she says again.

"I'm Leo," I say. "Your son."

"Bill?"

Fuck.

"No," I say, doing everything I can to keep my voice even. "Not Bill, Mom. Leo." *The only one that still kind of gives a shit about you,* I think, but don't say.

She squints in confusion again, blinks twice, then says, "Where's Bill? I need Bill." Which almost strikes me as funny, because whenever she'd needed my father, he was never around, so he was maintaining that perfect score.

I sit back down and, with no human shape to hold her attention, her eyes slip closed again.

Bill, I think. *Goddamn.*

Still, here I am, the dutiful son, the last one who conceivably does give a shit about her. The one that always shrugs awkwardly to all those that termed me *the good son.*

No, not the good son. I'm the guilty son, the one that stays by her side only out of duty, and so that, when she finally does give up that ghost, I can at least say I was there for her.

Surely that's worth something, right?

Maybe. Maybe not. Who the hell knows for sure?

Not me, I'll tell you that.

Sighing, I consider the book once again, but it holds no charms for me. I pull out my phone, but there are no messages, no one to really call, no one who'd call me. I slide it back into my pocket.

With hours to go, I consider heading to the kitchen and making myself a coffee. Maybe even a sandwich. Even if Mom wakes, she won't be looking for me, anyway.

I stand up from the uncomfortable chair to leave the cloying room. One last glance at Mom and —

—and I drop back into the chair hard enough for it to slide backward to the wall.

When I can find my voice, I can only get out a whispered, "Holy shit."

The room has gone *cold.* Painfully so.

And it's gone *dark.* As though every single shadow in the house wove a web around us.

Us. That's the weirdest thing. Instead of two of us,

there's three.

Mom is still on the bed, prone, sleeping. But Mom is *also* sitting *up* on the hospital bed, her hips occupying the same space as the prone figure.

My mother—old, slack-jawed, confused. There's frost in her hair.

My mother…another Mom—young, bright, smiling, alert. She's clothed in shadows and darkness.

I stare at this other Mom, and she smiles back at me.

"Hey, Lee," she says. I haven't heard that name in over thirty years.

I open my mouth, but initially, I can't get a sound out. My throat is locked up. But I finally manage a swallow, then try again. My breath fogs out as I speak.

"Mom?"

"Hey Lee," she says. "It's so good to see you."

I stare at her, then stand slowly, easing myself up. A part of me scared she'll disappear, a part of me terrified she won't. I glance at the prone form of my mother, the one I've been sitting with for the past few hours.

I look past her to the large windows. It should be sunny out there. Instead, it looks like midnight during a power outage. The blackness is overwhelming, no streetlights to cast reflections of metal. No moonlight.

No light whatsoever.

The darkness pushes against the glass and seeps inside, freezing the air into silence. Little movements no longer reach my ears.

I have so many questions, my squirming brain can't decide which to ask first.

I say, "Did you…?"

I say, "Are you…?"

I say, "Is she…?"

"She's not dead," the other Mom says. "That's not going to happen for—" Then she laughs and the sound is muted, yet musical, a memory from long ago. "Oops," she says. "Spoiler alert."

I lean in closer to her, and that's when I realize she's translucent. "If she's alive, then who are you?"

"Right thought," she says, raising a finger, "wrong question."

"What's the right question?"

"Well, hon, the who is obvious. I'm your mother. The right question is, 'What are you?'"

"What?"

"Exactly."

"No, I mean—" I give up. "What are you?" I say, asking the right question.

"I'm Mary, hon. Your mother. Except," she says, then lets out a sigh, "except I'm the ghost of Mary."

"How can that be?"

She laughs again, enjoying my confusion entirely too much. "You think your body has to be dead for the ghost to be freed?"

"I don't even believe in ghosts," I say.

She looks down at the frost and darkness on the prone body on the bed, then back at me.

"Well, then you'd be wrong on both counts."

"I'm not following."

"Of course you're not," Mary says. "It's a lot to take in. Okay, how about this…think of a time you were unbelievably overwhelmed."

"Probably when Jordan was born."

"Your child?"

"Yeah," I say, unable to disguise the distaste in my mouth, "Your granddaughter, who you ignored for the next—"

"I wasn't there for her birth. I wasn't there for her growing up."

"No," I say. "You weren't. You just blew her off—"

"You're not understanding me, Lee. Listen to what I'm saying to you: I have never met your daughter. I wasn't there for her, because I'd left by then."

I stared at her, trying to not notice the conjoining of the two bodies. I had to look away, shifting on the uncomfortable chair. No sound. Everything, silent. Just her voice.

"What do you mean," I say, turning back to her, you'd

'left by then'?"

"You felt overwhelmed when Jordan was born?"

"Of course. I was now a parent, and I felt completely unprepared for it."

"There you go," she says. "In the months between you telling me you were going to get married, and the day you did, I felt that same sense of being overwhelmed. My baby was getting married and didn't need me anymore."

"I did," I say. "Of course I—"

"Let me finish," she says. "I'll rephrase that to I *felt* you didn't need me anymore. I was alone; I had no one. You were starting a new life. So, yes, I was overwhelmed. And, not long after I watched you marry Lea, I...just..." She flutters her hands up and away from her. "...I just left."

"What do you mean?" I put my hands under my armpits to get some warmth back into them.

"I mean that—call it what you will: my personality, my spirit, my consciousness, my ghost, whatever...whatever made me *me* exited my body." She stabs a finger down at the prone form of my mother on the stretcher. "That body," she says. "I chose to leave it behind."

"What the *fuck* are you talking about?"

"Let me ask you a question, Lee. Think back to your wedding day...to later that evening. Think back to the reception. I'm guessing you interacted with me. Was I the same? Or was I somehow...off?"

"You've been off for thirty-odd years, Mom."

She cants her head to the side and cocks an eyebrow as she smirks.

"When did it start?" she says.

"When Lea and I were saying goodbye to everyone at the reception as we were leaving."

"What happened?"

"I said goodbye to my new father-in-law, and he told me Lea was mine now, and to not bring her back to him." I can't help but smile at the memory, because we both had idiot grins on our faces. I always had a good time ribbing Lea's father, and he did me as well. "And then I went to hug you and instead you just grabbed my hands and stared at me. I asked if you'd had a good time at the wedding and you just shrugged your shoulders, then you gave my hands a squeeze and said goodbye. You didn't even do that much with my brand-new wife. She went to hug you and you turned and left the circle."

I remember the look of shock and disappointment and confusion on my new wife's face. I remember the turmoil I felt. Thinking, *should I go after her and find out what the hell is going on? Or let it slide and not cause a scene?*

I was younger then. Far less confrontational. I let it slide.

I just didn't know how far down it was going to slide before it hit bottom.

"Shit," she says. "I'm so sorry."

"So, tell me, Ghost Mom, if you weren't in there," I say, stabbing a finger at the prone body of my mother, "then who was?"

"I don't know."

"You. Don't. Know."

She gave me an unreadable smile and shook her head. "You keep track of the people who move into the homes you've moved out of?"

"Well, no. But it's not the same."

"It really is." She shrugs. "My old life was over. My son had moved on. I really didn't have anything to hold me there."

"No, not, you know, the idea of seeing your son move to the next stage of his life. New wife, kids, better jobs…"

She drops her head. Weirdly, her hair doesn't follow physics and fall with it. It just holds its position.

"So," I continue, "you decided to skip all that. Where'd you go? What'd you do?"

"Just like someone was doing with my old life, I moved into others and lived their lives."

"You decided other lives were worth more observation than those you birthed and raised?"

She flicks her gaze back up to me. "When you put it like that, it sounds terrible."

"How else would you put it?"

She mulls that over for a moment, her mouth working, as though chewing on the thoughts. Finally, she says, "I knew you would be fine. You always had a good head on your shoulders."

Oh, I think. *Well, shit.*

We both take in the silence, watching each other. My mother — my other mother — still prone and sleeping.

We stay like this for a long time, wrapped in cold and darkness and our thoughts.

How did she figure out she could leave her body? Did one person replace her? Or several? Was there someone else in her body right now?

Then I think something else…

"Why are you back?"

"Isn't it obvious?"

I start to shake my head no, but then, looking at the prone form of my mother, I say, "Is she dying?"

The ghost makes a finger gun and shoots me.

I get up and move to the stretcher. The cold is making me ache all over. My fingers and toes are numb.

"Is she…?"

"Am I?" the ghost says. "No, Leo, we're not dead yet."

"How long?"

"How long do you need to say goodbye to her?"

"I don't know…how am I supposed to know that?" I say. "That's my mother, but you're telling me that, for half my life, I haven't even known who the hell I've been dealing with."

"Shouldn't that make it easier?" she says. "To say goodbye?"

"Who's in there? Who is she right now?"

"Right now, the premises are vacant. I chased out the last tenant when I showed up. Squatters' rights don't count when it's your own body."

"You make it sound like it's a fucking apartment, not a human being."

"If the shoe fits, Leo…" she says. "And watch your language."

"Says the woman who literally taught me how to swear."

"Leo, I've made a lot of mistakes in my life. Your father. Walking away from you. A lot of mistakes."

I hug myself tighter against the cold and the dark. "I hope, now that you're here, now that your body's dying, you're not going to ask for forgiveness."

"I…"

I hold up a hand to stop anything else she might say. "Don't. Do not." I huff out a disgusted breath. "Don't you dare, because if I know one thing about life, it's this: when it comes to the day-to-day, when it comes to how you treat friends and family, you can do it right, or you can let it turn into a slow-motion car crash."

"Lee —"

"I'm not finished speaking," I snap. "I let you talk. You will let me talk."

She inclines her head and raises a hand in a go on gesture.

"Everyone fucks up, Mom. Everyone. I've fucked up. Absolutely I have. But I've tried to be a better person than what would have been expected of me, considering my lineage. I've kept jobs. I've bought my own house with my own money. I've stayed away from the drugs and booze. I've tried to do everything right."

"You did."

That stops me. "I did?" I say. I squint at her and say it again. "I did? *How would you know?*"

Her mouth opens, but only darkness falls out. No words. I fill in the silence.

"I didn't do everything right, Mom. But yes, I tried." I give her a pointed stare. "And how did my mother reward me?"

"Lee."

"You fucking ran away."

"Leo…"

"You asked me how much time I needed to say goodbye?" I say. "I think I just answered the question. I needed this long."

"May I talk now?"

I actually consider it for a moment. I really do. Then I say, "No, I don't think so. You had over thirty years to say the things you should have said. Instead, you wait until your body's dying and that's when you decide to come back and try to get it all in, in a few moments. So…no, Mom. Too little, too late."

She drops her eyes to the frost-rimed floor. "Okay," she says, "okay, I understand. Would it help to say I'm sorry?"

This time, I don't need to consider anything. "No, it wouldn't."

I stand again and move closer to the shell of my mother. I lift my hand to put it on her arm, but then I think I don't even know who she is. *I don't know who's been in that head for half my life.*

I drop my hand without touching her.

"Answer one question," I say.

She looks hopeful. "What's that?"

"When she dies, you'll be gone? Forever?"

"Yes."

"Good." The hopeful look dies.

"Goodbye, Mom," I say. I grab my coat, but leave the book I would never be able to finish now. I know if I see the cover, all I'll be able to think about are these last few minutes. Better to leave it here and let it die too.

"Leo."

I turn and snarl, "What?"

"I truly am sorry."

I stare at her for a long moment. Then I shift my gaze to my mom on the bed. Then I say, "Yeah, you should be."

But the ghost is gone.

I realize they're both gone now.

I take out my phone and pull up my wife's phone number as I walk out into the warmth of the midday sun on Fern Street.

I leave my past behind.
I look to my future.

107

KNOW THYSELF
Lennox Rex

I never have trusted mirrors.

Or, to put a finer point on it, maybe it was that Doppelgänger on the other side of the glass that alerted my lizard brain. Does it really matter? What truly matters is the way my face would make less and less sense, the longer I'd stare into my own eyes without blinking. The way, if you continue to stare at your reflection long enough, your face eventually becomes an abstract grouping of shapes and fleeting expressions that you never can be sure are forming of your own volition. Something about watching my reflected lips twitch and twist into such uncanny smiles and seeing my own eyes narrow and glint with a hint of malice always raised the tiny hairs on the back of my neck. I'd always pull away at that point, silently repeating, *That wasn't you, it's not you.*

I never did quite get over that inexplicable sensation of defiance, that feeling of *this is not you,* but I did grow accustomed to that strange Self glaring back at me from the glass. You could even go as far to say, I suppose, that we became friendly. I smile at that man now and watch him mimic me as I adjust my tie in Mom's full-length mirror.

It's a family heirloom, the looking glass, made a handful of generations ago by some male relative that made fine furnishings. The dark cherry stain on cherry wood, with its inlaid gold, makes it almost regal. The four feet are carved to resemble the gnarled roots of a tree, and seem to grow up into two separate trunks, with the mirror's hinges nearly resembling a tree's crown. The top of the frame holds a wonderful skyscape of wispy clouds that has always seemed so real as to be drifting lazily at the behest of the soft breeze. The same soft breath of air stirs up the golden leaves that scatter along the bottom of the mirror's frame. I've always marveled at this looking glass for its obvious beauty, but that's not to say I ever trusted it. After all, we all know how I feel about mirrors.

Mom appears in the glass, tilting her face up slightly as her thin lips curve up into an adoring smile. "Of course I'd find you here." I watch her movements in the glass as she reaches up to pat my arm. "No need to preen," she teases. "You always look like my perfect gentleman."

I turn away from our reflections and bend down to plant a fleeting kiss on her forehead. "Finally dropping the 'little', are we?" I tease right back.

She pauses to check her own appearance, giving herself an exaggerated smile and quickly rubbing a spot of lipstick off one of her front teeth. "Well, I suppose it had to happen someday." She punctuates her statement with a theatrical sigh before beaming up at me. "Thank you for making the time to visit. It means so much to your sister."

I choose not to remark on that. I think we both know perfectly well that Mom wanted me here more than Laura ever would. Though, I suppose, when you've moved back home to be with family while your husband deploys for who knows how long, you stop being so picky about the company you keep. The quickness with which she'd pulled me into a tight hug upon my arrival yesterday had certainly taken me by surprise. "Of course." I glance back to our reflections. "I'll be right down, okay?"

I give one last peck on the forehead, and she chuckles on her way out of the room. "I'm not sure if it's that mirror you love, or your own reflection."

An honest frown flits across my face as I give myself one last appraisal. To say I'm not looking forward to this farewell party is an understatement. Some would claim I'm a touch anti-social. Truth be told, I'm not exactly thrilled to be back home at good old 107 Fern St., either. I suppose I might be able to get out of my usual yearly visit, since I've come now. So, there is some silver lining to this cloud. "Here goes nothing," I sigh. At least I don't have to carpool with Laura. Between her puffy-eyed sniffling and my niece's hysterics, I'd probably–

My muscles tense and my eye twitches at the ungodly screeching that erupts out in front of the house. Does she really think she can stop her father from leaving by acting feral?

One deep inhale and one slow exhale. I compose myself, straightening my tie one last time and smiling softly. The glass reflects a menacing grin. I blink, and blink once more, for good measure. My reflection now matches the feel of my facial muscles, but the eyes in the glass are burning with an ominous glee. A jolt of shock stiffens my spine and I turn on my heel, hustling out to the hall as I remind myself, *That couldn't have been you.*

✳ ✳ ✳

As expected, the party had been an exercise in patience, and deploying both my charm and restraint. Here I am now, dressed down and zoned out on Mom's new sectional. The hardwood floor feels smooth and cool under my stockinged feet. It was a smart move on Mom's part to redo the flooring down here on the first story. Especially if my niece will be running wild around here indefinitely. Clean-up must be so much easier than it was with the polyester carpeting I grew up with. I wonder if Laura might convince Mom to repaint the cream-colored walls. Color would probably hide the messes children make better. My lips twitch in amusement as I picture Mom merely covering up any mishaps with yet another framed family picture. In my opinion, there's already so many more than necessary littered all throughout the typical common areas. My gaze drifts over Mom's prized hutch in the corner, with her assorted knick-knacks and memories made solid. I wonder how they will fare. My eyes stop on the television once more, but don't take in whatever inane early evening sitcom is flashing on the screen. My train of thought hurtles back towards the party I've just endured. So many times, I would have loved the opportunity to enact my fleeting fantasies of casual violence. Nothing makes my fingers itch with the urge to wrap around throats quite like the obligation to socialize with mundane, dull-minded suburbanites. Can they really be considered intrusive thoughts if you enjoy them?

A sudden shout of "Uncle Travis!" startles me out of my thoughts and doesn't even serve as a warning before a towheaded little monster plunges into my lap and starts pawing at me. The only thing that could make this worse would be if the kid had sticky hands. "Play with me," she whines. "I wanna play hide-n-seek!"

Thankfully, Laura appears while I'm still trying to compose my expression into something socially acceptable. Without missing a beat, she pulls her spawn off me and turns them to face her. Immediately, they wrap around her like an octopus and snuggle their face into her neck. She angles her head down to kiss them gently atop their head, and speaks softly but firmly near their ear. "I've told you already, leave Uncle Travis alone. He doesn't want to play, Baby." Another kiss, and Laura sets them down on their feet. "I think Grandma is going to make cookies," she says slyly. "I saw her taking out her best cookie cutters." Their doe-like eyes widen comically, and they let out a little gasp before spinning around and barreling towards the kitchen with a shout of "Grammy, I wanna help!"

Rude though it may be, I can't help but shake my

head in distaste. I don't know why my sister, or anyone, bothers to have children. "Thanks," I offer as an afterthought. I turn to see her watching me with a stiff smile. Unaffected, the smile I return is much looser. She hovers, not sure if she really wants to sit with me. She tucks a stray strand of strawberry blonde hair behind her ear and scratches the back of her earlobe–one of her tells. I don't even attempt to shift my body language to make her more comfortable.

"I know we don't really talk much," she finally starts, "but I appreciate that you're here right now." Still unsure what to do with herself, she straightens the hem of her blouse and begins wringing her hands ever so subtly.

With an internal sigh, I grant her a bit of mercy. "At the end of the day, family is family." I get up and pull her into a hug. Her body relaxes only slightly, and I don't hold her very long. We pull apart with a fair bit of awkwardness on her part, and she excuses herself to go take a nap. I have no doubt she could use one. I'm very much looking forward to going to bed later, myself.

❋ ❋ ❋

The sensation of weight shifting beside me and a hushed murmur near my ear coaxes me into consciousness, and I open my eyes to find I'm no longer alone in bed. There's no way I can truly be awake because my new bedmate is none other than the Doppelgänger that's always peering out at me from every mirror I've ever looked into.

As I blink, desperate to get more light focused on my retinas, I notice this second self is not actually my exact twin. His hair, just a touch wavier than my own, and kept an inch or so longer, is a deep chestnut, rather than my own light auburn. His hazel eyes, boring into my own, are flecked with green instead of gold. There's something unsettling about his face—a nearly imperceptible malevolence etched deeply into every feature. "You're–" My brain fails as his–mine? our?–blunt fingernails ghost along my skin, down my sternum and back up towards the hollow of my throat, again and again. Of course, he'd know to touch me just like that. Even if I wanted to, I'm unable to keep my eyelids from fluttering as a groan rises from the depths of my diaphragm. He chuckles and presses himself closer against me. His skin feels amazingly warm and soft, despite its pale and unyielding appearance, like moonlight and the hard glass reflecting it.

"You're not me," I finally manage. My voice strains as his fingernail starts to lightly scratch down further, towards my navel. "I must be dreaming. Reflections don't come to life." He circles my navel with that bare-ly-there touch and travels back up towards my throat. My skin flushes with warmth as a larger volume of blood rushes that much faster through my veins.

Another chuckle of amusement slips past his smirking lips as he gracefully shifts to sit up, straddling me. He captures my wrists and pins them up above my head. Usually, I'd be the one to pull such a move, but I'm transfixed by that startling gaze that's somehow both strange and all my own. "Who said I was a reflection?" His voice is the same husky timbre I employ to seduce. I'm just as susceptible to it as every former bedmate I've had the pleasure of knowing. My pupils expand, taking in the knowing edge to his sharpening grin. "I'm a part of you, Travis." He pouts playfully as he adjusts, to be better able to run a fingertip down my right oblique. Another unstoppable groan escapes as I squirm. "The part that you will insist on running away from." He releases my wrists, and yet I stay frozen in place as he slowly comes down onto his forearms, pressing our bare chests together and brushing his lips against the side of my face. I let out a shocked gasp and shudder at the puff of his breath against my skin. It's electrifyingly cool, like glass covered in morning dew. "I'm done being ignored," he whispers in my ear. He nips at my earlobe, and I instinctively wrap my arms around him, letting out a soft hum of arousal as I roll my hips up against his. He laughs against me and presses his lips to my jaw. "It's time to accept me." He trails his lips across my skin as he moves his mouth to meet mine, finally whispering against my parted lips. "Time to become who you're meant to be."

The deep, throaty laughter is coming from me now, as I slip a hand up into his hair, wrapping the silky strands around my fingers. "And who am I meant to be?" I allow my eyelids to gently slide shut and sigh when he bears down with his pelvis, pressing me further into the mattress.

He catches my lower lip between his teeth and tugs playfully. "Let me remind you," he mumbles. He bites down hard on the center of my lip, shifting the pressure from his front teeth to his canine. He cuts my pained gasp short by pressing our lips together, using his tongue to push the metallic taste of my own blood into my mouth.

I grip him more tightly as I surrender to the overwhelming tide of complete, perfect pleasure that I would be able to get only from myself. Our breaths synchronize as lips slide and tongues tangle together. As we thrust our hips, matching wet spots forming at the fronts of our boxer briefs, I can feel the steady thrum of his pulse as if it were my own. While we seem to melt into each other, the memories flood my brain, firing off a fuzzy ecstasy all throughout my nervous system. A stray spark of joy releases itself as a near cackle as I remember Jenny Tiller. That first time I truly leaned into my instinctive callousness. I had simply regurgitated and embellished stories about inverted men from upside-down houses that could never close their eyes, and littered the rest of that night with warnings that those lidless eyes were always watching in the dark. All it took after that was a few well-timed growls just outside Laura's bedroom door, and Jenny had been in tears as she all but ran out into the street and all the way home. She never did return to our house, and I had manipulated my mother into turning a blind eye so easily. Knowing I had that power to hurt people, and even to get away with it–I had felt godlike.

His voice interrupts my reminiscence. It's smooth and enticing, far in the back of my mind. *Remember the gerbil?* Pride surges through me as I recall the memory, eliciting a happy moan. *It was so small, wasn't it? So warm and soft in your hands.* I feel my lips curve and curl smugly. *Wasn't it such a thrill to feel it struggle? Hear it squeak? Watch its eyes bulge when you finally gave it that last squeeze?* To this day, Mom and Laura think the pointless little rodent merely escaped, never to be found again. *Haven't you secretly wondered, all this time, how exquisite it would feel to play with people the same way?*

Gasping as if I've just pulled myself up out of the water, I throw my eyes open and blink the room into focus. Clean, cream walls with one artistically bland yet suitably pleasant landscape hung above the sturdy, plain desk. The old, worn drafting lamp sitting on the desk next to my laptop, and the squeaky office chair pushed in neatly. My suitcase laid down and opened beside the unstained chest of drawers. Moonlight, unhindered by blinds or curtains, fills the entire room and gives the scene an ethereal feel. Nothing out of place, and no longer anything extra. It's just me, but that's perfect.

I am here now, all of me; and I was exactly right. It's time to enjoy the life I've spent so many years denying myself.

My brain buzzes with excitement as I slip silently out of bed and cross over to pick out a fresh shirt and my favorite pair of lounging joggers. After all, I'm not a heathen. Being properly dressed lends my task a certain level of civility I much appreciate. Just as I reach out to grasp the knob and ease my door open, I hear it: the squeak of neglected hinges, followed by a light but careless footfall. They pass by my door, and moments later, I hear the click of a light switch. My niece, no doubt, needing the bathroom.

She seems such a delightful place to start.

THERE'S SOMETHING WRONG
WITH BARBARA
Reece G. Donnell

It all started when Cole saw the bag. Everyone had left after fawning over football practice, but Cole always opted to stay. He liked the peace and quiet of the school grounds when they were deserted. From the top of the bleachers, he saw the bag and recognized it immediately. He'd looked out for it plenty of times in crowded halls or classrooms and when he saw it, his heart was all aflutter. With one quick sprint, Cole was off the bleachers, scooping up the backpack and jogging out of the school grounds.

Pacing wasn't usually how Cole spent his Friday nights, but he was now. The checkered backpack sat on the end of his bed. Should he open it? Would that be crossing the line? He eyed the name tag stitched atop it once more...

Ethan Kirsch.

Cole already knew that, but he didn't know what address to bring it to.

"Aw, screw it," he whispered.

He pulled the tiny front pocket open and immediately confirmed what he suspected. Ethan Kirsch kept his library card there, too.

"Great minds," Cole said with a smile, and felt his

stomach tingle.

He closed his eyes and centered himself before studying the card. He had to concentrate. Not go googly-eyed over Ethan's rather adorable picture. His eyes scanned the information quickly.

108 Fern St.

"Ha!" Cole grinned triumphantly.

He turned to admire himself in his full-length mirror and smiled with great pride.

"Guess I have plans tomorrow," he told his reflection, inwardly stunned at his own bravado.

❋ ❋ ❋

The sun had been beating down on Cole all the way here, but when he reached Fern Street, it seemed to grow dim. He passed a few beige looking homes as he made his way down the street. Soon he stopped, acquiescing to his churning stomach.

"What am I doing?" he uttered. "I don't even know if he's..."

The sound of the lawnmower broke off Cole's thought. He turned to see a middle-aged man flick a glance at him from sunken, almost haunted eyes. Embarrassed that his startled jump might've been noticed, Cole tried a friendly nod. There was no response. The man just returned to his rattling mower. Cole took a deep breath, raised his head to the sun, and let the tension go.

"So what?" he said firmly. "If not, I'm just doing a good deed."

He nodded his head in agreement and set off walking again, passing the last house between himself and Ethan Kirsch.

"Hey! Cole!"

Cole didn't dare say a word. He was completely unprepared for the sight that met him before 108 Fern St. He never made it to the front door. From the sidewalk, his eyes craned up and took in Ethan Kirsch, spread lazily on a beach towel atop the porch roof. He had on cargo shorts and a tank top as he tapped his bare foot to the music he was quietly playing. Cole felt his stomach flutter and his mouth water simultaneously. All he could muster was a weak wave.

"What's up?" Ethan asked, running a hand through his dark, curly hair.

Cole wanted to die. But slowly he raised the backpack in his hand and words came in a sad croak.

"I... you... left this," he managed. "After the game, I wanted to—"

"Oh, cool, thanks." Ethan smiled. "Hey, come on up here. The door is open. Just come right up the stairs, you'll see the open window."

Cole still wanted to die, but this time, he thought his elation might just kill him.

❊ ❊ ❊

Up on the porch roof, time seemed to have no meaning as Ethan and Cole talked. They went from one topic to another, surprised at how much they had in common. They both loved horror movies, 80s music, and were both fascinated by the macabre world of true crime.

"Y'know..." Ethan began. "This street has... quite a few stories. Some have to be true, right?"

"I know," Cole responded meekly. "That's why I almost didn't come here."

"I'm glad you did," Ethan said softly.

Before a beat could pass, Ethan's hand had taken Cole's and their fingers were interlocked. Cole dared to look up at Ethan and saw that the sun backlit him. Ethan looked beautiful.

"See..." Ethan began carefully. "I didn't know if the plan would work."

"Plan?" Cole managed as pleasant chills raced through his body.

"Leaving that bag there," Ethan whispered. "I see you look at me. I'm looking at you too, but you always look away. I thought this'd give you a reason to..."

"Look?" Cole finished.

"Yes," Ethan whispered, coming closer and seeming slightly breathless. "It just so happens my Auntie Barbara is out of town. We've got all weekend, if something were to… happen."

Cole took Ethan's lead, raising a hand to his face, and they kissed softly.

"I've always wanted to do that," Cole stammered.

Cole just watched as Ethan climbed back through the hallway window and removed his shirt as he sauntered down the hallway. Stopping in an open bedroom door, he turned back towards Cole.

"No pressure," he purred.

Almost in a daze, his body fizzing with excitement, especially beneath his jeans, Cole climbed through the window and walked towards Ethan. They met in the doorway and kissed once more.

"Be gentle," Cole whispered. "I've never…"

"Of course," Ethan responded with a slow nod and another kiss. As he pushed Cole's jacket from his shoulders, Ethan also pushed the bedroom door closed.

❊ ❊ ❊

Suddenly, it was dark outside as Cole lay on his back, turning the events of the evening over and over in his head. Ethan lay sound asleep next to him, breathing peacefully.

"I can't fucking believe this," he whispered.

Turning onto his side, Cole stared at Ethan in the darkness, so peaceful and innocent looking. He wondered how one so angelic was capable of things they'd done, things that made Cole feel highs he never knew existed. He shook the thought off and snuggled closer to Ethan, as he did so, a blue flash lit up the room.

"Lightning," Cole muttered.

As if on cue, a rumble of thunder shook the house, but Cole didn't care. He was living his dream. It was only as his eyes grew uncontrollably heavy that Cole noticed something seemed wrong with Ethan's pale skin. He hadn't noticed in the heat of the moment, but the young man appeared to be covered in bruises. But Cole's consciousness had slipped too far, and sleep took over before the thoughts registered.

❊ ❊ ❊

Cole awoke as another lightning flash illuminated the bedroom. He'd rolled over onto his back and that's when he saw her. A woman, seen just for an instant in the flash, staring down at him. All his brain had time to process was her shock of auburn hair and her blood-red lipstick. As fear shot through him, something stung Cole in the arm and within seconds, he was rendered useless. His legs and arms refused to budge as the world began to fade away. As everything became blurry, Cole watched the redheaded specter walk around the bed and stop over the still-slumbering Ethan. Before he faded away, Cole heard her speak distantly.

"You dirty, dirty boy. What *have* you done now?"

The stabbing white light made Cole wince. His head pounded, and he immediately shut his eyes against the intrusion. Images flashed before his eyes like on an old projector. Ethan, making love, that *woman,* and there was something else, he recalled tumbling. Watching the world go head over heels again and again as something dug into his body.

"Here you come now." The voice was sweet, almost melodic.

Despite the pain, Cole wanted to know where it came from and so he opened his eyes. There she knelt in front of him, the redhead. Her face was much clearer now in the blinding light of the small bathroom. She was obviously older, but stunning. Her hair, perfectly coiffed in soft waves, and makeup, impeccably applied. Her face held a concerned smile as she knelt before him in a silk robe.

"Where?" Cole managed.

"Don't try to speak, dear," she said as she stood. "You really can't for a while yet. *Ooh*, and I'm terribly sorry about the stairs. A small lady like me couldn't lug you all the way down. It was just easier to roll you."

Cole could hear her chirping words, but they sounded so far away.

"Anyway, I'll be back later. I've got to wash that stink off you, dear," she continued. "I swear, you try to teach the boy and he *never* learns. He never learns. Now, I am sorry, honey, but I must lock this door. *Oooh!* And I'm sorry about the ropes. Just for safety, you understand?"

A door shut and there was a heavy *click*… But Cole didn't care. He needed to sleep.

❋ ❋ ❋

The shrieking from above him woke Cole up. Suddenly, his head was much clearer and the bright bathroom no longer pained him. However, something else did. A distant throbbing emanated from his ankle and he was just about to follow the discomfort when the shrieking came again.

"Yes… yes… *yes!*"

The three affirmations were screeched in complete ecstasy and followed by a long howl that chilled Cole to the bone. Then another voice came, one he recognized.

"No! No, *please!* No more… *NO MORE!*"

It was unmistakably Ethan's voice, muffled but clearly crying out in agony.

"Oh *yes*, more!"

Now Cole was quite sure the accompanying voice was the redheaded specter that'd spoken to him in such a soothing manner.

"Much, much more for you, filth," she cried with a harsh merriment.

The sound of footsteps overhead heralded silence. Cole followed them and heard the sound of someone coming down a staircase to his right, then the knock came on the bathroom door.

"Hello?" that same angelic tone questioned. "Are you awake in there?"

Cole froze, lifting his bound wrists before his face as if to hide, and that's when he noticed it.

"I suppose not," the voice murmured. "Oh well! Patience, Barbara."

The bindings on his wrists were incredibly loose, he spied. As footsteps padded away from the door and back up the stairs, Cole wondered if he could slip the thick rope past the balls of his hands. With one pull, he realized tying clearly wasn't this strange lady's forte, as his left hand immediately came free.

"Yes!" he whispered triumphantly as he shook his right hand free.

Now his ankles, although tied tighter, his free hands enabled him to undo the pathetic knot in seconds. That's when he noticed the large bruise on his ankle and located the discomfort he felt.

But it didn't matter now. He had to get out of here. Obviously, the bathroom door was impossible. He'd heard her lock it, but…

Yes!

A quick turn of his head confirmed there was a window above the sink. Cole pulled himself up using the ceramic, only for the pain to explode from his swollen ankle.

"Fuck!" he hissed as he hopped on his one good foot.

Pain didn't matter, getting free mattered. So, with gritted teeth, Cole clambered onto the toilet and reached for the window ledge. Rain spattered against the glass and lightning lit up the sky every few minutes.

"Please!" Cole whispered. "Open."

Bearing down on his screaming ankle, Cole lifted the window, and it slid up, disappearing and revealing the rain-soaked yard beyond.

"You're shitting me!" was all Cole could muster.

Bracing for the discomfort, Cole stepped over the sink and out onto the ledge beyond. The rain hit his skin with force, pleasantly warm, but immediately soaking him as he only wore his underwear. With a squelch, Cole managed a hop down onto the lawn below, his bare feet sinking into the wet grass.

Go!

He began an uneven, limping run across the back garden, setting the side of the house in his sights.

"Auntie Barbara! Where are you? What are you *doing?* I'll be good! Just please, let him go."

It was Ethan. Cole's head snapped around to a dimly lit bedroom window above the kitchen. It was open.

He sounded desperate and, in an instant, the incredible day they'd spent together flashed before Cole's eyes. He had to help him.

Go get the police… that'll help!

By the time the thought had entered Cole's head, he was already standing on the back porch with his hand on the doorknob. For the second time in just a few minutes, he willed something to open, but this time he knew it could spell his end.

Click!

The back door slowly opened. Gingerly, Cole pushed it aside and stepped into an immaculate kitchen. The counters were spotless, and the cutlery gleamed in the bright overhead light. Turning, Cole saw a door, and beyond it a staircase heading to the second floor. That's where the footsteps had come from. Immediately, Cole knew the closed door to the right was the bathroom he'd just escaped.

"Okay… Okay," Cole soothed himself.

"Auntie Barbara!"

Ethan's cry propelled Cole forward, through the doorway and onto the staircase. He was careful with each step he took on the cold wood. If it creaked, or if his puffy ankle gave out, he'd be found out.

"You just wait," came Barbara's reply, further off than Ethan's cries.

Cole was halfway to the top.

"I'm not done with you tonight," her melodic voice continued. "Not if you think you can bring *that* sort of *thing* into my home."

Cole reached the landing, keeping his feet on the rug running down the hallway's length. He could move without a sound now and sped up his pace.

"I-I'm sorry," Ethan sobbed. He sounded closer.

Looking to his left, Cole saw Ethan's bedroom. The door was open. Peering in, he saw it was empty; the bed was unmade from their encounter and their clothes covered the floor.

"You've been sorry before, fella," Barbara answered

with a chuckle. "And you know what happened to *them.*"

Barbara still sounded a ways off, so Cole ducked into the empty bedroom and hurriedly retrieved a pair of jeans and a hoodie. Clothing should've been the last thing on his mind, but he was all too aware of his exposed skin and feared sharp objects. Back in the bedroom doorway, Cole listened again.

"What are you gonna do?" Ethan choked.

He was in the very next room, and the door was open. Cole followed the dim lamplight to the doorway and was faced with the pinkest of boudoirs he'd ever seen. The carpet was fluffy and pink; the walls were papered with pink roses; the drapes were pink silk. To Cole's horror, he saw the sheets were pink too. Upon the four-poster bed lay Ethan, a limb bound to each bedpost. His body was covered in fresh welts, cuts and bruises. He was not wearing any clothes. A slight intake of breath drew Ethan's attention, and he spotted Cole in the doorway, his eyes immediately widened. Cole raised a finger to his mouth.

Shh...

Ethan complied and let Cole enter the room, giving an awkward nod to the louver closet.

"What are you gonna *do?*" Ethan screamed.

Cole understood he was giving him cover. He bounded to the closet and ducked inside as Ethan rattled his handcuffed wrists.

"You know." Barbara waved away as she swept back into the room.

She had emerged from an adjoining bathroom and was still clad in her silk robe. Through the slats, Cole took in more of her bedroom. Pictures, there were lots of pictures. Cole recognized each one.

Liberace. Tab Hunter. Anthony Perkins. Roddy MacDowall. Farley Granger.

Then, one that was unfamiliar. It was Barbara, beautifully made up as a bride with a golden-haired man on her arm...

"No," Ethan cried softly. "You can't kill Cole the way

you killed the others!"

"Oh!" Barbara cried as she shook out her luscious auburn hair. "Cole, is it? Not for much longer."

A knot formed in Cole's stomach. *Would* he get out of this alive? The knot rose into his throat as he saw the glamorous woman drop her silk robe as she stood over Ethan.

"Now..." she purred. "Let me fix you."

"Please," Ethan whispered pathetically. "No more."

For the next several minutes, Cole listened as Ethan cried out in protest to the unhinged woman's mounting of him. Eventually, everything reached a sickening crescendo, and Cole heard that same shriek that had awakened him from his drugged slumber. He felt truly ill.

"*Ahh,*" he heard Barbara groan.

Ethan said nothing.

"Smoke?" she asked as she took a cigarette from an elegant gold case. "It's always the best when you smoke after."

But she wasn't looking at Ethan, she seemed in a world of her own. After a dainty puff, she rose and retrieved her silk robe from the floor.

"I know," she said triumphantly. "A drink, that's what we want, let me just go get that!"

Easing into high-heeled slippers with ridiculous pom-poms, Barbara swept from the room in a flurry of billowing silk. Cole steeled himself and listened.

Tac... Tac... Tac... Tac...

She was going down the stairs, it had to be now.

Emerging from the closet just as 40s jazz came up the stairwell, Cole made his way to the side of the bed. Immediately, he saw the rotary dial phone on the bedside table, also seeing the padlock attached to it.

"Cole..." Ethan whispered breathlessly. "Cole, I'm sorry. This wasn't supposed to happen. I let us both fall asleep and I... Just *go!* Just please go..."

Cole looked down at his stricken crush and remembered how stunning he'd looked in the afternoon sunlight. Remembering how he'd made him feel, and how for hours it seemed they were as one.

"No," he said. "I'm going to get you out of here."

"It's no use, Cole!" Ethan replied, his eyes wide with panic. "She has the keys in her *pocket!*"

To amplify his point, Ethan shook his handcuffed wrists against the bedposts. His legs were bound with the same rope as Cole had been.

"Shit," Cole whispered. "There's... really something wrong with Barbara."

Cole looked towards the bedroom door as a rumble of thunder rattled the window.

"NO!" Ethan demanded.

Cole never looked at the stricken young man, just made his way across the room and out the door.

Barbara swayed to the mellow jazz instrumental coming from her old wireless radio. In her hand she swilled a glass of bourbon filled with ice. She felt good.

"Getting drunk again?" she pondered aloud with a girlish giggle. "Oh, darling, why not?"

She sipped her drink leisurely, before pain erupted across the back of her head, propelling her to the floor. Momentarily, things went black.

Cole watched as the Barbara hit the floor before him. The glass fell from her hand and shattered on the tile floor, spilling bourbon everywhere. As she hit the ground, she let out a startled cry and reached for the counter above for stability. Her eyes focused slightly and she registered Cole standing over her.

"How do you like it, bitch?" Cole screamed.

He held a heavy wooden cutting board in his hand.

"How did you get out?" she cried.

"I'm Superman," Cole responded dryly. "Now, give me the keys."

She backed up against the counter and raised her hands.

"Okay, that's alright," she answered with a nod. "I'll give you the key, I will."

Cole extended his free hand expectantly as Barbara reached into her pocket.

"Boy, you must really like Ethan, huh?" she asked breathlessly. "Well, that's good. I only want the best for him."

A shriek filled Cole's ears as Barbara withdrew a glinting chef's knife from her pocket. Before he could react, the massive blade had swung through the air and penetrated his open palm. He screamed as pain exploded up his arm and blood began to gush from the wound. Cole's attacker cackled as she ripped the blade free and swung once more. With only time to raise his butchered palm to his face, Cole felt more searing pain below his busted ankle. He cast his glance downward and saw the knife was embedded in his foot, pinning him to the floor.

"*FUCK!*" was the only thing Cole could muster.

In a flurry of swishing silk, Barbara had gotten to her feet and charged forward at Cole. He didn't have time to see the skillet she'd procured off the stove until it made contact with his jaw. He pinwheeled backward, ripping the knife from his foot and landing in a heap near the stairway door. Slowly, Barbara approached him, as he lay dazed and barely moving.

"Think you can *fuck* with me, you little fag?" she hissed. "You don't know what it's like, do you? To lose *everything*, to have a whole town laugh at you. When I went out, they'd crow, "Oh, there's the poor bitch whose husband fucked the garden boy." Well, no more! You think you can beat me? I've seen off tougher than you, you pathetic little runt. They couldn't have him, and neither can you! He's mine, got it? I was going to do you like the others, but for this, you're going to suffer."

She gave Cole a quick poke in the ribs with her foot. He didn't move.

"This is going to be a fun night," Barbara crowed as she turned back to the counter. "You hear that, Ethan? A fun night! Now, another drink, I think."

Setting the skillet down, Barbara reached into a cabinet for a new glass.

"What a waste of good bourbon," she lamented. "Want

one?"

As she spun with the bottle in her hand, a tiny cry escaped her lips. The floor was empty.

"What…" was all Barbara managed before her head was yanked backward.

She let out a screech akin to a feral cat as fingers pulled on her auburn locks and a knee was jammed into her lower back.

"Not the hair!"

Cole shoved her over the kitchen counter, using his capable knee, before slamming her head into the wood. Her forehead connected with the countertop once, twice, and finally a third time. Barbara cried like a banshee with each blow. She howled as Cole ripped a chunk of her hair from the scalp and mercilessly pinned one arm to the countertop. In a lightning-fast move, he reached for the switch within arm's length and started the whirring of the food processor. Not missing a beat, Cole took the shrieking woman by her pinned wrist and forced her hand into the blades. Blood exploded as Barbara made sounds that seemed completely inhuman. One finger popped off, and the stump began spurting, then another jumped from the food processor completely. Cole wanted to see more.

"Fucking die already!" he screamed over the noise.

In response, an elbow was driven into Cole's ribs and he stumbled backward. The air knocked from his lungs. He crashed down as he attempted to put weight on his mutilated foot. Shaking the tumble, Cole spun on the spot and turned his attention to Barbara. He saw her sweep the whirring food processor from the counter with a furious motion. It shattered on the floor and was immediately silent. As she lurched towards Cole, she no longer looked human.

"Dirty little bastard," she growled.

In a grotesque tableau, Barbara held her mutilated hand before her face, the two stumps still spurting.

"Do you have any idea how long it takes to do this *manicure?*"

"Your skills need work…" Cole smirked from the floor.

With a guttural growl to the heavens, she began to charge towards him, but Cole wasn't worried. With his non-injured hand, he swept up the knife that had once pinned his foot to the floor. As she began to bend over him, Cole jutted both arms outward and heard a satisfying wet crunch.

"Oof!" Barbara cried, dumbfounded.

Cole met the disbelief in her eyes with a steely confidence and wrenched the knife upward. Barbara took in a hissing gasp and cried tears of frustration as she fell to her knees.

"Bobby!" she cried as blood ran from her mouth. "Bobby, *I love you!*"

She collapsed forward and began to bleed out on the tiles. Cole gingerly leaned over Barbara and slipped a hand into the pocket of her stained silk robe. His fingers closed around the cool metal of a petite set of keys.

"Bobby…" Barbara whispered weakly. "Please, come back… Bobby."

Her chest rattled for the last time as Cole slowly began to inch backward toward the stairs.

❖ ❖ ❖

"She never got over it, ever," Ethan finished.

He and Cole sat in a tiny hospital room with an overweight sheriff sitting at the foot of the bed.

"You say she drowned the victims?" he asked.

Cole winced and clasped Ethan's hand.

"Yes," Ethan affirmed. "Only she was baptizing them. Making them… uh, clean, y'know?"

The sheriff nodded.

"And where are they? The bodies, I mean," he asked.

Ethan sighed wearily and shut his eyes. "In the basement," he confessed as he hung his head. "Some are under the floor, some are… well, not buried. She never let anyone go down there."

The door opened and there stood a man in a long white coat.

"Ah, Doctor Peck."

"Sheriff." Doctor Peck nodded. "I think it's time you gave these young men some rest, sir."

With a groan of effort, the officer hoisted himself up and moved toward the door.

"Yes, that'll do it, anyway," he stated with a dismissive hand wave. "We have everything we need."

Doctor Peck frowned after the sheriff, unapproving of his indifference.

"Everything okay here?" he asked with a smile.

"I could use some more pain relief," Cole said, his voice small and weak.

"I'll sort that out right now," Peck assured. "Oh, Mr. Kirsch, do you have somewhere to stay? You can't go home, you know?"

Ethan gave Cole a reassuring glance and squeezed his hand.

"I'm staying right here, Doc," Ethan stated with a nod.

Doctor Peck smiled and mirrored the nod. "Given the circumstances, I'm sure we can make up the other bed," he said and turned to leave.

Doctor Peck froze momentarily in the doorway before turning back to face the two young men.

"Oh, Mr. Kirsch," he began slowly. "Did you know that your aunt was pregnant?"

Ethan's face turned stony. Cole felt his stomach knot.

"No…" Ethan managed. "I did not."

"Hmm, about eight weeks," Doctor Peck said absently as he looked at a clipboard. "The only shame about this whole thing, really. Do you have any idea who the father might be? It might be courteous to inform him."

"No," Ethan repeated. "I have no idea at all."

TOTALLY RUINED THE EVENING
Mallory

"I'm telling you, man, my new place is awesome!" Colin said as he and Zach walked down the street, away from the grimy bus stop. "I managed to find this house—like, an entire house—with cheaper rent than most of the *apartments* in this city."

"Yeah," Zach muttered. "You've mentioned that. A lot."

"Just imagine the parties I could throw here!" Colin went on. "And the girls! I don't have to ask my roommates or nothing. I can have chicks over any time I want!"

"You don't have any friends except for me," Zach grumbled. "And girls don't really... *like* you, Colin."

"That's just 'cause every time I'm about to get lucky, someone walks in on us!" Colin said. "Remember last year when we were in the dorms, and *you* walked in on me with that one chick?" He scowled at Zach. "Totally ruined the evening."

"Um... see, I remember her muttering 'oh thank God' under her breath as soon as she had an excuse to leave," Zach said. "And then she came up to me in the cafeteria and thanked me the next day. She was nice."

"But incidents like that are a thing of the past!" Colin

said triumphantly. "As soon as I tell them I have my own entire *house*, they're not gonna be able to resist! Girls can't resist a guy with a house, everyone knows that!"

Another bus shuddered past them, leaving a cloud of smog that sent Zach into a coughing fit, but Colin didn't seem to notice. "And, I mean, yeah, the commute kinda sucks," Colin continued. "It takes me like an hour to get to campus on the bus, but with the money I'm saving on rent, I can probably get my own car pretty soon."

He shot an excited glance towards Zach. "Then, when I have a house *and* a car, they won't be able to resist me even more!" He paused for a second and furrowed his brow. "Uh, I mean… *less*. I think. Wait, is that right…?" He trailed off, and then just shook his head, and shot Zach a beaming, crooked grin. Zach just rolled his eyes.

They reached a stoplight, and instead of crossing, Colin gestured for Zach to turn right and follow him down Fern Street. Zach felt the temperature drop as soon as he made the turn; it wasn't that there was anything noticeably different between these houses and any of the others they'd just passed on the cross street, but it felt like these houses… *carried themselves differently,* somehow? Even in his head, he couldn't quite find the right words for it. It didn't help that they had gotten off the bus just as the sun was dipping below the horizon, so by the time they reached Colin's house, the sky had turned a milky shade of twilight.

A small black cat with white paws trotted out from the front porch of the house on the corner, meowing plaintively at them as it crossed the front lawn. Zach smiled faintly, knelt down, and held his hand out for it. The little cat sniffed his fingers momentarily, then clumsily head-butted his wrist.

Colin was already in front of the next house over, continuing to talk. He didn't seem to notice that Zach had stopped following him or listening. Finally, he turned back to Zach for an affirmation of his latest joke, noticed the man wasn't there, and whipped around to stomp back over.

"C'mon, dude!" Colin said, making no attempt to hide his annoyance. "Do you want to see my new place or not?"

"Sorry, sorry," Zach said, trying to stand up even while the cat made its best effort to crawl onto his lap. "Is this cat okay, dude? It *really* seems desperate for attention."

"Yeah, yeah, Mittens has seen some shit. We've all heard the stories," Colin muttered, finally grabbing Zach's arm and hoisting him back to his feet, much to the cat's dismay. "Now come *on*—"

Colin practically dragged Zach a couple doors down before stopping abruptly in front of a chain-link fence surrounding a modest two-story building and saying, "Well, this is the place!" with a beaming grin. As he pushed the gate open, he added, "What do you think?"

"Uh…" Zach muttered, as he shuffled into the yard, gazing at the structure that loomed over them both, at the peeling paint, at the cracked windows, at the lawn that consisted of nothing but dead weeds and bare dirt. "I think it's a dump."

"So are most frat houses," Colin said nonchalantly as he opened the front door. A couple of rusty metal numbers nailed next to the door designated this as 109 Fern St. "And have I mentioned how cheap it is?"

"*Yes,*" Zach said as he strode inside. "Yes, as a matter of fact, you—"

Zach froze. There was barely any light inside the house; the building was so old that he couldn't even tell if it had been wired for electricity. The furniture was sparse, there were spider webs in the corners, and every flat surface seemed to be covered in dust—but that wasn't what had made him stop.

What made Zach stop was that, on the wall opposite the door, the words "GET OUT" had been scrawled out in fresh, dripping blood.

"What the fuck, man?!" Zach shouted, scrambling back. He almost lost his balance and fell, but Colin caught him by the arm just before his butt made contact with the creaking hardwood floor.

"Oh, yeah, that happens sometimes," Colin muttered as he pulled Zach back to his feet. "I've got a couple of those *Magic Eraser* sponges in the kitchen. That should take care of it."

Zach just stood there, mouth agape, shaking his head slowly as Colin strode into the other room, whistling tunelessly under his breath.

"What the fuck, man!" Zach sputtered out again. It was all he could think of to say.

"Hmm?" Colin muttered as he returned, holding a squishy white rectangle in one hand and a spray bottle of cleaning solution in the other. "Oh, yeah, why do you think the rent is so cheap here?" he said with a grin, glancing back over his shoulder as he sprayed bleach on the first letter. "This place is haunted!"

❋ ❋ ❋

Colin was lying back on his couch, idly throwing a rubber ball into the air, high enough that it usually bounced off of the ceiling and fell back into his hands with a rhythmic *thap*. Zach was sitting on a milk crate across from him, both his feet planted firmly on the ground a shoulder's-width apart, hands folded tightly in his lap, staring down at the floor, his eyes focused on some vague point in the middle-distance. There was a beat-up old lamp in the corner, casting appropriately eerie shadows across the inside of the living room. It looked like Colin had picked the thing up extremely cheap from a yard sale, or maybe even just found it abandoned on the side of the road. At any rate, Zach supposed, it meant that, yes, the house was wired for electricity, since the lamp seemed to be working, albeit barely.

"So," Zach muttered slowly, "you *chose* to live in a haunted house."

"Uh-huh."

Bounce-thap!

"Because the ghosts drive down the rent."

"Yep."

Bounce-thap!

"And because it will get me laid," Colin added, holding the ball for a moment longer before he tossed it up again. "I think that part is very important."

Bounce-thap!

Zach scrunched his eyes shut, raised his hands to the bridge of his nose, and took in a long, slow breath.

"Colin?"

"Yes, Zach?"

Bounce-thap!

"What girl *in her right mind* is going to want to sleep with you in a haunted house?"

Colin caught the ball and sat up.

"Dude, you would be *amazed,*" he said, his eyes wide with enthusiasm. "You know that goth barista at the café down the street from campus? The one with the huge tits who wears that weird jewelry made out of, like, animal bones and shit?"

"Uh… yeah," Zach said slowly. "Not the words I would've used to describe her, but I know who you're talking about. I think her name is… Margaret? I actually haven't seen her in a while."

"Yeah, she *loves* witchy shit like this!" Colin continued. "As soon as I told her this place was haunted, she couldn't wait to check it out!" Colin leaned in close, with a childishly gleeful grin on his face. "You know, while we were bangin', she actually said she *liked it* when the ghosts watched."

"Oh, God," Zach groaned. "Colin, you perv, that's — " he paused. "Wait. So you know for a fact that there are ghosts here? Like, you've actually seen them?"

"Uh-huh," Colin said. "See, there's one of them in the hallway right next to you."

"Wha — JESUS GOD!"

Zach turned his head to the side and then almost fell off his milk crate. There was… *something* floating down the hallway that led into the living room. It looked like it might have once been wearing a wedding dress, but now had little more than a few strips of discolored fabric clinging to its rotting body, billowing in a nonexistent breeze. Its feet didn't touch the ground—if it even *had* feet anymore—and its face was a grinning skull, caked with dirt and spots of putrefied flesh, a few limp strands of hair still clinging desperately to what remained of its scalp. Its loose jaw seemed to open a little wider into a silent scream as it cocked its head to the side and lifted one bony arm, the index finger extending out to point menacingly at Zach while the rest of its fingers remained clamped tight around some dead stems that might have once been a bouquet of flowers. By the time it made its way into the living room, Zach was already off his milk crate and pressed up against the opposite wall, his legs scrambling to take him even farther away even though there was nowhere else to go.

Colin stayed on the couch with a slightly bored expression and took a lazy sip from one of the beer cans scattered on the surrounding floor.

"What—what are you—" Zach stammered, looking frantically back and forth between Colin on the couch and the ghostly bride in front of him. "Why aren't you—why are you just—wha...?"

"Because she's a *ghost,* stupid," Colin said, slightly annoyed. He lobbed his rubber ball at the bride, and it phased straight through her chest with no resistance whatsoever, then bounced against the wall behind her and passed through the bottom of her dress again as it dribbled back.

"She can't hurt you. She can't even *touch* you. See?" Colin pushed himself up off the couch, strode confidently over, and poked his index finger straight into the side of her head. Nothing happened; half of his hand just seemed to disappear at the boundary where her skull began. He pulled his hand back out, and his fingers were all there. Not even any residue.

"Heh-heh, watch this," Colin chuckled, and he stood there for a couple seconds, repeatedly poking his finger in and out of the bride's head while muttering, *"Poke, poke, poke, poke, poke,"* under his breath. The bride slowly turned to face him, her mouth still hanging open, and she swiped the arm with the dead bouquet straight through his chest, but it had no effect.

"See?" Colin said, turning to face Zach and spreading his arms with a shit-eating grin. "Not gonna lie, I kinda reacted the same way you did the first time I saw 'em, but as soon as I realized they were harmless..." He quickly waved his hand back and forth through the bride's head, causing it to dissipate like mist for a few seconds before reforming as soon as he was done. He turned back to Zach and shrugged. "They really wanna float there and watch while I'm jackin' off, that's their own business."

"So there's... more of them?" Zach said, without taking his eyes off the bride as he slowly pushed himself back to his feet.

"Yeah," Colin muttered tersely, suddenly glancing off to the side. "Or, at least, there used to be. Seems like there were a lot more when I first moved in, and then they started disappearing or something. I don't know exactly how this ghost stuff works. There used to be this one, looked like he was a lumberjack or something, had a plaid shirt and this big axe stickin' out of his head, but I ain't seen him for a week or two." Colin suddenly glanced back at Zach, and his grinning idiot smile returned. "Hey, who knows? Maybe the 'final wish' he needed to fulfill before moving on to the 'Great Beyond' was to watch me makin' that goth chick squeal like a stuck pig. You know what I'm saying?"

The bride's head stiffly cocked to the other side, then one billowing arm waved gracefully through the air next to her. Behind her, the wall started to bleed again. Zach took an involuntary step back without even realizing it. The blood was forming itself into letters, just as it had before.

This time, the message on the wall read, "SHE WAS FAKING IT."

"Hey, *fuck you!*" Colin shouted bitterly, his face contorting and starting to turn red. "How would you know, anyway?"

Zach tried to stifle a laugh, but still exhaled so sharply he thought he was going to choke on his own spit.

"You know what, never mind," Colin grumbled, abruptly turning away. "This is a decent-sized house. Let me give you the rest of the tour." Zach hesitated, but Colin enthusiastically gestured for his friend to follow him. "Come on," Colin continued. "I can't wait to show you what's in the basement!"

❋ ❋ ❋

The cramped wooden staircase tucked away in the corner of the kitchen led down to a dirt-walled underground chamber that was deceptively large for a house of this size. Colin had hung a couple of strands of cheap "fairy lights" around the top of the chamber, just as he had in their dorm the previous year, and attached them to an extension cord that led back to the kitchen. It didn't provide a lot of light, but it was enough to keep them from tripping over something. One wall even had a tunnel dug into the side that seemed to lead to another chamber elsewhere, leading Zach to privately wonder if several of the houses on this block had interconnected basements — that is, until his thoughts were abruptly interrupted.

"Oh, God," Zach groaned, instinctively throwing a hand over his face. "What the fuck is that smell?"

"I don't know" Colin muttered. "I think one of these buildings used to be a speakeasy or something. So who knows what kind of weird shit they might've abandoned down here back in the day. I'm not even sure where exactly that tunnel goes, though." He shrugged. "For all I know, it could connect to the sewer or something if you go far enough."

"Wonderful," Zach grumbled, his voice coming out as a nasally whine, since he was still trying to block his nose. "So is that why you brought me down here? To finally explore these tunnels and figure out what the hell is going on down here?"

"Uhh..." Colin said nervously.

Zach closed his eyes and started shaking his head.

"You stupid bastard," he said, tentatively taking his hand off his nose. It was hard to talk with his face covered, and the longer he was down here, the more he begrudgingly acclimated to the smell. "You couldn't just man up and fuckin' ask someone to help you explore your creepy sewage hole. You had to be all sneaky and invite me over 'just for the hell of it' and then spring this on me at the last minute."

"Well, I mean," Colin stammered, "if you knew the real reason I invited you, you wouldn't have come —"

"Of course I would have," Zach snapped bitterly. "You're my friend, you idiot. I give you a lot of shit — and you deserve most of it — but I don't want you to fall down a hole and break both your legs and starve to death just because you decided to explore down here on your own."

"Oh," Colin said quietly. "That's. Um. That's really nice, Zach."

Zach rolled his eyes.

"That's called not being a sociopath, you fucking sociopath." His hand covered his nose again. "Now do you at least have some masks or something we can wear while we're down here so I don't choke to death, Jesus Christ..."

"Masks!" Colin suddenly shouted, his eyes going wide. "Shit, I knew I left something upstairs!"

Hand still covering his face, Zach just closed his eyes and shook his head with a quiet grunt.

"Uh, hang out here for a sec," Colin said quickly, already heading for the basement door. "I'm gonna run upstairs and get some —" He hesitated. "—masks."

"I mean, I could just go back up with you," Zach said. "I don't really love the idea of being left alone in a basement full of sewage —"

But Colin hadn't even waited for a response before hurrying out the door. Zach just rolled his eyes and sighed.

Zach tentatively took his hand off his nose again. He

could tolerate the smell down here for brief periods — at least long enough to keep his face from getting sore — but he really hoped Colin would be back with those masks soon. In the meantime, he started pacing idly around the inside of the chamber, his hands in his pockets, looking around at nothing in particular. He made a full lap around the inside of the chamber — the light was too dim for him to see what was on the other side of the tunnel — and turned around to make a lap in the opposite direction when he almost had a heart attack.

The ghost bride was hovering right behind him and had apparently been following him for who knows how long. Zach took a moment to catch his breath — then immediately regretted it because he'd just breathed in a lungful of stench — but after a couple seconds of hoarse coughing, he managed to straightened his posture and puff his chest out a little.

"Oh, hi," he said, as casually as he could. "Nice place you've got here. Sorry you've got to share it with… you know…" he gestured in the direction of the staircase Colin had just disappeared up. The bride just cocked her head to the side again. Suddenly, a cold breeze blew through the chamber, mussing up Zach's hair and loosening some of the dirt beneath his feet… which shouldn't have been possible in a closed, underground chamber. The bride floated closer to Zach until her skeletal face was almost touching his.

"…*Gggeeettt… ooouuuttt…*" she hissed.

"*O… kay…*" Zach said, slowly backing away from her as cold sweat trickled down the side of his head. "I, um, I'm starting to think you have a point. Y'know, I didn't really mean anything by… *anything,* you know? I'm sorry about Colin. He and I aren't even really friends. He was just assigned as my roommate last year and —"

Crunch.

Zach had stepped on something. He glanced down and saw something glittery half-buried in the dirt floor. His eyes rapidly darting back and forth between the ghost in front of him and the object in the floor, he slowly knelt down and gave the object a solid yank, dislodging it from the caked-on dirt, and held it up to the light.

It was a bone.

But… a bone with something attached to it. Something metallic. It looked like… the chain of a necklace?

Colin's words from earlier flashed across his memory.

"That goth barista who wears jewelry made out of, like, animal bones and shit?"

And before Zach could stand back up, the blade of a shovel slammed into the side of his head.

* * *

Zach's vision was blurry, but he knew Colin was standing over him. Holding a shovel.

So was the bride.

So was… someone else.

Zach's vision was slowly coming back into focus. He recognized her. The barista. Margaret. Except she looked even paler than usual. And she wasn't saying anything; her eyes just bugged out and stared down at him, unblinking. And the side of her head was caked in blood.

And her feet were hovering a couple inches above the ground.

"Colin…?" Zach tried to say, but the word came out slurred. His whole body was sore and covered in a thin layer of dirt. The chamber he was in was significantly smaller than he remembered. It dawned on him dimly that Colin must have dragged him through the tunnel into the other chamber while he was unconscious.

Zach painfully shifted his weight until he rolled onto his stomach.

He could see something now, on the far side of the room, against the wall.

A large, dark lump, half-obscured by shadow, but he could still make out —

Bodies.

There were at least half a dozen bodies piled against the wall of the basement.

One of the only faces he could make out in the pile was Margaret, her eyes bugged out, her face caked with blood, looking exactly like the… *other* version of her that was floating above him.

Slow, crunching footsteps started behind Zach, as Colin calmly strolled around to where Zach's head was now facing.

"I don't know how this ghost stuff works," Colin said, his voice trembling. "But they've been disappearing, one by one, since I moved in here. And if all the ghosts are gone, and this place isn't haunted anymore, the landlord won't have any reason to keep the rent so low." Zach could barely lift his head high enough to look up at Colin's face. "I'm sorry, dude," Colin said, with a hint of genuine apology in his voice. "But I *really* need to hang onto this place, you know? And if the ghosts are going to keep disappearing, well… I guess I just need to keep a steady supply of new ones coming in."

"Colinnnn…" Zach whined helplessly as Colin lifted the shovel once again and wound his arms back, ready to strike…

* * *

Zach floated at the back of the room and watched with muted disinterest as Colin swung the shovel again and again, turning what had once been his head into bloody mush. The bride had just shaken her head and floated off a while ago, but Margaret had stayed down there with him, hovering next to him in silence until Colin finally decided he was finished and dragged the bloody shovel back upstairs, panting and wheezing the entire way.

"I'm sorry," she said quietly, as Colin clicked off the lights strung along the top of the chamber, enveloping them both in darkness. "But we *tried* to warn you."

GILDED REFLECTIONS
Danielle Robertson

"I'd kill for a drink."

Mona Samson's voice cracks as she speaks aloud. It happens, some days—on those days where she's alone for the morning and afternoon, with only talk shows and the *tch tch tch* of the lawn sprinklers for company—her normally velvet voice comes out like sandpaper.

Even more reason for that drink.

Lines of orange sunlight filter in through the blinds of the living room of 110 Fern St. Ted will be home soon, and he may be cross at Mona for not having dinner on the table—pot roast is his favorite, you know, and that takes ages—but Mona is too irritated and tired to care. It's the kind of tired that sinks deep into your bones, so you hardly know if you're sleeping standing up. Her head is throbbing; tension grabs the back of her skull and squeezes. She's sure her lipstick is feathering at the corners. She's sure her curls are falling, limp with too much hairspray. But she can't bring herself to look in the hallway mirror.

The gilded mirror is a thing of beauty, all burnished gold. It was a wedding gift from Ted's parents, presented to them after Mona and Ted's courthouse wedding. They had been shy, handing the newlyweds the mirror right there on the sidewalk after the ceremony. Mona shuffled her bouquet into the crook of her arm to hold the damned thing, squashing her pink roses to a pulp.

110 Fern St. had been a wedding gift from Ted himself. They'd seen the house listing in the window of a real estate agency after walking out of the movie theater one Friday night, and they'd booked a visit for the next morning.

The classic farmhouse had wide plank floors, exposed wooden beams, and a yard with a tree majestic enough for a tire swing one day. There were surprising details—like the wall-mounted ironing board in the kitchen and the stained-glass cupid in the bedroom window—that made Mona and Ted laugh in delight.

"It's the kind of house that really could become a forever home," the real estate agent had said. And Ted had looked into Mona's eyes, all soft, as if to say, "I want forever with you." Ted was a man of few words, but when his eyes got like that—Mona knew exactly what he meant. With his tender looks, and the soft swoop of his dark hair, and the hard angles of his jaw, Mona felt as if she'd married a movie star.

Ted carried Mona over the threshold on the day they signed the paperwork. They'd coughed as dust motes swirled in the air, and they'd laughed about their good fortune, and they'd had a belated wedding night celebration—much better than their time in the honeymoon suite at the Seafoam Motel after the courthouse. The stained-glass cupid in the bedroom smiled down on them, glowing a dreamy deep maroon in the moonlight.

Mona preened in the mirror afterwards, her curls a pretty compliment to the curlicues of the gilded frame.

"You're the lady of the house now," Ted said, and kissed her shoulder. She truly felt like the lady of the house, dressed in her pink silk robe. Four bedrooms and one-and-a-half baths to oversee: it was an embarrassment of riches. Mona and Ted clinked glasses of champagne on their freshly painted wraparound porch while jazz music played from a neighbor's open window and cicadas shrieked in the summer air.

* * *

The honeymoon lasted, until it didn't.

"All the men at the office have wives who keep the house clean." Ted poured himself a finger of rye. "They have wives who keep themselves styled, who have a hot meal waiting for them on the dining room table."

"How charming for those men," Mona said. The couple sat at the empty dining table with a bag of potato chips opened between them like a consolation prize. It was just so hot out, Mona thought. Too hot out to even think about turning on the oven. Back when they were dating—before they moved to Fern Street—they'd think nothing of going out to dinner instead. And Mona's headaches seemed to thrive on the heat: squeezing, squeezing, squeezing her skull. In an old house like 110 Fern, the heat settled like a blanket, so its inhabitants fell into a stupor. The ceiling fan turned lazy circles overhead. She was doing them both a favor, really, not turning on the oven.

Ted crunched on the ice cubes in his glass with a *chuk, chuk*—a sound Mona had tolerated up until that point.

"I'm just saying, it'd be nice to come home and feel appreciated," Ted said.

"Appreciated," Mona echoed. She stretched her bare feet beneath the table, cracking her unpolished toes. "And if I wore high heels to clean the toilets, you'd feel appreciated?"

"Don't be dramatic."

"You're the one soliloquizing over your drink."

"Listen to yourself," Ted sighed. "In the time it took you to say that word, you could've turned the oven on."

"It's too hot!" Mona stood up from the table. Her chair scraped across the hardwood with a noise that rivaled the crunching ice. She felt the vice grip of tension press against her skull, and she nearly swooned.

"I liked you better before we moved in here," Ted said, draining his drink.

I liked you better when you were a man of few words, Mona

nearly replied. But the heat, and the throbbing in her head, and the shimmering of tears behind her eyes kept her silent.

In the hall, Mona peered at herself in the mirror, her features fuzzing in and out with each throbbing pulse of her skull. The blur of her husband passed behind her like a shade on his way out of the house. When the front door slammed, the mirror shuddered in its frame.

❋ ❋ ❋

"A drink, a drink."

Mona repeats the word aloud now, her unused voice gaining strength with each repetition. Each pronouncement is a prayer as she makes her pilgrimage from the living room to the bar cart in the hallway. On the way, she bumps her shin against a low end table and curses.

That was against the other wall, Mona thinks. *I know I put that against the other wall, because the light looked so nice dappling the glass candy dish.*

She reaches down and rubs her shin. Her head throbs. The bar cart feels so far away now.

❋ ❋ ❋

There's only so much overseeing that can be done in four bedrooms and one-and-a-half baths, Mona realized. She began to spend more time on the front porch. Its beauty still felt charming when other memories of her first night in the house with Ted soured in her stomach. If she shut her eyes, she could still hear the rowdy cicadas' song. She could remember the first time she gazed upon the tree in the front yard, and imagined it would one day hold a tire swing. Coupled with the sight of the neighbor's white picket fence, the whole scene had been idyllic—ripe with possibility. She could still taste the fizz of cold champagne on her tongue. Those moments were a respite from that terrible heat trapped inside the house.

And then Mona found herself peering out into the side yard, where a rotting wooden garden bed sat languishing like a forgotten pool raft in a sea of crab grass. She felt such a pull towards that garden bed, like it was her kindred spirit. Both had high hopes moving into this place. Both had fallen into neglect.

Maybe there'd be hope for the garden, at least.

Mona changed out of her slippers and ventured out of the house. She went into town, past the movie theater where dates with Ted once tasted like peppermint and buttered popcorn. She walked past the realtor's office where they had dreamed together, noses pressed against the window's glass. She walked into the garden center, where she saw the infamous wives: they were poised, and polished, and prettily picking out plants. A potted daisy for a child's schoolteacher, perhaps. A Monstera plant for a screened-in porch, its green leaves as promising and refreshing as a tropical drink.

Mona went with sunflowers.

She spent hours outside — the heat didn't bother her out there, not really. Away from the prying eyes of cupid and the lazy ceiling fan, Mona breathed easier. Her face turned pink in the sun and her shoulders freckled with spots. Ted grimaced when he saw her, like she was a cinnamon raisin cookie when he'd been promised chocolate chip. When Mona looked in the mirror, she liked the wild reflection that stared back. She liked the dirt under her fingernails.

The rooms of 110 Fern grew a layer of dust. Coffee mugs collected in the sink. But in the yard, Mona thrived. In the yard, everything was in order.

She liked how tall they grew, the sunflowers. She liked how she could sit between them and feel their cool shade. How she could look up and smile at their dark seeds and bright petals.

❊ ❊ ❊

Now, the light filtering into the house is so bright that Mona can hardly keep her eyes open. Her head screams in protest. She reaches blindly for the handle of the bar cart and comes up empty. It should be right there.

"I'd kill for a drink," she says. Her voice is a croak.

She feels funny, nearly laughs. She feels like she's been here, in this exact moment, dozens of times.

❋❋❋

When Mona was in the garden bed, she was worlds away from 110 Fern.

She was so cleverly hidden in the shelter of her plants that Ted thought her somewhere else altogether. Maybe she was finally taking his requests seriously, he'd thought. Maybe she was out shopping, or getting her hair done. He loved when her hair was styled in those big, soft curls, like a Hollywood starlet. He loved when her hair was shiny gold.

Maybe things will be different, he'd thought. The smallest flutter of hope knocked on the door of his heart. But his secretary's hand was in his, and she was warm and pretty on the wraparound porch. It'd be a shame, Ted had thought, not to invite her inside.

He'd felt a touch of remorse as he opened the front door, like a chill on his neck. But he shook it off. He brought his secretary inside. She looked at home in the hallway, touching up her lipstick in the gilded mirror. He kissed her against the bar cart, messing up her perfect pout. He could have watched her touch up that lipstick a hundred times, and each time he'd be just as eager to muss it all up again.

It was the natural progression of things, then, to show his secretary the bedroom where not too long before Ted and Mona had their happy honeymoon.

❋❋❋

Mona stepped inside the house.

She was smiling. She had a touch of dirt above her eyebrow. Her flowers had staved off the ennui for the afternoon. Now, standing in the living room, the sunlight filtered in through the blinds in bright orange lines.

Her headache surged to the front of her head, reminding her of its existence. Even the sunflowers couldn't keep it away forever.

"I'd kill for a drink," she said aloud, and made her way to the hallway. The bar cart was in view —the promise of ice cubes and vodka, a cool balm after an afternoon spent outside —when she stumbled. The sight of two sweating rocks glasses on the table below the mirror set her pulse racing. She'd been known to put a glass down before and forget about it, seeking refuge from migraines or heat or Ted's barrage of criticism, but never two, surely?

And then, from upstairs: Ted laughed. It was a deep rumble of a laugh, intimate and warm.

Mona didn't stumble again. She charged up the stairs. Her insides twisted with fear. She threw open the bedroom door.

It was the first time she had felt — truly felt — anything through the haze of the spell 110 Fern had weaved through her in ages.

There was a part of Mona that processed the fact that Ted was in bed with another woman. There was a part of her that noticed the woman had golden hair, and a flushed face, pretty with blush and shadow. She had discarded her heels next to Mona's nightstand. She could be Mona, really, if Mona wore shoes, and put on makeup, and made anything other than cold cut sandwiches for dinner.

There was a part of Mona that processed these things. But there was a larger part — a part overcome with heat, and headaches, and rage — that won out. And this part of Mona, with her dirt-streaked face and her gardening shears gripped in her fist, stepped into the room.

And those gardening shears found their way straight into that woman's naked back.

The cupid in the window looked on, pointing his bow and arrow, staining the scene red.

❊ ❊ ❊

Mona has been here before.

"I'd kill for a drink," she says. She can't blink past the bright light that stipples her vision. She can hardly open her eyes from the pounding in her skull, like she'd been struck in the back of the head.

❊ ❊ ❊

Ted chased Mona down the hallway, shouting obscenities, his arms and chest slick with his secretary's blood.

Mona clambered down the stairs in her clunky gardening boots, trying to forget the resistance of the shears against that woman's back before they gave, tearing into her. Trying to forget her garbled choking, and Ted's guttural moan, and the scream that tore from her own throat like something feral.

She knocked into the bar cart and the bottles shattered on the hardwood floor. Behind her she heard Ted's shuddering breaths, and the hiss and curse as his bare feet stomped through the broken glass.

And then Mona howled as Ted gripped her arm and pulled, dislocating it from its socket. He grabbed her tight enough to pull her back against his body, not unlike a lover's embrace. The two wrestled against each other, screaming and spitting, tacky with blood and sweat.

Mona wrenched herself away from Ted, but she only made it a few steps before he grabbed her again and shoved her against the wall. The back of Mona's head struck the gilded mirror—the wedding present that promised so much and saw so much—and the pain of the past and the pain of the present surged forward until—

❊ ❊ ❊

"About that drink," Mona says, squinting through the pulsing pain of her headache. "I'd kill for it."

But there's something all wrong about the living room. The throw pillows are on the opposite side of the couch, and she knows Ted wouldn't have dared to do something as womanly as touch throw pillows.

She stumbles into the hallway. She bumps her shin against the end table that she knows should be on the opposite side of the room. The candy dish on the table rattles, dull without the sunlight nearby to make it sparkle.

So she does it. She pries open her eyes, fighting past the ache in her skull.

She finally looks in the mirror.

❊ ❊ ❊

It's a funny thing, realizing you are your own reflection.

It's a funny thing, but Mona forgets to laugh. Because

she's been here before, and she knows how this ends.

Still, Mona screams and slams her palms against the mirror's surface. Her hands sting. Her scream is trapped behind the glass. The striking of her palms against the surface is a dull *thunk* that's hardly noticeable over the *tch tch tch* of the sprinklers. She watches through the mirror as Ted takes his secretary in his arms, looking at her with eyes that once told Mona a million stories. Eyes that offered a million possibilities and a Hollywood ending.

Mona's head throbs. The mirror's glass shimmers and warps. Beyond the heads of the kissing couple, Mona sees, framed in the picture window, her sunflowers growing so tall they've begun to bend towards the ground. And between the stems, there's a glimpse of a woman — happy in their shadow, and unaware of what she's about to find when she walks through the door.

She watches herself leave the haven of her flowers. She watches herself walk towards the house, her gardening shears glinting in the sunlight.

111

THE CULT FROM DOWN THE ROAD
Emily Holman

As a teen who lives just a few streets away from the row of homes, you were always warned not to walk by. Not having a lot to do this summer, you've opted to climb onto the roof of your family's home to watch what goes on at the so-called haunted houses that you lived so close to on Fern Street. Naturally, those houses are all you can think about. Now, you have found that it is way too hot and conspicuous if you sit on your rooftop in the middle of the day, so you've found that observing at night, when the sun is down, and the mosquitoes are out, keeps you a lot less sunburnt and sweaty. Besides, night, in the shroud of darkness, is when all the creepy stuff happens anyway.

Since you've started these observations, one house, in particular, has caught your attention. It could have been how you could see more happening at this house than any of the others at night, or the sheer amount of people you see gathering at the doorstep at the same time every night, but the house in the middle of the row of mismatched houses of horror has been the center of your thoughts and attention all summer long.

During the day, since you cannot really watch the houses like you want to, you stay inside, partially to keep yourself out of the god-awful sun and temperatures that should be impossible to live through, but you've found a second pastime. In your room, you draw what you see. You have drawn the houses, first just sketches, then in more detail. You have tried to bring your sketchbook to the roof a few times, but trying to draw by flashlight is hard, and you don't want to draw attention to yourself with any more light. The neighbors might snitch to your parents, and then you wouldn't be allowed on the roof anymore at all, and you can't risk that, so you draw inside. You've drawn the figures you have seen lurking in the darkness. You have especially gotten good at drawing the people that arrive in red robes and white masks to the particular house at 10PM, which you figured out is house Number 111 on Fern Street. Despite watching them nightly, you know very little about this group. You wonder why they meet, what they do, and who they are, but all you know is what you've seen yourself.

What you have seen makes you want so desperately to know more. You already know that many people—you have counted around thirty each night, but it fluctuates day-by-day—arrive at the house dressed in dark red robes. When they have turned around at all, which they rarely do when fixated on what is to come when they enter the house, they have been wearing plain white masks, featureless besides two small holes for the eyes to peer out of. You have seen them silently stare at the door of the house, and when another red-robed figure opens the door, they all file in, two-by-two. You cannot see them once they are in the house, but you can catch glimpses of the house's backyard when they end up outside. You can see the red robes standing in a circle, a giant stone slab in the center, and you can see them because of the various sources of light that make the backyard—thankfully—easier to see in the darkest hours of the night. You've seen them pass something around, and although you can't tell what exactly it is, you assume it's wine, like when you go to church with your parents sometimes.

You can hear them, sometimes, too. You have listened to them chanting before, or maybe they were singing. They are too far away for you to tell and for you to make out anything specific they're saying. Sometimes there are loud sounds, possibly screaming, but you tell yourself that many things can make a screaming sound. Hell, it might even be a pet peacock or a fox that keeps getting through the fence. However, if you think about the screams for too long, you know what they are. You know the screams are human, but letting that sink into your mind on any given night gives you chills and keeps you from sleep, so you try to talk yourself out of it.

You do not want your parents, or anyone else for that matter, to find out you are staying up late to watch the creepy houses—you know your parents would worry that you were in danger, or needed therapy, or that you're not getting enough sleep, or that you'd fall off the roof, the list goes on—so you've hidden your drawings in the drawer of your desk in the hopes that they would not be found.

During one of the days you are inside, trying to stay cool and remember what you'd seen the night before, you hear the doorbell ring. Startled, you quickly shove your drawing into your desk drawer, making sure it wouldn't be seen if your parents were home from work early, and head downstairs to answer the door. When you look outside through the peephole, however, there isn't anyone at the door. This is odd to you, but you are curious if someone was ding-dong-ditching your house for whatever reason, so you unlock the door to peek into the street to see if you can catch the kid that pranked you. You don't get the chance to look around for anyone. Instead, you look down, and on your porch is a box with a gold-bordered note on top.

You look down both sides of your street, but see no one. You wonder, for a moment, who could have dropped the package off until you pick the note up from the top of the box and read it. In scrawled, swirling handwriting, it says: *We've seen you take an interest in us. You've piqued our interest, too. Bring whatever you've written about us. You know when and where.*

Glancing around again, you take the box and run back into the house, up the stairs, and into your room. You shut and lock the door for good measure, too. Once inside, you practically tear the box open, and inside is a red robe, on top of which sits a white mask. You gasp. You have been invited to 111 Fern St.

You are buzzing with excitement the rest of the day, feeling physical pain as you sit through dinner normally and wait for your parents to sleep. Finally, around 9:45PM, once it is dark enough, you find an old school binder to shove all your drawings and notes into and slip the robe over your head. It fits perfectly. You don't ask yourself why; you don't have time, so you shake it off and put the mask over your face. This, too, hugs your face as if it was made for you, but this time it feels like it is molding to your facial features, creating perfectly sized holes for your eyes to see from. You stand dumbfounded at how these clothes work, until you look at the clock and see that it is already five minutes 'til ten.

You decide that going out the window would be your best course of action. Your parents would not see you if they did wake up, and it is how you usually get to your roof, so you are pretty sure it's the best course of action. You're almost sprinting when you reach 111 Fern St., out of breath, your heart already pounding from nerves and having run a few blocks down the street. When you look at your watch, you are right on time.

You sigh, a little out of breath still, but you try to muffle the sounds of your heavy breathing as you notice all the other red-robed figures standing fairly still, silently staring at the door in front of them. It is the first time you have seen this house up close. It looks a bit old, with dark paint chipping in places and exposing the wood of the walls, a couple of shingles loose or missing here and there from the roof, and the wooden door having noticeable splinters in it. The only thing that separates it from any other older house is a rather large window at the top of the door, above the door knocker. Embedded in stained glass amongst the tired old wood is a big blue eye, staring right at you, with two large yellow wings protruding from either side. You do not know what it means, but before you think about what it could be, you startle as the door creaks open. Standing before you now is a figure in a robe similar to yours, although you can see a symbol very similar to the one in the window embroidered on the top left side. The figure says nothing as they open the door wider and step back.

Once the door opens, each red-robed figure files through it, two by two, as you have seen them do countless times. Only this time, you walk next to them as a red-robed person yourself, and you are almost shaking from nerves and excitement as you cross the threshold of what has been your summer's greatest mystery.

The house inside looks a lot nicer than its outside. The walls are decorated with black and gray patterned wallpaper, the furniture is all made up of dark wood and black fabric where necessary to match, and there are even some paintings hung on the walls, giving the foyer extra color. Most of the paintings consist of figures in red robes, as you are now, but one stands out to you as you look around. This painting has no red, only bright yellows, oranges, and whites. It depicts a human-like figure, but there are no discernable features. It's like a shadow of a person, but made of light. It feels like it does not belong in this room with you, but there it hangs, confusing you like everything else today.

"Welcome, everybody," a distorted voice startles you from your thoughts as you turn your attention toward the figure speaking. It is the person with the embroidered robe. You assume they live in this house and are the leader of whatever this is.

Nobody says anything in response. Instead, they nod, and you follow along. When you lift your head back up, you can see the two eyes peeking from the unidentifiable mask of the leader looking at you. When you look around, you see more and more of the figures' eyes on you as they figure out who their leader is looking at. You feel self-conscious—*Am I doing this right? Did I offend them? What should I do?*—but you hold on tight to your binder of drawings and bow your head again to the leader.

You still feel eyes on you as the leader tells you to come to them, and you oblige without hesitation.

"You are the one from the roof, yes?" you're asked, and you nod in response. "You have information about us. Let me see it," they tell you, and you realize they are talking about the binder. You hand the binder over to them, and they open it, flicking through page after page of notes and drawings from the past month or so.

The robed person closes the binder with one hand, making you jump, and the leader looks at you, then at the rest of the group. "Come outside, all." They wave and head towards the door. "We will begin our night's ritual."

With no protest or even looks of fear in anyone's eyes, the line forms again, two-by-two, and you follow them. Outside is the backyard you have seen night after night, but you get to see it up close this time. The lawn is high, as if it hasn't been kept up in a few weeks or so, maybe longer. Part of the lawn is sunken, though, where people start to place their feet to join in a circle. There is a big stone slab in the center of the yard, and the center of the circle that is forming, and you can see stains, maybe from food, perhaps something else, splotching the otherwise clean gray stone. A circle of rocks sits a little way over from the stone, and it looks like it's typically used as a fire pit, although you start to wonder if it is for roasting marshmallows and having backyard parties—or something else. A faint acidic smell hits you once you've been in the yard for a minute or so, almost like the smell of rotting mangoes, but you shrug it off. Maybe they have a compost pile or something.

Joining the circle, you realize there is not much else to the yard except for a metal wire fence covered in vines, making up three of the four sides of the yard's border, the fourth side taken up by the back-most wall of the house. There is not much to look at, so you stare into the center of the circle as it closes up, the leader standing at the head of the stone slab near the fire pit.

The red-robed leader looks at you again, making you feel uneasy this time; growing anxiety forms in the pit of your stomach. They hold up your binder, not breaking eye contact, as they place it into the center of the fire pit. "You cannot have any outside information about us," they say before pulling a match from their pocket, scraping it against the stone, and tossing the lit match into the fire pit.

You want to lunge towards it, grab your month's worth of work, and save it from getting utterly destroyed, but that uneasiness you felt looking at the leader is still there, and you think it's best if you remain where you are. Besides, they could just be a little overprotective of their organization.

The red-robed leader seems unfazed as they turn to the person standing next to them in the circle. The leader holds out a hand and is passed a large metal goblet that looks like it has come straight out of a knight-and-princess movie. You cannot see if there is anything in it, but the leader, whose hand is around the goblet's stem, takes a sip and passes it to the person on their right. You do not know how they're sipping from a goblet when the masks go over their mouths and your hands shake as the goblet gets to you. As you look into the goblet, you see what you believe to be a thick wine, like they pass around in a church. You think you are starting to understand: this must be a religious group of some sort.

You bring the goblet up to your lips as you had watched everyone else do, and the mouth of your mask opens up slightly, enough for you to tip a sip of the supposed wine into your mouth. It takes a lot of energy to keep a straight face as you pull the goblet from your lips. Instead of tasting a sweet wine, the liquid is heavy and hard to swallow, filling your mouth with a rich, metallic flavor. You force it down your throat as you hand the goblet off to the next person.

Once the goblet makes its rounds and ends up back with the leader, you start to feel your head beginning to ache at the temples and behind your eyes. You attribute it to the smell of burning plastic from the binder melting in the flames.

There is silence for a moment, and then the leader points at you. "We need you to lie down on the stone bed." You do not want to question the group's leader, so you are quiet and hesitate momentarily. The group's leader must have noticed because they give you a brief explanation: "Initiation." Hearing this makes sense to you, so without asking any more silent questions, you step forward, aware of all eyes on you, and hoist yourself onto the tall, heavy stone slab. Your hands sting from where they scraped against the rock, but you follow instructions and lay down, head facing the group's leader. They approach you and, standing over you, gently touch your wrists, then move down and do the same to your ankles. You do not understand why, at first, until you feel a material similar to your mask wrap around you, moving on its own, holding you against the stone and rendering you unable to move. You try to pull against it, break it, and escape, but the material strains tighter around the flesh of your appendages, and you have no choice but to lie still against the cold stone.

You can barely see what's happening around you. The restrictions placed on your movement limit your vision, and it does not help that you feel your head pounding now, or is it your heart? It could be both, but that's the least of your current worries. You look towards your feet, one of the only places you can look if you strain your eyes and neck, and you notice one of the members of the group—although now you're considering that this could be a cult—holding something relatively long and shiny, the flickering light from the fire making it glimmer ominously: a knife.

Approaching the foot of the stone bed you've been made to lie on, the cultist looks at your body briefly, as if contemplating the best way to murder you for some type of sacrifice. Then, raising the blade above you, they bring its tip down towards your chest. The knife is sharp and cuts right through your skin, and although it is not deep enough to kill you, not just yet, you cry out in pain. The cut stings as the air hits it, and the knife doesn't stop until it reaches the bottom of your stomach. You are relieved but still insanely panicked as the red-robed figure lifts the knife from your skin. You try to thrash around, but the mask-like material that binds you keeps you still for the most part.

As you begin to think this ritual is over, two more red-robed figures step towards you, adorning velvet pouches in one hand and a white candle, the wicks already lit, in the other. The hands with the candles reach out over you, and you feel hot wax drip onto your skin, in and around the already-bleeding cut, and your face is wet with tears. Once the small candles have melted what felt like buckets of hot wax onto your exposed skin, the figures switch to the components in the pouch. You do not know what is in those pouches, but as the substances fall into your open wound, you scream in pain again. It feels like they are pouring salt into your cut, and maybe they are, but you are helpless to stop them, so all you can do is writhe in pain as much as your limited range of motion allows you.

As the two cult members step back towards the circle, you hear one start chanting in a language you don't understand. The others follow suit, and as you hear their voices grow louder and louder all around you, the heat and the pain from your cut flare up. You can feel the heat from the fire nearly burning the side of your face. Your head is pounding; it feels like someone put ice picks through your eyes and a hammer through your skull. As your vision becomes blurry from the tears and the pain, it keeps getting worse and worse as the chanting gets louder and louder. Finally, when you feel like your head's going to explode, you scream, crying out as loud as you've ever yelled in your whole life, so loud the neighbors, your parents, and everyone else in this and the surrounding neighborhoods can hear you.

As soon as you cry out, there is a blinding light. You close your eyes. It's as if everything has stopped at once, the pain, the screaming, the chanting—everything. Everyone is silent and still. Even the fire beside you has gone out. A figure, just like the one in the painting in the house, has shot its way out of your body, out of your blood and flesh from the cut the cult made straight over your stomach and chest as if you had given birth to it. It turns to you—you are still trapped, tied down on the stone table, helpless to whatever this thing is— and you can see its body is covered in eyes, with wings protruding from multiple places out of its back. You want to run away—you're scared of this thing—but you know you can't, so you keep staring, and that's when the figure turns around. Where there would be eyes on the face of a human, on this thing's face, there are two large holes filled with fire. You make eye contact with it; it tells you not to be afraid, and then you feel a heat grow on all sides of you as your world turns black.

112

THIS COULD BE YOUR HOME, YOU KNOW

C. Mae Thomas

1954

After the second football game of the season, Abner Rose walked home alone down Fern Street. It wasn't on his way home, but Abner didn't mind the extra time. He whistled a little tune to himself as he walked, under a cooling dark September sky still smeared with a dusky pink.

Abner couldn't care less what color the sky was. The only color he cared about right now was the color of the eyes he'd spent all evening looking into.

Ettie's eyes, those big hazel pools rimmed with green. God, her dark hair falling out of its pins and framing her smile, her hand hovering over his at the concession stand.

It had been a perfect night. From the moments spent sneaking away to smoke cigarettes, to the hot dogs and soda, even down to Abner's best friend Jeff scoring that last-minute field goal to win the game. The crowd all jumped and screamed in unison, and Ettie's face, contorted in a shriek of joy, had turned to him rather than the scoreboard.

His lips were still all warm and tingly from how she had kissed him. His stomach was in a similar state from the way that she had smirked after the second time, throwing a glance over her shoulder while walking to her dad's car before the stadium lights thudded off at the end of the night.

Abner was so distracted, in fact, that he had absent-mindedly let his feet take him wherever they wanted. He had been so absorbed with thoughts of Ettie's skin, soft and pink and pale, the smell in the crook of her shoulder, her breath, hot and halted in the night...

Abner hadn't realized until he was standing squarely in front of it that his feet had brought him to this house, 112 Fern St., as marked in wrought iron numbers on the front siding.

Someone had left the door open.

The house loomed, solitary and black and dark against the creeping fog from a humid end-of-summer evening. Suddenly, it was like someone pulled the plug on Abner's heart like a drain and all of the pleasant thoughts gurgled down, chunks getting caught in the garbage disposal, until it was empty.

The last few months of him and Ettie were slurped down, too. She *had* been looking at Jeff a little too closely from the bleachers, with something like adoration in her eyes — hadn't she? Maybe she was just teasing Abner, leading him on, *just like all girls do*. A little gurgle of sour-sick jealousy touched Abner's gut.

The open door yawned, and there was something jealous about that, too.

Abner couldn't see anything in the dark hallway beyond walls and floor, but it didn't seem empty. It had something to it, something warm and hurting and lonesome in the shadows. *Everyone's left.* Abner felt a pang of hurt for the abandoned structure, left all by itself after it had probably been someone's home.

Home. Some thought said, and it seemed to come from the very cracks in the sidewalk. *This could be* your *home, you know.*

There was something lonely in the thought, and something yearning in the feeling.

Abner brushed off the seed of the bad thoughts about Ettie like a piece of lint on a jacket and reached for the good ones once again.

She was so beautiful in the stadium lights. He thought of her slim fingers woven in his, thought about sliding a ring on one of them. They'd need a home after graduation. They'd need a place to live together, a Good American House™ with a picket fence and a yard for the kids, whenever they came along.

There was no white picket fence on 112 Fern St., but there was a fresh sign on a post in the overgrown yard that cheerfully proclaimed FOR SALE.

Abner smiled. He went to the front door and pulled it closed with a satisfying click. How awful it was that such a nice house was left neglected by some hasty real estate agent who couldn't even shut the door all the way.

I won't be like that, Abner thought.

He took one last glance at the house before he put his hands in his pockets and turned on his heels, whistling the whole way home.

❋ ❋ ❋

1965

"Abner!" Ettie's voice trilled up the stairs and into the master bathroom. "Lunch, hon. It's going to get cold."

"For God's sake, I'm coming," Abner muttered to himself. His face was covered in shaving cream, now melting as the aerosol in the cream deflated. A white glob slid and slopped onto the hand that held his weight.

"Be down in a minute!" he yelled. Abner slid the razor across the rest of his face in four swift motions, enough to get the rest of the cream. He slipped a little bit with the last stroke, and cursed at the telltale sign of a nick.

"Ab?!"

The window whistled and hissed. Damn old house, always making noises. Abner tried to slam the window even more shut than it already was.

With the movement, a splinter chipped off of the old wood and burrowed itself into Abner's finger. He flinched, and swore.

When he examined his finger, the splinter was so far buried beneath the skin that he couldn't even see it. Abner sighed and patted the windowsill as if to apologize. It wasn't the house's fault.

Wasn't the house's fault his wife was a nag. Wasn't the house's fault she hadn't touched him for months. Wasn't the house's fault that from the very day he had carried Ettie across the threshold of the front door, she'd been different. Cold. Unappreciative. Harsh.

Abner had heard stories before of beautiful, laughing, young women undergoing some transformation into lumpy shrews as soon as they had the ring, the kid. Abner had given both dutifully. And what had he gotten in return?

His dad had warned him. Jeff had warned him. But no, he hadn't listened. Had to go and saddle himself with something that forgot to get the groceries he wanted and screamed at him on a Saturday.

"Abner! Food!" Ettie's voice came up again, a little thinner this time. The *tone* on that one. It hadn't even been two minutes, and she was nagging. *Again.*

No, it wasn't the house's fault his marriage was in the pits.

"I'm almost ready!" Abner yelled back. He splashed his face and patted it dry while grumbling to himself. *That tone.* It made him want to linger, to go even slower, just to show that woman that she didn't control him.

After turning off the sink, Abner crept out of the bathroom to the phone by the bed, careful to avoid the two floorboards that always creaked. He picked up the receiver, listened to make sure that Ettie wasn't on the line downstairs, and dialed.

"You with me again tonight?" Jeff's voice came without so much as another greeting. In the background, Abner could hear the sound of a game blaring on the TV, and the *hisssssss-crack!* of a bottle opener on a beer.

"If you don't mind."

Jeff laughed on the other side of the phone, and it

was a gristly sound. "You could actually come over if you want. State game's on. They're getting spanked. You could be good luck."

"Another time."

"Alright," Jeff said. "But listen, we should actually get beers soon. It's been a while."

"Yeah," Abner said. "Soon. I gotta go. 'Preciate it."

"Hope she's worth it." Jeff chuckled. "I'll see you when I see you."

Abner hung up.

"Jesus, Ab," Ettie said when he lumbered down the stairs into the kitchen. She almost looked pretty in that floral dress and white apron around her waist, face flushed from the heat of the stove. "I've asked you a thousand times to take the stairs more gentle-like. It's frightenin'."

"My house," Abner said, approaching the counter where the food was laid out buffet-style. "I take the stairs however I damn well please."

"Language," Ettie chided.

"Daddy, daddy!" Ella said, bouncing from her chair at the table with her mouth full.

Ettie handed Abner a plate." Did you see the sunflowers next door? Opened up yesterday. Gorgeous, fat blooms."

"Guess what we did in school yesterday!"

"I wish they'd do something like that down the road. You know, a few doors down at the Rainey place."

Abner slopped food onto his plate — roast beef, green beans — *from a can, of course, it was too damn much to expect anything fresh around here* — and a helping of instant mashed potatoes.

"Daddy, guess!"

"What, hon?" he asked.

"We made pictures! Can I show you?" Ella stood up on her chair and waved her spoon in the air toward Abner. A big fat dollop of mashed potatoes slid off with the movement and made a resounding splat on the tablecloth.

"Such a shame they don't keep it up," Ettie continued,

brushing away a strand of dark hair stuck to her face. The spoon grated across the bottom of the serving plate as she scooped potatoes for herself. "Beautiful old Victorian like that should at least have some decent landscapin'."

"Get down off there," Abner said to Ella. "You're old enough to know better."

"You can show Daddy your picture after you finish eating," Ettie said. "Now sit down. Greens first. I've got ice cream for dessert."

The promise of ice cream did its trick, and Ella plopped back down to pluck the beans off of her plate one by one. Ettie sat at the table next to Abner and delicately spread a napkin out on top of her lap. Abner was halfway through his meal already when she picked up her fork.

"Abner, Jesus, could you slow down? The way you eat's like a wild animal," Ettie said.

Somewhere upstairs, the house groaned. No one paid it any mind. Living in an old house, you eventually got used to the noises — eventually got over the thought that something somewhere was trying to talk to you. Abner grunted and swallowed.

"Oh, hon, you cut yourself." Ettie reached over and ran her thumb over the side of his jaw. There was a smear of red on it when she pulled it away.

The splinter in Abner's finger pulsed, insisting upon itself.

"What're you shavin' for on a Saturday?" Ettie asked. She picked up her napkin and went for his face. Abner swatted her hand away.

"C'mon, let me wipe it." Ettie reached again.

"I'm fine."

"You sure, hon? There's some hydrogen peroxide in the cabinet —"

"I said I'm fine, Ethel. Jesus! Just leave me alone. It'll stop bleeding in a minute if you just leave it."

The silverware clinked against the plates. The splinter throbbed. Abner swept one last spoonful of mashed potatoes into his mouth and shoved himself away from the table. "Goin' to Jeff's."

"Again?" Ethel asked, and the thinness in her voice reappeared, conjuring an angry rumbling at the back of Abner's spine. Or was that the upstairs floorboards again?

"We're just gonna sit out back. Have some beers, do a little shootin'. You know how torn up Jeff is. Misty leavin' him and all. Don't want him alone right now."

"That was months ago, Abner. What about leavin' us alone?" Ethel leaned her palms on the edge of the table so that her fingers pointed at him like daggers. "Just to go play marksman with beer cans and rabbits?"

"Daddy, my picture," Ella said forlornly, a bit of potatoes smeared near her mouth.

They were always on his back, these two. Couldn't be left alone for a goddamned second without them pulling him in all directions. Always *needing, needing, needing.* He wouldn't *have* to leave if it was more goddamn *welcoming* in here.

"Who do you think you are, Gary Cooper?" Ethel trilled.

Abner grabbed his coat with shaking, furious hands and put it on, one pocket weighed down with the gun.

It wasn't his fault that it was so loud in here all the time, that it was always such a mess. *It isn't your fault that you just can't stand it after such a long day. Isn't it enough that you paid for all of this? The house, the food on the table, the clothes on their backs?*

"I'll be back later," Abner said. He moved for the front door.

"Abner Rose," Ethel said, and her voice was no longer thin. "Don't you dare walk out that door."

She's right. Something creaked.

Abner stopped.

For once.

Abner turned.

You can bear it.

Abner inhaled.

"Honestly, Ethel, how dare you…"

∞

"How dare you," Abner sighed to himself, caught in the

limbo between a half-drunk exhaustion and stone-cold sleep. "How… how dare —"

"What was that, baby?" the voice from the crook of his arm murmured, and Abner startled. An orange light from the neon sign for the storefront outside illuminated the interior of the bedroom with a soft glow, muted by the cloudy haze of snowfall outside. The apartment was mostly bare, but for a chair in the corner with Abner's coat thrown over it, the clothes on the floor, the bed in which they laid, and a mirror leaned lazily against the wall across from the bed.

It was in this mirror that Abner could see the barmaid's hair falling to her shoulders as she lifted her head groggily. She — Amy? Allie? Annie? — smelled like hairspray, cheap perfume, and cigarettes, a smell that had reached across the bar that first night, an extension of her arm when she handed him his beer.

"Nothing," Abner said. "Go back to sleep."

The barmaid rolled over and turned to face him.

When Abner met her gaze, it wasn't her face at all.

Another woman was in the crook of his arm, looking up at him with big hazel eyes rimmed with green.

A dark liquid gurgled and dripped out of her parted lips, and it took Abner a moment to realize it was blood.

"What the —" Abner startled and jerked away, pushing himself backwards off the bed to stand.

"What's the matter?" the woman asked, and when she sat up, it was the barmaid once again. The blood on her face was gone.

Abner shook his head. He was still groggy with the booze; he must have been half-asleep.

"No, it's okay, I just — what time is it?" Abner looked at the clock beside the bed, but his vision was too fuzzy to read it. "I have to go."

"Jesus, Abner. Always something with you. Too much to ask you to stay one night?" The barmaid lurched out of the bed and went for her clothes. When she stood up, her reflection in the big mirror across from the bed caught Abner's glance.

The other woman was there again in the mirror, as still as a statue. Her eyes seared into him from the reflection. The blood bubbled and gurgled out of her mouth, down her chin, onto a floral dress and white apron.

"Ettie," Abner whispered, and the words caught in his teeth. She choked, and a spatter of pink hit the mirror like fireworks.

In the mirror, Ettie's gaze turned to the barmaid, who was now tugging on her bra in a frustrated fury.

"It's Addie." The barmaid sniffled a little, and it was a half-sob, half sardonic chuckle. "Get out. I can't even look at you anymore."

When Abner looked back at the mirror, there was only the glow of the sign, growing stronger as the remnants of the day outside faded.

"Alright," he said. Ettie's face burned into his vision, like the afterglow after staring directly into the sun for too long. A low dull ache crept into the back of his head. "I'm sorry, okay? I got startled. Trick of the eye."

There was no response. The barmaid, whatever her name had been, was gone, and Abner was alone in an empty apartment, paused at the door.

He looked once more at the mirror where Ettie had stood. From this angle, he could see two soft house slippers attached to two pale legs.

Then, there was the hem of a floral dress, glowing in the neon from the window and starting to drip.

Abner fumbled for the door handle, and it slipped slick and wet through his palms before it managed to turn. He burst into the hallway outside, his head throbbing.

The booze. The booze, Abner pleaded with himself over and over again. He had to believe it was the booze that was nesting in his skull, its claws scraping and suckling to get out. The pain was bursting out the back of his head, gripping him from throat to spine. He tripped down the stairs but caught himself with a thud on the railing, and kept sprinting down with no regard for the possibility of another impact.

When he rounded the last corner of the flight of

stairs, the floral dress was there again, a blur in his peripheral vision.

Abner kept his eyes on the floor and willed his legs to move faster to get away from the staring, staring, staring. He pushed past the dress and burst out the front door of the apartment complex.

The sun had begun its descent, a day dissipating into an evening cloudy haze. Everything in the air was muted with moisture and the advent of dusk, with no real shadows to cast.

Abner closed his eyes, and Ettie's face pulsed there with every heartbeat. Abner opened his eyes, and she stood in front of him.

He burst into a run as if it would free him from the vision gripping his spine.

When Abner finally slowed and stopped, he was in a park, the one just a couple of blocks away from Fern Street. From *home.* A familiar monument was just feet from him, a cold statue of some war hero.

Your head. Your head.

He had to sit down. Abner found the park bench with his hands and crumbled.

"Finally saw her, huh?" A voice came, and Abner whirled to meet it.

Jeff was sitting on the park bench beside him, casually tossing bread crumbs out of a paper bag that rested on the beer gut that had developed over the last few years. The other hand held a cigarette, freshly lit.

"Jeff," Abner said, and clung to the relief that washed over him. A *friend.* Maybe Jeff could talk him out of this nightmare and sober him up. "What are you doing here?"

Jeff chuckled. "Feeding the birds. What does it look like? Have a seat. You look like you could use a smoke."

Abner tried to reach out for the outstretched cig, but his hand shook too much to find a grip. Instead, he leaned back and pressed one hand to either side of his temple.

"Head, huh?" Jeff mused. "Here."

He put a hand on the back of Abner's neck, and Abner could feel infinite tiny hairs that resided there tingle with Jeff's touch, even colder than the air outside that surrounded them. Two fingers pressed firm, and in half a moment the pain loosened. His head was no longer quite so heavy. It still hurt, but it was manageable. Like a hangover.

"What the hell was that?" Abner asked. "What did you do?"

"A little relief." Jeff shrugged and tossed another handful of bread crumbs. "This ain't going to be easy."

"What are you talking about? Why are you being so weird?" Abner did feel a little better. "What was that you said? When I sat—"

"I know you saw Ettie," Jeff replied. "You saw she's dead."

"What the hell are you talking about?" Ettie's bloody face swarmed back into Abner's memory a hundred times, like he was viewing her from the kaleidoscope eyes of a fly. A nausea rose in his stomach to replace the headache.

Jeff shrugged again.

"Look, Jeff…I don't know if it's the booze, or if this is some dream, but this is too fuckin' weird. I'm goin' home." Abner stood up and turned to leave. He'd had too much at the bar. He'd been too drunk, and too sloppy, sleeping at that filthy apartment with whatever-her-name-was, and his head was playing tricks on him.

"I'm afraid that isn't a possibility for you, hon." Ettie's voice came from behind him, cool and crisp, like a song in the movies.

Abner whirled around to meet the bloody face, the floral dress. He found neither.

Instead, it was just Jeff, taking another drag of the cigarette, absent-mindedly tossing out more crumbs to the greedy pigeons. One of the birds cooed remorsefully.

"You're not Jeff," Abner said, his stomach freezing over with the realization.

"I'm something like him," Not-Jeff said. "On our end, it's usually best to relay any communications with a face, you know. A face you trust."

Abner opened his mouth, but could do nothing except

inhale. The being that was not Jeff turned back to the birds.

"Do you know where we are?" Not-Jeff asked. Their cigarette was finished, and they stubbed it out on the side of the bench before tossing it. One of the pigeons plucked it up in its beak and swallowed it.

"The… the park," Abner stuttered. "We're at the park."

"Brevity is the soul of wit." Not-Jeff snorted. "Look again."

Abner did. He didn't know how he had missed it the first time, but there it was, right in front of them across the street: the house. 112 Fern St., as looming and beautiful as ever. There was a tricycle in the yard that Abner didn't recognize: forest green, covered in snow. On the driveway, a gangly figure bundled in a coat and hat meticulously moved a snow shovel across the pavement, creating a cacophony of scraping and crunching that threatened to bring on Abner's headache again.

"My house," he said. "Who's that guy in the front yard?"

Not-Jeff eased themself to standing from the bench, leaving the bag of bird food. "Let's go."

"Seriously, what's this jerk-off doing at my house?" Abner said as they crossed the street.

"It's not your house anymore," Not-Jeff said.

"What are you talking about?" Abner said. He jogged ahead and stopped at the white picket fence that he had put in the year after he and Ettie moved in.

"Hey," he said. The man didn't stop shoveling, didn't look up, didn't even flinch. *"Hey!"* Abner said, louder.

The man stopped, and the scraping sounds of the shovel against the driveway ceased. He craned his neck curiously towards the house, the street, the sidewalk — right through Abner and Not-Jeff.

"June?" the man called. "You say something?"

"What?" A woman's voice came from inside the house, and then its owner appeared. She was young, petite, with flour on the apron tied around her waist, swelling with a pregnancy that was only just beginning to show.

"No, Jack. And will you shut the door next time? It's freezin'. The kids are going to catch a cold."

"Who are those people?" Abner turned to Not-Jeff. "Where's Ella and Ettie?"

Not-Jeff didn't say anything, but lifted their hand to point to the door, a thick hairy finger arced in warning.

The woman was gone. The door was open, and at first there was only the black beyond, a chasm that chilled Abner in a way the snow outside never could.

When he focused, he saw a familiar entryway—oak floors, a credenza beneath a mirror on the wall that was covered in a white sheet. Pale blobs in the shapes of furniture lurked further beyond: a sofa, a lamp, a chair in the hallway.

Something murmured to him through the cement, something black and bleak and strong. A magnetic need to step forward started to tremble in Abner's bones.

"You wanna go inside?" Not-Jeff asked, and Abner almost chuckled at the thought that there was anything *wanting* about this feeling at all.

Abner stepped forward. Despite the fact that the woman had been there—moments before the man had been shoveling the driveway—now, there was not a soul in the vicinity, not even a hint of presence or sentience in anything but the house itself.

When Abner took the first step inside the hallway, the house creaked with all of the familiarity of an old sweater.

Creaking Friend.

Creaking I missed you.

Creaking You came home.

And then, the memory hit Abner like a slap.

❋ ❋ ❋

"How dare you, in my own home—"

Ella immediately whimpered, and started to cry, startled by the sudden yelling.

"Abner, I—"

"Will you shut up for one goddamned second—" Abner lunged forward, and went for the weight in his pocket with the movement. Ettie's eyes widened. She staggered backwards over her chair,

and it toppled, tangling her legs with it.

"Abner, n —"

"How dare you—" Abner screamed and shot twice in rapid succession, then three times more, even though he knew that his wife was already dead.

Ettie lay on the floor, eyes agape. Blood dribbled out of the corner of her mouth and pooled into a deep scratch in the hardwood floor.

"Daddy!" The little girl's shriek was like the pitch of a fire alarm and Abner recoiled, his eardrums vibrating so rabidly that they threatened to explode. The scream was too high, too high, *TOO HIGH TOO HIGH TOO HIGH,* and he whirled to snuff it out.

A spray of red flecked the popcorn ceiling in a red mist so thin it looked pink. *My baby* said a thin small voice at the back of Abner's brain, but it was drowned out by the roar of rage baptizing the forefront of his consciousness as he fired once more. His ears rang now, not with the screams, but with the aftermath of the gun, hot and trembling in his hand. A thin wisp of smoke curled upwards from its handle and the acrid stench of gunpowder filled his nostrils.

It was quiet.

Abner thought dimly of the shooting range, the last time he had fired the gun. He saw the paper target, both human and geometric in its form of colors, expanding outward with measured precision. It twitched and burned and tore with every bullet that made contact.

Nice shot, the range officer had said.

Nice shot. Abner turned to the body on the floor in the kitchen that had once been the vessel of his wife. A body he had loved, written love letters to, made love to…

Nice shot. Under the kitchen table, a little leg twitched in the last protests of a nervous system in distress. One shoe dangled halfway off the foot. On the floor lay an empty spoon surrounded by mashed potatoes, fresh red gravy seeping into the starch.

Nice shot. Abner opened his mouth wide and placed the barrel of the handgun inside it, the heat from his last shots searing sensitive pink flesh and tongue. He pulled the trigger, and the last thought that seared across his brain was the jeering voice *of the range officer, Nice shot.*

***

Abner could feel the gun in his hands even now, could feel the barrel in his throat — could feel the heat of it, could taste the metal, could feel the black, the black.

He felt it even as the vision dissolved, and Abner stood in the hallway once more with Not-Jeff facing the veiled mirror. The pain in his head had returned, as cold as white flame on his neck and throat and spine.

Not-Jeff pointed to the mirror, and Abner understood.

He gripped the sheet with damp palms and tugged. The sheet fell away to expose the surface underneath. The mirror's sheen was muted in the dim light, but the reflection was clear. Half of the face Abner knew looked back at him.

The other half was gone, gaping, peeled back to flesh and bone and brain.

From Abner's left cheekbone to where his ear should have been all the way down to the back of his throat was an exposed, throbbing mess of brain matter, bloody flesh, and shards of bone. Dark liquid seeped into his shirt, flecks of white and yellow splattered on top like sprinkles. Abner's eyes were puddles of black pupils, all semblance of white gone. The thing in the mirror couldn't be him. Was not him. Was Not-Abner.

Abner raised a hand to touch his face. A slick, spongy surface met his fingers and squished sickeningly when he exerted pressure. Had the gun that had killed his wife and daughter taken a third of Abner's head, too?

No. A voice streaked across his brain. *The gun didn't do it. We did.*

On the intact side of his face was a small nick, raw and no longer bleeding.

Inside his finger, a splinter throbbed.

Abner walked to the dining room, no longer shrouded by white, but with furniture that he remembered. This was the lamp that was a wedding gift. This was the coffee table from Ethel's parents. This was the couch that a coworker had given him in his first job, the couch that he had slept on many times when he had been fighting with Ettie. His Ettie, now dead on the floor—the floor next to the kitchen table around which Abner had done countless laps trying to get Ella to sleep when she was just a colicky infant.

Ella—Abner couldn't look.

Ella

Ella

But,

It wasn't Ella he wanted to see.

Abner went to the third body. It could still be a dream.

He rolled up the sleeves on the corpse's arms and furiously searched for the scars, the ones from childhood, the ones from that bad accident on his bike.

"What, the mirror wasn't enough?" Not-Jeff said, a stain of boredom on their voice. "It's real, Abner."

The knobby white lines were there. Abner sat back on his knees, defeated.

"Could have just looked at its face." The cigarette crackled and fizzed.

"I killed them," Abner said. "I killed myself."

"Pretty gruesome stuff," said Not-Jeff. When they tapped their cigarette, the wind from the open door carried a bit of ash and it flickered and dissolved into the puddles of blood. "Look at 'em, will you?"

Abner shook his head, and the pain in his neck grew worse, so much worse with the movement. "I can't."

"Course you can't."

Not-Jeff snapped their fingers, and in a heartbeat the two of them sat back on the bench, on an ordinary park bench, just two people sharing a cigarette under a monument at dusk. There were children playing just yards away, parents trying to shepherd them to get home before dark.

"I killed myself," Abner said, and his voice pitched upward on the last syllable. "I..."

"Bingo," Not-Jeff said. "Most people just sort of 'pass on' after they do it. Dissolve, like the ash from this cigarette here." Not-Jeff paused and inhaled deeply.

Abner watched the smoke settle, and waited for the rest.

"Once in a while, though, we get one like you. Someone still floatin' around, relivin' things they're not s'posed to. We have to tell 'em. Have to help 'em leave. Make their peace."

"But I was just…" Abner faltered. "I had just left. I was just with…" He hesitated again. Allie? Amy?

From around the corner came a familiar hissing and lurching. A gray bus lumbered forward, farting exhaust.

"Time's a funny thing, Abner," Not-Jeff said. "Never really works how you expect."

The snow had started to fall again. "Seriously, Je— whoever you are. What the hell is this?" Abner asked. "Some kind of purgatory or something?"

Not-Jeff leaned back and guffawed, and Abner shuddered at how much it sounded like his friend. "There is no Purgatory, Abner. Not for you."

The bus lurched forward and came to a stop in front of the park bench.

"This is you," Not-Jeff said, and gestured to the doors as they opened. The interior of the bus was gray, empty, devoid of even a driver.

Abner thought about just going. Just stepping on the bus, and hoping that there would be something blank, something empty beyond. Anything but the pain in his spine, the faces in his head, the blood on his hands.

Not yet, the voice cooed.

"Alright," Abner said, and stood. "I'll go."

"Very good."

"Just… can I see the house again?" Abner said. "Since I can't… Just one more look, before I… one last goodbye. Maybe we can even grab a beer again after, you and me. That last beer I always said we'd get."

The shadow of the "Not" blew out of Not-Jeff in a shuddering breeze for half a breath and then returned.

"Sure, Abner." It chuckled and slapped Abner on the shoulder. "Say your goodbyes. Make your peace. Whatever helps you let go. We'll get you on the next one."

"Thank you."

"I'll be around." Not-Jeff nodded and sat back on the bench. "Oh, and Abner?"

"Yeah?" Abner turned, already impatient to leave.

"No beer."

❊ ❊ ❊

Abner picked up his pace until the *hssssss-chk* of the bus was no more than a faint echo in the distance behind him. Fat snowflakes were falling from the sky, adding to the white blanket already on Fern. It was December already. At the first house abutting the park, someone was outside starting to hang up lights. A few houses down, someone was putting up their wreath. It would have been perfectly lovely on any other day to walk around the neighborhood and spot the Christmas decorations that were one by one starting to announce their twinkling appearance on Fern at dusk. But this time, Abner wasn't in for an aimless walk.

This time, he knew exactly where he was going.

The first time Abner had walked this road, he had been drawn to the house without even being aware of its presence. With every step toward it, the connection had gotten stronger, and with every step away from it, he could still feel it whimpering at him through the concrete.

The house had wanted him then, from the very first moment he had been drawn to its door all those years ago. He hadn't realized it then. Now, he knew the call for his embrace, his presence, his touch.

Abner went willingly.

By the time he got to the house, the sky was fully and completely dark. All the same, 112 Fern St. seemed illuminated, like the exposure on a dark photograph turned all the way up. Like many of the other houses on the street, there were thin strings of lights hanging from the house's awnings and a festive wreath on the door. A collapsed snowman adorned the lawn, its silhouette fading in the accumulating blizzard.

The curtains to the dining room were open. From the sidewalk, Abner could make out a family bustling around the dinner table. The woman was calling something to a boy hunched over something glowing and beeping in his hands on the couch while she struggled to fasten another smaller child into a highchair at the head of the table. The man had his back to the window, fussing with something on the counter. The boy reluctantly trudged to the table, where his mother started cutting up a piece of meat on his plate.

They look happy, Abner thought. Normal.

You probably did too.

Abner crossed the yard, leaving no footprints in his wake. He walked directly through the bushes that pressed up against the siding and stopped at the window for the best possible view of the house that used to be his.

Still is.

The man turned and came to sit across from his wife. He sent a thin smile her way and turned back to his plate.

There it is. The slightest bit of tension in the smile, the lack of acknowledgement from her gaze.

Of course. The housework, the bills, the kids. A tired man returning from his work to a tired woman still saddled with hers, and the rest that they both sought, but neither was quite able to find.

Abner wanted to go inside. There was something intoxicating about the family in a warm light from a window. Family. He'd had that once.

That's not why, it hummed. *You know that's not why.*

"Jack!" the wife shrieked, and she was looking right at Abner. "There's something outside, look!" Without waiting for her husband's response, she was standing and backing into the kitchen.

"Calm down, June, what did you—"

"Something moved. In the bushes."

Abner wasn't *moving*. He was just looking. For a moment, it looked like they were just looking too, a picture-perfect image of a horrified Norman Rockwell family frozen in fear.

Abner didn't know why, but he raised his hand and waved. He felt a smile tickle his lips. Invisible strings seemed stitched to his cheeks, pulling his face upward into the enormous grin of a dark marionette.

"I don't see anything," Jack said. "It's windy out, June. It's winter."

"Please. Please, just go check."

Jack exhaled in a weary sigh and raked his fingers through his hair. Abner felt the annoyance in the gesture. His puppet smile spread wider, arm still waving, ticking back and forth like a metronome.

He has one of those nagging ones, too.

"Fine, I'll look. It's nothing."

Do you see?

The kids had already gone back to their food. June watched as Jack tediously pulled on first one shoe, then the other. He plodded to the front door.

Abner stopped waving and let his hand drop to his side, the grin still plastered on his face.

Isn't it enough that you paid for all of this? The house, the food on the table, the clothes on their backs?

The front door creaked open, and Abner turned. The man stepped outside and sighed.

He's just like you.

It was true.

There was *something* in the man that Abner could cling to, something that he could take hold of—a wispy black thread of anger that had tickled his facial expressions at dinner, and was coaxed even stronger with the disruption at the window.

The man shuffled a little as he clumsily navigated the landscaping.

When he got closer, Abner sensed the blackness in the man once more, and realized that it was a void. A ripe, plump, gaping void.

Not a void. A *vessel*, came the hum.

Jack bent over and poked around the bushes, shivering a little when he came close to Abner, close enough that Abner could see goosebumps on his arms.

Abner reached out his hand and let it rest on Jack's shoulder. For a lingering, delicious moment, an expression crossed the man's face and furrowed it like soft clay. But then Jack shook his head like a wet dog. He went back to the front door. It creaked, and clicked.

"Must've just been critters," his voice said from inside. "You're just jumpy. That's all."

"I swear, Jack. I swear I saw —"

Jack went over to her and took her into an embrace. "You're fine, doll."

He leaned down to kiss her. She reluctantly accepted, finally moving her gaze from where Abner stood.

The smile finally melted off of his face.

"Jumpy," she affirmed.

Jack patted her shoulder and went to the window, where he closed the curtains and Abner's view was swept away.

"Wait," Abner said. His voice was so firm it was almost a shout, but the curtains stayed closed. "Wait!"

You can make them hear you, if you want, the hum came again.

"You can't, Abner." Not-Jeff was behind him in a flash, like they had been watching the whole time. "You had your chance at this life. You have other chances now. Different ones. You had the choice to live or die. Now, you can linger and languish, or accept your final consequence."

"You won't even say what that is," Abner said. "You were supposed to be my friend."

"You're selfish, Abner. You didn't just take your own life, but that of your wife. Your child. Flesh of your flesh. A little thing, a child who loved you. And now, even now, all you can think about is saving your own skin."

Stay with me, 112 Fern St. cooed. *This is your home.*

"What happens if I don't listen?" Abner rasped. "What happens if I —"

You're why I did it, isn't it?

"You aren't meant to stay here, Abner. It upsets things."

"What things?" Abner scoffed. "Where exactly will I be going, Jeff?"

"Does it matter?" asked Not-Jeff. "If you stay, *it will upset things.* There is only pain and suffering for you here, and for everyone you touch. Everyone you infect."

We did it, the house whispered. *Together. Is it really all so bad?*

But then, Abner thought. But then, Ettie had never really loved him.

Stay home, Abner. Stay home forever.

The house had loved him.

We'll make something together. Something that will last.

His house.

She rumbled now in a great crackling purr. Abner started towards the front door.

"Don't go in there, Abner," not-Jeff said. "I don't know if you'll ever be able to come back out."

"Maybe I don't want to," Abner said. "This is my home. I belong here. I never should've left."

"We are trying to help you, Abner—I promise. Please. Don't do this."

"You can't reach me," Abner said. "You can't get rid of me, as much as you want to."

"There was good in you, Abner, I know it. I've seen it. I've seen you love Ettie once. You loved your daughter once. Choose that. It's too late for you, but you can do something good if you leave this world peacefully. One small good thing. Choose something that gives you even the smallest shred of redemption. These people are innocent. They don't deserve your poison. They don't deserve the horror and hate that you inflicted—"

"Did you see how he looked at her?" Abner snarled and whirled to face Not-Jeff. "He's already mine."

Not-Jeff's eyes went wide then, and Abner turned back to the house, satisfied that the expression was the last of the being he would see.

"You'll *rot,* Abner. The parts of you that are human—the parts of you that used to be. The good parts. They'll fall away. The energy you left in this place, everything you did here—it's a disease. A *disease,* Abner, do you understand?"

"I'm not going," Abner said. "Whatever the hell you are, I'm not playing your stupid game."

Not-Jeff's energy hummed. Abner could no longer see it, but there was a pity in its tone, even though Not-Jeff was no longer in view, and Abner was sinking, sinking, *sinking* into the dirt.

Something exterior started to disintegrate, and then collapsed. He was no longer bound by the flesh that kept him human — by clothes, by laws of physics or gravity.

Abner sunk into the ground, and the electrifying energy of *His House* was embracing him and pulling him deeper, enveloping him. Finally, it seemed to say. *Finally, you are here with me,* and Abner was glad for the ground, was glad that he was no longer imprisoned above it. Not-Jeff's presence grew dimmer.

"Think of Ettie."

Abner did. Even if she hadn't left him, he had seen the way she looked at him, had seen the resentment glistening behind those eyes. He had given up everything for her, worked for her, provided for her, and she had never been grateful.

"Think of Ella," Not-Jeff pleaded, so far away now.

Abner intoned, and it was not so much speech as a hateful gurgling groan that seemed to croak out of his lungs without being filtered by throat or muscle.

You'll rot, Abner. Rot.

Abner thought of things that rot.

Meat, that would first turn gray and then wax fetid and swell until it was overrun with tiny little maggots, burrowing holes in the flesh.

An old tree, wasting away, being torn apart and digested by a hundred million different tiny organisms, dissolving it at a cellular level.

A corpse.

Ettie's corpse, Ella's corpse, his corpse.

Corpses that would forever succumb to the bloating, the insects, the stench. *Oh, the stench.* It was the one thing that held them all together, all living things. It was once easy to suppose that humans are some sort of superior organism, some sort of superior form of life. But when it comes to death and decay, everything that once held the elusive term we call *life* is vulnerable.

Trees. Fungus. Meat.

Human meat is still just meat. It is still vulnerable to bacteria, still vulnerable to mold, still vulnerable to yeast and heat and sweat.

These processes had already taken hold of Abner's old body, wherever it was, turning it into something that would feed the things that crept beneath the earth. It didn't matter how he had gone, how Ettie or Ella had gone. The creeping things would take them all. The creeping things in the cemetery were the same creeping things everywhere — in the park, in the sidewalks, underneath this very house.

Things always creep underneath the floorboards. Abner would become one of these creeping things, now, too.

What remained of his flesh was tingling with anticipation, with a pleasure so dark and so vibrant that he could hardly contain a groan. The energy clawed at him with frozen, twig-like fingers. It loved him. *It loved him.*

There was life in this house, and he could take hold of it. He could creep into it and turn it gray, take hold like bacteria over the things that were dying and press them further and further into decay. Abner's energy shivered at the thought, the sheer pleasure of the power he would derive from snaking his own tendrils into that man (vessel) upstairs. He could rot him from the inside out, play with him, pull him into Abner's ever-sinking *nothingness.* And then, maybe, *there will be others too.* He was alone — but he wouldn't be for long.

You'll rot, Abner, and the voice was no longer a voice but a memory that would soon rot too. Abner still vibrated, and it was as if the rotting things, the creeping things were in his very flesh now, taking over his consciousness.

You're home, Abner. 112 Fern St. said, and it was an electrifying sound. *Feel my bones. Feel my foundation. Feel the cement, the floorboards, the insulation in my walls. You're home.*

This is where you belong.

We will find you a new body.

We will make you strong.

It would be a pleasure to rot.

DESTROY ME
Kaos Emslie

The house at 113 Fern St. was dark and quiet at 3AM, just like most of the other structures on the street. Standing on the pavement, looking at it from the road, it was a typical house—four walls, a roof, windows, doors, and stairs leading up to the porch. The street lamp made shadows dance through the curtains onto the far wall of the bedroom. Lottie Kirkham gripped her chest as her heart raced. The nightmare still haunted her. She sucked down breath after breath, but to no avail. Shadows, like menacing claws, reached for her as she fled down the hall. The low, rumbling growl still shook the walls. It was the squeal of the faucet that finally snapped her back to reality. She splashed herself with ice-cold water to wash away the last pangs of adrenaline. Only then did her breathing slow.

When she was able to breathe normally, she turned the lights off and walked to the little room she and her husband had initially planned on being a nursery. After dozens of failed attempts, they decided to give up and turned the room into an office. Books lined the far wall, and in front of the window was her painting desk and easel. She went to the desk with the ancient computer.

She sat down in the desk chair. Leaning down, she

turned the tower on, then pressed the button on the monitor. She could feel, in her head, the screen buzzing as it turned on. They needed to replace this dinosaur.

She opened an internet browser, pulled up the search engine and started typing in her query:

Nightmares.

Thousands of results lined up for her. She narrowed it down to her specific nightmare.

Growling and grabbing in nightmares.

She scrolled through the results, but nothing made sense. She attributed this to her morning brain fog. She stood from the desk and left the room, heading for the kitchen downstairs. The hall was cast in shadows streaming in through the window, and she tried not to focus on what looked like hands reaching through the glass. She hurried past it and down the stairs to the first floor. The creaking of the stairs sent shivers up her spine and gooseflesh down her arms. When she made it to the kitchen, she flipped the switch on and slammed her back against the wall, her breathing back to gasps. She peeked around the corner, into the hall, and saw the entryway in question across from her. The darkness breathed, and the movement was palpable. She could feel something, someone, watching her from that darkness. They were there, waiting for her. She bit her lip and turned back to the kitchen, resting her head against the cool wall and closing her eyes.

After a few moments of deep breathing, she opened her eyes again. The clock on the wall over the sink read 4AM—it wasn't too early, she could get away with making coffee and starting her day now.

Lottie needed normalcy, something simple to keep her mind from focusing on whatever was going on across the hall. She pushed away from the wall and grabbed the coffee grounds and filled the pot with water. She started working on breakfast when movement from the corner of her eye caught her attention. Something had peeked around the corner at her from the hall. She stopped and turned, slowly, to look at the entryway.

There was nothing there. With a deep breath, she laughed at herself and turned back to the stove. It was residual fear from her nightmare. There was nothing there, she kept telling herself. She grabbed the little radio and turned it on, needing something to fill the silence of her early morning solitude. She fiddled with the knob until she found the classical station, then placed the radio on the counter near the coffeepot.

With breakfast done and plated, she set the table and made a cup of coffee for her husband. Without looking at the dark doorway across the hall, she slipped up the stairs with the cup and into their bedroom, where she set it beside his sleeping body and took a moment to admire his peaceful face. He was an amazing man. She had gotten lucky with him, she knew that. Things could have turned out so much worse than they had. She reached her hand out and pushed a few strands of hair aside, causing Norris to groan and open his eyes.

"I brought you coffee. Breakfast is ready," she whispered, leaning down to kiss him on the forehead. He offered a sleepy smile as he sat up and stretched.

"What time is it?"

"Four forty-five. I had another nightmare and couldn't get back to sleep." That was a lie, she hadn't even tried to go back to bed after waking up. She realized how frequently it was happening now—every other night. Norris looked at her through a veil of sleep-tousled hair, his tired eyes concerned. "I'll be fine. I can take a nap if I need to."

"You should talk to the doctor about these nightmares. Maybe see if there's something you can take for them." She flinched at the suggestion, and he let out a sigh. "You know that's not what I mean. They are going to start causing issues, Lottie—it's not wrong to ask for help."

"You know how I feel about medication."

"And therapy."

"I'm not crazy," she said, crossing her arms and looking away. The sun was starting to rise, sending rays of yellow and orange into the otherwise black sky beyond their bedroom curtains.

"I never said you were crazy. But you've been through some rough times, and trauma is a real thing that a lot of people deal with." He reached out and touched her shoulder, and she wanted to melt into his arms and stay there for the rest of time, but she was stubborn and refused to give in. She moved her shoulder out of his grasp and huffed.

"I have my coping methods, and they seem to be working just fine."

"Right. Well, I'm going to eat breakfast before it gets too cold. I'll see you downstairs?" She felt the bed shift as he stood and the air pressure in the room changed when he left. She could feel the loneliness in the room, and it scared her. She shivered against the feeling. She glanced around, making sure she was alone in the room, and when she was satisfied, she began getting ready for the day.

Monday

Lottie leaned over the sink, peering out the kitchen window into the side yard. She thought she had seen someone walk by, but apparently, it had been her imagination. With a sigh, she continued washing the dishes from breakfast. She peeked over her shoulder at the kitchen doorway, out to the hall and beyond to the living room entryway. It was still black, as if someone had drawn a curtain over it. Impenetrable shadows leaked out of the edges, threatening to reach for her.

The crash of a glass snapped her attention back to the sink and she shrieked. Shards sprayed out of the basin onto the counter and the floor. She gripped the edge of the counter to steady herself as she focused her mind on what was in front of her. Her nerves were shot. She reached for a washcloth and began gathering all the pieces of glass, then tossed them in the bin. She needed a break from reality.

The entryway followed her as she snuck up the stairs

to her shared bedroom. She kneeled beside her side of the bed and pulled out a small cigar box. Inside was a bag filled with pre-rolled joints. She pulled one out, grabbed her lighter, and went to the office. The shadows from downstairs threatened to come up to the second floor — she could see them from her perch on the windowsill. Reaching, begging for something, grabbing at the wallpaper and dragging their jagged nails through it until nothing was left but wisps hanging from the walls. They'd wreck this house, given the chance. She lit the joint and drew in a hit, holding it for a few seconds before letting it out with an audible sigh.

They receded. The darkness backed off enough to where she could see the sunshine coming through the window, shimmering across her paints and papers, inspiring her. She sat down in her chair and uncapped her paint water. Everything was already set up. She just needed to do it. Another night sky, with trees — this time with a full moon! Blues and purples. She sucked down another hit and held it longer until she coughed out the smoke and laughed at herself. She snuffed the joint in her ashtray and started work.

When she finished the painting, she set it aside and leaned back in her seat, her arms folded behind her head, satisfied with her progress. With a smile on her face, she looked out the window at the late afternoon sky, but something caught her attention in the reflection. A figure stood behind her, in the doorway. She turned, half-expecting her husband to be watching her from the hall

It stood there, black shadows dripping from its jagged fingers, a horrible grin splitting its face. Lottie screamed and stood from her chair, scrambling back against the bookshelf, and putting herself between the wall and her desk. She slid down to the floor, but the creature didn't break its gaze on her. She couldn't make out its eyes, and something about that terrified her more than the blood dripping from its teeth. It reached out, long fingers pointing at her, beckoning her, but she shook her head against it and screamed out again. She wouldn't go to it. She had to keep telling herself to stay still, don't look at it — if she looked, it could control her.

She sat there, scrunched up into the smallest ball she could muster, minute after dragging minute. Finally, Norris came home after what felt like hours of waiting, and Lottie screamed out for him. The creature was gone, she was free to move, but she was too terrified. She listened to him run up the stairs and watched his concerned face as he focused on her form on the floor. She wrapped her arms around his neck and let him carry her to their bed as she sobbed out her explanations. She wasn't sure she was making sense, but she also wasn't sure she cared much. He was home, he would save her. He would make sure the creature stayed away.

Tuesday

"Have a wonderful day at work!" Lottie waved at Norris from the front door. He waved back as he slid into their ancient wood-paneled station wagon. She watched as he pulled away from the curb and left her in the darkening doorway. She gave a genuine smile to the neighbors and offered waves to those who passed her as she stood in the sunny morning air. For a few moments, at least, she could feel normal.

She put a hand on the frame and gripped it tightly as she turned to look down the hall into the house. On the left, she could see the bright kitchen — on the right, the gloomy living room entryway shrouded in shadows. She closed the door and locked it, then moved to the left side of the hall and made her way down to the bright entry, shying away from the living room. Nothing could get her to go in there. It was a void, her home did not exist beyond the wood that framed the shadows.

She felt comfortable in the kitchen, safe in the yellow-wallpapered haven. She went to the freezer and pulled out a pound of hamburger meat for dinner — Taco Tuesday, how cliché, but it worked. She set the meat on the counter and turned around to survey the rest of the kitchen. It needed to be swept and mopped; the counters wiped down.

Lottie reached over the sink and turned on her portable radio. A loud crack and static came over the speaker. She winced at the sound and grabbed it to adjust the knob. As she moved it back and forth, trying to locate the classical station, a cacophony of whispers came through the speakers. She strained to hear them at first, but as they grew in volume, she was able to pick out one word:

Mommy...

She stopped and looked down at the radio in horror. The whispers continued, distorted and echoing through the speakers. It was like they surrounded her, filling the kitchen.

Mommy...

She threw the radio on the floor and backed up against the wall, her hands jerking to her ears. She wanted to hide from the voice, but there was nowhere to go in the kitchen. She was stuck, surrounded by the crackling growl.

Come here, Mommy...

She let out a scream and finally tore away from the wall and scrambled out of what was supposed to be her haven to the stairs. She shot up to the second floor, barely touching the steps, and made her way into the bedroom. She slammed into the closet and closed the doors against the still echoing sounds from the radio downstairs.

She stayed there until Norris opened the doors and reached down to help her up. An entire day spent hiding in the closet — she blushed as she tried to explain it to him, but her words came out jumbled and confused. He led her to the kitchen and poured her a glass of wine and sat with her as she calmed herself.

"The radio," she was finally able to say coherently. He looked behind her at the portable radio on the counter. "Someone said my name on the radio."

"That's strange, but I'm sure there's another Lottie

in this city."

"No, it wasn't on a station. I was turning the knob and this weird sound came out and then my name. It called me Mommy." She shoved her glass aside and buried her face in her hands, sobbing. "Why would it say that?"

"Maybe you imagined it? Did you smoke before you messed with the radio?" She knew he was trying to be helpful, but something in his tone felt accusatory. She bit her lip and narrowed her eyes.

"No, Norris, I wasn't high. And I am not crazy!" She jumped as the phone rang and was ashamed at how on edge she was. Norris went to the phone and answered it. He said a few quiet words into the receiver, then turned to her and held it out.

"It's for you."

Lottie slowly rose from her chair and made her way over to the counter. She grabbed the receiver from her husband and held it to her ear. At first, there was no sound, not even the crackle of the connection.

"Hello?"

The whispers started low, as if they were far away. She could barely make out what they were saying. She strained to hear them and pushed the receiver closer to her ear, trying to get a better angle to understand what they were saying.

"I can't hear you."

The same whispers from the radio grew louder, but they weren't saying anything she could understand. She narrowed her eyes, as if that would help her hear, and leaned forward on the counter. Norris stood beside her, his face knitted with concern. She could finally hear them, but there were so many voices she couldn't pick one out to pinpoint what they were saying.

Something was wrong. She could feel pinpricks in her feet, as if they had fallen asleep, leading up her legs. She was rooted to the spot, her body refused to move. She tried to put the phone down, but it was glued to her ear. The whispers began to even out, slowly, and words started to form.

It is time, Mommy…

Finally able to move, she threw the receiver down and screamed, her hands finding her hair, twining in between the strands, pulling until it came out. She pulled away from Norris as he tried to comfort her and returned to her wine, draining the glass. She sat in her chair and buried her face in her arms, tears streaming down her cheeks. She wanted to hide from them, but they echoed between her ears, the same sentence over and over again. She could see Norris's mouth moving, but his voice was lost somewhere in her mind's distorted and static void. All she heard were the whispers.

Wednesday

The afternoon sun streamed through the bedroom window and hit her in the face. Lottie drew the covers over her head and buried herself deeper in the surrounding pillows. She wanted to go back to sleep. She didn't want to get out of bed, but she couldn't spend all day under the covers. She threw them back and sat up, stretching her arms over her head. She stood from the bed and wrapped her robe tight around her body, belting it at her waist. The bathroom was her next stop.

The house was a vacuum, every little noise swallowed up by the shadows on the walls. She made her way to the stairs, but there was no sound to be heard. As she stood at the top of the staircase, staring down at the first floor, she felt something shift behind her. Something was standing behind her. She froze, trying not to startle whatever it was. As she took in a deep breath, she started to turn. Before she could catch herself on the railing, she was falling down the stairs. Head over feet, she tumbled down until she landed, crumpled on her side, on the first floor.

She went to stand, but something rushed at her and dragged her toward the dark living room. She kicked and pushed at whatever had a hold of her, but its grip was so tight it burned. As the darkness swallowed her, she could feel dozens of hands grabbing at her arms and legs. Fingers laced in her hair and pulled until she screamed, nails dug into her flesh as she struggled to get free. She could see the light of the hallway just beyond the doorway, so close but out of reach. She tried to scream, but every time she opened her mouth, hands would crawl inside and choke her.

"Lottie!" Norris's voice broke the silence and she was no longer lost in the void. His hands gripped her arms tightly to her sides as she struggled to free herself, but he wouldn't let her go. She looked around, frantic, her heartbeat racing in her chest. "Lottie stop! You're alright!"

She looked down and saw ribbons of blood decorating her arms and legs. She screamed and the sound was so loud in her ears that it made her eyes water. Norris wrapped his arms around her and held her to his chest, cooing at her, trying to calm her down as she heaved heavy breaths in and out.

Thursday

Lottie woke to an empty bed and sunlight peeking through the curtains. A still-warm cup of coffee sat on her nightstand and a short note rested beneath it. She read it and let a smile creep across her face. Norris was too good. She winced as she moved to grab the coffee, her heavily bandaged arms awkward. He had relented when she refused to go to the hospital, which was more than she could have hoped for. She knew they would have wanted to keep her, and she didn't want that. He had only dropped the pursuit because she had agreed to call a psychologist. And she would. She had made a promise, but that didn't mean she liked it. She didn't appreciate the insinuation that she was bad enough to need to talk to a professional.

Sitting up in the bed, coffee in hand, she breathed in the aroma of the liquid and let out a sigh. After a few sips, she set the cup back on the nightstand and stood from the bed. She stretched her arms over her head, careful not to twinge the wounds under the bandages.

With fresh clothes on her body and a quick trip to the bathroom, she almost felt ready to take on the day.

The shadows in the hallway didn't move or reach for her as she made her way to the stairs. As she stood at the top of them, looking down at the first floor, her vision blurred and she wobbled on her feet before catching herself on the railing. Gripping her coffee cup in her right hand, she took in a deep breath. It was okay. She took the first step down — nothing happened. Another step, and still nothing happened. Satisfied that she was safe, she walked down the stairs and into the kitchen.

The kitchen phone sat on the counter, mocking her. She picked up the receiver, then replaced it, repeating this motion three more times until she bit her lip and narrowed her eyes. She dialed the number Norris had written on the notepad beside the phone and waited. It rang and rang, and she was about to hang up when a woman came over the receiver.

"Doctor Lang's office. How may I help you?"

"Hi, hello," she started, her chest tightening. "My name is Lottie Kirkham. I need to set up an appointment."

"We've got a nine o'clock on Monday that just opened up." Oh, that was fast. She grabbed a pen and wrote the information down on the notepad.

"Yes, that works. Thank you."

"Bring your insurance cards and a picture ID, and arrive fifteen minutes early. We'll see you on Monday."

The line went dead before she could thank the woman.

She went to the refrigerator and pulled out the brisket and vegetables for dinner. Norris had already set the crock pot on the counter for her, along with the cutting board and a sharpened knife. She picked up the knife and thumbed the edge of the blade, caught for a moment in the reflection of the light on the stainless steel.

With the vegetables lined up, she began the process of chopping them. First, the potatoes were cut into quarters — she picked them up in handfuls and placed them in the bottom of the crock pot. Next, she lined up the carrots and began slicing through them. She closed her eyes and smiled. As she chopped, she met more resistance and a slight pain in her fingers caused her to open her eyes.

She looked down and, at first, the image didn't register. It took a moment for her brain to catch up with her eyes. There was blood, and the tips of flesh-colored carrots rested with the orange ones on the cutting board. And she couldn't stop cutting. She moved the knife up and felt the blade cut deep into her flesh, where it scraped against the bone as it pushed and dragged, forcing the pieces away from her hand.

Lottie let out a shrill scream, but even as she pulled away from the cutting board, she was rooted in place — she looked down and saw the clawed hands of the creature wrapped around her ankles, forcing her to stay where she was. She kept sawing through her fingers until they were in pieces on the cutting board, her blood pooling on the wood, dripping in rivers onto the floor around her feet.

Norris found her huddled in the corner between the table and the fridge, clutching her left hand as if it were mangled. He tried to show her that she was fine, but all she saw was her bloody stump of a hand and the bits she had cut off on the counter, still resting in the coagulating blood. He carried her to their bedroom and tucked her in for the night, but Lottie couldn't sleep knowing that her flesh was rotting in the kitchen downstairs.

Friday

The room was dark, save for the light from the street lamp coming in through the closed lace curtains. Lottie stirred, rolling from side to side, a grimace tugging at the corners of her mouth. She opened her eyes and sat up in bed, letting the comforter drop from her chest as she stared at the closet on the far wall.

Norris lay fast asleep, snoring beside her, and it made her wince to recall the argument they'd had before bed. She didn't want to hear him nag her anymore, so she crawled over him and rested on his lap, legs straddling his hips.

Something dark and angry stirred in the pit of her stomach. She could feel something stretching through her, up into her arms and neck, settling into her hands and head. She snaked her fingers up his chest until they rested on either side of his neck. For a moment, she looked at his sleeping face. He was so peaceful. She wanted to wipe the calm look off his face and make him scream and beg. Her fingers tightened around his throat, just a fraction at first, just enough to make his breathing skip. His eyes fluttered open.

"What are you—" She tightened her grip on his throat, cutting his words off. His hands flew to hers. He tried to pry her fingers off, but her grip was too tight. She continued to squeeze until he was choking and his eyes bulged from their sockets.

"You think you're so special," she growled. The voice that came out was not hers. It was deeper, more animalistic than she had ever heard a voice sound. "She doesn't need your help. I'll help her."

Lottie felt her arms weaken, and her eyes were so heavy now. She gave one final squeeze to her fingers and then Norris was able to push her aside. He jumped from the bed and backed against the wall, holding his throat, his eyes wide with fear and confusion. She felt her eyes close as she drifted back to sleep, caught in the darkness behind her eyes.

Saturday

The darkness whispered to her. Something scratched at the walls, the sound filling her ears. It called to her, and she answered. She slid out from under the covers and down the hall to the stairs. The wood creaked under her weight as she descended, the scratching louder. Shadows surrounded her on the first floor, drawing her closer to the living room entryway. As she stepped up to it, she began whispering.

"It's coming. It's coming now. It's almost here."

The words meant nothing to her, she couldn't understand them. The scratching echoed in the night, coming from the walls and floor. It surrounded her. She tried to scream, but the void held her captive and she remained standing in front of it, eyes staring into it, her voice whispering into the blackness.

Sunday

She looked on from the doorway. The garage was a jumble of projects Norris hadn't finished yet, and he was starting a new one. He was building another bookshelf for the office. Lottie ran her fingers up and down the rough wood of the frame as she watched him work. It was almost like watching a movie from behind her eyes. She moved forward, but it didn't feel real, as if she were moving through a pool of thick fluid, pushing toward the workbench to her left. When she finally stepped up to it, her legs wobbled under her weight and she had to steady herself against the bench.

Her fingers went straight for the circular saw, and she rubbed them against the blade, feeling the bite of the cold metal nip into her flesh. Yes, this was what she wanted. This was what the creature wanted. She lifted the saw off the rack and plugged it into the power strip. As she turned it on and the sound filled the room, Norris jumped and turned around, his eyes wide with confusion.

"Lottie, what are—" She cut him off with a loud cackle as she raised the saw and brought it down on his shoulder. Blood sprayed into her face and coated her arms as she raised it again and went for the other side. He screamed, the sound so loud she could hear it over the tool. He couldn't move his arms now, but he was trying to scoot away from her the best he could. She lashed out with the power tool and cut through his shirt, slicing into his belly. It was only a superficial wound. Nothing came spilling out as she had hoped. She needed to get closer.

Lottie jumped forward, landing with her feet on either

side of her husband, and she raised the saw over her head. She needed to do this. She dropped the blade onto his head and watched as it cut through his skull, sending little bits of bone and brain matter into the air.

The deed completed, she backed away from her husband's corpse and put her back flat against the far wall. She looked down at the saw, still spinning, still shrieking in her ears, and understood what was wanted of her. She lifted the blade, ran it across her throat, and then dropped it. This was necessary. As her blood spilled from her neck to pool around her limp body, she had a moment of clarity. They were not the first, nor would they be the last, to fall victim to this house.

114
THE RED LADY
Jason A. Jones

At 3AM the bleeding woman stood at the end of Jenny's bed, screaming in the house on 114 Fern St. The little girl covered her face, her eyes wide and watering underneath her threadbare Sesame Street blanket. Through it, she could see the old lady's bloody grin, her eyes rolling into the back of her head. A few minutes passed and Jenny managed to crawl out of her bed and escape through the bedroom door. She hurried down the staircase where her mother sat, falling in and out of sleep in a recliner, trying to read.

"Mommy?" Jenny said, her eyes looking towards the blackness up on the staircase landing.

"What are you doing, Jenny? You're supposed to be in bed." She lovingly caressed her daughter's cheek. Jenny was hot and her pajama top felt too tight around her neck. She held her blanket close to her chest. Finally, she crawled into her mother's lap and whispered in her ear.

"The Red Lady is smiling at me."

Brenda felt the room go cold. Icy, skeletal fingers caressed her spine, and she laid her book beside her slowly. Jenny huddled close to her mother, her small hands and arms reached around Brenda's waist and squeezed like rubber bands. She looked at her daughter and tried very hard to keep her composure. She couldn't display any fear. She had to protect Jenny, but who would protect her?

"Wanna build a fort on my bed?" Brenda managed a smile, hoping Jenny would feel at ease. She did. With Jenny in tow, Brenda walked towards her bedroom and opened the door. She turned her head as she led Jenny inside the room and shuddered to see eyes floating in the darkness at the top of the stairs. Brenda locked her bedroom door.

Throughout the rest of the night, Brenda tossed and turned while Jenny lay next to her, the Sesame Street blanket wrapped around her tiny body. The clock displayed 5:30 AM and she took a sip of the bottled water on her nightstand. She slowly slid across the bed and lowered her feet onto the floor, tiptoed to the door, looking over her shoulder to see if her daughter was still asleep. She was.

Within the moonlit living room, Brenda could hear the creaking of feet on the wooden floor. She thought she heard groans and crying coming from her surroundings. All of a sudden, deadly silence filled the air, and she knew The Red Lady was in the blackness, waiting.

As she crept silently through the house, something sinister gurgled from the shadows.

"Hello, child," a thick, gravelly voice called. The voice was hideous, and Brenda's skin became gooseflesh. Her hand slowly reached for the lamp by her recliner and turned it on. Sitting in the chair was an old lady in a bloody nightgown. She was smiling hideously. This grotesque thing sat there, blood and pus running down her chin and neck into her wrinkled cleavage. Brenda instantly recognized her.

It can't be, it just can't be. The thought raced quickly in her mind and she stood in place, glaring into the eyes of her dead mother.

"Yes, little girl, it's me. You know why I'm here."

"No, please. Please don't take her." Brenda knew her

pleading would go nowhere.

"You are the same whimpering little bitch you always were! I should've killed you when I had the chance!" the old woman screamed into the darkness. Brenda's blood ran cold, and she knew this couldn't be her mother. Her mother was gentle and kind, and always there when Brenda needed her. Brenda didn't need or want this evil thing before her now.

"I'm taking your little brat that's lying in your bed right now," the woman whispered, a widening smile engulfing her face. She stood and approached Brenda, blood running from her lips, mottling her gown. Brenda was frozen in place, her hands at her side, eyes staring into this monster before her.

Please…

In the bedroom, Jenny let out a blood-curdling scream.

Now The Red Lady stood at the end of Brenda's bed, her head tilted like a dog. Jenny's eyes were wide and terrified, and she could feel the heat of urine escaping through her clothing.

"Don't be afraid," the creature said. "It's so wonderful where we are going. It's a forever place filled with constant delights beyond your wildest imagination. You don't want to be here, do you, Jenny, my sweet?" The Red Lady's voice was deep and frightening. Her eyes blackened, and she walked slowly to the edge of the bed, where Jenny was huddled under her blanket. She kneeled down beside the child, her hot, hideous breath spewing onto her skin, dampening it.

Brenda screamed from the living room and she fell to the floor, her legs refusing to move. Little by little, she began to crawl. The thing that wasn't Brenda's mother came close to Jenny and whispered in her ear.

"You don't need her. I remember when you were in that cunt's belly; I wanted to rip you right out of her!" It laughed and spit. Jenny stared into the darkness of the creature's eyes, the evil behind them piercing and menacing.

Brenda managed to get up on all fours and lift herself, holding the edge of her recliner. She struggled, finally reaching the kitchen, where she pulled a butcher knife from the wooden block sitting on the counter. She headed toward the bedroom and opened the door. The Red Lady's mouth was open wide, and she was trying to eat the little girl.

In an instant, Brenda hurled herself toward the thing, burying the knife deep in its back. It howled, flailing its arms. One of the arms swung wide and struck Brenda in the face, knocking her to the wall. She got up and attacked the old lady again, shoving the knife deeper and deeper until all that was left was a bloody handle.

Jenny was screaming now, and the thing was clawing at her, ripping her Sesame Street blanket. Brenda could see the terrified look in her daughter's eyes. It was enough to send her on a rampage. She jumped on the creature's back and dug her fingers deep into its eye sockets. It hissed and screamed, frothing blood and long strands of saliva fell from its horrid mouth.

"You'll never have her! Run, Jenny!" Brenda screamed.

Jenny grabbed her torn blanket and ran for the bedroom door and escaped into the living room, her tiny legs taking her to the staircase. She raced to the top and into her bedroom she went, slamming her door. Horrible screams emanated from below, and she hoped her mother would be okay.

Jenny crawled to bed and waited, her fingers gripping her only friend, which by now was just a ragged, torn piece of cloth. She looked at it, horrible sobs escaping her lips. A bloody likeness of the Cookie Monster was smiling and staring at her with his large, lifeless eyes.

"You fucking little bitch!" the monster screamed as she tore Brenda off of her, throwing her on the floor. Brenda's head hit the floor with a thud and she saw stars. The monster was on all fours now, crawling toward her. It was naked and its entire body was covered in blood, the knife sticking out of its back. It slithered slowly like a snake, making bloody trails on the floor.

It finally stood and hovered over Brenda, who was now getting her bearings.

"You're not…my mother," Brenda whispered, her breath labored. The creature bent down beside her and caressed her daughter's face, its lips forming upward into what resembled a mother's gentle smile. Brenda turned her head. The hideous thing forced her head towards it, dirty fingernails digging into her jaw.

"This is futile, dear one. The inevitable is going to happen." Calmly, The Red Lady leaned her grotesque mouth to Brenda's ear and hissed, "She's mine now."

Suddenly and unexplainably, Brenda wasn't sure if it was a dream or a nightmare in what she was seeing, but the creature before her eyes was now her mother, the way she remembered. The eyes were as blue and calm as a cloudless sky and her skin was radiant. Blond hair flowed from her head, and the smile was definitely gentle now. There was no more blood or gore coming from her lips. She lifted her daughter from the floor and hugged her for dear life.

"This has to be, you know that, right?" her mother said, arms around her tightening. Brenda could feel digging in her back as if small knives were cutting her skin. She could feel dampness across her backside, small grunts escaping her mouth.

"There, there now. It'll be over soon," the mother thing said, claws continuing its course through Brenda's skin. "I love you," the creature gurgled. Brenda struggled in her weakened state, but it was too strong and she slowly gave in to the monster's desire. After a while, she accepted her fate and made her way to Jenny's bedroom.

"Honey, it's Mommy, are you okay? Everything is over now," Brenda said. The door creaked a little and Jenny peered through the crack. She opened the door and reached for her mother without hesitation, the tattered blanket still in her hands. They held each other for a long time and Jenny knew she was going to be okay. Jenny yawned as she laid her head against her mother's shoulder.

"Let's get some sleep, babe." Brenda carried the little girl to her bed and covered her up. Jenny continued her slumber, dreaming a funny dream about Oscar the Grouch and how the Cookie Monster was playing a game with Kermit the Frog to get some chocolate chip cookies. While she slept, her mother watched over her at the foot of the bed with a horrid bloody smile across her face.

$$\underline{\quad\quad 115 \quad\quad}$$
TOLD YOU SO
Torrence Bryan

I told them not to build the house at 115 Fern St.

I told them countless times.

I showed up at every town hall and council meeting I could. Posted signs, sat on the curb, sometimes alone, sometimes with a friend. Days passed, then weeks. Seasons changed. My broken arm healed. The bruises on my face slowly disappeared. The internal damage would take a bit more time.

The emotional scars would take even longer.

I sat. I sat, and I waited, and I protested, and I complained. I tried to explain. I told them what would happen if they continued. But in their eyes, the plot of land was empty. A blank slate in the neighborhood. A fresh start for a young family.

And so the house at 115 Fern St. was built, despite my moans and arguments. Despite every road block I put in their way.

The house was built, spring gave way to summer, and up, up, up the building sprang. An outside source might see it as a beautiful home. The perfect place to raise fat-cheeked babies and watch them grow into long-legged children. Two stories, with grand windows, and a massive porch. Rich mahogany siding, and a pretty white front door ready for the seasonal wreaths. Neighbors next door that smiled and waved, and a perfect white picket fence across the street.

I saw it for what it really was. A grave.

The first family moved in, even as I sat and protested.

They lasted three months. Three months until the mother was the last one standing, tearing out of the door in the middle of the night, crying that something was wrong with the house. It was alive. It had taken her children, her husband, and it was out to get her. The walls were painted with blood, dripping. Something had been screaming, something horrible. Inhuman. A sound she would never forget.

Silly, really. The idea that a house was alive. But the story stuck, the mother found herself a nice place with padded white walls, and the house was declared cursed.

I thought that would be enough. That it had proved me right. That they now knew that the house shouldn't be lived in. But the realtors simply dropped the price and twisted their words, and soon enough, another family with another moving truck was rolling up to the house. The house that should've never been built.

So much unique character! A home where three people were killed, and one was committed. Definitely different.

Floor to ceiling windows! Windows where the daughter had hung, her body swinging, until the police made it inside to cut her down.

Fresh paint! Freshly painted to cover up the blood that streaked every wall—the blood the mother screamed so loudly about.

I tried not to worry too much about it. They would learn their lesson soon enough.

I sat and watched it all. Sometimes from up close, sometimes from far away. I'd watch them go about their lives, eating dinner together like the perfect family. They'd go to school and work, never realizing they were living on borrowed time.

So here I sat, now. This was the third family to move

in, or was it the fourth? I couldn't remember. None of them lasted long. You'd think they would learn their lesson after a while. That people would stop buying the house, quit moving their families into a place where other families met their gruesome demise. But with each horror the house experienced, the house just got cheaper. And families got more willing to forgo their morals for *a bargain you'd never again see.*

A chance to leave a legacy for your family.

I wondered if the first family that moved in thought that. That they were leaving a legacy for their children, only for it to be snatched out of their grasp for trying to build a life on tainted ground.

Enough space for Grandma to stay!

Grandma had been staying with the second family when the whole bloody ordeal went down. The newspapers picked up on that tidbit, blasting it around until everyone and their neighbor knew that Grandma had tried to escape out the second-story window, breaking first her leg, and then her neck on the way down. The mailman found her in the morning, his scream alerting the neighbors, who called the police.

A piece of me felt bad for family number four—it was definitely four, wasn't it? They thought this was the start of their lives. A new home, ready and waiting for them. And wasn't it *a bargain?* Could they believe they were here? That all of this was *theirs?*

But I tried to tell them. I tried to tell all of them. And none of them ever listened. But I had to try. For Robbie's sake.

You see, Robbie wouldn't have minded. He was always good like that, easy-going, with a ready smile. Nothing fazed Robbie. That's what he had me for. His mother always said we were a good match. That he needed a girlfriend with a backbone to offset his happy-go-lucky attitude.

We weren't just a good match. We were the perfect match. We were going to get married, spend our lives together, have beautiful children, like the family moving in now. They should be us.

But that couldn't happen, because I'm here watching the family move in, while Robbie's lean body decomposes under the dirt. The only thing I couldn't protect my sweet, perfect boyfriend from was what we couldn't see — black ice on the road. I watched him swerve, over-correcting his mistake. I saw what was going to happen seconds before it played out. There was nothing I could do. Robbie's scream split the night air sharper than the ice we skidded on.

Robbie wouldn't have minded that they built this perfect house on top of where he died that night. Because Robbie was good like that. He would've wanted the families to be happy, content. To have made a good memory out of something so tragic. Me, though? I have to protect him.

I told them not to build a house at 115 Fern St.

Now I sit here, hidden by the wide front porch — *perfect for watching the world go by in a rocking chair as the sun sets* — the axe gripped tightly in my hands. It's like an old friend. A dance I've done a dozen times before, and I'll do a dozen times again.

I told them not to build a house at 115 Fern St.

Now I'll make sure they realize their mistake.

DIMINISHING RETURNS
Derek Heath

The attic was locked.

There were enough problems with the new house that Rob scarcely found the time to look up, let alone consider the fact that there might be an entire storage space or even another bedroom up there. 116 Fern St. was subsiding, ever-so-slowly sinking into the ground—something that the surveyor had only discovered on his second assessment, three days after Rob had signed the preliminary contract—and among other things, trying to gauge the extent of the problem had kept him fairly busy for most of the week. Not only was the entire property destined to burrow its way into the earth within the next eighty years, but the kitchen desperately needed ripping out and replacing, and the upstairs bathroom was a wreck.

"Hi, love," he said wearily into the crook of his neck, bent up in the cupboard beneath the sink. The phone was crushed into the sweaty space between his cheek and his collarbone, and he could barely hear Hayley's voice through the erratic squawks of static in his ear. There was something about the service 'round here. Yet another fucking thing. "Yeah, I got your picture. I did. It looks great, love. You look beautiful."

He had asked about the attic when he'd first viewed the house, enamored by the traditional brickwork fireplace in the lounge and the spacious bedrooms upstairs, and had received a fairly vacuous answer. Since then, he'd forgotten all about it. He'd sunk a good three-hundred grand into this place with the expectation of making three-fifty once the renovations were done.

"I am listening," he grunted, twisting the wrench in the dark space beneath the sink. With one eye closed, he thrust his elbow into the corner of the cupboard, immediately gluing a clump of dusty cobweb to his cracked, red skin. "No, I mean it. It's a beautiful dress. And it doesn't—"

Another round of static buzzed in his ear and he sighed.

"—doesn't have to look exactly like your wedding dress, no, that's what I was saying. Yeah. Yeah, I know. Yeah. Okay, but we're only renewing our vows, we don't have to recreate…"

He closed his eyes as a bright bolt of pain crisscrossed the back of his skull. He had another migraine coming on.

"Listen, love, I think you're beautiful. Really. Always. And it's a really nice dress. No, I… no, I didn't mean 'only' renewing."

He backed up out of the cupboard, stifling a yelp as he reared up too quickly and smashed the top of his head on the frame. Clamping a hand down over the sore spot, he stumbled back into the kitchen, looking out onto the street. The houses across the road were little more than vague silhouettes in the fading sun, boughs of gold tinging the bottoms of deep pink clouds. The sun was already slipping away from him.

"I love you too, sweetie," he said. "Not long now, all right? I promise I'll be done with this shithole in a few weeks, and then I'll be more helpful with all the invitations and—oh. I didn't realize you'd done it, I'm sorry. Yeah. Yeah, I will. All right. Bye."

He turned around, rubbing the crown of his head as

deep, throbbing waves of agony swelled through the spongy tissue of his brain.

116 was a bit of a fixer-upper, but it shouldn't have been anything he hadn't dealt with before. He'd made calls to all the right contractors, lined up a couple potential buyers before he'd even started work—this should have been a six-month job, tops. Six months' work, a few hundred cups of coffee, and thirty-thousand dollars profit. Easy.

If only the damn house wasn't caving in like everything else around him.

* * *

Rob stood at the bottom of the stairs with his *White Buffalo* cap wedged on his head and a steaming mug of coffee in his hand. His shirtsleeves were rolled up past the elbows and his arms were caked with grease, knuckles flashing white through the cracked smudges of oil on his hands. The knees of his overalls were stained green. He had momentarily zoned out as he wandered absent-mindedly from the kitchen to the staircase, and as he tipped the mug up to his mouth to drink, his eyes flitted to the ceiling.

The hatch was embedded in the plasterwork, the wood and frame pale-white and almost indiscernible from the rest of the ceiling; were it not for the brassy glint of the padlock, he would not have registered that he was looking directly at it.

"Huh," he murmured, lowering the mug. Around him, a mess of flaky plaster pieces and shredded scraps of wallpaper littered the hallway floor. The carpet had been torn up and the floorboards beneath were rough and pale. Here and there, tiny nails poked up through the wood.

Setting his coffee on the floor, Rob reached into his overalls for the hammer swinging against his hip. He withdrew it, his eyes still on the hatch. A long-handled claw hammer, its head speckled with rust.

Climbing up to the landing, he retrieved a stepladder from the bedroom and unfolded it, placing it directly beneath the hatch and struggling up onto the top step. His big feet clumsily balanced on the step, a sudden surge of vertigo nearly sending him backward.

Without sparing the padlock a glance, Rob punched the hammer upward and smashed the head right into the bolt to which the glinting brass thing had been attached. There was a sound like the ricochet of a bullet in one of his dad's favorite Clint Eastwood movies and the bolt keened into itself, folding into a right angle. This sound was followed by the dull tinkle of the padlock hitting the rungs of the stepladder as it fell, then the *thwump* of it sinking into the carpet.

Gingerly, Rob tucked the hammer into his overalls and reached up to push open the hatch.

It was a phenomenal effort to haul himself up into the attic, and he was out of breath when he finally bundled his legs over the edge and rolled onto his back. Only now did he realize that it was almost entirely dark up here, the only light coming from down below; slowly he sat up, giving his eyes time to attune to the pitch. Eventually he made out the thin snag of a frayed cord hanging above the open hatchway, and he leaned forward to tug it sharply.

Light exploded into the attic and flickered. Dull blossoms of amber washed the rafters.

Rob crouched awkwardly, immediately deflating when he saw that the attic was only half the size of the bedroom and about a third of the height; indeed, the rafters slanted inward at such an angle that even perched on his ankles right in the middle of the loft, his head thumped the ceiling. So much for a third bedroom. In fact, he thought, blinking as the flickering light assaulted his eyes, there wasn't much room for storage either: even the previous owner had only left a couple boxes here, stuffed against the back wall.

Curious, he crawled around the hatch and fought his way toward the boxes. He was acutely aware that the day was running away from him again, but there were only so many hours per day that he could waste deciding whether to spend a few more thousand dollars on resin injections and underpinning or just try and convince the buyers that the place would still be standing when they retired. A minute away from it all wouldn't hurt.

He spent far longer than necessary trying to pick away the tape securing the first box before deciding to rip the lid off instead. Inside was a selection of porcelain mugs and figurines, carefully wrapped in newspaper. He tucked them back in, largely disinterested in the contents but aware that even stuff like this could be worth something; crockery was more Hayley's forte. He'd have to call her this evening and ask her about the mugs.

The second box was more difficult to open; whoever had stored them up here—presumably the same person who'd locked the attic—had taped all around the corners and edges so that he had to spend a full ten minutes gradually ruining his nails in an attempt to get inside. Eventually, he found a lip in the tape casing and worked his way in.

More newspaper. He sighed softly, expecting more figurines. Still, what was he hoping for? A few grand bundled up nicely? A couple gold bars?

Digging into the newspaper, he recoiled as his hand brushed something cool and wet. "What the—"

No.

Not wet, he realized, wiping his hand on his overalls. *Scaly.* More cautiously this time, he poked at the newspaper and burrowed a small hole until he could see what was hidden inside. Polished leathery scales glittered in the dim light of the attic: he caught a glimpse of a yellowed, serrated tooth. A flash of gold.

"Holy balls," he whispered.

✳ ✳ ✳

The kitchen was a mess. The cupboard doors were gone, exposing the hollowed-out cavities beyond; the tiles had been ripped up and the new tiling had only begun to creep out from one corner in the past few days, forgotten as he spent hours on the telephone with contractors who told him, time and time again, exactly what he already knew: that by the time they were through with the underpinning, the house on Fern Street would have cost him more than he could afford to lose.

He cleared the table quickly, shunting everything onto the floor and planting the thing from the attic right in the middle of the new, hastily polished space. Now Rob stood in the kitchen doorway, staring into its eyes. His stomach twisted nervously as it stared back.

As far as he could tell, the thing was real.

It was enormous, but still he got the feeling that it had only been a juvenile when it had been killed. There was a shallow black scorch-mark between the ridges around its eyes that he imagined was the carefully treated scar of a gunshot wound. Tiny, almost imperceptible stitches around the stump of its neck, sealing the polished bone and stuffing inside.

It was disgusting.

His guts turning with revulsion, Rob reached for the phone in his pocket and dialled quickly. Holding it to his ear, he kept his eyes on the thing and swallowed.

After a moment, he hung up.

Take a moment, he thought. *Really* think *about this, before you do anything stupid.*

The alligator head watched him, its mighty jaws split open by a cruel, ululating grin.

It was three times the size of his own head, with a great flat snout exploding into a mess of smashed ivory teeth. The lips and gums were a pale, sickly yellow, the inside of the mouth a black hole. The leathery skin was ridged and spiky in places, such a dark emerald that it was almost black too. Flared nostrils were framed by frilled horns; the paler scales of the thing's lower jaw and neck were smooth and speckled with brown.

Its eyes had been removed and replaced with two perfectly spherical balls of solid gold.

Each was an inch and a half across and sunk perfectly into the spiny mounds of the thing's brow, glinting viciously in the light of the kitchen. Some of the teeth had been replaced too, and little curved spears of shining yellow protruded from the thing's stuffed, leathery gums as though they had grown there naturally.

A beat, and then Rob lurched for the kitchen counter. Swiping aside a couple of empty takeout containers, he fumbled for the cutlery drawer, digging around inside with a dreadful rattle before clamping his fingers around a plastic-handled teaspoon. Whirling around, he faced the grinning alligator head and swallowed.

"This won't hurt a bit," he said, and he surged forward.

Gritting his teeth, Rob clamped one hand down on the alligator's skull, right between the eyes where the bullet had entered its brain. With the other he poked forward with the teaspoon, thrusting it into the tiny sliver of black between the first golden eyeball and the scales that erupted into irregular whorls around it. There was a wet slithering sound, and the teaspoon curved around the back of the gold ball. With a grunt, Rob slammed the heel of his hand forward—

The alligator's golden eye flew out of the socket, punching into the wall behind him and dropping to the floor, where it rolled between his feet. Triumphantly, Rob grinned, bending down to pick it up.

The house trembled.

He froze, doubled over with his fingers splayed around the gold ball. For a moment, he thought he must have imagined it in his excitement, but then the house shuddered a second time.

An earthquake?

Now?

Rob grabbed the golden eyeball and straightened up, slipping it into his overalls. His eyes moved to the window above the sink: outside, the low roofs of the houses across the road were still. Number 116 was still. He *had* imagined it.

His attention dropped to the alligator head, and he balked.

A steady stream of gluey, bright red drizzled from the empty eye socket he had raided.

He could swear the thing's grin had widened a little.

* * *

Rob slept uneasily on the mattress in the smaller bedroom, eight inches off the carpet and tucked awkwardly into a striped Lifesavers sleeping bag. The house would be sold unfurnished, of course, but he regretted not ordering a cheap bedframe for his temporary living quarters. Every day that he grew more deeply involved in the chaos that was saving Number 116 from the ground, he became more certain that he never should have bought the damn place; all his buyers had backed out, and even the contractors he'd hired seemed reluctant to do work around here for anything less than the asking price of the property itself. What the hell was it about Fern Street that made people so goddamn *scared?*

He woke up a little after midnight to the sound of slithering in the bedroom wall.

Rob's eyes snapped open. The room was dark, only the faintest halo of moonlight filtering in through the blinds and dappling the carpet with spangles of dim gray-blue. His skin was drenched in sweat and he shivered as he instinctively grabbed for the sleeping bag, tightening the casing around him. For a full minute he lay there, groggy and half-dazed, wondering if the sound that had woken him up had been a part of his dream.

Another minute passed, and the wall shuddered again.

Rob bolted upright, wheeling as the mattress sagged beneath him. The sound was like something enormous and long snaking through the cavity in the wall: he heard the scuffling of rats amplified by a thousand, and then the *smack* of a long, leathery tail against a supporting iron rod. He turned his head to look in the direction of the sound, but it was moving fast: before he could pinpoint the location of the thing in the walls, it had scuttled toward the landing and disappeared.

Silence.

"What the fuck…"

Rob heaved himself out of the sleeping bag and staggered half-blind across the room, his boxers clinging to him, gray tee soaked with sweat. Rubbing grit out of one eye, he paused on the landing and listened. A few beats passed, and he realized he was swaying gently, his legs fatigued from the day's work.

Nothing. He had imagined it. "Oh, for fuck's sake," he whispered, turning around to get back into bed. He paused, realizing he needed to relieve himself and deciding instead to head for the bathroom. Might as well, while he was up. He'd only have to go in a couple hours, anyway.

As he turned for the bathroom, something scuffled in the wall across from him. His head snapped round and he followed the wet, slithering smacking sound as it boomed across the stairs. There was something moving in there; it dragged itself loudly downward, and he lowered his gaze, following it down, down to the entrance hall…

"No," he muttered. Jesus Christ, on top of everything else… was he really going to have to call in pest control?

He thundered down the stairs, following the sound toward the front door. Here it paused before the thing in the walls careened in the opposite direction, heading past the kitchen and lounge to the small downstairs bathroom. It was larger than a rat, that was for sure. Moving like a snake, its body scraping the edges of the crawlspace as it sluggishly plowed through the plaster.

"Are you shitting me?" Rob called angrily, refusing to acknowledge the fact that the rat-cum-badger-cum-elephant in the walls probably couldn't understand him. "I'm renewing my vows in a fucking week and I need this house *done,* you hear me?"

The sound stopped.

The house was still; only now did he realize that it had been trembling around him. Quickly he moved into the bathroom, sharply tugging the cord to turn on the light. Cringing as it flooded the room, he surveyed the walls, breathing heavily.

The thing was gone.

Well, fuck it. As long as that thing—whatever it was—kept quiet while the realtors were showing buyers around, he could deal with it.

* * *

In the morning, he pried loose the second golden eyeball and the rest of the teeth. Wrapping the lot of them in a sandwich bag and tucking it into his pocket, he drew in a deep breath and locked eyes with the defiled alligator head on the kitchen table. It stared blankly back at him.

There must have been a pound and a half of gold in that sandwich bag. If it was solid, like he thought, then…

Well, then everything would be different.

"Back in a while, crocodile," he quipped dully, then he swiped his keys from the table and turned to leave for the jewelers'.

* * *

Rob was halfway across the drive when he saw the monster in the backseat of his car.

"What the…"

He froze, the keys for the old Jazz gripped tightly in one hand. Within moments the knuckles had turned bone-white, but he didn't notice, his gaze locked on the rear window of the little hatchback.

Bright hungry eyes looked back at him from inside, the piercing yellow scarcely dulled by the greasy rheum coating the glass. The shape curled up in the backseat was enormous and somewhere in the terrified goop of his brain, a voice screamed out that this insane thing was real; it had to be, because the weight of it had made the back of the car sag right down onto its axles so that it was almost scraping the tarmac. As it reared up its head, the hatchback's suspension jounced with an awful squealing sound. The creature was a titan of black scales and ridged, bumpy spines, its tail slung over the headrest of the driver's seat, its jaws puffing great blooms of vapour onto the inside of the window.

The creature grinned, flashing dozens of sharp white

points.

Rob cursed under his breath.

Then the beast's gargantuan snout plowed forward, and the window shattered, a great bellowing roar exploding from the darkness inside the car. Rob staggered backward, awkwardly fumbling for the front door key as a spray of glass and scales showered the tarmac. The car tipped forward, and the shape slithered out through the ragged hole, jaws clamping shut hard and then opening wide, impossibly wide, head swinging from side to side as thunder rumbled in its throat —

Eyes locked on the beast's impossible maw, Rob scrambled for the lock and the door swung open, nearly dragging him onto his butt in the hallway. The alligator thrashed its tail as it crashed onto the drive, smashing a great volcanic dent into the side of the car. Then it was moving toward him, slamming its enormous claws into the tarmac and propelling its low, black body forward.

The door slammed shut just as the creature snapped its jaws. Rob yelped as it punched into the wood behind him and the whole front wall of the building shuddered.

"Fuck!"

He scrambled for the nearest window and yanked back the curtains, almost slamming his face into the glass as he looked desperately outside.

Nothing there.

The car was empty, the window unbroken. Rob's attention was momentarily snatched away from his own driveway and he glanced toward the house across the road; 115's front yard was a hive of chaotic energy and swelling red-blue lights. He hadn't heard the siren above the mania pumping through his body, but he saw now that there was an ambulance parked on the curb, that they were loading something into the back. Something bent and broken.

Not his problem, he thought bitterly, his mind racing a million miles an hour, and he returned his attention to his own car. There were no shapes in the backseat — nothing on the drive, either, though he could smell the dank swamp water that coated the creature's spiny back, the thick ripe meaty scent of its breath…

"What the fuck is happening?" he breathed, glancing at the door. He could have sworn the weight of the beast had splintered the wood panels into ruins.

The door was untouched.

❋ ❋ ❋

Rob hunched over the toilet bowl, the acrid taste of bile in his mouth, his stomach churning violently. His skin felt cold and clammy and the hands that gripped the edges of the bowl were pale. He could almost see tinges of blue in his nail beds.

Nothing else came up, his stomach having emptied itself fully in the last half hour or so. Wearily, he eased himself into a half-standing position. Then, unable to sustain that for more than a minute, plonked his rear onto the toilet seat.

There was a gurgle from the water beneath him. Almost imperceptible, like the minute sound of a tadpole swimming about in the bowl. He didn't notice.

Absent-mindedly, Rob reached into his pocket, searching for his phone. It was probably about time to give Hayley another call. Tell her that he'd be coming home this weekend. Whether the house was finished or not, he wanted out of here. They could push back the sale for a while; wasn't like anyone was biting *(ha!)* anyway. And so what if they couldn't afford to go on the second honeymoon they'd planned? Hawaii had been great the first time, but right now, all he could really remember was the awful food poisoning he'd gotten.

Another gurgle from deep within the U-bend, a meaty belch that sent ripples through the water.

Rob's fingers brushed the sandwich bag in his pocket, and he paused before digging it out. Inside, two golden balls and a collection of twenty-four-karat teeth, jostling against each other as he massaged the bag in his hands. They shone brightly in the unpleasant bathroom light.

Was this the problem? Had he messed with something he didn't understand?

"Don't be a fucking idiot," he murmured, shoving the gold pieces back into his pocket.

Inches from his rump, something thin and dark grinned in the toilet bowl. A juvenile, its face narrower and paler, its eyes no less hungry.

"You're just tired," he whispered, clamping his hands over his temples. "Tired of this fucking house, this fucking street, tired of fucking *life,* you're not—"

A sudden bolt of movement as he stood up, face flashing red with anger. Absent-mindedly, he reared back to slam his hand down on the flush. The explosion of water in the toilet satisfied him somewhat, though he didn't see the dark, wide-jawed shape slipping back down the U-bend, retreating with its long, slender tail coiled around its claws.

"Get off your butt," he told himself a little redundantly, "and sort yourself out. You're going crazy, that's all."

He turned to the sink and screamed as it exploded off the wall, the long jaws of an alligator hatchling snapping around his wrist as its slim, black body shot out of the tiles in a gush of hot, swampy water. The sink smashed into the bathtub as a bright hot pain shot up his arm and Rob staggered back, eyes widening in horror as another hatchling, slightly bigger than the first, slithered out of the gaping crack in the tiles. Then came a third—and a fourth—and finally he ripped his eyes away from the black hole in the wall and looked down at the creature clamped to his arm. He batted it into the wall and the thing squealed as its teeth slid out of his skin and it fell onto the cistern tank, setting off the toilet's flush again.

"Jesus *fuck!*" Rob yelled in agony as a thick network of glossy red webs spread across his arm. Stumbling for the door, his foot keened through a spreading pool of water and something bit down into his calf, sending another shooting pain up his leg as it tore away a warm chunk of flesh. Behind him more and more alligators slithered through the hole where the sink had connected to the wall: a dozen of them—two dozen—flooding the bathroom and sliding about in the spray of sewage that followed, snapping their jaws as they scuttled after him. Quickly, Rob jammed down the handle and tumbled out into the hall, turning to look back as he kicked the door shut. In that frantic half-second he saw that the bathroom had filled with black, spiked shapes, that the tiles had teeth and the bathtub was crawling with snapping gray animals —

Rob screamed, slamming his back into the door. His leg trembled, threatening to buckle beneath him. How many pints of blood before he went into medical shock? Was he there already? Was this whole thing a hallucination?

Mania pumping through his veins, Rob hurtled forward. He had to get out of the house, at least get onto the street —

A black shadow fell over him and he looked up.

"Oh, Jesus Christ almighty," he whispered.

The ceiling was a rippling vortex of black scales and deep, half-healed slashes. Smears of pale flesh bulged between bloated ridges of leathery green and dozens of winking reptilian eyes watched him from within the swirling, contorting mess, the walls popping and ripping open as plaster blackened and turned to leather. Behind him, he heard the bone-shattering thumps of dozens of tiny creatures punching their bodies into the bathroom door. The carpet squelched wetly beneath his feet; the gushing water from the exploded sink had begun to seep into the house.

Rob whimpered and lurched for the front door, recoiling when it swung open and flashed its teeth. The outside was gone — Fern Street was gone — and all he could see through the mouth-shaped doorway was the deep, red tunnel of a scarred, ancient throat and a knotted mass of lashing, wet muscle that he could only assume was the great throbbing tongue of the beast.

Wheeling away, he glanced toward the bathroom door and saw that the creatures had started to break it down, tiny snapping jaws poking through great ragged wedges in the wood. "Fuck," he whispered, starting for the stairs.

The carpet clawed at him as he grabbed for the banister. He tried to wrench his hand loose as the cool scales of reptilian skin brushed his palm, but it was too late: an impossibly long coil of ribbed, black tail snapped tightly around his wrist and pinned him to the newel post.

"What do you want from me?" he yelled, yanking his whole body back to withdraw his arm from the banister rail's grip. His eyes shot up to the landing, and he moaned as he saw that the bedroom door was open; inside, an enormous, scaled shape writhed off his mattress and started toward the landing.

There was only one thing he could do.

As he lunged for the kitchen, the hallway buckled beneath him, the great ribs of some impossible beast splaying like the hood of a cobra and shunting the floorboards apart. The whole house was spinning now, subsiding into the earth a good few decades too soon, and as he threw himself toward the kitchen door, his left side smashed into the frame, enveloping his bones with a thick coat of pain. "I'm giving them back!" he pleaded desperately, fumbling in his pocket as he staggered into the kitchen. "For G-god's sake, I'm trying to give them back, if you'd just *let* me —"

He froze.

The kitchen was a great black maw, hundreds of thousands of smashed, white teeth bursting out of the fleshy walls. Swamp-water pooled over the tiles, each one now a rubbery, black-green scale shivering with hungry anticipation. The table was still there, but it was covered in spines and sinking into the fleshy muscle of the alligator tongue beneath.

And the head was gone.

"No..." he moaned, the gold eyeballs heavy in his hand. The alligator head had disappeared. His only hope.

A titanic hand clamped down on his shoulder, and Rob screamed. Another twisted into his thinning hair and he realized they weren't hands, not really—they were claws. Enormous, lengthened alligator claws.

Slowly, he turned around.

The beast grinned down at him, half of its teeth missing, its eyes gone and the deep, sunken pits of the sockets bruised and purple. Its body was gargantuan, the smell of its breath, fruity and rotting.

"I'm sorry," Rob said. "I'm so sorry. I let you down, I know that. I never meant… please know that I never meant to let you down. Not once. This isn't what I'd planned on saying, G-god knows it isn't, but… please… please know that I never meant to hurt you. Please."

The beast's gruesome smile widened as the blind, wide-faced creature leaned forward and bumped Rob's forehead with its snout. A long, purple sliver of tongue drew a wet path across his face.

"Your apology is… lacking," the monster rasped hungrily.

"I know," Rob whispered, "but it wasn't for you."

Rob closed his eyes and hung up the phone in his hand.

As the creature's teeth closed around his head, he prayed that Hayley would find the money somewhere to take herself on that second honeymoon they'd been planning.

117

THE MISSING GOLD RIBBON
Nadine Stewart

I wish everyone would just leave me alone, little Sally thought to herself as she kicked the dirt in the driveway with her toe. Mother would be so mad if she got her pretty lace socks dirty or her best Sunday shoes scuffed. But she didn't care. No one else cared about her, so why should she worry about her dumb old fancy clothes? Sally continued to sulk and kick the dirt and gravel all the way up to the backyard. Her brother, Benji, had left his red rubber ball by the fence. Next to it, in a mound of dirt left behind by some pesky critter, lay some of his *G.I. Joes* and *He-Man* action figures. It looked as if an epic battle had just occurred; some were missing an arm or a leg and others were half buried under the remains of a make-shift fort made out of sticks.

Sally picked up the red rubber ball and started bouncing it off the wooden fence separating her house and the grumpy old man's yard next door. *Thwomp…thwomp… thwomp.* She turned her head, looking back at the house just in time to see the worn, sun-faded curtains in the den flutter closed. Father wasn't going to be happy with all the noise she was making. "You're making enough noise to wake the dead," he'd say. With one final hard, swift kick, Sally watched as her brother's red ball missed its mark and flew right over the fence into the neighbor's yard. *Oh well,* she thought to herself, *we won't be getting that one back.*

Sally tugged on one of her long, golden braids; she had a nervous habit of twirling the ends between her fingers when she was feeling worked up or anxious. She noticed one of her pretty rainbow ribbons was missing. Mother wouldn't be happy if her long plaits came undone and her naturally curly hair became a wild mess. Begrudgingly, she made her way to the back porch, stomping up the stairs and stepping over broken flowerpots and her brother's rusting yellow Tonka Trucks. Stepping into the dimly lit kitchen, Sally looked around, worried that Mother might see her sneaking past but, to her relief, her mother was gabbing on the phone again.

When Mother wasn't doting on Benji, worrying about her older sister Jane or fussing over Sally for one thing or another, she was sitting at the orangey oak dining table winding and unwinding the long telephone cord extension around her hand as she gossiped with her friends about all the comings and goings of their neighbors on Fern Street. But Mother was looking a little odd this morning, and surprisingly, she wasn't doing a lot of talking. Her red eyes made her look very tired and her face and hands were a dull pale blue. The long coils of telephone cord were wrapped tightly around her neck. *Just like a scarf!* Sally giggled to herself. *Mother must be really cold.* Sally didn't have time to stick around for fear of getting caught, so she darted down the hall and took the stairs two at a time up to the second floor. Loud music was booming from her sister's bedroom as Sally sprinted down the hallway and ducked into her room before anyone noticed her.

Sally's bedroom was painted a bubble gum Barbie pink. She had a matching set of white wood furniture; a night stand, dresser, vanity mirror and a white metal daybed with brass knobs. She sat down in front of her vanity mirror and slowly opened the cream-colored box that held all her pretty baubles. She had hair ribbons in every color of the rainbow which she dug through to the bottom, looking for her favorite gold ribbons. She found one and pulled it out; it was so soft and sparkly and glimmered from the sunlight streaming through her bedroom window. She continued to scrounge through the box, becoming frustrated that she couldn't find the one that matched. Sally took the whole box and dumped its contents onto her bed. There were little plastic animal barrettes, round marble-like baubles and dozens of colorful ribbons, but no matter how hard she scrounged through them like an animal digging a hole, Sally couldn't find the second gold ribbon. *Where could it be?* She must have lost it somewhere in the house, but she was always so careful when wearing her special gold ribbons.

Twisting one of her braids between her fingers, Sally made her way back down the winding oak staircase, running her hand along the grooved, spindled banister and carefully dodging her sister's roller skates on the landing. "Mother?" she called. "Have you seen my gold ribbon, the gold ribbon for my hair?" No answer. *She must be on the dang phone still,* Sally thought to herself. She would check the family room first; she remembered wearing them while watching *Muppet Babies* and *She-Ra* last weekend. She remembered because as much as she loved her gold ribbons, she was mad at herself for not wearing her *Rainbow Brite* ones for Saturday morning cartoons.

As she reached the bottom stair, Sally heard the distinct *ching-ching* and jovial *boings* of *Super Mario Bros.* escaping the family room into the foyer. Her brother was hogging the T.V. still; earlier she had wanted to watch *Punky Brewster* but he just ignored her as always. Entering the room, she called: "Yo, dummy, have you seen my gold ribbon, the gold ribbon for my hair?" The Nintendo was on pause and Benji was slumped over on the couch with his Hulk Hogan Wrestling Buddy pillow over his face. "Hey, stupid! What the hell? If you were just gonna take a nap, I could have watched my show!" Sally gave him a quick kick to his shin, but Benji didn't move. Instead, he flopped further over, his Hulk Hogan pillow falling to the floor. *Bonehead must have been up too late playing video games again,* Sally thought to herself, *he's really dead to the world.* She did a quick look around the room, sweeping her hand under the couch and the coffee table. No luck. She would check Father's den next.

Heading back through the foyer towards the den, Sally opened the front door to let Mickey, their little grey poodle out; he had been whining and scratching at the door for what seemed like hours. She left it open for him to come back in as she poked her head into her father's den. "Father?" she whispered. "Have you seen my gold ribbon, the gold ribbon for my hair?" She never knew which version of her father would greet her. The one where he took her and sat her on his knee and told her spooky bedtime stories (Sally liked these better than stupid princesses and castles), or the angry mean Father who threw things and yelled after he drank too many glasses of his grown-up apple juice. Stepping into the den, Sally saw her father had fallen asleep in his chair again, a half empty glass of brown liquid on the end table next to him. A medicine bottle was lying on its side next to the glass with a few scattered pills spilling out. *Father must have had one of his bad headaches again.* He was sleeping so still and quiet, he usually snored really loud. He sounded like a freight train, Mother would often complain. Father must be sleeping very soundly because he was drooling all down his chin and weird foam was bubbling at his mouth. Benji drooled in his sleep too and Mother always said it was because he was sleeping hard after a long day.

She took a quiet look around, careful not to wake her father.

No gold ribbon.

It was then Sally remembered her sister, Jane. Jane had asked her to borrow a gold ribbon for some dumb football game. Jane was a cheerleader, and their team colors were blue and gold. "No way!" Sally had told her. "They're my favorite ribbons and I don't want you to lose one." Jane lost everything. Her room was a mess, and Mother was always getting on her case for leaving things all over the house. Jane had not been happy and had stomped off and slammed her door in a rage. *I bet she stole it!* Sally thought, angrily.

Sally didn't want Jane to hear her coming, so she quietly tiptoed back up the stairs. She was so mad thinking about it, she almost tripped over Jane's roller skates again. Jane's bedroom was at the top of the stairs. Her door was closed, with a KEEP OUT sign on it. She could hear Cyndi Lauper's *Girls Just Want to Have Fun* blaring from Jane's little pink ghetto blaster. Sally silently approached her door, even though there was no way Jane could have heard her over the deafening music. Opening the door ever so slowly, she saw Jane lying on her bed, staring at the ceiling. *Probably daydreaming about Michael J. Fox or Kirk Cameron or David Hasselhoff again,* Sally thought, rolling her eyes. Jane had all of their posters taped to her ceiling above her bed, torn from one of her *Teen Beat* magazines.

"Jane!" she yelled, hoping to scare the hell out of her sister, but Jane didn't even flinch. "Jane!" Sally shouted again. "Have you seen my gold ribbon, the gold ribbon for my hair?"

When Jane still didn't move, Sally walked cautiously across Jane's bedroom, trying to avoid piles of clothes and magazines strewn haphazardly on the floor. Jane was lying on her bed, wearing her blue and gold cheerleader uniform. As she got closer, Sally noticed a big red stain on the front of Jane's white sweater. *Oh, Mother is going to be so mad. Jane's in big trouble now,* Sally silently giggled to herself. And then she saw it, out of the corner of her eye, a flicker of gold.

Jane's long side ponytail was flowing off the side of her bed, and there it was! Sally's gold ribbon!

"You stole my gold ribbon, the gold ribbon for *my*

hair!" Sally screamed; she was beyond mad, she was infuriated! With one quick motion, Sally yanked Mother's long, sharp sewing scissors out of Jane's chest and cut off her ponytail, gold ribbon and all. *That'll teach her,* Sally thought as she ran out of Jane's room before her sister could chase after her.

"Mother, Mother..." Sally yelled as she ran down the stairs. Jane would call her a tattle tale or little baby, but she didn't care. No one else cared, so why should she? Fuming and distracted, Sally hit the landing fast and, before she even had time to grab the banister, her left foot stepped right on her sister's forgotten roller skates. As if time and space froze around her, Sally flew through the air in slow motion. She landed with a sickening *thud,* face down at the bottom of the stairs.

A few moments later, Sally picked herself up and smoothed out her wrinkled, ruffled dress with her hands. Turning around, she stared down at her lifeless body. A pool of dark crimson was slowly seeping out from under her head. One of her arms was bent at an unnatural angle; she still clutched Jane's ponytail in her hand. Her right foot was twisted grotesquely; it looked like someone had sewn it on backwards. Sally's left leg was squirting blood from where a fractured bone pierced through her skin. Shivering slightly, Sally shook her head and shrugged. She turned back towards the open front door and skipped out into the yard.

❋ ❋ ❋

Jackson wrapped his sleeping bag around him and looked around at his friends. "And that's how my parents got this house dirt cheap. No. 117 Fern St. It sat empty for twenty years. No one wanted to buy and live in a haunted house." Jackson's friends laughed nervously. "Some nights you can hear little Sally repeating the same thing, 'Have you seen my gold ribbon, the gold ribbon for my hair?', over and over."

"Oh, piss off! That didn't really happen," James muttered skeptically.

"I swear, man, it did. Ask my parents. A couple of

Mormon missionaries found the front door wide open and discovered the bodies."

"Whatever, I'm going to sleep." James lay quietly, listening to the other guys mess around and tell dirty jokes until, one by one, they all fell asleep.

Every one of them snored loudly except James. He lay tossing and turning; he'd never admit it, but Jackson's story had freaked him out. Maybe he was really just a big chicken; he couldn't even watch horror movies because they gave him such paralyzing nightmares. Just as James was finally drifting off to sleep, he heard a faint, melodic sing-song voice. He squeezed his eyes shut tight. Surely his mind was just playing tricks on him...

An icy blanket creeped over his body; it wrapped so tightly around him that he almost felt like he couldn't breathe. His skin tingled with the heavy feeling that someone was close by, watching him, and James couldn't help but snap his eyes open.

Staring back at him, mere inches from his face, was a little girl sporting long blond braids with one ribbon noticeably absent. With bulging bloodshot eyes, she jutted her crushed grotesque face even closer to his and, with an unearthly growl, she screeched:

"Where's my gold ribbon, the gold ribbon for my hair?"

118

INVERT HOUSE
Louie Sullivan

"Have you heard about Invert House?"

It starts out on a schoolyard, not far from Fern Street but far enough that the kids whisper and gossip and lie, spreading the legends in hushed tones between hasty sandwich bites about all the horrifying things that have happened on that strange and unfortunate road.

"Tommy Sambora told me it's called that because the guy who lives there is all inside-out. Like, his skin's on backwards and all his blood and guts and bones and shit are all stuck to the outside of his body. Said the guy can't close his eyes because his eyelids are on wrong, so if you see him, he's got these bugged-out eyeballs that are just staring at you all the time. And his lips are on the inside so he can't talk right, he just groans and growls like in *Dawn of the Dead*. Tommy said this girl Gina from his block tried to go over there one time to get a look at this freak, and he never saw her again. Because if the guy from Invert House catches you, he grabs you with his messed-up bony hands and turns you inside out next!"

The crowd that had gathered around Jake Bryan jumps back, their eyes wide. He grins, knowing that his story is a success... until Ricky Torres steps forward to challenge him.

"Tommy's full of crap, Jake, and you're a dipshit for believin' him! That doesn't even make any sense—a guy who's inside out? He'd be dead in like two minutes!"

"Well, why do they call it Invert House, then?" Jake sneers.

"Because the house is flipped on its head. It looks normal from the outside, but if you go in, the whole place is upside down."

A voice from the back of the crowd: "I heard it's upside down on the outside too!"

"Shut up, loser! Whoever told you that is a dumbass. It wouldn't be able to stand up—the whole thing would fall over! Everybody knows it's the inside that's all weird. That's how it gets ya."

Jake is unable to hold back a shudder, his imagination running wild.

"What do you mean, gets you?" he asks, to Ricky's delight.

"I mean, when ya go in and it's all upside down, you float up to the ceiling and you turn upside down, too. And the place sucks you further and further up. You go up floor after floor until you end up at the door to the roof. And then you go outside and that's it—you float off forever until you're dead."

Jake can hardly imagine which is worse: the gross inside-out man that Tommy had told him about the other day, or Ricky's assertion that if you go into the house, you just drift off to your doom. He hopes neither is real and prays he'll never have to find out. Only one of these wishes will come true.

"I think it's probably all bullshit anyway," he tells Ricky. It's the wrong move.

"What do you know, jerk?" Ricky shoots back with a shove. "You've probably never even been over there!"

Jake barely takes a second to think before taking the bully's bait. "Of course I have!" he says, putting on a brave face to try and hide his lie. A sick smile spreads across Ricky's face.

"Perfect—then you can lead us there. You know the way, right?" And in a single moment, two traps are set in the school playground: Ricky's plan to get Jake to the house, and the House's darker plan for them both.

❋ ❋ ❋

As the sun sets, a swarm of bikes descend on Fern Street. It's a dangerous place to be after dark, and the kids have heard the legends, but their curiosity outweighs every survival instinct that warns them to stay away, every internal alarm screaming for them to turn back. They pass something that looks like a frat house (and Billy Jackson swears it's loaded with ghosts), and another house that Veronica White claims is headquarters to a cult or something. Biking recklessly over the cracked sidewalk as they weave into and out of the empty street, they pass the sites of countless monsters and madmen, regaling each other with tales you surely know by now, and some you have yet to learn. After what feels like hours, they arrive at their destination. Their bikes screech to a halt, with Jake and Ricky at the lead, dumbfounded, as they stare in awe at their quarry: Invert House. They are, for the moment, blissfully unaware that the house has hunted for them just as eagerly as they have hunted for it.

Invert House stands upright (sorry, kid in the back of the crowd, you're the first to be proven wrong) at 118 Fern St., toward the middle of the block. But even in the center of this row of strange and storied houses, Invert House creates a sense of unease unlike the others. Standing near it produces a feeling of wrongness that echoes through the bones, tingles throughout each nerve ending, and sets the entire body on edge. To get the sensation of being in proximity to this cursed place, imagine your mother, your husband, your brother, your girlfriend, or some other person you care deeply for and see very regularly. Now imagine them speaking in someone else's voice, assuring you that nothing has changed, that this is the way they always sound. Imagine their unblinking eyes as they tell you this, in tones you have never heard, a cadence perhaps not quite human even, and you will come close to the discordant feeling that Jake, Ricky, and the rest felt as they beheld the house for the first time.

Invert House was built on a foundation of unreality. It is at its core a place that is, plainly put, wrong. From the very base layers of its bones, it was created backwards, inside out, upside down. Unwalled rooms jut from its center into the street, bearing furniture crudely exposed to the elements, boarded windows that hide unimaginable views. The interior is a mystery barely contemplated at first, so obscured is it by the outlandishness of the outside. The rooms, though outdoors, still give a sense of interiority — this is not merely furniture on a porch, but a full inside of a house somehow juxtaposed onto its outside. It stands at odds with reason, like a double-exposed photograph in the sense that, though you may be looking at it and can decipher individual pieces of what you see, your mind knows that as a whole the thing that is before you cannot exist.

For Jake, this is already almost enough to cause him to pedal as fast as he can, as far as he can, to anywhere on earth but here. He can feel his brain struggling to grasp the optical and sensory illusion that stands before him, the leaps in logic he is trying to take in order to make this place make sense. Ricky, however, is too stupid to have a similar problem. His brain, which has hardly ever comprehended anything more complex than basic math, just accepts that this impossible place simply is, and doesn't question anything beyond that. So he puffs up his chest and begins to harass his favorite punching bag yet again.

"Gonna go in, chickenshit?" he taunts. "Or is little baby Jakey gonna run home to Mommy?"

But it's not enough. Jake is floored by the sight of the place, too busy trying to reconcile its architectural impossibility to pay any mind to the small threats of his onetime aggressor. He can hardly speak, but he manages the words "If you're so brave, why don't you go in?"

The change in dynamic is palpable — the others aren't quite as dense as Ricky, but they aren't hit as hard by the unreality of Invert House as Jake is either. Still, it's enough to make them stop caring, enough to override their playful curiosity and force them to be wary instead. Ricky has no power here, a feeling he's never experienced in his brief years of life. He scrambles for a way to regain it, thinks for a moment as hard as he can, and makes his decision.

He climbs the carpeted steps toward the front door of this impossible façade and stands beneath the archway like a king lording over his subjects. "Nothing to be afraid of if you're not a pansy-ass like Jake!" he declares, but it's too soon. A sudden gust of wind encircles him, throws him off-balance.

Ricky stumbles back, hands fumbling for anything to grasp onto and finding only the door to Invert House. With the fullness of his weight against it, it bursts open, and he loses his grip, tumbling backward into the inky black void beyond that rises up to envelop him. The other children barely catch a glimpse of it as Ricky falls headlong into madness, but to them two things are clear before the door slams firmly shut behind him: first, that perhaps they are already Inside, and always have been; and second, that whatever lies behind the walls of Invert House, whatever dwells Outside, must never be allowed in.

119

MOUNDS
Dr. Stuart Knott

Earl Ward fumbled with his keys. Gilligan barked at his heels and Earl shot him a glare through squinted eyes.

"Yes, thank you!" he admonished as the key finally slid home. "Twenty-five years I spent listenin' to your mother's bitchin', I don't think I need t'hear it from *you!*"

Gilligan darted into the house and went straight for his battered, slobber-stained bed. Earl shuffled in, haphazardly tossing his keys into a small bowl that sat on the windowsill near the door and struggling with his slowly disintegrating bags of groceries.

Stubborn old fool, Lynn's voice echoed in his head; it seemed to be coming from Gilligan.

"You kin shaddup an' all!" Earl rasped.

The house was musty, cool, and eerily silent as ever as Earl dumped his groceries down on the kitchen counter with a grateful sigh. The bags split open almost immediately and a few apples and rolls of toilet paper bounced to the floor. His joints screaming in agony, Earl snapped his hand out just in time to save the eggs from being crushed by the milk and, muttering curses, set about picking everything up.

He was a step too slow, however; Gilligan came padding in, tongue drooping from his daft face, and Earl swatted his nose with a packet of mince as the dopey beagle tried to gobble up the spilt groceries. "Git back in there, yah mutt!"

Twenty minutes later, Earl was settled out on the back porch, a steaming mug of coffee in one hand, a smoldering pipe in the other, and that day's newspaper open in his lap. Next to the hustle and bustle of the outside world and the dead silence of his house, now more a tomb since Lynn had passed, Earl would take his modest back porch and well-kept yard any day.

Unlike some of his neighbors down Fern Street, Earl was incredibly proud of his neat little patch of grass. He counted himself lucky that he even had this small space to putter around in; others weren't so fortunate and had to make do with unsightly paved patios or dirty old garages. Were he a richer man (or, as Lynn would put it, if he could ever "get off his damn ass"), Earl would have installed a nice little greenhouse to grow tomatoes and other salads, but he was happy to make do with a well-trimmed square of grass bordered by beautiful rows of flowers.

As he sat, half-dozing, his coffee growing colder and the paper slipping further from his lap, Earl could almost see himself and Lynn busying themselves amidst the geraniums, the sunflowers that sometimes grew taller than either of them, that ungodly little rose bush that she insisted on pruning year after year and, of course, his prized crop of hydrangeas. Flanked by a smattering of lavender and a trail of orchids, Earl's hydrangeas might not have won any awards (they weren't "ribbon worthy", as Lynn would say) but he was always calmed by their beautiful violet glow and tended to them most fastidiously of all.

A rough, wet tongue lapped at Earl's dangling fingers, snapping him awake.

"Geddoffit!" he grumbled, fetching a half-hearted kick at Gilligan; he hissed with pain as a bolt of stone-cold arthritic agony shot up his leg.

The excitable little beagle scampered into the grass

and began sniffing around fervently. The dog had been Lynn's idea, something to "keep them company" now that the kids were older, with kids of their own. Earl had been resistant at first, but had been begrudgingly won over by Gilligan's big, chocolate-black eyes and curious tortoise-shell patches of brown and white. If nothing else, the dog was one way to keep the grandkids off their damn Nintendo machine, with its incessant bleeping and blinking, when they came to visit and eat all of Earl's cookies.

"My ol' dad would've tanned my hide but-good!"

"Oh, hush!" Lynn would snap back, elbowing him right in the ribs. Even now, Earl could feel the phantom pain lingering there.

"*Oi!*" Earl leapt to his feet…and instantly regretted it as another jolt of pain shot down his spine. He half-tripped into his slippers, his pipe and paper forgotten, and limped into the grass where Gilligan was busy digging away, his paws a blur of excitement.

"What have I told you?" he admonished, one crooked finger wagging. "Not. In. The. Peonies!" Earl delivered four light taps to Gilligan's hide to emphasize his point; the dog simply stared up at him sheepishly, obliviously, and tottered off.

Earl sighed and turned back to the pink, blooming flowers. The peonies had always been Lynn's favorites; she'd carried a whole bouquet of them at their wedding and he'd had a small matching corsage tucked into the breast pocket of his suit, his medals lined neatly alongside it.

"Blasted mutt…" Earl grumbled as he inspected the damage.

Thankfully, the peonies were largely unscathed, save for a few torn petals, but Earl bit back a string of curses when he spied a small plastic ball in amongst the flowers. His glassy, pale eyes glared at the chain-link fence that separated his cherished garden from 117; their rowdy little girl was always kicking balls and tossing shit into his garden and, without Lynn around to admonish him,

Earl reminded himself to give her parents a piece of his mind the next time he saw them.

Can you really afford to lose a part of that daft old brain? Lynn asked.

"Jus' watch me," Earl sneered.

Earl steadied himself to endure the effort of stretching up and heading back to the house; he had a particularly grim-looking chicken and potato microwave meal he was looking forward to crapping out in a haze of curses waiting for him in the freezer. However, something caught his eye; a mound of dirt, dark and muddy and neatly piled, not unlike Gilligan's frantic shit holes.

Earl frowned.

It was a molehill.

❉ ❉ ❉

A few whacks with a shovel may have sorted out the problem, but it had also all but wiped Earl out, and he was at his wit's end when the doorbell rang, tearing him away from *Family Feud*. Earl yanked open the door to find a couple of well-dressed young lads holding a spread of pamphlets in their hands.

"Good evening, sir," the fresh-faced boy with the sweep of brown hair (*Hippie hair,* Earl noted) greeted. "Do you have some time to talk —"

"No," Earl snapped. "I damn well don't. Don't you have anythin' better t'do than disturb people at this hour?!"

The boy's companion assumed a beaming smile. "We're here on the Lord's behalf, sir. Did you know that —"

"*Oh!*" Earl interrupted with feigned interest. "The *Lord's* work, is it? Well, *that* changes ev'rythin'! Tell me, where was *your* God when *my* wife was lyin' in th' hospital bein' eatin' away by cancer, hm?"

"Well, I…that is…" The boy's face flushed a deep red.

"And *you…*" Earl jabbed a finger into the other boy's perfectly ironed shirt. "I s'pose *you're* gonna tell me ev'rythin' happ'ns f'r some 'divine reason,' right?" The boy could only stare, dumbfounded at his outburst.

"We…w-we believe that—"

"Oh, *fuck* what you believe!" Earl roared. He swept his hand at the boy's pamphlets and sent them fluttering to the ground. "Pick that shit up an' get dah fuck outta here before I set the dog on you!" The idea of "setting" Gilligan on anyone was ridiculous, of course, but it was an effective (if empty) threat.

"You, er…you have a good day, sir," the other Mormon said politely, frantically pulling his partner down Earl's small, paved pathway.

The busybody from 117 appeared in her doorway, aroused by the fracas, and Earl snarled at her. "An' just what the fuck're you lookin' at?!"

She huffed and disappeared into her house. Earl sneered and sucked on his bottom lip as Lynn's voice chastised him from the depths of his memory…and imagination. He paused to polish the brass number etched into the door frame—119—before slamming and locking his door. Gilligan was sat staring at him with those big old eyes, silently judging him, but happily clambered upstairs when Earl clapped his hands and ushered him off.

After popping a variety of colored pills and rising four times to pee, Earl had finally drifted to sleep in a bed that now felt large, strange, and alien to him. Lynn's scent lingered on the sheets, the pillows…everywhere, infecting his dreams. In them, she staggered to him, arms outstretched, her face an unsightly, dripping mess of gore as it melted from her skull.

Earl awoke with a start, a heavy weight on his chest. He jerked and Gilligan spilled to the floor with a yelp, then damn-near tripped him as he shambled to the bathroom to shower dand shave for the day. Over a plate of half-burned toast and the first of his two obligatory morning coffees, Earl stared into space, rattled by the constant nightmares of his beloved wife. He hated that she came to him in such a state and hoped, wherever she was, she was in a better state than that.

"Mebbe I shud ask the feckin' Mormons…" He grimaced as he swigged back his coffee.

The sun was out, the air was cool and dry, and Earl was ready to get to work in the garden. Lynn had always said he was too much of a perfectionist for his own good but, as he always said, if he didn't tend to the plants, then who would? It was too easy to just hide away inside and leave the flowers to wither and the weeds to run rampant, and he wasn't about to let all that hard work — and one of his last links to Lynn's memory — just succumb to neglect.

However, as he stepped onto the porch dressed in his tattered gardening overalls, a dusty fedora on his head and a portable radio in his gnarled left hand, Earl's heart just about froze solid in his chest.

The lawn was in shambles; piles of dirt littered the entire space, as though dozens of small rocks had dropped from the sky.

"What the…?" Earl's wrinkled face creased into a frown, then screwed up into a look of anguish and despair.

The hydrangeas were a shredded mess; scattered petals lay strewn on muddy piles like the bodies spread across a battlefield, and fat, ugly worms wriggled freely in the warm daylight air. Earl wandered over to the peonies, hands shaking, and kicked flutily at the mounds of dirt that had also ransacked his wife's cherished flower patch. Enraged, he smashed his radio down on the nearest pile; globs of mud flew into his face as he beat at the ground and hacked out curses that would've turned Lynn's skin pale.

❋ ❋ ❋

"Yessiree," the clerk had told him. "This here'll solve your problem, no sweat. The little creep tunnels through here…" He pushed his hand through the metal loop to demonstrate, "and *shwooip!* He's snapped up nice and clean as you like!"

Earl had nodded along impatiently and had the boy bag him up a few of the metal traps. He had briefly considered letting Gilligan have free rein in the garden to root out the troublesome moles, but thought better of it; Gilligan was about as useful as a one-legged man in an ass kicking contest when it came to hunting. Hell, he regularly needed his food bowl brought to him since he was too lazy to go to it himself.

Instead, Earl had bought the traps and set them strategically throughout his garden. He stamped them into the soil and dropped a special concoction on top of them for good measure: slug pellets and rat poison, just to give the little bastards something to think about if they burrowed their way above ground.

A patient man with little else to fill his days, Earl sat in his favorite wicker chair and waited for the traps to do their work. The neighbors and their bratty little kids came and went; Gilligan sat and lapped at a bowl of water by his master's feet; the newspaper was read cover to cover; coffee was sipped, tobacco was smoked, and still Earl sat and stared unblinking out at his garden as day turned to dusk turned to night.

Earl imagined the moles burrowing underground, oblivious, going about their moley lives, thinking moley thoughts and then suddenly finding their stumpy limbs caught, their stout necks choked, and their useless little eyes bugging from their heads as they became entangled in his traps.

His stomach rumbling, his back aching, Earl rose from his chair, eager to review the fruits of his labor. He grabbed ol' stumpy, his favorite pitchfork, and dug each of the ten traps up one by one. The first two were empty, so he forced them back into the dirt, but all the others but three held a squirming, chubby black/brown little mole in their clutches.

"Fucked with th' wrong peonies, didn't you, yah little bastard?" Earl smirked with glee as the moles squeaked and writhed on the very lawn they and their brethren had left a muddy, disheveled wasteland.

Now what? Lynn asked. *You keeping them as pets?*

"Mebbe I'll have a little mole pie!" Earl answered, but it was an empty threat; somehow, he imagined the squat little mammals would be too chewy and gristly even for his iron-clad palate.

His first thought was to toss them onto the porch and let Gilligan tear into them, but he quickly thought better of it; not only would he have to clean up afterwards (assuming the stupid dog didn't simply nuzzle at them like they were his playmates), but the last thing he needed was to deal with an over-gorged beagle hacking up chunks of mole onto his carpets.

No. In the end, Earl had simply stuffed the squealing moles, their stumpy, clawed arms thrashing weakly, into a burlap sack and tossed them unceremoniously into the water butte at the end of the garden.

"Good riddance," he sniffed.

❋ ❋ ❋

Lynn rose from her hospital bed stiff as a board. Her eyes, once so impossibly blue, were swimming with a murky, creamy liquid; her brow furrowed into a look of disappointment.

She held out arms as gaunt as autumn twigs; the pale blue veins throbbing beneath her paper-thin flesh twisted into tar-like gouges that tore through her skin, up her neck, and burst from her split lips in a spew of muddy gunk.

Peonies, bright and full, tumbled from her vomit; shrieking, half-digested moles splattered down her front. Her lips moved slowly, like the creaking of an old barn door, and a rapid, piercing yelping jumped from her throat.

Earl's eyes snapped open with a start. He rolled onto his back with a groan and slapped his palm to his forehead; it came away sweaty. Incredibly, he could still hear that whining yelp in his ears; he whipped his head around, certain that he would see Lynn's emaciated corpse lying in the bed, arms outstretched to welcome him to oblivion, but he was alone in the dark.

That was unusual. Gilligan was nearly always curled up at the foot of the bed, or at least in his ratty dog basket.

The yelping continued, frantic and panicked. Earl leaned out of his bedroom door and peered down the dark stairs and could hear it echoing up from the back door.

"Gilligan?" he called, as if expecting an answer. "What've you gotten into, boy?"

Wrapping his robe around himself, Earl gingerly made his way downstairs, gripping the banister tightly with each step and chastising himself for leaving the television on overnight. Static blared into the lounge and cast a faint light across his humble abode, which he kept as clean and tidy as he could, if only to keep Lynn's voice from nagging him.

The shuffling of paws and a steady, rhythmic whining led Earl into the kitchen. He snapped on the light and balked as he saw he'd stepped his bare foot on a dirty, bloody paw print. Earl stepped aside and half-collapsed against the kitchen counter at the sight that awaited him by the screen door.

Gilligan was lying on the floor tiles, his back legs kicking involuntarily, his tiny tail wagging weakly. His face and snout were a mangled mess of fur, blood, and flesh; one eye, weeping from a deep slash, rolled pathetically up at Earl. Gilligan's breathing was shallow; a shallow, wheezing howl accompanied each strained breath. Blood was streaked everywhere and pooled beneath the beagle's weak, eviscerated body. His abdomen had been torn to shreds; Earl could see the jagged spikes of ribs jutting from the bloody remains of the dog's chest. Steaming lumps of entrails were strewn across the floor, tangled in the beagle's limp limbs; little chunks had been bitten out of them, out of Gilligan's fur and flesh, and what remained of his belly was unnaturally swollen.

A pained, guttural cry left Earl's throat as he moved to help his wounded dog. Lynn, always the pragmatist, told him it was already too late, that there was nothing he could do, but he dropped to his knees and stroked uselessly at Gilligan's blood-matted fur anyway. A shriek escaped his lips as a sudden pain, like pins being driven into his flesh, flared up from the web of skin between his thumb and index finger.

Earl scrambled backwards, bashing the back of his head against the kitchen cupboards. He held his shaking, bloody hand up and was stunned to see a chubby little mole gnawing into his skin. Panicked, disgusted, Earl slammed his hand against the cupboard door repeatedly, splintering the wooden panel and bludgeoning the mole into a mess of guts and bloody fur. He clamped his good hand to the gaping wound the mole had left and watched, horrified, as two more tumbled weakly from the ghastly remains of Gilligan's corpse. They slid across the kitchen tiles blindly, their little claw-hands weakly moving as if swimming.

Earl hauled himself up using his elbows, blood dripping from his wound and his joints screaming in protest. He watched, horrified, as the moles crawled to their fallen friend and pushed their pointed noses into the meaty remains. One flopped across the floor towards the fresh blood spilling from Earl's hand in a steady stream and began lapping at it with its worm-like tongue.

Gagging, Earl lifted his leg to stamp the vile vermin out of existence but paused with his gangling, hairy leg raised halfway. Gilligan's little dog flap was stained with blood and matted fur; it swayed open, gently nudged ajar by the muddy head of another mole. It wobbled briefly before plopping to the floor and sniffing around, licking at the gore spread across the floor tiles.

It was followed by another.

And another.

Earl kicked away the mole nearest to him, hissing as its talon nicked the flesh of his foot, and peered out through the screen door. The garden was a war zone of molehills; the unsightly mounds of dirt were piled all over, the flowers plundered, and a writhing, snuffling stream of bulbous moles crawled their way from each one and across his porch towards the dog flap.

* * *

Babbling, half-crazed, Earl fled up the stairs, tripping up

every other one, and sought refuge in his bathroom. He slammed on the lock and collapsed onto the toilet seat, panting and barely able to comprehend what he'd seen.

Any attempts to explain it away as another vivid nightmare were completely washed away by the burning pain in his hand. Earl shakily stood and washed his wound under the faucet; he sucked on his bottom lip as the cold water sent jabs of searing pain up his arm, then reluctantly peered down at his hand to inspect the damage.

The mole had bitten a small chunk from his flesh, but the damage didn't seem to be any more serious than that time he'd accidentally caught himself when chopping potatoes. Like so many superficial wounds, it bled with surprising vigor, so Earl grabbed handfuls of gauze from the medicine cabinet above the sink and clamped them tightly onto the bite.

He was just fastening the makeshift bandage to his injured hand with a piece of tape when the bathroom door shook violently. Earl turned around so fast that he almost tripped over his own feet.

"You gotta be fuckin' kidding' me…!" he moaned as the door rattled again.

Cautiously, he pushed aside the towels hanging on the back of the door and pressed his ear against the panel. His hearing wasn't what it had once been ("You're as deaf as a dormouse!" Lynn had been fond of reminding him) but he could just faintly make out the sounds of scratching, mewing…

Thud!

The door shuddered as if slammed by a weighty force. Frowning, taking a step back, Earl's mind raced with a myriad of insane possibilities: were the moles charging into the door like mini quarterbacks? Perhaps rolling up into little voracious balls of fur like in that awful movie Lynn had dragged him to one evening?

Thud!

A splinter appeared in the bottom panel.

Thud!!

Earl scanned the bathroom; it was a small space of white tiles, housing only a toilet, sink, medicine cabinet, and a bath. It was hardly a well-stocked armory!

"Hell, I'd settle for the garden shed!" Earl spat bitterly. "At least then I'd have ol' stumpy…"

Thud!!

Incredibly, the door panel fragmented just enough from a bloody, dirty little claw hand to poke through. His options limited, Earl grabbed the toilet plunger and beat pathetically at the appendage, fending it off briefly but not enough to stave off the constant banging and the emergence of more of those shovel-like feet. They grabbed at the broken wood, snapped more of it off, and a disgusting, octopus-like snout of pink tendrils poked its squinty-eyed face through the hole.

Revolted, Earl reacted instinctively and stupidly threw the only weapon he had on hand at the dirt-encrusted mole; the plunger clattered uselessly to the floor, completely missing its target. The strange-looking mole briefly sniffed at it, the many tendrils of its star-shaped snout quivering as they investigated the plunger's wooden handle, then it turned back towards Earl, as if smelling his blood…or fear…and clawed towards him, lugging its rotund body across the bathroom floor as more of its pointy-nosed kin burrowed their way in behind it.

Backed against the wall with no other options available to him, Earl started stomping away like a madman. The heel of his foot came crashing down on a few of the dirty, squealing vermin but more just forced their way through the opening. When he missed, a jolt of numb pain spread across his feet; when he hit, he had to swallow back bile as his knobby heel crunched down on the rough fur and tiny ribs of half a dozen moles.

Earl shrieked as one clamped down on his toe; he kicked his leg out frantically and sent the mole flying against the wall, only to find two more lugging themselves up his bare leg, their dagger-like claws digging into his skin like pinpricks. Earl pinwheeled in a panic, crushing two more under his heels and beating at the moles now gnawing on the flesh of his calves and forearms.

As he flapped his arms to try and shake them off, Earl caught sight of his wizened, terror-stricken face in the mirror of the medicine cabinet. Bright blood oozed from his left ear in a steady trickle and, when he turned to get a better look, he saw a rancid, star-snouted mole nibbling on his earlobe.

Appalled, Earl roared with anger. *"Gerroff you little…!"*
Vomit, hot and chunky, spilled down his robe as he grabbed the wriggling abomination in one bloody, liver-spotted hand. He grimaced with disgust as the thing's stubby arms flailed uselessly; its snout, like the pouting embrace of some eldritch abomination, rippled hungrily, its button-like eyes glaring at him sightlessly.

Ignoring the stabbing pains at his ankles and calves, the blood dripping from dozens of wounds as more and more of the moles chewed on his flesh, the startling geysers as they nicked arteries, Earl took the mole in his hand and prepared to dunk it, bizarre snout and all, into the toilet bowl. He longed for the rush of superiority from hearing it splashing around in the tepid water before he pulled the handle and sent that disgusting little mammal spiraling down the drain.

He moved to have his vengeance, moles splattered into a furry paste under his cracked toenails, but just as he was about to dispose of the mole, another of its kin scrambled down the length of his arm and bit into the thin skin of his wrist. Earl yanked his arm back, the pain sharp and lancing throughout his body, and the freakish mole tumbled from his grip and disappeared into the scrambling litter covering his bathroom floor.

Earl fell to one knee, his vision growing gray and blurred. Blood and moles fell about him; he could see them, impossibly multiplied through his hazy eyes, as they suckled eagerly on his life's blood and gnawed at his flesh. Their fur, black and muddy, was slick from blood and their incessant mewing echoed around the small bathroom in a cacophony.

Moles crawled and clawed over Earl's crumbling, trembling form. One bit into the fatty flesh of his cheek; another scrambled over it to clog his mouth and started nibbling on his tongue. Through the pain, the madness, the mess of squealing, gnawing little vermin, that nauseating, revolting, star-nosed mole sauntered across the floor, nudging aside its kin to clear a path towards Earl.

The strange mole, its snout more tentacles than nose, sidled between Earl's legs and the last thing he felt before the world fell away to a swirling, inexorable darkness was the mole's needle-like teeth sinking, sinking, sinking…

120

THEY COME WHEN YOU SLEEP
Jack Finn

Katerina turned her head to hide her tears in the straw-filled pillow as she clutched her favorite doll, Sarah, close to her chest. She always tried to be brave for her parents and older sister when they hid in the cellar. The cellar was cold and damp, and she missed her soft bed and warm blankets.

"Hey now, Kitty Kat, what's wrong?" Her father sat on the edge of the bed and ran a gentle hand over her hair.

"I'm fine," Katerina sniffed, holding back tears.

"Well, what about Sarah? Is she okay?" He poked softly at the small raggedy doll.

"Sarah is scared," she rolled over to look at her father's kind face. "She's afraid the bad things are going to get her."

"No, Kitty Kat, we're safe in the cellar. There's nothing to worry about."

"How long do we have to keep sleeping down here?"

"Only until it's safe to sleep upstairs in our beds again. But tomorrow, we can go for a walk in the woods together." He ran his fingers through his dark hair, a habit he had when he felt stressed or worried.

"What if they get into the house?" Her eyes were

suddenly wide with fear.

"If they get into the house, Sergio and Andrew are upstairs; they won't let anything hurt you."

"But Sergio is just a gardener, and Andrew is an old man."

"They are good men; they will protect us," he smiled down at her reassuringly.

"Papa," Katerina sat up with a concerned look. "I forgot my flower up in my bedroom."

"It will be okay," He gently eased her back onto the small bed. "When Sergio comes to check on us, I will ask him to bring it to you."

"You won't forget?"

"I won't forget. I promise."

"Oh, sweetie, there's nothing to be afraid of. Why don't you try and get some sleep?"

"Because they always come when you sleep, Papa."

❋ ❋ ❋

Elena sat on the stairs and watched her husband in the dim candlelight of the cellar as he tried to calm their youngest daughter. Viktor was a good man, a good husband, and a good father. She smiled as she watched him; he looked just as young and handsome as the day they had met so many years ago. A lifetime ago, it seemed, as they sat hiding amongst the shelves of winter preserves and trunks of old clothes in the manor house's cellar.

Beside her sat her eldest daughter, Petia, staring gloomily at the earthen floor.

"What's on your mind?" Elena nudged the brooding teen playfully with her elbow.

"I was just thinking about Tatiana." Petia tried to give a weak smile, but her eyes filled with tears.

"Oh, Petty, that won't happen to you." She ran a hand soothingly across the girl's back.

"Mama, she was my best friend, and now she's gone. She had so many hopes and dreams, and those monsters took her while she slept. No last words. No final thoughts. She went to sleep, and they ended all that she was. Do you remember when Papa brought down that deer last month, and we shared it with Tati's family? How happy she was that night."

"I remember. She was a wonderful girl."

"It's not fair what happened." A tear ran down Petia's cheek.

"No, dear, it's not."

"I want to sleep in my bed. I want to go to sleep and not worry that those monsters will take me while I sleep. Or someone that I love." She ran her thumb over the carved wooden ring on her finger, turning it to see the etched rose in the candlelight.

"You're worried about Tomas." Elena smiled at her daughter and hugged her close.

"I just want a life with him, like you and Papa have."

"You'll have that, Petia. You and Tomas will have a long life together."

"Why is the world like this? Why are there monsters like that?" Petia searched his mother's dark eyes, pleading.

"Just like we hunt the beasts in the woods, the monsters hunt us."

"But we hunt the deer to eat; they hunt us for sport."

"That is why they are monsters."

❋ ❋ ❋

"How is Katerina?" Elena looked searchingly into her husband's eyes; the strength she found there always calmed her.

"She's resting, but she refuses to go to sleep." He wrapped his arms around Elena and hugged her.

"Do you blame her?" Elena pressed her head against his chest and held him close; he smelled like elderberry flowers.

"No, of course not. How is Petia holding up?"

"She's still upset over Tatiana and worried about Tomas."

"These are dark, sorrowful times," Viktor kissed his beloved's forehead. "So much death, so much loss. We need to bring the girls someplace beautiful and peaceful.

Do you remember that lake in Iskar Gorge?"

"The one with the waterfall," despite all her worry, the memory made Elena smile against his firm chest, feeling safe in his arms. "How can I ever forget our time there?"

"Let's go back there. Take the children to swim in that lake under the moonlight."

"We'll have to wear clothes this time." She pressed her face into his chest and squeezed him tightly.

A knock on the cellar door rang out, followed by another long knock and four in quick succession. Elena turned in alarm, and Petia stood from her perch on the stairs and stared at the door.

"Papa?" Katerina sat up in alarm.

"It's okay, everyone. Calm down. That is our knock code. It's just Sergio," Viktor looked at each of them assuredly. "Let me go see what he wants."

Viktor climbed the aged stairs and unbolted the thick wooden door. He cracked it open and saw Sergio's dark eyes and bearded face peering at him.

"Mr. Viktor, I'm sorry to disturb you," his deep Spanish-accented voice came across in a hushed tone. "Andrew has seen movement in the garden."

"Thank you for informing me," Viktor's countenance visibly showed his worry.

"You have been very good to me and my family. If it's them, we will do all we can to protect you."

"I know you will," a wordless exchange of respect passed between the two men.

"Good luck, Mr. Viktor. May God protect you."

"I think I'll leave God with you, Sergio. Take care of yourself and Andrew." Viktor closed and bolted the door.

He tried to fix his face into a mask of calm as he walked down the stairs to his family.

"Viktor, what did he want?" Elena spoke the words that all of them were thinking.

"It's fine. It was just Sergio wanting to...." The sounds of a loud crashing noise upstairs cut off his words.

They all stared at the ceiling as a cacophony of noise rang from the floor above them. Breaking glass and banging sounds, followed by a second loud crash.

"They're through the outside door!" gasped Elena as gunshots echoed from the upstairs rooms.

"Girls, I need you to hide." Viktor tried to keep the calm in his voice. "Kat, get behind the shelves. Petia hide in the herb storage under the bed."

Katerina leaped out of bed and ran to the shelving holding the preserves. The space between the shelving and walls was narrow and dark. She hesitated momentarily, thinking of the spiders and creepy crawling things that could be hiding in a place like that. But a banging at the cellar door urged her forward. She wriggled her small body into the tight space until wholly concealed.

"It's all going to be okay, Kitty Kat. I need you to be brave and not make a sound, no matter what happens. Your mother and I love you very much," Viktor reassured her as she leaned several old, dusty rugs against the side of the shelves to conceal the small opening.

Elena was helping Petia move the bed to access the trap door when the cellar door smashed inwards, sending shards of splintered wood tumbling down the stairs. The sound of a mechanism releasing echoed in the darkness, followed by a feeling of something swooshing through the air and a thwacking sound.

"Mama," Petia said softly and stood straight up, a wooden bolt protruding through her heart and chest.

Elena screamed as her daughter's eyes rolled upwards in her head, and she fell lifelessly onto the bed.

From her hiding place behind the shelves, Katerina peered through a crack and saw dark-cloaked men in hoods running down the stairs, followed by a wild-eyed priest holding a gleaming silver crucifix aloft. Spittle flew from the priest's lips as he screamed verses in Latin she did not understand.

She watched as her father flew across the room and tackled a man struggling to reload a crossbow into the narrow space. Her father's strong arms wrapped tight around the man as he sunk his elongated canines into the man's neck. The man screamed and kicked his legs as another hooded man plunged a wooden stake through her father's back, and his body went limp.

Two men rushed towards her mother, but she quickly batted both men aside, and they landed in crumpled heaps on the floor. She snarled at the priest and flashed her two sharp fangs at him. The priest retreated in terror and raised the silver crucifix. Katerina saw her mother laugh and smack the silver cross from the priest's outstretched hand. Crossbows releasing their bolts sounded from the top of the stairs, and two wooded shafts flew out of the darkness and embedded themselves into her mother's chest. She reached one last time for the priest and then collapsed to the floor.

"Father Grigori, help me," cried the man her father had bitten as he reached out towards the priest.

"He's been bitten. Kill him," the priest ordered dispassionately.

"No, please," the man pleaded as one of the hooded figures stepped forward and thrust a wooden stake into the man's chest, silencing him.

The priest surveyed the room as the hooded men carried their dead and wounded up the stairs. He kicked at her mother's corpse and loudly proclaimed, "The Lord's will has been done!"

Katerina shook with terror and held her mouth closed tight, fearing that she would make a sound and give herself away. She watched as the hooded men sunk gleaming silver hooks into her family and dragged them up the stairs like pieces of meat. One of her father's black shoes came loose and tumbled down the stairs to land on the floor.

She stayed hidden behind the shelves for a long time, trembling and crying. Only when she heard the hoot of a barn owl outside did she feel it was nighttime and safe to go out. Katerina pushed aside the rugs and wriggled out from behind the shelves. She was covered in dust and cobwebs, but did not attempt to brush herself off.

Bending down, she picked up her father's shoe and walked up the cellar stairs and through the shattered remnants of the door. Sergio lay dead in a pool of blood in the house's foyer, his body riddled with bullet holes. His eyes stared sightlessly at the ceiling, and she knelt, gently ran her hand over his face, and closed them so he could rest peacefully.

She found kind, old Andrew hanging from the staircase, his hands bound behind his back and a tight noose around his neck. Katerina tried not to look up at his face, choosing instead to remember him as she saw him every evening when she awoke with his wide grin and boisterous laugh.

The house felt strange to her, lacking in the warmth and laughter that used to fill its halls. She walked to her room and retrieved the small flowerpot from the window. It was a night-blooming cereus, and its white flower reflected the bright moonlight. She smiled down at the little flower, remembering the day her father had given it to her. With a sad sigh, she placed the little flower pot in the opening of her father's shoe. She cradled it in her arm and left her room and all its happy memories for the last time.

The night air was cool on her face as she walked outside. The fluttering wings of an owl broke the silence of the night as it came to land on the old light blue Dodge Spirit in the yard next door. A burnt smell filled her nostrils, and she looked sadly at the three scorch marks on the lawn where the sun had turned her family's bodies to ash. The very place they had all laughed and danced together under the moonlight only a week before. Then her back went rigid, and a shiver of fear ran down her spine as she realized she was not alone in the front yard.

A dark figure stood by the scorch marks with his back to her; the shadows cast by the moonlight had hidden him from sight until her eyes adjusted to the night. Katerina watched as the figure stooped down and laid a single red rose on one of the darkened patches of grass. He cocked his head to the side, sticking his fingers into the scorched grass. Then the figure stood up and stared down into his hand.

Katerina walked silently up behind him and saw that he held a small wooden ring, a rose finely etched on its surface. He sensed her presence and turned, his handsome face a mask of alarm that quickly gave way to relief.

"Katerina, you're alive," the man breathed deeply, as if he had been holding his breath. "I feared the worst."

"Tomas," the little girl collapsed into the man, finally letting herself give in to her grief. "I hid when the monsters came."

"You're safe now; I won't let anything happen to you."

"I'm sorry about Petia," her chest heaved with great sobs, the tears streaming down her face. "She loved you so much."

"I loved her too. She was my little rose petal," he looked down at the wooden ring in his palm as a tear slowly escaped his eye.

"I am going to miss them so much."

"I am too. Every moment of every day."

"Will the monsters find us?" She looked up into his face, the streaks of tears on her cheeks glittering in the moonlight.

"No, Katerina, the monsters won't find us," he looked down at her and then over at the three scorched patches of grass. "Because we are going to find them first."

121

BUMP
Billie Karras

I believed in God no more than I believed in ghosts, but still I prayed: *Please. One more bump and we can get this over with.* We were in my bedroom, the paint peeling, the drywall cracked, and I bent over and felt a tickle as he tapped more cocaine into my asshole. There was a sniff, a cough, and then the slimy worm of his tongue was burrowing into me again.

"Are you ready for me?" he asked, the absurd redundancy of his words muffled by my flesh. His breath back there was hot, moist, and it made my stomach turn. I was never ready for them.

"Yeah, baby," I moaned, doing my best to play the part of the eager whore. He lifted his face out of my ass and gave it a slap. "Oh, yeah." Then he entered me.

He was only half-hard on account of the coke, and I thrusted backwards, trying to speed our coupling along as best I could. Meanwhile, my mind was elsewhere. I looked up at the wad of bills he'd set on the dresser; the prize that awaited me at the end of all this.

I thrusted harder, faster.

"Hey," he said from behind me, out of breath and alarmed. "Wait, I don't wanna—" And then he was out of me again and the thin, watery putts of semen were dribbling onto my ass—warm at first, then almost instantly cooling in the ceiling fan breeze.

"Ahhhh *fuck,*" he hissed.

I was already up—wiping myself off with the towel I'd set on my nightstand, stepping into my panties, sliding my t-shirt over my head. "That was *so* good," I said, not looking at him, not bothering to smile. "I got an early morning tomorrow, so—"

I stepped toward the dresser, reaching for my pay. Suddenly he was beside me, hand shooting out with the speed of a striking snake. Then it was gone.

I rounded on him. *"Hey!"* I said it in a furious whisper; I couldn't be too loud. "Give me my money!"

His lip jutted in a pout that was ridiculous on a man at least twice my age. His pants were still off and his penis, still slick with the KY Jelly I'd slathered us with, poked limply out in front of him like a metastatic tumor. "I paid for an hour, and it's only been," he made a grand show of checking his watch, "twenty *minutes!*"

"Listen, buddy," I said slowly. "You *came.* You wanna *fuck* me double, you gotta *pay* me double."

His fists clenched, his jaw tightened. "If you think I'm paying full price for fifteen minutes, you're out of your mind."

This wasn't the first time something like this had happened; the kind of men that had to resort to hookers to cheat on their wives were often cheap, entitled bastards. "Give me my money. You cum, you pay. That's fair."

"Fair?" he cried. I shushed him, but he ignored me, face contorting in so much self-righteous outrage. I could see my money crumpled tight in his sweat-shined fist. "I *paid* for the hour. I should *get* the hour. *That's* fair."

No, this wasn't the first time this had happened. I had a backup plan. When a woman's in business for herself, sometimes she has to get her hands dirty.

Especially in a business like this.

"Look, just—keep your voice down, okay? You want your full hour?" I leaned my body against the dresser. Behind my hip, I let my hand fall to the second drawer from the top. I fingered the crack, prying it open just enough to slip my hand in.

"I mean, I'm not paying for something I didn't get. That's ridiculous, I mean, treating your customers like that."

"I'm sorry."

"Well," he said with a satisfied smirk. "Frankly, I think you should be."

I bit the inside of my cheek until I tasted blood. "Okay," I said. "How do you want it?" I watched him think it over as I felt around the drawer, trying not to let the pain from contorting my wrist show on my face.

His brow furrowed. "Hey," he said, stepping forward. "What—?"

At last, I felt the cold metal of my little snub-nose revolver. I flung the barrel in his direction; *the words give me my fucking money* ready to fly off my tongue.

But he was too fast.

Before I could even get my finger on the trigger, he was on me. The gun slipped from my hand and skittered away as we crashed to the floor. The air in my lungs rushed out of me in a great wheezing gust as all his weight pressed firmly down on my chest. There was a loud *crack* as he punched me in the side of the head, black stars exploding into my vision.

"Pull a gun on me, huh?" He was panting. "Fuckin whore thinks she can pull a gun on me!" He hit me again, this time on the chin. My teeth cracked together, and gritty flecks of chipped enamel dotted the insides of my cheeks like grains of sand and tears squirted out the corners of my eyes.

"Please," I whimpered, "please stop, y-you can keep the money, just please—"

"Oh, I'll keep the money." I was dimly aware of the sound of fabric tearing somewhere. "Don't you worry about *that.*"

When I realized what he was doing, I tried to scream. He wrapped his big hands around my throat and it cut off with a squeak. Panic filled me like electricity, making my muscles jump, and I thrashed about, hitting him, kicking him, trying to free myself.

He held tight, his teeth bared, and his eyes bugged and a vein bulging angrily at the top of his forehead. "Think you can scam *me?*" he said, straining, punctuating each word with a hard thrust of his hips. "You dirty, saggy, skanky, ugly *slut*—"

My vision began to dim. I could no longer feel the rape that was ripping through the flesh between my legs. All I knew was the pain in my lungs, the blood in my throat. I felt that at any moment it would surely pop, my neck like the belly of a child's pet frog held tight, too tight, until finally bursting open in a glut of blue blood and cold, gray innards.

Blessedly, for a moment, his grip loosened, and I hungrily sucked in air that was *so* much like broken glass. Then he squeezed tighter than ever. I felt the blood vessels in my eyes pop. I smelled the piss as my bladder let go, and for a moment I was warmed by the pool of it below me. Then it was cold.

In the next room, my baby began to cry.

And then I was dead.

* * *

It would be impossible to fully describe the passing from one plane of existence to another, so I won't really try. There's a feeling of weightlessness. A mild, yet seemingly endless nausea. All in all, it boils down to this: one minute, everything was horrible, and the next, well.

Everything was worse.

People like to believe that death is an end to suffering. You hear it all the time. About a month before my father's forty-fifth birthday, he was diagnosed with cancer. We were all hopeful at first, but things didn't take long. By the end, he was bedridden, incontinent, sedated on so much morphine it was incredible he could even open his eyes; propped unceremoniously up in front of the television. It broke my heart to see him like that. But what could I do?

After he was gone, my mother wiped tears from her

eyes and my brother hugged her tight and I heard him as he whispered thickly into her red-dyed perm, again and again and again like some ritualistic chant:

It's all over now, Momma.

My brother was wrong.

There was no peace, no empty restfulness to wash over me as my heart stopped beating and my brain starved of blood and oxygen. There was only more pain, as all at once my soul was ripped from my body like the wings off a baby bird. It—I—hung over the room, an invisible mist of hurt and despair and silent screams. And although I no longer had eyes, still I had no choice but to watch as my death scene went on and on and on and on below me.

His body stiffened, climaxing again, and suddenly I knew his name: William Brite. Sweat beaded on his upper lip and hung there. He wasn't looking at my corpse below him; his eyes were closed, and his face was twisted up in shame, in anger, in bleeding ecstasy.

My baby was still crying.

His eyes opened, slowly, and he saw me at last. My body's mouth hung open. His mouth opened, too. As he did, a drop of sweat fell, landing in the hollow of my neck. I was surprised to find how clearly I could feel it as the thoughts clanged about inside the walls of his skull. *Oh, fuck,* he thought. What had he done?

It wasn't quite like hearing, not really. It was more like having the thoughts myself, only they weren't mine. And I couldn't help but have them. The irony of this filled me with ugly despair: the physical rape had ended, and yet here he was, continuing to invade me.

He wasn't high anymore, and the comedown had left him with a massive headache that I felt as if it were my own. His mouth was still numb, bone-dry, and his tongue sat swollen between his teeth like a fleshy rock.

He looked toward the wall where the crying was coming through. *There's no other room,* he thought, but he wasn't sure about that. In his guilty haste to get it all going, he hadn't noticed. William got off me, pulled his pants on, walked out the door. He pretended not to see it as he shuffled down the hall.

The room my daughter was in.

He paused at the front door, and I could feel it as he considered turning back. Checking on my baby, calling the police. He could find a payphone, be anonymous. No one would ever know it was him.

YES! I wailed at him, not making a sound. *YES! Please, please, pl* —

But then he thought of his wife. Sarah was her name, and I could see her through the cloud of his thoughts, and she looked good for an older woman. A little thick in the middle, but pretty (it came as no surprise that, through his thoughts, the only impression I got of her was of the way she looked).

He thought of his children, and I could see them, too. A girl of six or seven, smiling, a tiny ray of sunshine and innocence. A boy of ten or twelve, with a moody mop of hair and a *Star Wars* tee shirt.

He'd lose them all if he got caught at this. His wife, his children, his *life*. And for what? Some junkie whore's crack baby? *Hell* no. Hell no.

I fell to his feet, pleading.

William didn't notice. His nose was running, and he sniffed. I felt the bitter dregs of his last bump of coke pull out of his sinuses as clearly as if they were being pulled out of my own, sliding along the back of his tongue, my tongue, slipping down our throats with the numbing taste of aspirin and gasoline. If I'd still had a face, I would have grimaced. As he did.

William Brite grasped the doorknob, using his shirt to prevent the leaving of fingerprints, and turned it. Pulled. Gave the direction of the cries one last harried, wide-eyed look. And then he was gone.

He took me with him.

* * *

The road was clear as it was dark; there were no street-lights on my side of town. William drove home slowly, not wanting to be pulled over. And all the while, I screamed. He couldn't hear. I reached over his shoulders, wrapping the ectoplasmic tendrils of what could be called my fingers around the steering wheel and wrenched, trying desperately to turn the car around. It wouldn't budge.

If I'd still had lungs, I would have been hyperventilating. My baby was in my house, crying, probably *screaming* by now—for me, for her mommy, and I was only so much stiffening meat on the floor in the next room. Would the widower next door hear and call for help? In the two years since I'd moved in, I'd seen him only sporadically, and the last had been, what—five, six months ago? He'd been in his garden, by the peonies; muttering to himself, stuffing what looked like some strange sort of rats into a burlap sack. I'd watched from my front window, frowning, pressing a protective hand over my pregnant belly. The house had been dark ever since. Was he even still alive in there? Who could know?

I flung myself against the car's windshield, trying to smash through it. Nothing happened. How long could my baby wait there, alone? A day? Two? I pictured her in the crib, not crying, breathing shallow and lethargic, heart rate slowing, organs shutting down, brains turning to mush. I sobbed, and I screamed, and I wanted to peel the flesh from William's bones. I'd wear it like a suit of skin, and I'd turn the car around. I'd get back home, and I'd call the police, and I'd go to my daughter and I'd plant a ghostly kiss on her forehead and we would wait together for the last time, and then she'd be saved.

I dug my fingers into William's throat and squeezed, praying desperately for a victorious glut of blood to spray out onto the dashboard. *Please, God.* Ghosts were real, after all; I knew that now for myself. Maybe God was, too. *Please, please, please,* I prayed. *She needs me.*

There was no blood. He simply sniffed, slowing at a stoplight, and scratched absently at his neck as if I were nothing but a probing mosquito on a warm summer night. The sobs that wracked my spirit were shuddering, painful, so loud they should have shaken the car off the road entirely.

But they didn't.

* * *

He entered his house quietly, dragging me after him like a leashed dog. The house was huge compared to my run-down single-story shack. It was almost a mansion. The door was an oak monstrosity, inlaid with decoratively cut frosted glass and arched on top like the entryway to a castle in a fairytale.

It was late. He slipped his shoes off in the sleepy darkness, leaving them by the door, and softly padded toward his bedroom. The door was ajar, and he pushed it open just wide enough to slip through.

I remained at the front door. It seemed the tether that kept me tied to him was not quite as short as I'd feared. I tried to open the door and leave. Nothing happened, of course. I tried to squeeze beneath the crack below. Again, nothing; it was as if some invisible barrier were there, trapping me inside like a force field in a science fiction novel.

Meanwhile, I could hear the exchange between William and his wife as clearly as if I'd been right next to them. I moved toward their bedroom, passing leather furniture and red Tiffany lamps and painstakingly posed-for family photos. In them, William Brite wore a mustache. I wanted to spit on it. At the other end of the hall, I saw another door tacked and taped with crudely colored drawings. *The kids' room. Or one of them, anyway.*

"Will? That you?" The woman's voice was sleepy, unconcerned. I knew he came home late often, and, over the years of their marriage, she had long since grown used to it. I slipped inside. He was standing at the foot of the bed, unbuttoning his shirt, thinking about me. She was a lump of covers in the bed. I watched.

"Hey, honey," he said. "How was your day?"

"Fine. Chuck keep you late again?"

"Yeah." The lie came easily. In his head, the image of my strangled face played over and over again like a looping film reel. He pushed it away. "You know how it is."

She made a mumbled response in the affirmative and wrapped herself more tightly in the comforter. "Could you turn the heat up? It's cold."

"Yeah," he said, and disappeared into the bathroom.

I floated over to his wife — Sarah, I remembered. She'd already fallen back asleep. I leaned in, getting close to her face, and spoke: *wake up.* She didn't. I reached out to shake her. *Wake up!*

Nothing.

Frustrated, I went to the bathroom door. It was shut, and I paused. So far, I hadn't been able to walk through anything at all, but somehow this felt different. *He's inside there. That might make a difference.* I closed my eyes and moved forward, bracing for impact. It never came. I'd passed right through.

I thought I was starting to understand the limitations of my phantasmic abilities. If I was inside somewhere with him, I was free to roam where I wanted, as long as I stayed inside. I could pass through doors, through walls too, I assumed; I just couldn't leave. Okay, fine.

But I also couldn't *move* anything, couldn't *say* anything, couldn't appear to anyone. I'd seen a hundred horror movies at a dozen drive-ins, and not once had I ever seen one where the ghost didn't *do* anything the whole time. My baby was going to die if I couldn't get back to her somehow. There had to be *something,* some trick to this I just wasn't getting.

But then again, I realized, I'd never seen a ghost before, had I? Maybe this was why. Maybe this was just how it was.

Then I remembered how I'd tried to rip out William's throat in the car. It hadn't worked, true, but he *had* felt something, hadn't he? Yes. He'd scratched. But I couldn't just *itch* him to death. There *had* to be something I could do, had to be something I was missing.

* * *

Inside the bathroom, the shower was running and William, naked, stood leaning over the sink. His image was a fleshy blur in the mirror, which had already fogged up in the steam. The little glass vial of coke he'd had when we were together sat on the counter before him.

Fury burned in me like bile at the back of an alcoholic's throat. This man, this *man,* had raped me, he'd murdered me, he'd abandoned my child to die a slow and painful death alone with nothing but the corpse of her own mother for company, and here he was—*here he was*—weighing the pros and cons of having another fucking *bump.*

Just call it a night, Willie, he was thinking, *you don't need it.*

Do it, I said. *I hope it gives you a fucking heart attack.*

"Fuck it," he muttered, and tapped some out onto the flesh between his thumb and forefinger. He brought his hand up to his nose and sniffed.

I felt it as the drugs stung his sinuses, as bitter mucus dripped down his throat, as his senses sharpened and his heart rate quickened and he felt, all at once, oh, so much *better.* I didn't realize what was happening at first; I was too angry. But as I'd been hearing his thoughts, as I'd been feeling his feelings, so, too, did I feel his high. My disincorporated soul buzzed with it, *thrummed* with it, and for the first time since I'd died, I felt something other than helplessness and pain. I felt *electric.*

Suddenly, I knew what needed to happen.

I leaned forward, right up against his ear. I whispered: *another.*

William leaned over and tapped a fat line out onto the counter. Dug into his pants, which lay crumpled on the floor, and found a twenty (one of mine, I thought), and rolled it up quickly, hungrily, thinking the phrase *just one more* over and over again like it was a blinking neon sign hung outside an inner-city strip club.

He snorted it in one fluid motion, quickly straightening his body and kicking his head back to force every last bit of it all the way back.

Another, I said.

He obeyed.

Another.

Another.

I felt myself growing stronger, stronger, ever stronger —

At last, he lifted a fist up to the mirror, wiping away at the fog to check his mustache for any errant white flecks —

Then he froze. His eyes widened. His mouth opened. I felt it as every hair on his trembling, disgusting body stood on end — smelled it as the sour odor of fear hissed from every one of his pores like poison gas from a mustard bomb. I'd been missing something, alright, and now, oh yes —

I thought I'd found it.

In the fog, just beyond the sloping lump of his shoulder, was me, perfectly visible. Perfectly *physical.* I grinned at him. My face was moon pale. My eyes were black. My hair floated around me in wild tangles, as if I were underwater. My grin stretched wider, and wider, and wider, until the skin at my cheeks split open, papery and bloodless, to reveal my molars and my rotten tongue and the shiny white of my jawbone beneath them.

William screamed.

I wrapped my long, wispy fingers around the back of his neck, lifted him up off the floor tiles, and then I flung him through the glass shower door beside us. It shattered, cutting him in a dozen different places, and I felt every one — a gash in his thigh, a cut along his spine, and a slice into the meat of his forearm so deep the glass squealed against the bone. And it was nothing, that pain — *nothing* — in the corpse-cool face of my undead fury.

Sarah was pounding at the door. *"Will?"*

I moved toward him, my feet gliding over the floor as if I were standing on a dolly. He lay folded over, legs draped over the side of the tub. The spray from the shower mixed with his blood and ran pink down the drain. I stood over him and watched the cut on his thigh bleed. He cowered. I reached out and gave it a flick.

He yelped, legs kicking, and scuttled backwards like a crab, trying to go deeper into the tub, trying to get away from me. But there was nowhere to go. I reached in after him and jammed my finger into the cut, digging in, feeling his pain, loving it, relishing it. The feeling of being inside living flesh again, even just a little, was amazing. And the coke only made it better. In my life, I'd always been pretty take-it-or-leave-it with the stuff. But this was *exhilarating*.

"Stop, stop, please!" he cried. Outside, his wife continued to beat on the door.

I giggled and swiped the vial off the sink. Snapped the top off and brought it up to my nose. I gave it a monstrous sniff, and his bladder let go then. I watched with amused glee as piss squirted out of his sad, shriveled penis, running down between his quivering thighs, mixing with the blood and the water and the glass beneath him.

The coke hit me like a semi-truck. Strength rippled through me. My hair lashed around my face like flames of a pale fire. He screamed. I laughed.

And then I was on him.

Suddenly, the door burst open, and his wife tumbled inside with us. "Oh my god, Will, what—"

Then she saw what I was doing. Her jaw dropped. Her eyes twitched. A low, mewling sound came from deep within her throat. Then she was gone, running from the room.

I'd turned him over, holding him down with both hands. His hairy buttocks were spread open before me, his asshole staring up at me like a puckered mouth. Distantly, I heard a child cry, "Mommy, don't leave me!" Then I heard the child's cries rise up, twisting into alarmed and horrified shrieks. A door slammed, and then somewhere outside, a car started.

Below me, William was thrashing, kicking. His feet passed right through me like I was nothing more than empty air, despite my newfound stimulant fleshliness.

I held him tight. "Please, stop," he sobbed into the porcelain. "My children, p-please, my *children*—"

"Shh." I chuckled, its sound the creak of a gate in a graveyard. "Don't you worry about *that*." I leaned forward.

"What—hey—*uk*—"

And I shoved my head into his asshole.

I could feel it as his skin tore around my cheeks, bathing my neck and my shoulders and my back in warm sheets of bright, sticky crimson. His screams, muffled to my ears, rattled his bones around me and I squeezed my arms in, compressing myself like a rat in a drainpipe, digging up through his organs, going farther, and farther, and farther. His pain was blinding; it was a gutting, tearing, ripping, splitting, horrible pain. And I felt it—all of it—as if it had been my own. And as his screams rang from outside his body, so too did my screams burble from inside him just as loudly.

But still I went on.

My fingers walked up his ribs, searching for the places where his arms met his torso. At last, I found them, and I pushed my arms into his like sleeves on a sweater. I pulled my legs up into him and down, and my feet slid through muscle and tendon until finally settling into the insides of his soles. I pushed my head up through his throat, past his nasal cavity, and tasted the residue of coke-snot built up back there, and then I went further, pushing my head up against the spongy mass of meat in his skull—

It wouldn't budge. I pushed again, straining. *Please.* Nothing.

Just—

One—

More—

There was a wet, meaty crunching sound in the dark. And then I watched, through his eyes, as his brain exploded out of his nose. It splattered thickly onto the porcelain wall before him like a chunky soup: Campbell's Blood and Spinal Fluid and Slick, Graypink

Brainmeat. Ninety-nine cents. Find it on aisle nine.

I blinked the splashback out of his eyes and lifted myself up out of the tub with his arms. I stood shakily on his feet and watched as the shower's spray began to wash the mess away. The pain was gone. My thoughts were my own.

William Brite was dead.

I was free.

"I hope it's cold down there," I said, my voice passing through his throat. "And I hope it *hurts.*"

Then I was digging into the pants on the floor, finding his keys. I grabbed the last bit of coke off the counter.

And then I was gone.

✶ ✶ ✶

When I got back home the door was still shut, still unlocked, just as William had left it. Inside, however, it was silent, and fear prickled at me from within William's shredded guts. *Please, let her be okay. Please.*

I was buzzing—I'd done the last of the coke on the way over, fearing a quick comedown on the road. I was terrified to be driving when William's corpse suddenly grew heavy around me, too heavy for me to move. I could imagine his car veering off the road, could almost feel the impact as it smashed into a tree. That couldn't happen. I had to get home to my baby. And now here I was, standing outside her door.

Please.

And then I heard her: *"Mmum-mmum-mmum-mmuh…"*

I burst into the room and ran to her. The paint was unblemished, the walls hung with the paintings of animals that I'd done for her. "Hi, baby!" I scooped her up, hugged her tight. "Mommy missed you, oh, Mommy missed you so much." I felt the sting of tears as they welled up in William's eyes. "Are you hungry? Oh, you must be so hungry."

She began to cry then, as if she'd forgotten all about her hunger and I'd just rudely reminded her. I took her out of the room, through the hall, into the kitchen.

"Yes, baby, yes, let's get you fed," I said as I mixed

a bottle, and now I was crying too; full, ugly, sobbing cries. This would be the last time I'd ever see her. I didn't know what would happen after the drugs wore off, but I had a feeling I wouldn't be able to follow her wherever they took her. Maybe there would be another place I'd go. Or maybe I'd just cease to exist completely. It scared me because of how much I'd miss her.

I'd miss her so much.

I sat us down on the couch and with one hand, held the bottle to her lips as I used my other hand to lift the phone to my ear. I cradled it on my shoulder and dialed.

When I hung up, I stared into my baby's eyes. They were so beautiful, so perfect. "I'm so sorry," I said, sniffing. My head was starting to hurt now; nose congested, mouth dry. This was it. The comedown.

She finished her bottle, and I lifted her up to my chest, resting her head on my shoulder, and patted her back. She burped, and I laughed, softly, and kissed the top of her head. I imagined the life she'd have after this. The family that would adopt her. The perfect mother, the one I never could have been. I smiled. But it soon soured. Would this really be it? *God, don't let it be—let me haunt her; please; please, please, pretty please. With ghostly kisses. With spectral snuggles. With everlasting love.*

Outside, a car pulled up, and I heard the heavy clunks of doors opening as flashing blue and red lights bled in through the blinds. The fine blonde hairs on my baby's head glowed with them in the darkness, and the tears were no longer flowing. I blinked, trying to start them up again, desperately wanting to mourn my motherhood just a little bit longer. And as my hands began to grow heavy, as my eyelids began to droop, I wished, I begged, I *prayed*—

For just one more bump.

122

DINNER ON FERN STREET
Julie Aaron

I've watched the house at 122 Fern St. for five months now. The chipped gray paint peeling off shutters that are wrapped around the grimy windows. The weak bottom step leading up to the squeaky screen door with the slit in the bottom left. The guest bathroom window that she always leaves unlocked. The creaky board in the hallway you have to step around or else it whines loudly into the quiet night. The light above the oven she keeps on to rid the empty house of scary things in the dark. The house itself isn't very special. A build from the late sixties untouched by modern remodels. What's drawn me here is her. The smell of the hairspray she doused herself in to get ready for work that morning. The TV dinner she microwaved for herself before watching whatever movie she rented at the video store next to her job at the bank uptown. The smell of her skin painting the walls of this house. Like a magnet, I have been drawn to her.

I lean against the kitchen sink. I've gotten comfortable in her space. She's made it so. Why else would she always leave the window unlocked and the oven light on for me?

We locked eyes in the checkout line. I was watching her read the front page of the latest Reader's Digest when she felt my stare. She looked up from her page and smiled at me so I know she felt it too. We couldn't act on it then. Our love, the love of two women, would have to be shared behind closed doors. So after her groceries were bagged and her check was written and handed to the young cashier, I watched her push her buggy through the double sliding doors. The outside evening air blew through her teased bangs. I abandoned my cart to chase after her. I threw myself into my old Datsun and hunched over the steering wheel to keep my eyes on her. She is so beautiful loading paper bag after paper bag into the trunk of her light blue Dodge Spirit. Her arms are strong and long. She's pale. Her brown hair in permed curls runs down her shoulders onto her dark green Mickey Mouse crewneck. She wants me to see. She wants me to know. Why else did she smile at me like that?

So I followed her home. From the grocery store down Main Street. Stopped, suspended in time, at the traffic light near the Episcopal church, right onto Clinton Street, over the railroad tracks, past the baseball field and a left down Fern Street. The third-last house on the left. The grass is a little overgrown and the tree in the front yard has seen better days. The house itself is nothing special. Boards and nails and chipping paint. But it keeps her safe for me.

Tonight as I drink her wine from her cornflower blue glass, I think of crawling into bed with her. How soft her hair might be. Does she sleep only in her panties? The faded pink ones she often leaves in the broken plastic basket in the laundry room. Would they smell just as good on her as they do before they go into the wash? It would only be a short walk through the living room and down the hall, past the creaky floorboard, past the bathroom with the window she leaves open for me and through the particle board door that makes no noise when you sweep it open. I've been all over her home. So much so that I've come to think of it as our home. I know the ins and outs of 122 Fern St. better than she probably knows them herself. It was me who fixed the flusher in the bathroom, me who started the dryer when she ran off to work late and forgot. She's welcomed me into her life. Why else has she not been scared to find my glass on the counter every night or my fingerprints on the windows?

I've made my choice. Tonight is the night. I will march across her house, our home, sweep her quiet bedroom door open and gently pull her floral bed cover back and slide myself against her warm body. God, I've dreamed of this. Touched myself to this. Planned for this. She'll feel me, strong against her back and breathe a sigh of relief. *Finally,* she'll think, and turn in my arms. Facing me. I'll taste her. Drink her in like I've fantasized for months. In the cover of night, these four walls will expand for our love, our new lives. Together. We won't be judged or prosecuted. We can just be. After all this time watching, protecting, caring, hiding. I set my glass down in the metal sink next to her dirty dinner fork and the mug with its ring of morning coffee painted across the bottom. Cracking my neck, I suck in a gulp of her air and place my right foot in front of the left when I hear it.

A scratch so faint a trained dog wouldn't even pick it up, but I am better than any dog she could have. Another scratch. I close my eyes to pinpoint its origin. Where is it coming from? I know everything about this house. I've been inside of 122 Fern St. every night for four months. It took me some time to build the courage to go to her, but once I did, how could I ever leave?

In a stutter, I reach back to the oven light, clicking it off. In the pitch black, my heart drops to my stomach. I am not the only thing that haunts this house.

A shadow darker than the end of the world stretches itself, standing tall from the floor. There's a black void swallowing the light that's trying to pour in from the street lamps. Spreading itself across the windows of the house. The scratching is incessant now. The shadow drops its long arms to flex its fingers back and forth against the vinyl-covered concrete. It will wake her and take her from me.

I had heard the rumors, of course. The town whispers. The street lamps that never shine on the home, the beautiful owner six months new to town with no family and a ravenous appetite for raw steak. The missing neighborhood animals, the hair-standing quietness surrounding the dwelling. Hell house.

She looked tired when I met her. The kind of tiredness that isn't explainable or forgiving. Supernatural. Bumps in the night, flickering lights, bodies buried under the crawl space. But then I came to 122 Fern St. I slept in her favorite recliner for hours as she tossed and turned in the next room. I sat at her kitchen table while she was working and pretended we were having dinner. I stood over her dirty laundry breathing her in, and I never saw or heard anything worse than me. I guess I've become a part of her, a part of her home, and her ghosts have accepted me. A smile crosses my face. Just another way we've become one. Her demons are mine. God, I am bathed in bliss at this thought. The Devil himself recognizes me as hers. What else could I be but hers? What else could she be but mine?

Whatever has clawed its way out of the fire and into our home won't stop me. Tonight she'll know. Tonight I'll have her. Even if I have to devour her myself.

The shadow breathes in and out, pushing against the particles in the air, flexing the foundation of the house. My fist clenches at my side. Bloody palm from my nails pressing tightly into my skin. We move towards each other in tandem. One hesitant step. Frozen when we realize we've stepped at the same time. The shadow touches every corner of the house. Large and looming and a deep dark blackness. The kind of darkness that swallows you whole. She sleeps still; I'd know otherwise, I'd feel her breathing shift, I'd hear her rustle her covers. The covers I should be sharing with her by now. But I'm here. Face to face with her ghost. Her demon. Her hellish creature. Her curse. I can taste my fear. It sits, a pungent thing, humming under my skin, begging me to turn and run for the back door, not looking back. Damn the creaky floorboard, anything to get me out of here. My need for her anchors me.

I am not the only thing consuming here tonight. I cannot inhale without it creeping towards me. A slow drag, the darkness spreads, claiming the house as its own. And me with it. As some payment, a tax, a prize. It is polarizing how cemented I am when she is in the next room needing me. The shadow takes another step. Another step. Another step. It is upon me. We share the same air, thick with dread and craving. Breathing in and out against one another. Poison to poison. We stand face to face, the same smile splitting our lips bloody. If this is the only way to have her, then so be it.

I turn from the shadow and start my journey down the hallway. Past the creaky floorboard I'd always been so careful to dodge. Now I feel it dip and whine beneath my weight. I stagger in the complete darkness past her bathroom with the window unlocked just for me. I sweep her quiet particle board door open. It takes no time to be near to her. Like a spell, my body knows its way to hers. Swaying at her bedside, I watch her breathe. The floral blanket she drapes herself in rising slowly with intent. Up and down. Rhythmic perfection. I want to swallow her breath. I crave her. Wholly as holy consumption.

Like a struck match near a gas leak, the room explodes. In the heavy quiet, I can hear her eyes open. They're as dark as the shadow that towered over me, feasting on the light in the living room. Black as the death of galaxies, reflecting my fear back to me. Her hair is messy from sweating through the early night and being pressed against the tattered pillows we should have shared. I rake my wide eyes over her, the shadow is ripping at her pale skin, begging to be released. Her smile is calm and controlled; she is not afraid of the demon that exists behind her walls. Quickly she rises to her knees, denting her spot on the bed. The spot that should have been for me.

Her pupils dilate, her fingers flex. She is hungry.

Standing statuesque at her bedside as she stares me down, drinks me in, it dawns on me. I have not been the only one hunting in this house. I might not have been the one hunting her at all. The thought comes too late. I am already struck by her gaze. My feet pinned to the carpet like they've been buried under a thousand pounds of wet cement. The shadow is at my back, her at my front, ravished from months of me being in her space. She has not accepted me into her home. I am not welcomed; it is not ours. She did not invite me to crawl in through her forgotten window, share her dusty air, drink her cheap wine and pace her floors with burning want and indecision. She has trapped me. Like a deer in velvet antlers. I was caught by a mating call, strategic and cruel. I have been lured, seduced. I have been fucking ensnared. Like a common rabbit! She lunges.

I feel her claws dig into me, shredding my tan skin; a scream is frozen in my throat. My eyes locked onto hers as her jaw unhinges, bloody, to latch onto my shoulder and pull me apart. There is so much blood. In the silence of the night, she is a messy eater. Not a loud one, all that can be heard as I dip in and out of consciousness is her teeth striking roughly against each other while she tears through softened flesh and sinewy tendons. As my last breaths come, I feel the house sigh with relief; the shadow regurgitates the streetlight lumens into the hidden corners of the room, her eyes return to the golden brown I have spent months chasing after. She is fed. If this is the only way I can have her, so be it. I belong to her and to the house now.

As my body is rolled into the dusty crawl space beneath the creaky floorboard, I land atop the other figures buried inside of her home. Some half-eaten, others picked clean. I wonder if she ever comes back for us. Will I feed her for days to come? Will she be gluttonous with me? Will she relish in me? All this time I thought I would be tasting her.

123
FUN AND GAMES
Alex James Donne

The door was locked.

Lionel knew this, unquestionably, because not thirty seconds ago he had walked across the room, opened the door (briefly) to confirm that it was in fact *not* locked, closed it again, inserted the key and turned it firmly until he heard the satisfying click of the lock engaging, tugged on the door handle for confirmation before giving that handle a little up-down jiggle for luck, returned the key to his pocket, and stepped back to finally take the breath he'd been holding in for almost the entirety of those thirty seconds.

So the door was, beyond any shadow of a doubt, locked.

Nineteen agonizing seconds later, the door was opened from the other side.

* * *

In the last week and a half, he had become very good at assessing the passage of time. Not just counting minutes, but counting seconds. He could probably stretch himself to fractions of seconds at this point, straying into the nebulous realm of minuscule moments of time he would need a degree in particle physics to adequately comprehend. Time, after all, was something he had far too much of these days. He had given up on snatching more than two or three hours of sleep after the first three nights, and all the usual things he might do to make the time pass a little faster—read his Kindle, clean the house, or as an absolute last resort switch on the television—were no longer options for him.

It would not allow it.

Not when It wanted to play.

And It wanted to play all the time.

❋ ❋ ❋

For a while he thought he'd been clever by leaving the curtains open, so at least he had the option of observing the outside world (and Lionel very much thought of it in those terms now, the outside world where things were normal and the inside world where things were very far from normal indeed), as long as he wasn't too obvious about it. A casual glance to watch a car pass by along Fern Street or Gwenda Duncan from Hemlock Avenue walking her awful, yappy little dog, a surreptitious peek at the sky to assess the fine weather he dearly wished he could be outside enjoying. On the sixth day, he'd allowed himself a full two seconds to watch a grocery store delivery driver hauling two crates of groceries up the driveway of Number 126 when all the air seemed to be sucked from the room to be replaced by a droning, sonorous thumping from inside the walls, and the ceiling, and even from beneath the floor. The air, when it was returned moments later, was frigid cold, but the thumping remained and only stopped once he realized he was supposed to get up and close the curtains. In his urgency, he tugged the right-side curtain closed a little more forcefully than the left, leaving an inch-wide gap between the curtain's edge and the window, and the monstrous thumping actually rose in volume until Lionel had carefully rectified his error. His last glimpse of Fern Street, through that slender inch-wide gap, was of that same delivery driver rolling his now empty trolley back down next door's driveway towards his truck, and it may have only been his imagination, but Lionel was almost certain he'd been whistling.

Just to be sure, he'd taken it upon himself to close every other set of curtains in the house, as well as lowering every set of blinds on the windows—for example, those in the kitchen—where he hadn't hung curtains. He hadn't opened any of them since.

❋ ❋ ❋

As he watched the locked door glide silently open for the seventh time that day Lionel wondered, not for the first time, why the door game was Its favorite. He was forced to play it twice as much as any of the other games. Of course, he'd played them all multiple times by this point. Dressing in as many layers of clothing as he could manage, only to have items yanked off his body, one piece at a time, often out of order (and frequently rather painfully) but always miraculously intact. Or there was filling the bathroom sink with water hot enough to fog the mirror, shouting "It's t-too hot!" at the top of his voice, and watching as the water instantly froze to form a single sink-sized oval of solid ice. The worst part was waiting for the moment when the ice shattered into hundreds of glittering shards that would float languorously across the room, slowly melting, creating a mess. It was then Lionel's job to clean it up. And let's not forget standing in the doorway of his perfectly orderly kitchen, turning around, counting to three (once, he'd tried to be sneaky and only counted to two; he wouldn't try that again), and then turning back to see chairs stacked impossibly upon tins of kidney beans and table legs replaced with spindly towers of cutlery. Compared to all that, a locked door seemingly opening all by itself felt decidedly hum-drum. And yet, he was called upon to play his part in this particular trick numerous times each day.

How he knew precisely what It wanted from him was both less and more of a mystery. It was as though a voice was speaking inside his head, but not with words, and though he understood, he could not hear it. Door. Kitchen. Clothes. Sink. The first few times this happened his nose had bled (thankfully it was only the very first occasion that, rather embarrassingly, caused him to lose control of his bladder as well), but he supposed his body had acclimatized, and that particular side effect was a thing of the past.

And there were other questions, too. What exactly It was. Where the damned thing had come from in the first place. Why it had chosen him. He supposed it was, to all intents and purposes, a ghost. He was sure there was even a particular word for exactly what type of ghost it was, but unfortunately Lionel didn't know it. The point was, his house *wasn't* haunted; he'd lived there for five very happy years, and before It arrived, there hadn't been the slightest hint of unwanted supernatural presences.

Not at Number 123, anyway.

He could still remember the reactions from one or two of his colleagues after sharing the news that he'd put in an offer on the house on Fern Street. The place certainly had something of a reputation, and bargain or no bargain (and Number 123 certainly had been a bargain, an unbelievable steal), the jokey (and perhaps slightly nervous) comments about watching out for the attic and being careful where he dug in the backyard lest he rouse whatever slumbering evil might be lurking there, had a definite edge to them, almost as if they'd been delivered as warnings, but nothing even remotely like that had come to pass. Well, there was Number 118 across and down the street; a house Lionel could only describe as *wrong* without ever being able to adequately explain why, so much so that his initial sight of it was almost enough to make him reconsider purchasing a house on Fern Street at all… But he saw sense in the end, of course. The asking price of Number 123 really was too good to pass up.

So where had It come from? Had It simply followed him home one evening, latching on as he strolled home from his usual pre-dinner walk? And what about before that? Were there other houses, other victims, before him?

And what happened to those previous victims once It decided the time had come to move on?

The sound of the door slamming shut was so monstrously loud Lionel felt it rather than heard it, a punch of sound that sent him staggering back towards the sofa. He quickly fixed an equally monstrous grin onto his face and began to clap as though his life depended on it, which is what he should have done in immediate response to the locked door swinging open. He kept it up until the door swung smoothly open again, and then for a full minute afterwards. He counted the seconds, every last one of them.

※ ※ ※

He supposed he was rather a boring person. He had friends certainly, people he'd share an occasional meal with, chatted with every now and then on the phone, but he never felt particularly lonely when they weren't around, and in fact he much preferred his own company. He always had. He was much happier now he'd made the permanent transition to working exclusively from home, and he doubted he would mind in the slightest to know that his former colleagues missed him about as much as he missed them. He had plenty of interests, plenty of ways of occupying his own time, and if it was dull or boring or unsociable that he tended to shun company, then so be it. He didn't mind thinking of himself that way, and that others might think of him that way as well did not bother him at all. They didn't have to live with him, *he* had to live with him, and he had never once found that arrangement problematic.

But maybe It did. Maybe It thought he was lonely, and It didn't like that. Maybe It saw him and thought to Itself, now there's a fellow that could use a little fun!

The problem was, none of it was fun, not for Lionel.

He had tried talking to It, but his first tentative efforts to engage It in conversation ended abruptly when the belt he was wearing at the time unbuckled itself, yanked itself out of the belt loops on his trousers (tearing three of them) and slowly but firmly wrapped itself around his mouth. It took a frantic nod from Lionel confirming he'd received the message loud and clear to get the belt to unravel and drop to the floor.

After that he spoke only when he sensed that It wanted him to, like during the ice game or when he whispered "Night night, sleep tight," before retiring to bed. It didn't seem particularly bothered whether he actually slept or not, as long as he started his day promptly at 6:13 AM, the time It had set his alarm clock for at the end of their first day together.

It rather amazed Lionel that only a week and a half had passed since then. It seemed like so much longer.

❀ ❀ ❀

By the start of week two, the food situation was beginning to concern him.

It was fortunate that he kept his larder well stocked, preferring to cook and eat at home rather than eat out or order in (he did treat himself to an evening out a couple of times a year, perfectly content to dine alone), and it was either by luck or Its uncanny judgment that It first made itself known the day following his last big grocery shop. But now that one week had become two, Lionel couldn't help wondering if It was aware that, sooner or later, he would need to replenish his supplies. He was out of oat milk already, and very nearly out of butter. It didn't help that the kitchen game often resulted in burst cartons or irretrievably damaged tins, not that Lionel dared complain. What he did do was decide that the time had come for an experiment.

On what he was reasonably confident was a Tuesday morning, after playing the clothes game once followed by the door game three times in succession, he went to his desk in the tiny second bedroom for some paper and something to write with. Returning downstairs with a fresh yellow legal pad and a thick blue marker pen, he sat down on the sofa and, rather pleased that his hand wasn't shaking quite as badly as he'd feared it might, wrote in large, thick letters the single word: **HELLO?**

Then he waited. He could feel the nervous sweat begin to gather on his brow, but resisted the urge to wipe it away. The room, permanently dim like the rest of the house thanks to the always-closed curtains, remained silent. Lionel waited for one full minute, then for one minute more, before turning to a fresh page and writing again.

FOOD? RUNNING LOW. UNDERSTAND?

And he smiled to show that he wasn't in the least bit angry or worried about this situation, even though he definitely was.

In reply, the door, which he had closed behind him upon entering the room, slowly opened.

The pad was yanked out of his hand with such force he yelped in surprise, then winced sharply at what felt like the worst paper cut in history. He was looking down at the wound slowly opening across the palm of his right hand, cupping the hand carefully to avoid spilling too much blood, so he only heard rather than saw the pad slice clean through the balusters and embed itself into the opposite wall. The pen, clearly the least offending item, simply fell to the floor and rolled for a few inches across the parquet before coming to a gentle stop.

Lionel sat and stared at the pen for another five minutes before daring to stand up, and when it failed to fly up and skewer him in the leg or embed itself in his eye or do anything else equally unpleasant, he picked it up and deposited it into the nearest drawer.

Then, avoiding even looking at the stairs, he went to the kitchen to attend to his hand.

❋ ❋ ❋

Towards the end of that week, he came to a terrible realization.

It was either Thursday or Friday. Lionel genuinely wasn't sure. He'd had barely any sleep in the days since his failed pad and pen experiment. It wanted to play all the time now. Game after game after game after game. Perversely, it still allowed him to go through his usual pre-bed routine, whispering "Night night, sleep tight," and crawling into bed once he'd ensured the alarm clock was set for 6:13 the following morning, and then almost at the very second his head touched the pillow Door or Kitchen or Clothes or Sink flashed in his head, leaving him no choice but to get up and play.

He could not fail to notice that it was the door game It wanted him to play with more and more frequency, sometimes for hours at a time. Lionel became almost numb to it, responding by rote, muscle memory carrying him through the all too familiar actions, his thoughts adrift, floating away through the forever closed curtains and out into Fern Street, as though he was the ghost now, free to roam wherever he pleased…

But inevitably he became too untethered, his thoughts roamed too far, and It responded, perhaps interpreting this gradual unshackling of himself as some desperate attempt at escape. If he was standing close enough to the door, It slammed it closed into his face with enough force to send him flying back across the room. Or, if he was slowly approaching, key in hand, he would smell his flesh begin to cook as the key became a molten-hot version of itself.

It wanted him here. It wanted him paying attention.

And then came the awful realization; why the door game was Its favorite, why It wanted Lionel's full attention every time it was played.

One day, almost certainly one day very soon, the door would open to reveal It in all Its terrible glory. There could be no other explanation. And when that day came, all Lionel could do was clap and smile and hope that whatever came next was over quickly.

124

THE GRANDE DAME STILL LIVES HERE
Sirius

The front yard was overgrown with white heather and tall blades of grass that snagged Amy's skirt the moment she stepped through the gate. The path to the front door was broken and uneven—and the wooden wheelchair ramp that snaked around the side of the house had become inaccessible in its state of disrepair. The front door was blue, which she thought was an odd color—that old, powdery blue like the ribbon on a baby's bonnet. The paint was old enough that it curled up in long, heavy peels, and the brass Number 124 looked as if it had been beaten in with a fist.

Amy licked her lips and rang the bell. It buzzed, and the house groaned, swaying just enough with the hot spring breeze that it made her nervous.

Clouds gathered overhead, and a spinning weather-vane prophesied a storm. Amy rang the bell again and felt the unpleasant buzz in her teeth.

She wanted to be inside before the rain began. Spring showers were so frequent these days, and she regretted not bringing an umbrella. Her tilted straw hat with its cute, frilly bow did not stand a chance against the elements.

The door finally came open, although it seemed to

take some effort from the other side. The warped wood was intent on sticking to the jamb. A gaunt, severe face appeared—the face of a woman who had not had a good night's sleep since Elvis was being covered in the tabloids.

Amy smiled as brightly as she could.

"Good afternoon," she said. "I'm here about the room you have for rent." She reached into her handbag as she spoke and pulled out a newspaper clipping.

The woman on the other side squinted at the paper and then scoffed.

"It is not my room." She opened the door a little wider. "I am just the nurse."

"Oh." Amy fought to keep her smile intact as she stepped inside. "I'm so sorry, I assumed—"

"Ms. Rainey is taking her nap," the woman cut her off. "I can show you upstairs."

"I appreciate that," Amy said whole-heartedly. "My name is Amy Coulson. I rang earlier. I don't know if you're the one I spoke to, though."

"Unlikely. I switched shifts with the overnight nurse only about an hour or two ago," the woman said. "You can call me June."

Inside, the house was grand—although too dark to be enjoyed, even in the middle of the day. All the windows had been covered by layers of heavy cream-colored drapes and then thin white veils, embroidered with pink cabbage roses and soft blue butterflies. It smelled as old as it looked, and the dark hardwood floors were in bad shape. They creaked with every step, as if protesting the idea of a visitor.

Amy restrained a cough, not wanting to be impo-lite—even if the smell of old fabric and mildew was downright oppressive.

"It's a beautiful house," she said. The nurse, June, grunted as she led Amy from the front door to the stairs. There was a split landing before they reached the second section of the staircase, and then it led up to the second level. The walls were covered in frames—they were all of varying sizes, but most of them displayed some sort of needlework or crochet. The tallest one, at the top of the landing, was as tall as Amy—and it was a crocheted picture of the Lord's Prayer.

"Does she do all these…?" Amy asked, indicating the frames.

"No, that was all her grandmother," June said. "And trust me, if you get her started by asking—she will never stop talking about it. So, do yourself a favor. Here." They reached the top of the stairs. There were three sets of doors, only one of which was open. "That is the room that she advertised."

Amy waited to be led inside, but the nurse did not move. She hesitated only a second more before poking her head in. The room was more or less what she had steeled herself to expect—neatly kept, with a white metal-framed bed and a dresser provided. There was a set of French doors that led out onto the balcony, and they had been left open to allow a breeze in. It was simple, charming—and within her budget.

"I like it," she said, pulling herself back. Stepping into the room felt strange, like there was something that did not want her there.

"The bathroom is just down the hall." June indicated the door as she spoke. "It will be all yours, since no one else is up here. The other two rooms are closed off and have been since—forever, I don't know."

"Ms. Rainey never comes up here?" Amy asked. June rolled her eyes and shook her head.

"No," she said flatly. "Ms. Rainey has not been upstairs ever since she started using her wheelchair."

"Oh," Amy said, "my goodness. I am so sorry."

"Don't be." June held up her hands. "She doesn't need it. She doesn't even need *me*. She is forty-seven years old and fit as a fiddle. But she stays downstairs, and she makes us wait on her hand and foot. We do it because our agency does not like to ask questions."

"I see," Amy said, although she felt a little lost. "So, she doesn't need it, but she uses it anyway? Is she sick?"

"Only in the head," June said. "And you didn't hear

that from me. Are you done?"

Amy looked over her shoulder at the room again and nodded. "I think so."

The nurse started walking down the stairs without another word. Amy followed her while trying to ignore the odd, twisting feeling in her gut.

"June!" a sharp voice croaked from the hazy afternoon dark as soon as they reached the bottom step. "June, where have you been?"

"Upstairs, working outside of my job description," June said as soon as her feet touched the floor. "This is Amy. She was interested in renting."

"It's a pleasure to meet you," Amy said, squinting to try and get a glimpse of whom she was speaking to. "You have a lovely home."

"It is an old home." There was a soft rumble as something rolled across the floor, and from a wide entryway emerged an austere figure seated in a wheelchair. The chair itself was opulent—there was no other way to describe it. It was all curved, gleaming brass and worn velvet padding, more like a throne. And if Amy had not just been told her hostess' age, she would have never guessed that the woman seated was only forty-seven. She looked so much older—and maybe it was the way she styled her fading blonde hair in big stiff Victory rolls, or the white greasepaint makeup that settled into every crease of her gaunt face. The dress she wore was yards of white satin and lace and looked like something out of an old period film, with a high collar that looked tight enough to strangle her. She smiled, although it was more like a grimace, and she had bright red lipstick smeared on her teeth.

"I am glad to see that my little ad was effective," the woman said.

"Oh, yes." Amy tried to gloss over any unpleasantness that had accumulated from her staring. A nervous smile jumped back onto her lips. "Well—you run a tempting offer. $200 a month with everything included is much better than I could ask for in the city."

"And without city noises," her hostess added, crossing her hands over one another in her lap. "Or city crime rates. As a neighborhood, we keep to ourselves—I do not remember the last time the house across the street even opened its blinds."

"Seems like a match made in Heaven," the nurse said as she turned to walk towards the kitchen. "I think it is time for your medication, Ms. Rainey."

"My name is Vera." The older woman's eyes came up to meet Amy's. They were powder blue, the same color as her front door. "Vera Rainey—like the movie star."

"Oh." Amy touched her chest. "My name is Amy."

Her hostess' thin mouth turned down into a scowl. "I suppose you are too young to know who that is," she said, her words sharpening.

Amy was taken aback. "No," she said, "I know who that is—my grandmother loved her movies."

"So did mine," her hostess seemed to soften up again. "We would watch them together when I came to visit in this very house." She looked around wistfully. "I loved *The Upper Level.*"

"Is that the one where she gets into an accident and is confined to her room upstairs?" Amy glanced after June, wishing she could follow the nurse into the kitchen.

"Yes," Vera said. "I think she played it beautifully, don't you? She should have won an Oscar for that picture."

"I think so," Amy agreed, anything to keep the conversation moving.

June returned with a shot glass of little pills and a tall glass of water. Vera reached out to receive them and knocked the pills back with practiced ease.

"Perhaps we can watch that one tonight, after you bring your things," Vera said when she was finished.

"Oh," Amy paused at the blatant assumption, "I would love to, but I—"

"Half the reason I am renting out the room is for the company," Vera cut her off. "I will *insist* as part of your application. There is no fee to apply, and I have a maid to take care of the chores here. It is a very little thing for you to do, all things considered. I am practically giving half of my house away."

Amy took a deep breath. Her thoughts raced around the inside of her skull, spinning too fast to keep up with. Yet, somewhere in the center of the cyclone, she had already decided that she was going to do it. This place was her last stop on a long list of advertisements. Nowhere else had been willing to accept her, not while she was only working part-time hours as a waitress.

This woman did not seem like she cared where the cash came from, or even how late it might be, so long as she was indulged. And according to her nurse, she never went upstairs—so how bad could it be? At least there would be some privacy.

Amy swallowed and nodded, giving her hostess another smile.

"I would love to watch it with you," she said. "I'll bring some popcorn."

"For the stove," Vera added. "There is no microwave here."

* * *

The house epitomized its owner in many ways, in that it creaked and groaned with complaints day and night. It was something that Amy was quickly growing accustomed to—although it did not stop her from waking up in the middle of the night, wondering if someone was coming up the stairs or if there was something tapping on her door. Old houses settled, she knew that, but this one was restless. And she could swear that she felt it sway, sometimes like being on the deck of an old luxury liner.

There were times when she could not tell whether the bumps and groans were the house or Vera. She was not sure the woman ever slept. There was always a light on downstairs for the overnight nurse, who would read or knit something in the old yellow chair, which was kept tucked into a corner beside the piano.

Amy's only comfort was that the days were growing longer, and that the sun did not set until around eight.

She kept the doors to her balcony open to let in as much light and air as possible. It chased out the old, dingy smell and made her feel a little less stifled.

She kept her door closed, even though there was no risk of an intruder. She noticed that when she did, there was no lock. There was a broken hook at the top of the door, but no lock.

And the first time she saw Vera Rainey outside of her chair, the lady of the house was standing in the doorway of the second-floor bedroom. She was a shadow against the dim light coming from the hallway. If Amy had not been sleeping so lightly, she may not have woken up at all.

Her heart jumped into her throat and she sat up in bed, gripping her covers with the desire to pull them up over her head. Vera swayed on her heels, rocking back and forth with her head lolling around her shoulders as she rubbed her hands together. It was so quiet that all Amy could hear was the sound of the woman's thin, glossy palms sliding back and forth and the clacking of her many rings.

Amy held her breath, unwilling to draw any attention to herself. Vera stood there for what felt like hours, rubbing her palms and staring into nothing. Her powder-blue eyes were startling, even in the darkness, and looked glazed over — a dead fish.

Amy closed her eyes and pushed her face into her blanket. She did not remember falling asleep, but she must have — because when she opened her eyes again, her neck was cramped, and Vera was gone.

Soon, it was every night. Vera stood in her doorway and muttered to herself, whispering into her hands and rubbing them back and forth. Amy could not hear her, at first, but when she finally did manage to make something out — she realized that all of Vera's words were lines from *The Upper Level.* Not a single one of them made sense when pulled out of context. They were all random, punchy bits of dialogue from the main character.

It was enough that Amy bought a new bolt from the hardware store. She installed it herself when Vera was supposed to be napping. Four screws and a small drill, and she afforded herself some peace of mind.

She even slept before her dinner shift—two hours that left her far better rested than any given night for the past two weeks.

* * *

The sound that came from the downstairs level shook the whole house. Amy sat bolt upright and threw her gaze towards the door. It was still bolted, and closed—no one had come in, and it did not sound like anyone was trying. In her dream, someone had been banging on the door—but now that she was awake, she realized the sound was coming from the bowels of the house.

Amy crawled out of bed and flipped up the bolt on her door. It sprang open on its own, as if ushering her out. She made her way quickly to the stairs and looked down, trying to see past the split landing and to the bottom of the staircase. There was nothing but darkness below. The sound that came through the inky depths was like a sledgehammer being thrown against a wall. It rattled the house with dull repetition. *Slam. Thud. Slam.*

Odd, too, that there was no light downstairs—and no nurse on duty. She started down the steps, taking each one slowly, gripping the banister the entire way down so that her hand did not shake.

When she reached the bottom step, she saw a light coming from the kitchen. She leaped across the narrow hall that divided the living room and the kitchen with its adjoining dining area, and immediately threw up her hand to shade herself from the light. The kitchen was tube-shaped, and the yellow linoleum had peeling, dirty corners.

Vera was in her wheelchair, and she was slamming it against the kitchen cabinets. The source of the sound was her footrest banging against the wood with such ferocity that the cabinet in front of her had started to splinter.

Amy swallowed a gasp and raised her voice a little with a question, hated how much it trembled. "Ms. Rainey?" she asked, trying to treat the display as if it was nothing out of the ordinary. "What are you doing up this late?"

The banging stopped. Vera turned her wheels sharply and rotated the chair until she was staring up at Amy, her powder-blue eyes rimmed with red and burning feverishly bright.

"You think the house will defend you," she said, and her words came crawling up her throat with all the vitriol of a caged creature. "It won't."

Amy felt her blood run cold. "What?" She shook her head. "I'm sorry. Is there someone I can call…?"

"You do not think I need this chair," Vera said, lowering her chin so that her pale blonde hair fell over her face — bare except for the smeared remnants of greasepaint that never quite came off. "It keeps me trapped down here…and you do not think that I need it!"

"I…" Amy looked around the kitchen to see if there was a phone that she could use. She had to call someone — the nurse, the hospital — the woman was clearly having some sort of breakdown. "I believe that you rely on it, I do."

"You are lying to me!" Vera's voice climbed. Amy held out her hands to try and placate the older woman.

"I have seen you walk around upstairs," Amy said, keeping her voice as soft and soothing as she could. "At night, sometimes, and I—"

"No one believes me!" Vera grabbed the handle of a drawer in front of her and pulled it out. The drawer fell off its track and landed in her lap. Knives rattled inside, and she grabbed the handle of the first one she saw. It was a butcher knife — slightly rusted — and she swept the drawer off her lap. It crashed against the floor, landing on its side and splitting apart.

"Please!" Amy lunged forward. She reached out to try and take the knife from Vera, but the older woman turned the wheelchair away. The elaborate brass handles struck Amy in the ribs and took out her breath — and she had to skitter to avoid her foot getting crushed by the wheel.

"You don't believe me…" Vera muttered to herself. "But it is hard to argue when it is right in front of your face!" She gripped the knife and plunged it into her leg.

Vera screamed, and Amy shrieked at the sight. There was so much blood spreading across the crinkled white dress. Vera pulled the knife back out and stabbed herself again, this time in the opposite leg. Blood squirted out—dark and arterial. Amy felt like she was going to faint.

"Oh, my god!" Amy's voice was hoarse. "Oh my god, you're going to die, shit! I need to call someone—shit!"

"Who is there to call? What are you going to tell them?" Vera pulled the knife back and drove it down again and again, stabbing herself until her skirt was shredded and her legs were deep, bloody cuts of meat underneath. "Here it is, Amy, here it is—there is no denying it now! Do I need this chair? Do you think I need this chair? Do you think I can walk when my legs look like hamburger meat?"

"Stop, oh god, oh god…!" Amy's stomach lurched and bile surged up her throat. "Stop, stop, please, oh my god…shit…!" Yellow bile came spewing from her mouth and nose. She gagged on it and fell to the floor, her whole body shaking. She had to stand up. She *needed* to stand up. She needed to find a phone. Or she needed to run.

A thick, syrupy pool of blood was gathering on the floor. It crept towards her, soaking the hem of her nightgown. Amy retched again, vomiting froth onto the linoleum. All she could hear was Vera screaming, and the sound of the knife like it was being plunged into a ham.

Her world went white. Amy closed her eyes and curled her fingers into her hair. Her hands were shaking. She just wanted it all to stop.

And then the world was quiet and dark. She felt nothing; she heard nothing. It all faded away as she blacked out.

* * *

The splatter of eggs and the smell of frying sausage woke her up. Amy lifted her head—which was a mistake. She felt like someone had jabbed a nail through her temple. There was no blood on the linoleum or anything else, but she still had vomit on her nightgown.

Amy sat up, dragging her hand across her dry, crusted

mouth. June, the nurse, was standing at the stove — apparently content to let her lay there.

"Where is Vera?" Amy croaked.

"She is in the parlor, waiting for her breakfast," June said in that short, clipped tone of hers. "She is none too pleased about you stumbling in here last night, drunk and disorderly."

"Drunk?" Amy furrowed her brow. "Absolutely not!"

"I had to clean up your vomit this morning from under your head. Is there another explanation?" The nurse tapped her wooden spoon against the side of a cast-iron skillet. "If you are not feeling well, then go upstairs. I will not have her catching anything."

Amy stared at her, dumbfounded, but reached up to grab the counter for support as she stood up.

There were no missing drawers. No knives except for the one that had been used to slice up bread.

"I think I'm going crazy," she said softly.

"I hope not," June said. "Because one of you being completely mental is enough."

"Her chair…" Amy tried to peer past June and investigate the dining area. "Is she still in her chair?"

"Always. She thinks it makes her tragic. I think it makes her a pain in the ass. Lots of good people in this world need the things that she has." She shook her head.

Amy did not understand. She stared at the floor again, as if expecting all the blood to reappear. The night played back so vividly in her head.

"Would she ever hurt herself?" she asked. She could not help it.

June looked at her like she was nuts.

"I think you ought to go upstairs," she said. "Take some toast with you."

Amy pulled in a deep breath. She wanted to argue further, but she could see that it was not going to get her anywhere.

"I might need to find a new place to stay," she muttered.

"You do that," June banged her spoon again, "and tell me how it goes."

125

OLD DEAD-EYED JOHN
Todd Condit

Every town has some sort of legend surrounding it that, whether based on truth or not, is passed down from generation to generation through the most reliable means of communication: bored kids. There's always a local haunted house, a creepy dead tree at the end of a long dirt road, or the local crazy person that walks up and down main street mumbling to his or herself while pushing a baby stroller full of trash around.

But this town was a bit different. This town had a whole street dedicated to the occult, the local boogeyman, witchcraft, murder, and other crazy stuff, depending on who you asked.

So for three local kids with nothing but boredom and summer on their side, Fern Street was just ripe for exploring.

* * *

The moon was high and cicadas droned in the warm summer air as Max, Luke, and Donnie huddled inside Max's dad's red camping tent in Luke's backyard. The interior of the tent was littered with snacks, sodas, comic books, and a *Risk* board game that none of the boys were interested in since they were currently shoulder to shoulder peering at Max's older brother's new *Playboy* magazine by the gentle blue light of a small electric camping lantern.

"Holy shit, look at the boobies on her!" Donnie said as he leered at the nude model. Donnie was the typical chubby kid of this group because just like every town had some kind of creepy legend, every group of boys had a chubby friend. He wasn't the best at throwing the baseball around and always trailed Max and Luke when riding bikes, but he always had the best snacks and the biggest comic collection out of the three twelve-year-olds.

"Those are almost as big as your mom's, Donnie," said Max, who had found himself to be the default leader of the group since they all met in Mrs. Harrison's 1st-grade class. He was the typical athlete who, in a few years, would probably drift away from this group and fall in with the other sporty kids once he made it to high school. But for now, the group was inseparable.

Donnie laughed and put a meaty arm around Max's neck, attempting to place him in a chokehold that his hero, Hulk Hogan, would envy. But Max was strong and wiry and playfully shoved him away.

Luke, a nice balance between Max and Donnie in every aspect, gently gripped the corner of the page that showcased a big-breasted model and turned it. His eyes widened as he took in the centerfold.

"Hello, Miss June 1996," said a wide-eyed Luke.

Max and Donnie quickly abandoned their minor wrestling match and returned their attention to the forbidden pages before them.

"What I wouldn't do with those," Luke said.

"What *wouldn't* you do with those? More like what *would* you do with those, Luke?" Max asked with a leer. Max was six months older than both of his friends, so he felt more mature than them. He was set to turn thirteen years old soon, which would increase the growing gulf between him and his friends.

Luke, on the defensive now, shrunk back a bit.

"I mean, you know," Luke said defensively, not knowing that none of the boys knew what to do at this young age. But boys were boys.

"I'd tell you what I'd do," said Max in his pre-pubescent voice.

SNAP!

Suddenly, a branch snapped outside of their tent, causing the boys to momentarily freeze, the pages filled with sex temporarily forgotten.

"What was that?" Luke said in a shaky voice.

"Dude, chill," said Max. "We're in my backyard."

"Your backyard is in the woods, stupid head!" Donnie said as he grabbed his black *Jansport* backpack and reached inside it, pulling out a small *Star Wars*-themed flashlight.

"Give me that, you freaking nerd," said Max as he snatched the flashlight from Donnie, unzipped the tent entrance, and showed the meager beam outside.

The beam fell across a small section of grass that led to the thick woods beyond. Nothing moved except for the gentle swaying of leaves in the gentle summer breeze.

Luke and Donnie's heads appeared on either side of Max's as the flashlight moved across the forest's edge.

"See, nothing there but bugs and stuff," said Max as he clicked off the flashlight.

The three boys ducked back into the tent as Max zipped the entrance back up.

Luke reached for the lantern and moved the dial up, causing the light to increase as Donnie grabbed a bag of *Cool Ranch Doritos* and started munching on its contents.

"What do you guys want to do?" asked Luke, still obviously shaken from the snapping tree branch.

"I dunno, eat chips and talk about who would win in fights?" Donnie suggested with a mouthful of *Doritos*.

"You know what we should do?" asked Max as he flipped the flashlight back on and pointed it under his face. "Talk about Fern Street," he finished, making the words "Fern Street" sound spooky with a ghostly waiver of his voice.

"Ghost stories, no," Luke said with finality. "My mom

said no ghost stories and to be asleep by ten."

"Your mom's not here dumb dumb, and it's summer, dude!" Max guilt-tripped Luke. "We should be out exploring the woods, or throwing rocks at the Fern Street houses or something."

"I'm with Max, Luke. Plus, my dad said that house 125 on Fern has *Jason Voorhees* in it," said Donnie.

"Jason lives at *Camp Crystal Lake,* stupid," Max said. "Fern Street is like one thousand miles away from *Camp Crystal Lake.*"

"And Jason isn't real," Donnie added.

"Correct. Jason is not real. But you know who is real?" Max said teasingly as he paused for dramatic effect. Donnie and Luke looked at him with their full attention.

"Old Dead-Eyed John," Max said in a spooky voice.

"Bull crap, Max!" said Luke, shaking his head.

"No, it's true. My uncle Mike told me about it," said Max.

"Yeah, *bullshit.* He also told you about some ghost girl that asked him about a gold ribbon or some shit. Plus, isn't your uncle Mike in prison for stealing boxes or something?" asked Donnie.

"Yes, but before he went to prison, he told me all about the story. He and my dad used to ride their bikes down Fern Street when they were our age. He said that the street was always just *wrong,* like it shouldn't exist. It would be a bright sunny day and as soon as you started riding down Fern, it would get darker. Like a dark cloud was following you, blotting out the sun. Houses were always falling apart from lack of care but 125 was special," Max said.

"What made it special?" Luke asked sheepishly.

"Well," Max said, leaning in for dramatic effect. "It was special because Old Dead-Eyed John lived there. Uncle Mike said he ate raw animal meat and when he couldn't catch a wild animal in the forest, he would move on to kids, using his old sledgehammer to bash their heads in."

"Nope, no way, no way in heck," said Donnie, shaking his head vigorously as he reached for another bag of chips.

"Yes way, dude. He said that one day their friend Jimmy Ray was dared to go ding-dong-ditch 125, and he never was seen again. They found his bike in the woods, all bent up and soaked in blood."

"Why is he called that?" Luke asked

"Called what? Old Dead-Eyed John?" asked Max. The boys both nodded in unison.

"Well, for starters, he's *old*. And his eyes are cloudy and *dead*…and his name is John," finished Max.

Donnie and Luke stared at Max's illuminated face before turning their heads to each other and bursting out laughing.

Max lowered the flashlight and clicked it off, defeated that he wasn't able to scare his friends as easily as he normally could.

"Okay tough guys, okay. Don't come crying to me when you end up at the bottom of dead-eyed John's meat freezer," Max said as he grabbed a *Twinkie* from Donnie's backpack.

"Meat freezer?" Luke asked, as he stopped laughing.

"Meat freezer," Max confirmed. "That's where John would store his victims. Because Jimmy Ray wasn't his last victim, far from it. He was just his first."

"Well, why wouldn't the cops arrest Old Dead-Eyed John?" Donnie asked.

"Too busy, don't care. Who knows? But Old Dead-Eyed John is still there to this day, eating raw meat and killing kids."

Max stood up, his head pressing against the roof of the tent, grabbed his backpack, and flung it around his shoulders.

"What are you doing, Max?" Luke asked.

"Going to Fern Street, duh," Max said as he moved to the front of the tent and unzipped the entrance. He stepped out into the warm night air.

"Umm, why?" Donnie asked.

"To prove to you dicks that Old Dead-Eyed John is

real and that house 125 still contains him, that's why. Now let's go."

Max walked out into the backyard, and towards the boys' three parked bicycles. Max and his big brother Tommy had devised a plan to scare Luke and Donnie, and if Max's timing was right, Tommy would be at 125 now, finding the perfect spot to jump out and scare the two boys.

* * *

Reluctantly, Donnie and Luke followed Max on their bicycles to the entrance of Fern Street. Dark houses greeted them, the absence of light, moon, or lights from the houses seemed to reach out to them.

"Which one is it?" Donnie asked nervously.

"It's down at the end and around the corner," Max said.

"This is not a good idea guys, let's just go back to the tent. If my mom finds out I left, she'll kill me," Luke said.

"If you don't come with us, then I'll kill you, Luke. Now come on." Max took off down into the dark of Fern Street. The darkness seemed to swallow him up as he made his way slowly down the street. The boys, not wanting to be labeled a couple of wimps, reluctantly followed.

* * *

"That's the one," Max said as he got off his bike and kicked the kickstand out.

"So, we're here, now what?" Luke asked.

Max pulled out the camping lantern that he took from the tent and held it out. "We look around a bit," Max said as he carefully walked toward the dark house, careful not to step on a crunchy branch or a pile of dead leaves. Donnie and Luke watched Max silently as he made his way to a corner of the house and disappeared around it.

"This is hella stupid, Donnie. I am not going over there," Luke said with finality before proceeding to get on his bike and pedal back the way they came.

Torn between not wanting to stay but also not wanting to leave Max, Donnie just watched Luke's back as he faded into the darkness.

***

Damn pussies, both of them. I swear they still act like they are both ten years old still, Max thought as he walked along the side of the decrepit house. The moon was covered in dark clouds and the darkness seemed like you could cut it with a knife. He rotated the knob on the lantern to its lowest setting, which barely illuminated a couple of feet ahead of him.

Max came to the edge of the house and poked his head around it, hoping not to spring his brother's trap. Instead of seeing his brother, giant weeds that were as tall as he was filled the backyard. He spotted a staircase that led to the back door of the house and made his way toward it through the thick weeds.

He tripped and fell, pain shooting through his right knee as it came down on something hard and metallic. A beat-up old bicycle stuck up, weeds growing through its various openings like it had been there for a while.

Max rubbed his knee and gingerly got up, kicked the bike with his uninjured leg, and limped his way up the steps and onto the back porch. As he got closer, he noticed that the door was open a few inches.

Oh cool, it's abandoned. We could make this our secret club-house, he thought with excitement as he slowly nudged the door open with his shoe. More darkness greeted him as the small light from his lantern fought against the darkness. He stepped inside and held the lantern up.

A withered face with foggy white eyes stared back at him. A smile slowly spread across the old man's lips, exposing a mouth full of broken and missing teeth. Max gagged and tried not to vomit as the wretched man in front of him spoke.

"I'm hungry."

Max screamed.

***

Donnie was just about to turn around when he heard a muffled scream from inside the house. Emboldened by the likes of *Indiana Jones* and *Hulk Hogan*, Donnie pushed his fear down and followed Max's path. He came around the house and saw the lantern sitting in the doorway of the back door.

"Okay Max, that's enough, dude. Game's over!" Donnie said as he moved up the steps and picked up the lantern. A candy bar, set on the ground a few feet inside the house, caught his attention as he grabbed the lantern. Donnie moved inside the sour-smelling house and grabbed the candy bar. The light of the lantern caught the glint of another bar as he covered his nose and entered a living room of sorts. 1970s-era furniture in various states of decay and neglect cluttered the room. A thick layer of dust covered the floor and turned into little dust clouds as he walked around.

CRASH!

The back door slammed behind him, nearly causing Donnie's skeleton to jump through his gaping mouth. The heavyset boy ran to the door and yanked on it, but to his fear, a rusty padlock had been latched onto it, securing the dirty door to its frame. He started to panic and made his way to where the front door should be, but what greeted him were boards nailed across the door.

"Max! This isn't funny! I'm going to tell your dad!" Donnie yelled as he moved about the filthy house, looking for an exit.

He tripped and nearly fell as his foot sunk into something soft and wet. What he saw when he looked down nearly made him throw up. He had stepped into the open stomach of something red and squishy; his Converse shoe was soaked in blood and made a loud squelch as he pulled it out. A long piece of slick intestine briefly stuck to his shoe before snapping back into the open cavity with a wet smacking sound. He moved the lantern closer to the wet thing and instantly sprayed half-digested *Doritos* onto the face of the lifeless corpse of Max's big brother.

Donnie screamed as he ran to the nearest door and yanked it open. A dark staircase greeted him and he ran down it, the lantern held out in front of his vomit-covered face like a shield.

He made it down the stairs and stepped onto an

uneven dirt floor, the sour smell from before increased in potency and stung his nostrils. A gentle knocking sound was thumping from somewhere in the basement.

"Max?" Donnie called as he cranked the dial on the lantern to full illumination as he followed the sound of the knocking.

A low humming came from the dirty white, rusty ice box that came into view, and as he walked slowly towards it, chasing the darkness away with the lantern, he saw that a smear of fresh blood was dripping down from the edge of the closed lid. The muffled voice of Max called for help from inside the freezer.

Two things happened at once.

The cheap lantern that held the darkness at bay suddenly went out as the hairs on the back of Donnie's neck went up, and a rancid smell accompanied the raising of the hairs as a low voice brushed across his skin.

"I'm still hungry, boy."

❊ ❊ ❊

Luke rode his bike quickly back to the tent and went inside it.

Those stupid assholes, he thought as he grabbed the discarded Playboy and opened it back up, but he quickly tossed it aside since he really couldn't see anything without the lantern.

SNAP!

A tree branch broke outside, but this time he wasn't scared. A dragging sound could be heard, like the sound a stick or baseball bat makes when you drag it through the grass. The sound circled the tent and was joined by labored breathing.

"Nice try, Max," Luke said as he opened the zipper. A rancid, sour smell drifted into Luke's nostrils as he opened up the tent.

He looked up and screamed as the bloody face of Old Dead-Eyed John smiled back at him, bits of flesh hanging from his broken teeth. John raised the old sledgehammer he held at his side and brought it down onto the boy's head with a loud crack.

126

THE FRIEND
Loki De Witt

One of the last houses on the street, just at the edge of the cul-de-sac. Constructed in 1951, back when homes and dreams were built to last forever. It was built during a time of expansion in the suburbs when everyone was looking to stake their own piece of Americana so they could do their part to help build a bright future for a country that had just come out of a very dark time. Fern Street was one of those small neighborhoods that would help bring back the luster of the American Dream and help remind the world why the Stars and Stripes would shine brighter than ever before. I know all about 126 Fern St. I should. I was born there, after all.

It was a few years after the house was built that I came to be. First, 126 Fern St. had to come alive in a different way. I like to imagine it sometimes, a young family moving into their very own home for the first time. Daddy was a war hero who made his country and neighborhood proud when he went overseas to do his part in taking a stand for freedom. Mommy was his high school sweetheart, who waited anxiously for him to return home so they could start the rest of their lives together. They were truly and hopelessly in love, and everyone knew it. That was why there was so much celebration when they got married. Knowing they would need lots of space for all the kids they were going to have, they saved up money and eventually found themselves the proud owners of their dream home at the end of the cul-de-sac. It didn't take them long to settle in, and soon, they were pleased to share news of the fact they were bringing a sweet bundle of joy into the world. Her name would be Harriet, after her grandmother. Dear, sweet, Harriet. She is the reason I am here, to begin with. Harriet came along and brought new life to the house in more ways than one. Her cheerful giggles and tiny footsteps filled the halls of the house. Her parents doted on her. As much love as there was in the family though, Harriet was timid. She was so shy that for a very long time, she wouldn't go outside and play with the other children. She would watch them from her window, the boys riding their bikes in circles while the girls watched on, dolls clutched tightly against their chests. She wanted so badly to go out and play, but she was just so scared that since they were older than she was, they wouldn't want to play with her. So, she decided she needed a friend she could practice playing with until she gained the confidence to go outside and play with the others.

That is where I came from.

She dreamed me up over several days, deciding how I would act, what I would like, and the games we would play. She took her crayons and scribbled down what I looked like. As those colors spread across the white paper, I took form. I was nearly there. I could see her. I could feel her. I wanted to be her friend! I still needed one more thing to give me the spark of life needed so we could finally be friends forever. I needed a name. Then she spoke it. That one single word gave me the spark of existence.

"Buddy."

With the name spoken, I sprang to life. Buddy was a good name—the best name. And I would live up to that name and be the best buddy she would ever have.

That's just what I did, too. We ran around. She told me stories. We played games. I heard her secrets. I had to wait for her to come home from school, but the whole time she was gone, I dreamed of all the things we would do when she returned. For so long, everything was perfect. Then suddenly, it wasn't. As Harriet got older, she spent more and more time away from home. She started playing with the kids she had watched through the window before I came along. At first, I was happy for her. My friend was growing up and that meant new adventures! Only, it didn't. The older she got, the less and less time we spent together. I spent many nights sitting there, watching, waiting, hoping she would look at me and ask to play. Those words were never spoken. Soon enough, I wasn't Harriet's buddy anymore. Instead, I was something I had never been before: alone. I never lost hope that one day, things would go back to the way they had been. Then, Harriet's dad got a promotion, and they moved far away.

I thought that I had been alone before Harriet got in the car and rolled out of my life, but walking the halls of 126 Fern with no one living there was agonizing. When Harriet had been there, I could at least be happy watching her, but since they had left, the halls they left were empty, like my heart.

It took a little while, but eventually, a new family moved in. They even brought me a new friend. His name was Andy. Andy was a wonderful friend. As soon as he found me, he told me all about the place he had moved from, a great big city called Chicago. He also told me how he used to play with a doll when he was younger. Lucky for him, I was better than any old doll could ever be. He also gave me a new name! He called me Joey. He told me Joey was the name he always wanted for a brother. I was so excited to get my new name because it meant I wasn't just a buddy; I was Andy's brother. Andy was so much different than Harriet had been. She liked to have tea parties, and play house.

Andy liked to crawl around on the floor and pretend

he was a soldier. He also knew everything there was to know about baseball. I loved playing with Andy, and he loved playing with me. He even promised we were going to be best friends forever. It was too good to last, though. Andy's dad had been called back to Chicago by his old job, and that meant that Andy had to leave. Andy was smart, though. He decided that I was going to go back with them, and then he would show me all the places he had told me about before.

When the time came to leave though, I made an awful discovery. Andy headed toward the car and I went to follow him, only to find that as soon as I tried to step out of the house, I started to get weak. I reached out my hand to Andy, but saw that it was fading away. Andy reached back, but his dad scooped him up and loaded him into the car alongside their belongings. I heard Andy crying out the name he gave me as I dragged myself back inside the house.

Andy's dad came and shut the door in my face. I could still hear Andy calling for me as the car pulled away and took another friend away from me.

Once more I found myself alone, with just the walls of 126 Fern to keep me company. I tried to see if I could escape the house so I could join Andy in Chicago. It took a little bit, but I discovered that I couldn't leave the house. Somehow, my energy was bound to it. That meant the house I had been born in was also my prison. So, I did the only thing I could, and I walked the halls of the house, hoping and praying that one day, another friend would come.

When another friend finally came, they were much younger than the other two had been, barely able to speak. It was okay. I still understood them. I understood them in ways their parents never could, and they could see me, even though their parents couldn't.

He couldn't tell me his name, but I heard the adults say it. My new friend was called Charles. He was so small and fragile. I knew that he needed my protection. So I watched over him, keeping him safe from the other things his parents couldn't see. For some reason, I felt more attached to Charles than the others. Maybe it was because he was so young. Perhaps it was because I was his protector. It didn't matter. What mattered was that he was going to be the one that stayed.

One day, Charles surprised me. Though he still couldn't speak well, he looked right at me and with a smile informed me of what he would call me, Cookie. I was delighted that he had chosen to call me this because, in my time spent with him, I knew that cookies were his favorite thing in the world. Charles was the most precious thing I had ever encountered in my time in 126 Fern, but I knew he was something special. I watched him grow from a baby into a toddler.

Once he could walk, the fun really started. We played games. We shared snacks. He even told me stories. I watched as he drew pictures of us on the walls of his room. His parents didn't like them much, but to me, they meant everything. Every day, as he got older, our bond grew more potent, and I knew that Charles was going to be my friend to the end. As long as he was in 126 Fern St, I would do everything I could to keep my friend happy and safe.

Looking back now, it still breaks my heart. Charles didn't leave like the others did. His mom loaded him up to take him to the grocery store so they could buy all kinds of yummy treats. I didn't care much for the fact that he had to leave me alone while they went shopping, but I knew that they would be back soon. Only, they weren't. I remember Charles's dad coming home, crying, screaming to no one in particular. I didn't understand why he was sad, but I knew that as soon as Charles came home, everyone would be happy again.

Days passed, and Charles still hadn't come home. Others showed up, though — people dressed in black. They were all crying, like Charles's dad. They sat around and talked about Charles and his mom. After several of these visits, I came to understand that Charles was never coming home again. I finally understood why everyone was so sad because I was, too.

For several long nights, I watched over Charles's dad, our pain an unspoken bond. I wanted to comfort him, to make him happy, like I had his son so many times. I knew he couldn't see me though, and I knew the only thing that could make him happy was something that neither of us would ever have again.

Eventually, I was left alone in the house again, and the "For Sale" sign appeared in the yard once more. This time though, I wasn't just left with memories. The heaviness of grief stayed behind with me. Everywhere I looked, there were little reminders of Charles. From cookie crumbs that the broom had missed to the drawings he had made of us on his bedroom walls, his presence still lingered. Only instead of the sounds of his sweet laughter, there was that deafening silence I had come to hate so much. As much pain as I was in over losing Charles, he had given me something Harriet and Andy hadn't. I spent so much time in front of the drawings on his walls, remembering how proud he was when he showed them to me. They brought me so much joy, and at the same time, they filled me with pain.

The next time I had visitors, it wasn't a family. Instead, it was a small group of men armed with tools. Apparently, someone had bought the house and decided that it needed to have some new life breathed into it through some cosmetic repairs. At first, I ignored them. I didn't care what they did to the rest of the house, as long as they left my precious drawings alone. One of them had to try and cross that line, though. I knew what he intended from the moment he first came into the room to give it a look over. He made a comment about how he was going to paint the walls and erase the only happiness I had left. I knew that I had to stop him, but I wasn't sure how.

When he came upstairs with his paint and brushes, I made my move. As soon as he opened the door, I shoved him backward. Much to my surprise, my hands slammed right into his chest. He tumbled backward down the stairs, the can of paint tumbling behind him. His body landed awkwardly with a hard thud. His neck was turned at an odd angle and his eyes were beginning to go dim, when the paint can slammed into his face, finishing what the fall had started. The other men came running as I stared at my hands. It had never occurred to me that I could touch them, much less harm them. As they scrambled to help their friend, I looked into the vacant eyes of the one who tried to take away my drawings. I felt a sudden surge of power.

I rushed down the stairs and grabbed the nearest one by the back of his neck, and hurled him away from his vacant-eyed friend. Chaos ensued, and the ones that were still moving fled from the house. When the house went quiet again, I stood over the silent, contorted form of the one I had shoved down the stairs. As much as I knew, I should have been horrified, that was not what I felt. I looked down at my hands again, and a vicious smile crept across my face.

The adults had taken my friends from me before, but now I could stop them. I could punish them. A while later, the police and ambulances arrived to haul away the dead body. I could have hurt them too, but instead, I watched. I knew that seeing what I had done would let the parents know to never take my friends away again.

More time passed, and it seemed that the word of what I had done had spread much further than the confines of the house I was trapped in. I knew this because I heard the older kids talk about it in hushed whispers as they crept up to the porch. They were older than the ones I had played with before, but I still would have gladly had them inside. The older ones didn't see me as a friend though, they saw me as a ghost, a demon, something to be feared. They told embellished stories of the night that I punished my first adult. Their stories described a rampage I had gone on, where several adults had died at my hands. At first, I was heartbroken that they would think of me as a monster. Eventually, though, that sadness faded away and was replaced with anger. If they wanted some sort of monster, I would give it to them. Soon enough, their knocks that had gone unanswered were met with doors opening and then slamming. Whispers between friends as they slowly made their way to the house were met with me whispering back, and then roaring at them. I learned to relish the way they screamed as their bravery ran down their fleeing legs. I would never torment the younger ones, though. Even if they didn't know I was there, I was still their friend.

I watched the years pass through the windows of 126 Fern. The rest of the street changed. Houses were torn down, while others were built to cover up vacant lots. I saw the children that lived in those houses grow up, and leave, never to return. All I could do was watch, because nobody wanted the decrepit old house at the end of the block. Everyone knew that house was haunted, and someone had died there.

Soon enough, with the passing of time, the life that had once filled the house that was my prison did the same thing the crayon drawings Charles had left behind, they faded away. I hadn't been entirely alone while I watched, though. From time to time, the stray deviant would enter the walls of my home. Drug addicts and criminals decided that a house abandoned to time would be the perfect place to hide from their sins. The police would come looking for them, but those are bodies that they will never find. Needless to say, I had become quite skilled at punishing those who would harm my friends. None of that did any good though, because as long as I was alone inside the house, I couldn't do anything to protect my friends outside.

Eventually, the passing of time took its toll on me. I had been alone so long outside the occasional visitor that I became resigned to my fate. I would forever be the phantom that walked the halls of the eyesore at the end of the street. Just another urban legend from a forgotten time, that was there to scare the kids that were supposed to be my friends.

Fate had other plans, though.

It seems that the city council decided it was time to restore some of the older homes in town so that they could bring new blood into the neighborhood. At the top of the list sat none other than 126 Fern.

At first, I wanted to keep the workers from changing my house. Then I heard them talking about how the house would be perfect for kids once it was fixed up again. I was so excited at the prospect of new friends that I stayed out of their way. It took a few months, but eventually, the old house beamed with fresh new energy. Even though it didn't look like the house I had been born in, I loved it all the same. Then the families started coming. One by one, they explored the house. They would talk about how exciting it would be to raise kids in the house. Only one couple brought their children to see the house, though. Two of them, a boy and a girl. She was slightly older than him, but that didn't matter. I wanted them both to be my friends. Nobody would ever hurt them, not even the world outside. I wouldn't let it take them like it took the others. No, I will make sure they stay safe! I only know of one way to do that. That's to make sure they never leave me again.

Oh friends, we're going to have so much fun together!

127

THE BONES OF MILDRED MELLOWS
Jennifer Montgomery

Nobody lives on Fern Street anymore. At least that's what you hear. Decrepit houses rise up from barren yards, no one caring enough to replace broken windows or varnish the peeling pickets; neglected homes whose flaking paint flutter like snow in a stiff breeze, with windows that haven't seen a bottle of Windex in nearly a decade. That's not to say that the street is abandoned or in total disrepair — several attractive properties line the quiet, dead-end lane — but the prettiest of these is nestled at the end. With cream trim and green siding blending tidily with the surrounding trees of Coleclair Woods, 127 Fern St. is pristine. A lone edifice positioned at the curve of an otherwise deserted cul-de-sac, its manicured lawn and overflowing flower boxes looking every bit the cover of *Better Homes and Gardens*. The house backs to Knottingwood Place (known by the locals as Rottingwood), a civil war era graveyard, and although rumored to be haunted, Mildred Mellows goes about her day pruning rose bushes and sipping lemonade not a hundred feet from the nearest crumbling headstone.

Mildred is a sixty-five-year-old able-bodied soul, with just a few wrinkles that stretch across the happy places of her face. Unfailingly cheerful, she has a wave for everyone. Her routine is clockwork; at the grocery or library at noon, and once a week at the local nursery. On Saturday mornings you'll find her selling homemade lye soap at the flea market, except on this particular Saturday, stall number seventeen is empty.

* * *

Mildred Mellows can feel her nose twitching. She can't feel much else, but her nose seems to be *hunky-dory*. Hunky-dory. Such a strange phrase. It took Millie a long time to learn the language. The nuances and parts of speech were baffling, and some of the things that people said still made absolutely no sense to her, but she studied anyway, and used the silly words the most. People seemed to like silly words. They were comfortable with silly words. Silly words made her one of them.

Mildred knows it's after ten when the sound of *Mork & Mindy* drift in from the living room. She watches very little television herself, but a person has to blend, to fit in. The soft glow of *The Love Boat* flickering behind a drawn curtain after dinner meant she was tuned in, just like everyone else. She laughs when others laugh and frowns when it's expected.

Last week she'd stood in line at the grocery store, dabbing her eyes as mothers and wives talked about the latest disappearances. Six people, including a child, in the last seven months. Nine, the year before that, *but probably* more, Julie Ramsey had whispered. There'd been four runaways, or so the police claimed, but Julie thought they were lying. Several disappearances from surrounding counties in previous years, and the list went on and on. No clues, no evidence, and no connection. Mildred had no children of her own, so she could only imagine their horror.

* * *

Although her nose appears to be peachy-keen, it isn't going to help her get up off the floor. She wiggles the fingers of her left hand but the other arm lies useless, wedged between her body and the stove, as far as she can tell. The knife protruding from Mildred's back isn't a particularly large knife, but he'd thrust it in like the dickens. She wonders if she's dying, not in the traditional sense, but from a higher consciousness, a deeper place. Fear will take over, and her brain will shut down, but it's the after that concerns Mildred. What will happen after? When she can no longer depend on her brain and skin and heart for food and protection; for life? Where will she go then? Will it all just end? Like most, she can't remember a life before this body.

After several minutes of listening to TV chatter, it dawns on Mildred that her ears are still working, so she strains against the stillness, listening for *him*. Is he still in the house?

She tried locking him in the closet once he'd pulled the knife, but the stab had been so acutely sudden that she couldn't remember if she actually flipped the dead-bolt before tumbling down the stairs, an unfortunate incident that broke her hip and knocked her out for a few seconds. When she finally came to, she clambered through the foyer over brand new parquet flooring, gracelessly army crawling into the kitchen, her impotent arm dragging uselessly behind her as she trailed streaks of red in her wake. The plan was to grab her biggest knife and fight back. The body certainly wasn't in the best shape, no siree, but her resolve was pretty okey-dokey. Unfortunately, the strategy goes to seed when Mildred realizes that she can't reach the knives, and without a weapon, she wonders how on earth she will fend off her assailant. As she hypothesizes further possibilities, a line from last week's *Dr. Who* settles snugly into her brain matter: *Resistance is futile*. Indeed, it is. Once the realization sets in that she's a sitting duck, Mildred contemplates crawling to the garage. She thinks perhaps she can hide out in her trusty Escort until devising a better plan, but that idea skedaddles when she suddenly hears banging and screaming coming from the upstairs closet. It will take her a half hour just to get to the car, and she knows it's only a matter of time before he finds a way out, and once he does, he'll finish her off for good on the concrete floor.

Mildred might not be able to reach the knives on her own, but thinks perhaps she can use the drawer handles as a sort of ladder to help propel her upwards. If she can just get a good lean against the cabinets, she'll have no problem retrieving the butcher knife. She strains upwards with her good arm, reaching and pushing, her fingernails scraping against wood, clawing for the brass fixture. When she at last reaches the metal, Mildred curls the smoothness of it in her palm and pulls, bending her arm while dragging her leg beneath her. Her cotton-picking hip is useless, jutting outward at an unnatural angle, but she still manages to get a knee on the ground, and balancing her weight as best she can, Mildred pushes against all that is holy and bobs up the cabinet drawers, the lower half of her body bashing and dashing away like Morse code. After one final heave-ho, Mildred Mellows is upright.

Bang bang bang goes the knife handle on the closet door. The sound of it echoes down the stairs, slamming into her like a dump truck. *Bang bang bang.* Screaming, yelling, cursing, a nonstop assault of the rat in a cage. She slides her hand across the green flecked laminate, grasping the smooth, wood handle of the knife. The verbal assault upstairs hits a fever pitch with the man throwing himself against the door, again and again, and Mildred scans the room, looking for the best place to hide. Without warning, the deafening crack of splintered wood explodes from the bedroom, and in a panic, Mildred jerks towards the foyer. In doing so, she loses what little footing she's established, and her body jolts backwards, its dead weight propelling her downward. On her way to the floor, the base of Mildred's skull catastrophically cracks against the sharp linoleum edge of the peninsula. She lingers there for a split second as the nerves sever, and her fingers and legs turn to pudding. *There's always room for Jell-O.* She chuckles like a madwoman on her way down.

❋ ❋ ❋

Now, about twenty or so minutes later, judging from the kitschy end theme of *Mork & Mindy* exuding from the Magnavox, Mildred estimates it to be about eleven. She comes to in complete darkness, the unfortunate result of bashing her head on the counter. The hum of the air conditioner can be heard buzzing below the noise of the television, but other than that, the house remains quiet. Her last memory was the sound of the closet smashing open, and then everything went dark.

She meditates on the stranger for a bit, pondering his identity, wondering who he is and if he has any family. He's a small man, young, maybe late teens, or early twenties. Mildred had been in the graveyard, as she often was in the early morning. She'd stumbled upon him by pure dumb luck. It was as simple as that. She was always tinkering in the cemetery, a little dirt here, some chrysanthemums or bulbs there, and *poofity-poof,* he'd popped out from behind an elm just like a jack-in-the-box. The man offered to push her wheelbarrow back to the house for her. Mildred was leery, of course. She contemplated his presence and finally just asked him why he'd been there in the first place.

"Cutting over to the main road," he'd told her, and she had to explain that Coleclair Woods didn't open up in that direction. "Well then! No wonder I've been aimlessly roaming around in here for twenty minutes." He laughed, and Mildred laughed, and she relinquished the handles of the cart.

The man described his recent move from the coast and how he was looking forward to finding a job. He was quite the Chatty Cathy, but Mildred began to suspect that perhaps he was making it all up as he went. By the time they got to the garage, she had a pretty good feeling that the stranger was as full of bologna as a person could get. But by then it had been too late.

***

An echo reverberates in Mildred's ears, distorting the sound of the TV. She's sure that she doesn't have much longer. Memories, some she knows and some she doesn't recognize at all, sizzle across her brain like static. A little girl. The sky and stars. The expanse just beyond the planet. Someone riding a horse. Pink flowered teacups. Afternoon baseball games on the television. The unmistakable smell of popcorn. Floating on the edge of the universe, just one of a billion inestimable bodies comprising thought, desire, dreams, and pain. Press your luck! No whammies! A laundromat in New York in the sixties. Scratchy grass. Soft grass. Hard-boiled eggs. Bacon. Fat. Flesh. The sensation of skin crawling away from organs. Blood, on her hands, and in her mouth. Geraniums and bones, and bones and teeth, and teeth and screams, and soap and acid.

Clickety-clack, a commercial has ended, and a laugh escapes her lips, or at least she thinks it does, as the last words she'll ever hear float on a breeze from one room to the next. As always, the idiosyncrasy of the language is not lost on Mildred, nor is the irony, when Sonny Curtis does his darndest to assure her that *She's Gonna Make it After All*, when, in fact, she is not. Not on your Nelly, no siree Bob, she wasn't going to make it after all, because Mildred Mellows was no Mary Tyler Moore.

Mildred Mellows wasn't even Mildred Mellows.

❀ ❀ ❀

Clyde Turner shifts uncomfortably in a cheap plastic seat, his cuffed hands resting on a cold silver-topped table. As if the shackles weren't awful enough, the swelling, caused by breaking down the closet door, squeezes the metal bands even tighter. A mountain of a man on the other side of the table, Detective Clegg, looks like a steroidal gym rat with a porn 'stache. His beefy fingers squeeze and release the pen in his hand at least a million times, his eyes never leaving Clyde's face.

"Can I get a drink of water? A can of Coke maybe?"

"You can get a swift kick in the ass if you like," the detective responds. "I told you before, keep your yapper shut until the captain gets back."

"I've been in this damn chair for four hours! I didn't do anything wrong!"

"What planet are you on? My guys picked you up on the side of the road, running away from a damn murder scene."

"I tried to explain…"

"I don't give a shit," the detective snaps back. "You're covered in blood! You admitted to stabbing somebody to death. You catch my drift? That's all the explanation I need, son."

"You're not listening, dammit!" Clyde hammers his bound hands to the table in a deafening crash. "You didn't even get a doctor to look at my hands!"

"Does this look like a hospital to you? Shut the hell up or I'll do it for you. Not a word until the captain gets back here, or so help me God…" Clegg lets the comment marinade between them as he fixes his icy blue stare on Clyde. "Not one more syllable." He watches the twitchy kid on the other side of the table to see if he has any other bitches and moans. He does not.

The sudden crackle of the walkie at Clegg's hip jolts the pair to attention. With his eyes still trained on the bloody guy in the chair, the detective raises the black box to his lips.

"Clegg."

"Captain just called in." The voice on the other end seems unusually high-strung, and Clegg wonders what in God's name has put Grady's panties in such a wad.

"And?"

"He says," Grady clears his throat nervously, "he says to put that pecker head in the car right now and get him the hell over to that house."

"Bullshit!" Forgetting about the iron-clad shackles tucked tight around his ankles, Clyde Turner bounces out of his seat and stumbles with a thud to the faded yellow tile. "No way! No way in hell am I going back there." The detective peeks over the edge of the table and doesn't know whether to be amused or pissed about the bloody idiot scooting across the floor in the fetal position.

"Did the captain say why?" Clegg spins in his chair,

holding the walkie close to his chest.

"It's bad, detective. Something ain't right." After a brief pause, the voice on the other end continues quietly across the radio. "He sounded…off, Oliver. Freaked out, I think. He's hoping your guy can answer some questions."

"Not happening!" Clyde yells from the corner in a half-seated position. "I told that thick headed son of a bitch not to go. Didn't I tell him? I explained everything, and you assholes didn't want to listen. Well, you're listening now, ain't ya Kojak!"

"Shut your goddamn mouth! I can't even hear myself think!"

"I'm. Not. Going!"

"You are going!" Detective Clegg slams his chair to the floor, the sound like the bullet through a barrel. "And once we're in the car, you can start over, and you can give me your bullshit story one more time along the way, but you *are* going. Even if I, and every other damn cop in this building, have to drag you out of here."

"Why?" Clyde knows he's crying now, sniveling like a pussy in the corner, but he doesn't care. He didn't want to go back. It wasn't fair. He'd made it out, and now they were taking him back.

"Why? Because I've known the captain for over twenty years and I have never even seen that man flinch. Not once. Not ever. There's got to be some grade A shit going down over there for him to be so spooked. He wants answers and apparently thinks that you're the one to give them to him."

Twenty minutes later, Detective Oliver Clegg peels onto Fern Street and yanks the wheel over at the curb. Blue and red squad lights bounce off neglected houses, and residents over on Hemlock Ave. can be seen peering through their yards trying to catch a glimpse of all the excitement.

"So you admit that you went to her house in order to rob the place? That right?" Clegg flips his half-smoked cigarette out the window, turning and resting his arm on the top of his seat. Clyde stares wide mouthed in his direction, his head shaking in disbelief.

"Holy shit dude, you still don't get it, do you? Out of everything I told you, that's the one piece of info you're stuck on."

"I'm a cop, asshole. You've admitted a laundry list of felonies to me, so yeah, we're going to talk about that shit. The rest is fiction. You know it and I know it. Now I don't know exactly what you did in there to cause the captain so much damn grief, but your story ain't it."

"Okay then, get on in there and talk to your captain. See what he has to say!"

As the detective is popping open the door, two uniformed officers round the front of the house carrying an industrial size barrel. Teetering it up the hill unsteadily, they shimmy it across the grass, the liquid inside splashing over the rim. When the tallest of the two plows into a hydrangea bush, the army green container tumbles out of hand, landing with a thud. The officers trip over themselves, scrambling away from the mess as it seeps into the grass, discharging smoke and stench into the air. Clegg can very clearly see a pile of small bones lying in the puddle.

"What the fu…"

"I told you, man. I freaking told you! There's like ten of those things in the cellar. Poison and bones, all in different states of decomposition. I found them after I realized she was dead. It's all those missing people, it's got to be!"

Detective Clegg has seen plenty of dead bodies in his time, but something about those brittle bones laying there on that thick Kentucky Bluegrass turns his stomach. It's summertime. His boys are at home in their fort with no worries or concerns, just reading comic books and playing checkers in a makeshift hideout of pallets and their mama's old tablecloths. The little bones lying in the yard could very well have belonged to one of his own sons. There'd been over fifty missing persons cases, twenty kids in all in their area alone, since the early seventies. Babies as young as two years old, and Clegg wrestles with the probability that all those children died right here at 127 Fern St.

"Tell me one more time, Clyde, about the end." The detective's voice has turned eerily monotone, his eyes never leaving the remains in the yard. "Don't go all Poe on me with your bullshit horror story, just tell me one more time what happened. I'm listening."

"I was cutting through the graveyard, that part was true," he begins. "Can I have a cigarette?" Clegg pulls a gold pack of Winston lights out of his pocket. He puts two smokes in his mouth and lights them both, passing the second through the window to the backseat. "I see this old lady all by herself pushing a wheelbarrow, so I know she can't live far, and this is the only house on this part of the street. It's a nice house, man, and old broads always have jewelry."

"Yep."

"So I chum her up thinking whoa, this is way too easy. You'd assume old ladies living by themselves would be more cautious, you know? But she lets me jabber on for a bit and then I offer to help her back to her place. I wasn't going to hurt her," he adds. "For some reason, it's important to me that you know that. I would have tied her up until I was done, but I ain't never really hurt anyone."

"You're a saint. Give me the rest."

"So we get in the garage and she starts talking about this sewing box up in the top of a closet that she just can't get down. Says she's old and feeble and doesn't want to climb on a stool, so I'm like hell yeah, there's my in, you know? I follow her up, and she shows me the closet. I thought it was the perfect place to put her until I was done, but she grabs me by the back of the neck and sinks her fingernails right into the skin, right at the jugular. I get away easily enough, but then she takes a freaking bite out of my arm! Right here!" He holds his hand out the window, but Clegg has no interest.

"I've already seen it," he says. "I thought it was a

defensive wound on her part."

"Hell no, it isn't. The crazy bitch was trying to eat me, like literally."

"Keep going."

"So I push her away and she keeps coming at me, but I can't get past her. Then I noticed this purple spot on the back of her neck. I know for a fact I didn't see it earlier, so it's something that comes and goes. Anyway, it's…moving, or vibrating, or something. Like it's alive. Iridescent and ripply, not a bruise or anything, just this weird ass, nearly glowing, purple spot on her skin. I was transfixed on it, and I swear to God I felt like it was hypnotizing me. Like once I saw it, I could hardly look away. Freaked me the hell out and I hauled off and punched it, *bam,* just as hard as I could, right there on her neck. She lets out this scream that isn't human, man. Not at all. Sounds like some serious *Twilight Zone* shit, I'm telling ya. I didn't want to beat the hell out of her, but she goes and takes another big old chomp from my shoulder, so I pull out my knife and bury it up in her ribs somewhere. It was reflex, man. It just happened, and before I know what the hell's going on, she locks me in the fucking closet."

"Alright." Clegg tosses another butt towards the sewer and opens the door to the backseat. "Come on, get out."

"Hell no. I'm telling you dude, I can't do it."

"Listen. I can buy the crazy ass, geriatric, cannibal, murderer scenario. Really, I can. When I was a cop in New York, I saw shit that'd put you on Thorazine for the rest of your life, but I can't buy the rest, and because I can't, you have to come in and explain it all to the captain."

"Bring him out here. I don't mind telling the damn story, but I don't want to go back in there."

"You don't have a choice."

"Bullshit. Everyone always has a choice."

"Not you."

"I'm telling you, Clegg. She wasn't human. When I finally got out of that damn closet and found her in the kitchen, she was flayed open. From the inside out. Clawed open, scratched open. Something dug their way out of her body and left her meat sack laying in there on the freaking kitchen floor. I didn't even think about it at the time, just started stripping the place out, you know, jewelry and silverware and shit, but then I found the barrels, and a lot of other stuff that scared the shit out of me, so I go back and look a little closer at the old lady's skin suit. Something was living inside her, detective, and it was still in that fucking house. I heard it squishing around somewhere in the living room."

"And this is where you lose me, Mr. Turner."

"You ever had your boots stuck in the mud? I'm not talking about a little pothole. I mean a pigsty kind of slop. Up to your calves, really just mired down into it, you know? You ever heard the noise it makes when you go trying to get that foot out of there? That slurping, wet, mushy, sucking noise? That's what that thing sounded like. I sure as hell didn't wait around to see it. Now I'm telling you, those men in there are in danger, and instead of shooting the shit out here with me, you should be in there dragging their asses out."

"I don't buy it, Clyde."

"Whatever was in her is still in that house! Why in the hell would you want to run up against that? That psycho tried to eat me!"

"Yeah, and now she's dead. I'm not overly concerned about safety right now. There are bigger issues at hand."

"How many missing people you got around here? How many other bones are in the basement, or better yet, dumped over there in that cemetery? I've worked it out in my head. That's what she's doing back there." He motions toward the graveyard. "She melts down in those barrels what she can't eat and then buries in those old graves what she can't melt down. Go on! Dig some of those assholes up and tell me if you don't find new bones."

"And all that may be true, but she was just a sick old lady and now she's dead, so we're going to go in and substantiate the realistic part of your story, and then get down to the business of identifying victims so we can inform their families. Jesus Christ, I don't even want to think about how we're going to tell all those parents what happened to their kids. Makes me sick." Detective Clegg opens the back door and orders Clyde to exit. "I'm going to take these off," he says, motioning to the cuffs, "but you so much as look at me sideways and I'm going to beat the living shit out of you right here in the front yard. Either way, we're going in." As the pair moves toward the house, the same two officers that dropped the barrel burst through the front door. The short cop is covered in blood and the bald one is screaming incoherently.

"What's happening?" Clegg grabs the closest one. His neck is bleeding profusely and when he tries to speak, blood splatters from his lips. He immediately drops to the ground and twitches there for a moment before growing still. The other cop runs for his patrol car, but the detective intercepts him at the curb.

"What in the hell is going on?! Where's Cap?"

"There's something in there! It grabbed the captain. It…it tried to eat him, Clegg. It had this mouth… Oh Jesus, Mary, and Joseph, we got to get out of here. Call in the government or something, we're not equipped for this shit."

"You left Robert in there? Saved your own ass and left him in there?"

"It chewed off his head! What in the hell did you want me to do?" He yanks out of the detective's grasp and lunges for his car door. Once in, he spins his tires on the pavement and peels off towards the main road.

Oliver Clegg draws his pistol and walks cautiously to the front door. Clyde Turner, on the other hand, turns tail and runs toward the graveyard. With a deep breath, the detective pulls open the screen and enters the house at 127 Fern St.

* * *

Clyde Turner yanks up the living room blinds, letting the

early morning sun stream through. He kicks a couple beer cans out of the way and makes for the fridge to crack open a few eggs. The mobile home isn't pretty, but it is his, paid for by money he actually earned.

When Clyde took off from the house, he didn't look back. He just kept running until he found an abandoned building to hide out in for a while. He did a few small jobs, just enough to make a few bucks and get the hell out of Dodge, but he never fully walked away from that day. He didn't know what happened to Clegg and scoured newspapers for weeks, trying to figure it out. What he found was a big steaming pile of bullshit.

They pinned the murders on the old lady and Clyde had been right about her burying bones in the old cemetery. For years she got away with ordering industrial amounts of lye for her soap making business, but most of it was used to get rid of the bodies. During his interview, Officer Walker told Internal Affairs everything he'd seen, from his partner getting attacked to Captain Miller getting his head chewed off by a black blob in the old lady's living room. Of course, no one believed him, and a report, written up by the recently promoted Lieutenant Oliver Clegg, attested to harmful amounts of lye-based poison in the house, extremely dangerous levels which attributed to Officer Walker's hallucinations. In reality, Lieutenant Clegg explained, the old lady shot them both and then turned the gun on herself. By some miracle, Clegg made it out of the house just before it exploded, another convenient incident attributed to volatile poisonous fumes.

But Clyde knew better, and he paid Clegg a visit, incognito, in case anyone was still holding any grudges. When he confronted the ex-detective about the newspaper article, he was assured that everything he supposedly saw in the house was a hallucination, and that Clegg had also classified his stabbing of Mildred Mellows as self-defense. Clyde argued the hallucinatory bit until he was blue in the face, but it was apparent that the truth didn't matter.

"It's the way it has to go," Clegg told him. "Keep your nose clean, Mr. Turner, and mind your business. If I see you again, it won't be pretty."

Clyde let him go without any further argument, but as Clegg walked away, he saw the shimmer of a purple spot at the back of the lieutenant's neck. It glistened in the sunlight, pulling him in, transfixing him. He made himself break contact, stumbling backwards into a trash can. Clegg looked back over his shoulder, and with a toothy grin, he pointed at Clyde and gave him a wink.

That was three months ago. These days Clyde keeps to himself and habitually reads the local paper, waiting for news of the disappearances to start up again. He knows they will, and when they do, he'll be ready. He may not know exactly what the monster is, but he knows *where* it is, and that will just have to be good enough for now.

Caleb J. Pecue is the owner and editor for Terrorcore Publishing, which specializes in bringing back the vintage feel of the 80s. His short story, *The Turning of a Card*, was published in the second volume of Horrorscope, edited by Harriet Everend. Another of his short stories, *One More Time for Old Time's Sake*, will be published in Gridiron Gates of Hell for charity. By day, he works at a university in Illinois, advising students; by night, he works to find short stories to publish and writes his own that he hopes to publish.

Cameron Chaney was born and raised in a small Ohio town you've never heard of. He spent his childhood roaming his family's six-acre property and devouring one spooky book after another. He now enjoys writing spooky stories of his own in his home library and talking about all things spooky on his YouTube show, Library Macabre. Cameron also works as a youth services librarian aboard his local bookmobile. He currently resides in yet another small Ohio town you've never heard of. Don't feed him after midnight...

ABOUT THE AUTHORS

E.P. Clement began to appreciate horror when she discovered the monster in her bedroom was simply a creepy silhouette of her least favorite lamp. Though "Time in My Wake" is her first published horror story, she's written plenty of morbid poetry over the years with topics ranging from grief and loss to memory and honesty. When not writing, E.P. Clement is yelling at the girls on her TV to stop checking out the spooky basement and flickering lights by themselves.

Laura Mangi is a lifelong reader and lover of books. In addition to reading and writing, she also does photography. She is looking forward to writing more and getting published and finally getting a golden retriever.

A.L. Davidson (she/they) is a writer who specializes in massive space operas and tiny disturbances. She writes stories about ghosts, grief, isolation, space exploration, eco-horror, queerness, and the human condition. They live with their cat Jukebox in Kansas City.

Jackson Robinson was born in Colorado Springs but grew up in a small, midwestern town in North Dakota. He began writing early on in life after being inspired by the works of Stephen King, Clive Barker, and Joyce Carol Oats. He has now returned to Colorado to write full-time. His work has appeared on The NoSleep Podcast, Scare Street's Night Terrors anthologies, and more. He is currently working on a longer piece that you can look for around December 2023.

Tobin Elliott writes ugly stories about bad people doing horrible things. To prove this, he's published a six-book horror series called The Aphotic that includes Lovecraftian demons, werewolves, and vampires, but the worst monsters are the humans. Tobin has several novels, novellas, and short stories published. And you can find him at all the usual social media haunts.

Lennox Rex, an Oregonian raised in sunny San Diego, wrote his first story in second grade and just never stopped. When he's not reading or writing, he's collecting interesting facts and generally being a random geek. To him, life is best lived with music, body mods, and plenty of coffee and sweets. He lives with his husband and their three children.

Reece G. Donnell is currently a journalist for the world famous Scream Magazine. The Northern Irish lad studied film, English Literature and Drama However, his lifelong dream has to gain publication creatively. After selling over 40 pieces to various media outlets, it is hoped that *What's Wrong With Barbara* will be a creative breakthrough.

Mallory is a writer and cartoonist who lives near Los Angeles, California. Their previous work includes the novels "The President's Head Is Missing!" and "But It's for Charity!," the graphic novel "Egg Behavior," and a whole mess of short stories published by Ahoy Comics. Yes, their professional pseudonym is just the one name on its own, like Madonna or Cher.

Danielle Robertson writes character-driven novels and short stories. Her work has appeared in the print anthology The 12 Days of Book-Club-Mas (Volume 4) for Once Upon a Book Club, as well as in online publications including Breadcrumbs Magazine and Storychord. She lives in New Jersey with her husband, her daughter, and her overstuffed bookshelves.

Emily Holman, a 22-year-old autistic author, is currently a graduate student at California State University, San Marcos to obtain a Master's degree in Literature and Writing. She writes everything from fiction to poetry, and even full-length novels, but horror and the supernatural hold a special place in her heart.

C. Mae Thomas grew up in South Bend, Indiana, where she was homeschooled with her 8 siblings. She has a B.A. from the University of Dayton and has since resided in Ireland, North Carolina, France, and California, where she now works in commercial real estate. Her love of the spooky, strange, and surreal is reflected in her debut publication "This Could be Your Home, You Know". When she's not writing or working, she can be found devouring sci-fi, fantasy, or horror with her cats, Spock and Bones.

Kaos Emslie lives in Southern Arizona with her two children and a growing number of cats. They are surrounded by pens, paper, and books constantly. They love all things horror and gore, gothic and spooky. They are never far from a caffeinated beverage. Their current long-term project is a horror series based on their experiences with mental illness.

Jason Jones is an industrial painter by trade and is a fan and collector of vintage horror fiction. He enjoys writing poetry with a horror flare and stories as well. He currently resides in central Indiana with his wife.

Torrence Bryan loves control. She loves to control lives, to control stories, and most importantly of all, to control your emotions. Her stories will make you think, and leave you wondering exactly what goes on inside her twisted little head. When she isn't writing dark tales, she writes romance about rainbows and butterflies.

Derek Heath is the author of ENDLESS LIVING ORGAN MASSACRE (coming 2024 from D&T Publishing) and the OUTBACK TERROR series of books from Raven Tale. His short fiction can be found in anthologies from Eerie River, Splatter Ink Publishing, Skywatcher Press, Voices from the Mausoleum and more. Derek lives in the UK with his partner and a horde of semi-stray cats. By day, he is an accountant. (By night, he is asleep; the writing is sandwiched somewhere in the middle).

Nadine Stewart made her author debut this year in Horrorscope: A Zodiac Anthology. Since then she has had pieces published in the spring 2023 edition of Sirens Call, and the July anthology release Flashes of Nightmare. Her story "Shattered Reflections" is featured in Voices From the Mausoleum's That Old House - Bathroom Anthology. Born into a creative family of artists and raised in beautiful British Columbia, Canada she now resides in Washington state. Follow her on Instagram @nadine.stewart.author.

Louie Sullivan is thankful to have never come face to face with the Outside, though there's still plenty of time for it to get him. He is a graduate of Fordham University and Saint Peter's University, reads about a hundred books a year, and goes to the movies as often as humanly possible. You can also find his work in issue 62 of The Sirens Call.

A lifelong fan of videogames, comic books, and horror, action, and science-fiction films, **Dr. Stuart Knott** writes horror fiction with the intent on infusing the mundane nature of everyday life with dark comedy and macabre events.

Jack Finn is a folk horror and fantasy writer living in the wilds of the Pacific Northwest. He is a lifelong believer that the Tooth Fairy is proof that you can trade body parts for cold, hard cash. Jack's published works include

The Seven Deaths of Prince Vlad, Hell Shall Make You Fear Again, and The Legend of the Deer Woman.

Billie Karras grew up in the dusty Arizona desert with an ever-putrefying love of all things blood and guts and slime and sharp, rotten teeth. He spends his nights writing, his days dreaming about the 80s, and is truly a romantic at heart. That heart just happens to be green. Flyblown. And teeming with their squirmy little worm-babies. You can find Billie on Instagram via @billiekarras_author.

Voracious reader and wannabe poet **Julie Aaron** resides in Houston Texas with her loving wife and their rowdy German Shepard. Writing when she can, this is her first published work. Thank you to all who devour it.

Alex James Donne is a lifelong resident of West London, an unrepentant hoarder of books, and an occasional writer of dark fiction. His short story 'The Things We Do for Love' appears in the anthology The Monsters Next Door.

Cyrus Spears, who adopts the pen name **Sirius** for writing endeavors, identifies as a queer, nonbinary, and disabled author situated in North Carolina. Being a part of the Horror Writer's Association, Cyrus has penned a gothic horror novel titled "Swallow You Whole," set for publication in September 2023 through Curious Corvid Publishing, along with additional works in the pipeline. Notably, Cyrus's collection of dark speculative short stories has been featured in publications such as The Magpie Messenger, The Spectre Review, and the Siren's Call eZine, with more forthcoming contributions anticipated.

Todd Condit is an avid family man that loves to grill every type of food imaginable for his wife and kids. Rain, shine, or snow you can find Todd flipping burgers behind the grill. As a lifelong horror fan, he is always eager to write, read, watch, or talk horror! So if you're the type that wears a horror shirt to the store, dont be suprised when he comes out of nowhere to strike up conversation about the movie.

Loki DeWitt has lived in a number of different places but currently lives in Arkansas. He has loved horror since a very young age when he was introduced to the genre by watching a number of 80s horror movies with his dad (Despite his mom's protests). Years later he began writing in the dreaded land of fan fiction. While his stories were not original, they let him sharpen his skills for the days ahead when he would tell his own stories. Now an adult, Loki retains his overactive imagination and takes great pleasure in unleashing it on readers.

Jennifer Montgomery is a poet and author from Cedar Hill, Missouri. Influenced heavily by her mother, also a poet, and her father, a writer of horror poetry and fiction, Jennifer worked with her father on his small press Sci-Fi/ Horror magazine in the early 1990s. She's had several pieces of dark poetry published, as well as flash fiction and short stories. Jennifer is currently working on her first gothic horror novel, as well as two other full-length literary projects.

www.ingramcontent.com/pod-product-compliance
Lightning Source LLC
Chambersburg PA
CBHW020055310726
48970CB00002B/324